THE
SWORD
OF
THEBES

RORY HEADREN

Typeset in Sabon

Cover design: Kobir Miah
kobir_miah@live.co.uk

Design Consultant: Robyn Ricci
RobynRicci@yahoo.co.uk

Typesetting and publishing by UK Book Publishing
www.ukbookpublishing.com

ISBN: 978-1-914195-86-0

THE
SWORD
OF
THEBES

PROLOGUE

*A*fter seven long years of bitter conflict between Athens and Sparta, it was the Athenians who finally believed that victory was within reach - Spartan morale having collapsed.

During their failed attempt to recover the strategic northern peninsular of Pylos, nearly three hundred of their army, which included one hundred and twenty from their elite spartiate class, surrendered to the Athenians. This astounding event caused the Spartans to believe they must have offended the gods, and having no previous experience of such misfortune, they became nervous of bringing about a similar disaster. Now lacking confidence in their decision making, instead of being on the offensive, forcing the Athenians to hide behind their walls, it was now the Spartans who adopted a defensive strategy.

In contrast, Cleon, the assertive leader of Athens, buoyed up by his surprising success at Pylos, believed that any decisions he made, whether supported by forces large or small, would be victorious, and the Athenians now embarked on an ambitious, more aggressive plan of action.

Waiting patiently for such a change in circumstances were the exiled Plataeans. Having accepted the uneasy hospitality of the Athenians since the fall of their city at the start of the war, they'd fought alongside their powerful ally in every major campaign, *hoping that one day Athens would repay them by helping to retake their cherished fortress. As the war dragged on, they were forced to live on their wits; struggling against the odds to keep alive their dream of going home.*

Not every Spartan was stifled by indecision, however. Due to his courage and intelligence, an unusually dynamic and ambitious commander was making a name for himself. Unlike his fellow countrymen, he was not afraid to take risks. His name was Brasidas, and he was more than ready to fulfill his destiny.

Taken from the notes of Admetus (historian)

Mesembria

ONE

A DISQUIETING STILLNESS ACCOMPANIED the two men as they climbed their way purposefully up the pebble strewn path, lined by gnarled, tortured looking trees, to the burial ground. The twisted bare branches were filled with great black seabirds referred to by local fishermen as 'the black death', due to the devastation they caused to their fish stocks, and their malevolent forms like sinister statues stared down coldly on the mournful pair. The birds' eerie presence caused alarm in the younger man, and he stumbled, sending a cascade of rocks noisily down the hillside. Suddenly, the air was filled with their agitated grunting calls; their broad flapping wings spread out as if for flight. The youth cried out in horror, 'What is this place? They're like harpies! Are you sure it's here, Clytes?'

By the Temple of Ares on the sacred island of Aretias in the Black Sea, Clytes of Eleusis looked down on the grave, his whole body shaking, his mind overwhelmed by grief and anger. 'It's here, Angelos,' he answered, grimly. The unmistakable mound of earth covered with its white stones, concealed the body of an Amazon warrior, dressed by her tribe in full regalia; her hair pierced with an eagle's feather. Also in the grave were her weapons and her still-born child.

It had been a year since the lovers' hurried parting on the shores of Anatolia; a time of waiting and anticipation on the part of Clytes, for his return to the hunting grounds of the Amazons, to be reunited with his fiercely courageous Anthousa and to see the child she'd expected to bear him. From his first encounter with the beautiful Tanagrian in a Plataean brothel, seven years previously, to their adventures in Persia and the rescue of Plataea's golden shield, their relationship had grown in mutual love and respect.

His arch-enemy Lykaon, Wolf of Thebes, was now dead; killed on the shores of the Tigris while attempting to flee with The Shield, and after many years consumed in seeking revenge for the death of his family, Clytes felt his life had finally taken a turn for the better - but it seemed the judgemental deities on Mount Olympus had exacted the ultimate price for enabling him to kill Lykaon.

'Why?!' he raged at the gods, as he stormed angrily along the shore, back to their waiting vessel. 'What did I do that was so wrong?' All around them screamed enormous flocks of white gulls, constantly diving and attacking the men, and they suffered painful jabs from these persistent, ferocious birds as they fought their way along the strand.

The ever-faithful Angelos who'd accompanied his friend and protector on the long journey from Athens to Pontus, tried to give solace. 'You are not being punished, Clytes. It's not uncommon for women to die in childbirth. This is not your fault!' he yelled above the din.

'But I feel it is!' retorted Clytes, turning on his young companion. 'And the gods know it is!'

Eager to leave the mournful place and return to Athens while the winds were favourable, the pair returned to the Amazonian river-settlement on the mainland and in earnest, began preparations for travel. They were interrupted in their efforts when a group of wild horsewomen rode towards them at speed, quickly surrounding them.

'Leaving already?' called out Melousa, queen of the local tribe, and she jumped down to stride over to Clytes. 'Stay for a while,' she said, insistently. 'You are not yet rested from your long journey. You won't regret it,' she added, pointedly.

CHAPTER ONE

'Did you even *try* to save her?' demanded Clytes, ignoring her invitation, as he carried on determinedly with fastening up a bundle. 'I thought you were skilled in such matters!'

'We did everything we could,' Melousa answered, defensively. 'The baby would not come. When we could not save Anthousa, we cut the child from her, but it was already dead.'

'Was it a girl or a boy?' he asked, bitterly.

'A girl,' answered the leader, defiantly. 'If she'd lived, she would have stayed with us, to be raised as a warrior!'

Melousa moved closer to Clytes and thrust her hand between his legs. A familiar smell of incense rose from her leather clothing, bringing back memories of his previous encounter with these extraordinary, ferocious women. 'Father a boy next time, Clytes,' she said stroking him, provocatively. 'A boy you may keep for yourself. We have no need of males......except for this!' and she gripped him more forcefully.

'I think not, Melousa!' replied Clytes, angrily, as he firmly removed her hand. 'I have just left Anthousa's grave!'

'The dead have their own realm!' spoke the warrior, vehemently. 'We are very much alive, you and I.'

'Ha! Speak for yourself!' responded Clytes, harshly, still reeling from his personal tragedy.

'I could hold you here!' she said sharply, indicating the fierce warriors at her back, watching keenly, just waiting for her command.

'I have no intention of becoming one of your drugged captives, to be disposed of on a whim!' Clytes replied, hotly. 'I've experienced your herbal concoctions before, Melousa...... remember? Angelos and I will be forever grateful for the assistance your tribe gave us in escaping king Ataxerxes' men, but I'm in no mood for negotiations. I'll send more than one of you to Hades,' he said threateningly, 'if you attempt to stop us from leaving!'

Faces suddenly turned to watch as a warrior woman carrying a swaddled child, walked slowly towards them. She approached Clytes and pulling aside the woollen blanket, showed the infant to him.

'What's this?' he asked, confused.

'We believe Anthousa was not the only member of our tribe made pregnant by the Hellene soldiers passing through our territory,' answered Melousa. 'and this mother seems certain of her child's parentage.' Looking at her comrade, she said to the woman, 'Give him the name of the soldier.'

'He called himself Imbros,' the tattooed woman replied, staring boldly at Clytes. 'He said he was an Athenian. Tell him he has a daughter,' she added proudly. 'Tell him her name is Okayle.'

Clytes looked solemnly for a moment at the familiar serious expression on the child's face, then said, grievously. 'The child's father no longer lives. The Athenian you speak of was killed at Sardis, not long after we left your lands.'

'I'm sorry,' replied the young warrior. 'He was a good lover,' she added, reflectively, 'although a little intense, I remember.'

Melousa turned to face her followers, now numbering fifty or more, all equipped for hunting and looking increasingly threatening. Clytes and Angelos, knowing not to underestimate the pride or the ruthlessness of these women, grabbed whatever weapons they had within reach and took up defensive positions, standing back-to-back.

The Amazonian queen looked angrily at the two men for a moment, then quickly leaping onto her horse, indicated to her warriors that they were leaving. Laughing and shouting wildly, they urged their mounts nearer to the anxious pair, galloping daringly close around them, before riding off in the direction of heavily wooded foothills.

'Put down your weapons!' shouted Melousa, with barely concealed indignation. 'I won't keep you here by force. We also mourn the loss of Anthousa. She became a respected member of our sisterhood due to her fortitude. We will tend her grave, Clytes. She will not be forgotten.' The horse under her, eager to follow the others, was straining at the bit. Briefly, the warrior's eyes met Clytes' in a moment of mutual sadness. 'In her memory,' she said, with emphasis, 'you're free to go.' Impatiently, her spirited mount pawed at the ground. Its rider released the reins and let it have its head. As she galloped furiously away, they heard her shout, 'If you are still here when we return from the hunt, I may change my mind!'

Suddenly, the men were alone, but they kept their defensive positions until all horsewomen were swallowed up by the dense vegetation. All that remained was the sound of their terrifying cries, left ringing in their ears.

TWO

ON HIS JOURNEY BACK to war duty in Athens, a companionless Angelos stopped at the tiny island of Mesembria, just off the Thracian coast; winter home of fellow Plataean, Theomenes and his expanding family. He and Clytes had visited the island in the Black Sea, on their way to Pontus and had promised to call again on their return with news of Anthousa and the expected baby.

'You have no idea where he is, Angelos?' asked Theomenes, incredulously.

'He was badly affected by what he found on the island. He barely spoke on our journey towards Sinope. Glaucus stopped the Delias there, after we recovered The Shield, remember?'

'I remember. Glaucus would be sorry to hear about Clytes' troubles. Those two are like brothers. Go on.'

'I stayed a week looking for him, hoping he'd come back. I had Leukos to help me.'

'The lad who helped us get to the coast? I hope you found him well.'

'He's happy enough, Theomenes. He's working at Sinope harbour.'

'I'm relieved to hear that. I felt bad about leaving him behind, after all he'd done for us, but to get the ship through the Hellespont and save The Shield, we couldn't take passengers.'

'We checked the port as to any ship Clytes may have boarded. We questioned horse traders too. From the description I gave, no-one seemed to have seen him. He simply vanished.'

'He must have disguised himself. He's good at that.'

'I was hoping to find him here.'

'He obviously needs time to adjust to the sad news. He'll turn up.'

'I'm not so sure. When he did speak, and that wasn't much, he kept muttering about the gods punishing him because of his obsession in wanting to kill Lykaon. He seemed to think it wasn't safe for anyone to get too close to him.'

'The idiot! He needs his friends more than ever! We'll find him in Athens,' added Theomenes, hopefully. 'His fellow actors, Leon and Panthas are expecting him at the City Dionysia.'

'I don't think he will go to Athens. I'm worried. He took all his possessions but left this.' Unfurling a bundle of cloth, Angelos revealed an exquisitely crafted sword with a gold embossed hilt.

'Now that is strange! He would never be parted from that weapon. He must have told you how it was given to him by the Plataean garrison, for bravery during the Theban attack. It was taken from a Theban boetarch. Why would he leave it? I don't understand.'

'Wasn't the boetarch, Lykaon's uncle?' queried Angelos, pointedly. 'I think that's why he left it. He believes he's being cursed.'

'Cursed?'

'By Lykaon.'

'From the grave? Now, *I'm* worried,' said Theomenes, shaking his head. 'It seems our friend is in a bad way and capable of doing anything. I am to return to my cavalry unit by the end of the month,' he added, grimly, but also with barely concealed pride. 'Mydon is already making arrangements for the journey. We'll travel together, Angelos.'

'To get there before the fighting starts!' asserted the young Plataean, boldly.

'Ah, the rashness of youth!'

'You are only two years my senior!'

'It feels more, Angelos.'

Sensing his friend's anxiety, Theomenes gripped his shoulder, as an elder brother would. 'When we get to Athens, there'll be news of Clytes, I'm sure.'

'Is the entire household leaving for Athens?' asked Angelos, as they walked towards the villa.

'No! Amara and the child are remaining here. It's safer. Mydon won't be going back to Athens with me, either. Although a freedman now, he's of no use to the military. He's too lame after our arduous travels in Persia. He'll be fully occupied keeping an eye on my uncle's business interests in Thrace. Admetus will also stay. He's too old for war duty.'

As they entered the villa, Theomenes indicated the solitary figure bent over his desk and totally absorbed in frantic scribbling. 'No-one's allowed to go near him while he's working,' spoke Theomenes quietly. 'He doesn't want to interrupt the Muses. Since hearing of the death of the historian, Herodotus, he seems driven to emulate the great man's work. His account of what happened at Plataea and the consequences of those events, occupy all his time now.'

THREE

'**W**HY DIDN'T YOU JUST let him have it?' the stallholder asked Clytes, as she dabbed at the bleeding gashes on his face. 'He really gave you a beating!' Lifting his tunic to check for more injuries, she was shocked to find his chest tightly bound in a bandage. 'What's this?' she asked, shaking her head at him in bewilderment. 'Why is such a good-looking fellow like yourself, picking a fight when you're already hurt?'

'I wanted that bread!' answered Clytes, defensively.

'No, you didn't!' replied the woman. 'I saw you. You provoked him deliberately.'

'Well, what of it,' grumbled Clytes. 'Great oaf!' he exclaimed.

'Babak is a celebrity around here,' the stallholder told him. 'Wrestled a bear once. Killed it!' she said, with emphasis.

'Doesn't surprise me,' replied Clytes, wincing as she applied more pressure to his cuts. 'Probably sat on it!'

Wearily, he managed to stand up. 'How can I repay you?' he asked, as he dusted down his clothing. 'Your intervention with the broom probably saved my life!'

'I can think of a way, handsome' she answered, her face lighting up in anticipation. 'If you're up for it?' and quickly looking around she then attempted to push a reluctant Clytes towards the deep shadows of a warehouse doorway.

'Isn't your husband about?' he asked, hopefully, trying not to stare at the profusion of dark hair on her upper lip.

'Oh, he's busy. Don't worry about him,' she said, breathlessly. 'There's a camel train leaving today. He's supplying them with barley and fresh bread.'

'Going East?' queried Clytes, indifferently.

'No, south......Egypt!' replied the woman, making little progress in steering him through the crowded market.

Since deserting Angelos at the port of Sinope, Clytes had travelled without aim, finally arriving at the great trading city of Mazaka, in central Anatolia. Situated on the crossroads of the main highway from the Black Sea to the Euphrates River and the great Royal Road running east and west, it was a vital meeting point for merchants. The thought suddenly struck him that in this bustling centre of enterprise there could be opportunities.

'How do I find it?' he asked, with urgency. 'Which direction?'

'That way,' she said pointing. 'About a mile. They gather at the way station at the crossroads. You're not thinking of joining them, are you? It's a hazardous journey. Thieves are always a problem.'

Clytes, eager to escape his unwanted predicament, started to limp hurriedly away. She called after him. 'So much for your gratitude!'

Returning quickly, he took from a concealed pocket in his tunic a small leather pouch. 'Here!' he said, trying to thrust it into her hand.

'I don't want your money!' replied the woman, offended.

'It's a bracelet,' said Clytes, his hand shaking. 'Take it if you want.'

Curiously, the woman inspected the bag. 'It's beautiful!' she exclaimed, holding the shining object to catch the sun's rays. Suddenly feeling empathy with this obviously troubled stranger, she asked, 'Don't you have a wife to give it to? A sweetheart?' When receiving no response, she suggested, 'A sister, perhaps? I don't like taking it, if there's a woman in your life who would appreciate it.'

'I have no use for it...... and there's no woman in my life,' Clytes added, sharply. 'Do you want it or not?'

'I'll take it then,' answered the baker's wife, gratefully. 'Too small for me though,' she said, with obvious disappointment, as she tried to squeeze it over her plump fingers.

'Do what you like with it,' responded Clytes, and giving a last lingering look at the gold and silver bangle, he set off painfully in the direction of the hostel where he'd left Amir, minding what remained of his possessions. It occurred to him that the lad may have already sold them. In fact, when he'd left him that morning, he hadn't really cared about what happened to his belongings, or to himself for that matter. Now, he felt a sense of purpose. A faint one. Futile, even. But it was enough.

The boy was just where he'd left him, curled up asleep with his head resting on Clytes' travelling bag, but he leapt up, bowing eagerly, when he heard the door opening.

'It will be a dangerous journey for us, master!' Amir said in alarm, when he heard Clytes' plans. 'Many bandits!'

'Which is why you are staying here, Amir.' said Clytes, firmly. 'This is where we part company. I'll take you back to your uncle before I leave.'

The boy cried out in anguish and rushed at Clytes, clinging to him tightly.

'Agh!' Clytes, cried out. 'Watch my ribs!'

Accustomed by now to seeing this tall outlander return to his lodgings somewhat worse for wear, the boy asked anxiously, 'But who will look after your things, master, when you get yourself into trouble? My uncle Yazuv is always beating me!' sobbed the boy. 'You don't!'

'There'll be a first time, if you don't let go,' said Clytes, as he painfully released the boy's grip. 'I'm not safe to be with,' he told him, firmly. 'You will live longer if you stay with your uncle. But before I leave, I want you to find me a dog.'

'Why master? What kind of dog?' asked the boy.

'One big enough to look menacing but with no vices,' answered Clytes. One that will guard my possessions......and me, while I sleep.'

'But I do that master!' exclaimed Amir.

'Yes, you do, lad,' responded Clytes, almost breaking into a laugh. He was relieved when the pain of his cuts restrained him in time. He couldn't take the boy with him. No need to demean him further.

When he returned to his room, after settling his account with the landlord, he momentarily stared in astonishment.

'Is it a dog or a donkey?'

'You said you wanted a big one, master. 'It's a local breed. Used for guarding animals. Is it no good?'

'How much does the owner want?'

'Nothing, master.'

'Hmm. Probably something wrong with the animal then.'

'What name does it answer to?'

'It doesn't have a name. It's never had a name.'

'Doesn't have a name? It's got to answer to something. What on earth does it eat?'

'It doesn't eat much, master. A little barley and milk will do.'

'You seem to know a lot about the brute.'

'Yes, master. I've seen it around.'

'Well, I don't have much time. It will have to do.'

Leaving the dog in his room with his belongings, he walked with the boy back to where he'd found him, at the stable yard where his uncle worked. He was eager to leave. It had been some time since he'd felt any interest in anything, and he didn't want to miss the opportunity.

'Here, Amir,' he said, giving the boy a small pouch containing some coins. 'Hide it from your uncle!' he stressed.

Amir took the pouch, mumbled an elated thank you, but didn't look up.

'If you're thinking of following the caravan, Amir......don't!' said Clytes, sternly. 'I've told you why you must stay. I'll only have you returned. Do we have an agreement?'

'Yes master,' was the reluctant reply.

Yazuv was obviously not happy to learn he'd no longer be getting regular payments from the outlander for the hire of his ten-year old nephew, and although Clytes was in a hurry to leave, he felt concern for the boy's welfare.

Holding himself upright and trying to conceal the pain in his ribs, he said, threateningly. 'I'll be returning to this region, and if I find out you've been beating Amir, I'll break your ugly face so hard, you'll need the boy to feed you! Do you understand me?'

The man bowed, fawning, as the long shadow of Clytes fell over him. 'He's my own blood!' he whined. 'Come here, Amir!' The boy did as he was asked and Clytes watched frowning and suspicious as the uncle hugged the boy to him.

'Hmm. Just remember what I said!' Clytes asserted, and with a last guilty look at Amir, he left quickly.

Egypt! What was it the old historian, Admetus, had told him, he reflected, during those evenings spent with Theomenes at Mesembria? *'If you ever get the chance to see the Great Pyramids, Clytes, take it. It's a place everyone should see before they die!'* That was only a few months ago, he thought, with a sigh. Theomenes will be in Athens now, reassigned to his cavalry unit. Leon and Panthas will probably still be wondering what's happened to me. Well, their lives are in the hands of The Fates now and not Lykaon's!

Clytes was as unsure of the dog as it seemed to be of him. Concerned it might run back to its previous owner, he thought he'd better put a restraining rope on it. Approaching cautiously - it was a very large animal - he was greeted with a low warning growl and bared teeth. Thinking it was about to attack him, he held back. Well, this is a good start he thought, looking at the great hound, warily, but it has to know who's in charge. Approaching again slowly and talking softly, he could feel the animal tremble as he placed his hand on its large head, while slipping over the rope. His fingers immediately felt the raw flesh. Carefully stroking back the fur, he could see where a previous rope had left a deep encircling, weeping wound. He removed the leash gently, and bravely ignoring the snarling grin, made a thorough inspection of the animal, only to find more distressing evidence of ill-treatment. A previously broken jaw, now slightly crooked and a limp due to a badly healed fracture, being the most obvious.

'What have you left me with, Amir?' he muttered, as he looked at the afflicted animal, which was eyeing him suspiciously. 'Some guard dog!'

From the stable yard, man and boy had watched Clytes walk out of sight, then Amir broke free and tried to run. He was too late, the horse whip struck him across his back making him cry out as he stumbled to the ground. 'He won't be back, runt. He's lying!' growled Yazuv, standing over the terrified boy. 'Now! Where's the dog? Have you let it go again? Find it and bring it back. If I find it first, I'll break another leg!'

FOUR

'CAN'T SOMEONE STOP THE child from crying!' shouted Stephanos, as he entered, stooping, through the narrow doorway. 'This house is too small for a family!' he muttered to no-one in particular. Elissa, the housemaid, rushed past him from the kitchen area, heading in the direction of the wailing, and within moments there was silence.

'She has such a way with him,' remarked Micca, emerging flushed and dishevelled from the bedroom. 'I think he loves Elissa more than me.'

'My dear wife,' remarked Stephanos, kindly. 'You'll learn. It's your first child. Here, try this to pacify him,' and he handed her a small bronze pig. 'I bought it in the market earlier. Shake it and it rattles.'

'He has such a temper!' said Micca, wearily.

'He probably gets that from me,' Stephanos admitted.

Yet I tamed you, husband!' Micca replied, suddenly confident.

'Ha! You like to think so!' he replied, chuckling. 'I know I'm difficult to live with, Micca,' he confessed, as he gave his wife a quick embrace, 'but this existence in Athens is getting harder by the day for me to stomach!' Flinging himself down on their long couch, he declared, 'Now winter's over, all Plataeans must urge Cleon for action. There's never been a better opportunity to win back our city!'

'I know you better than you think,' said Micca, sitting down beside him. 'When I was just a girl, I used to watch you on the battlements with my father. You'd be pacing up and down like a caged animal. You were angry even then!'

'Diokles was a great mentor to me,' spoke Stephanos, seriously. 'The hours we must have spent on garrison duty, talking about the past and discussing world events. Sometimes, we thought we were the only two people in Plataea, aware of just how vulnerable the city had become. We'd become too used to relying on Athens for our protection.'

'I've had to make Athens my home for seven long years,' said Micca, sadly. Three for you, since you escaped the siege, but until this war is won, Stephanos, Athens will have to remain home for our boy, too.'

'Nicolaos is our hope for the future!' spoke Stephanos, forcefully. We can't continue to live like this; beholden to the Athenians for every crumb we eat. They may be able to till their own lands again, now the attacks have ceased, but we must return to *our* city and *our* groves!' he said, his voice rising.

'There, you've woken the baby again,' said Micca, looking askance at her husband, as wailing split the air, and purposefully shaking the bronze rattle, the mother returned to her son.

Stephanos took the opportunity to slip back through the doorway and crossing the shared, stinking courtyard, hurried back to the agora. Like many others, when he wasn't playing his part in defending the city, he was drawn to the prison building in the south-west corner of the marketplace, where, exhibited to the curious Athenian populace, were one hundred and twenty captured spartiates, the elite warriors of Sparta. The previous year, during the battle to keep the Messenian promontory at Pylos as an Athenian base, they'd surprisingly been captured alive, together with one hundred and seventy other prisoners. It was unheard of for Spartans to surrender, and the event had given a much-needed boost to the Athenian alliance. Although the initial frenzied attention had waned, he still had to push his way through the onlookers to reach the cells.

'They never fail to turn up!' called out one of the prisoners from behind the iron bars. 'Haven't they scrutinised us enough, Stephanos, to know we don't have horns and our dicks are just the same size as other men's?'

'Athens' greatest festival will be soon, Styphon. It's their City Dionysia,' the Plataean explained to the Spartan. 'You'll get many more spectators over the next few weeks. Get back!' he suddenly shouted, in exasperation, as some of the younger men crowding into the prison yard, began prodding the high- ranking Spartans with sticks and calling out taunts in an effort to get a reaction, but as always, every warrior stood firm and only glared back, stoically dismissive.

'What brutes!' the actor Panthas was heard to say to his companion Leon, as the pair found themselves pushed close to the bars of one of the cells. 'Don't look at them, Leon!' he exclaimed, shuddering, yet unable to resist a quick sideward glance at the hard muscled prisoners.

'Why did you want to come back here, if they make you so nervous?' asked Leon, tutting. 'You didn't sleep for a week after your last visit.'

'They could be returned to their homeland, Leon. We might never get another chance to see a spartiate this close. Unless he's cutting our throats!' he suddenly wailed, while clutching at his neck.

'Keep your dramatics for the stage, Panthas,' answered Leon, wearily. 'We are back in Athens to meet up with Clytes and for our own performances, not for you to get cheap thrills. If it wasn't for these 'brutes' we wouldn't have been able to leave the city. I never thought I'd appreciate the freedom so much.'

'It was good to meet up with old acquaintances,' agreed Panthas. 'Nice to know we'd been missed! But you're right, Leon,' he asserted, turning to scowl as someone behind him in the crowd pushed him forward, 'there've been no attacks by the Spartan army since the capture of these noble savages!'

The Spartan, Styphon, overhearing the remark, sprang at the bars with a loud roar, then fell back laughing, as Leon with the help of another spectator, assisted the slumped, trembling figure of Panthas out of the prison yard.

'What were they?' Styphon asked Stephanos, incredulously.

'Actors,' answered the Plataean, by way of explanation. 'Here for the festival. They're awaiting the arrival of a fellow performer. A very good friend of mine.'

The Spartan looked at Stephanos, quizzically.

'Oh, you couldn't scare *him*!' laughed Stephanos. 'You'd like him.'

Since the battle of Pylos, the previous year, more than one myth about the Spartans had been shattered. The fact that their elite warriors would fight to the death rather than surrender, being one. The belief that the Spartan populace would expect the prisoners to commit mass suicide rather than endure the humiliation of imprisonment in Athens, was another. The Athenians could not have been more wrong. The Spartans wanted their valued soldiers

17

back so desperately, they sued for peace, and the yearly brutal invasions into Attica, ceased.

To study and perhaps even re-educate so many Spartan elite was thought a unique occasion not to be missed. One persistent but unwanted inquisitor was the grey cloaked, paunchy philosopher, Socrates. Himself an honoured soldier, showing incredible bravery on the battlefield more than once, he failed to impress the Spartans. They were not very forthcoming when it came to discussing whether 'might makes right' and divulged little that would satisfy the driven man. Stephanos, on the other hand was a welcome visitor. He was a soldier they could relate to. No pointless questioning from him and, first and foremost, he was not an Athenian. He had also witnessed the astonishing bravery of their commander, Brasidas, during the Athenian defence of Pylos; a tale which the prisoners relished telling and retelling, with every detail recounted, helping to keep pride and hope alive.

'It certainly was a sight to see those triremes being driven ashore!' admitted Stephanos. 'Brasidas had some nerve to risk wrecking the ships like that.'

'He is unlike any other commander,' spoke up one of the prisoners, proudly. 'Absolutely fearless and a brilliant strategist. I was close enough to hear him shout, *'Perish the ships and force a landing!'* The other captains obeyed without question.'

'It's where I received my first serious wound,' admitted Stephanos. 'We had to fight like demons to stop you lot getting inland. When he came onto the gangway, we trained every arrow on him. I knew we had a hit when I saw his shield fall into the water.'

'We have one consolation,' spoke Styphon, confiding in Stephanos. 'If Brasidas had not been taken away by the medics at that time, he could have been captured with the rest of us, when Cleon's reinforcements arrived. That would have been hard to accept. As it is, we know he will not have given up the fight for victory, *and* he'll be working on a plan for our release!'

Shouts of, 'Brasidas! Brasidas!' suddenly rose up fiercely and loudly, spreading from cell to cell. The din reverberated around the prison yard as the guards rushed in, unsuccessfully attempting to quell the commotion. Only when Styphon finally raised his arm, did his fellow Spartans cease their chanting. He was their commander when they put down their shields and surrendered to Cleon, and he remained so, even in imprisonment.

'Brasidas!' muttered Stephanos, as he left the prison and made his way back to the undesirable neighbourhood where he and Micca had their home. He had seen the man in action. He'd experienced at first-hand how this audacious leader of men inspired those around him. His fingers felt for the deep scar on his shoulder, the result of a Spartan spear thrust. He tried lifting his right arm, still feeling the stiff resistance. As much as inactivity irked him, he seriously hoped he would never encounter this most dangerous of adversaries again.

FIVE

THE NOISE OF THE camels drew Clytes towards the crowded way station at the crossroads. Their grumbling as cargoes were loaded or unloaded filled the air, and the dog pressed itself close to Clytes without the need for any leash. There must have been two hundred or more, and together with braying donkeys and bellowing oxen, they created the loudest din imaginable. Clytes urgently needed to find the camel train master, and he eagerly pushed his way through the colourful seething mass of humanity, seeking out the one man he thought could get him to Egypt. He was told by a sweating caravaneer, busy loading carpets onto the back of a resisting camel, that the headman was called Masoud. After pausing briefly from his labours and giving Clytes a critical look from head to foot, he felt compelled to warn the stranger that the master was a suspicious bastard who trusted nobody, and he didn't like trouble.

A fellow camel handler gave a sideways glance, as Clytes, dishevelled and bruised, accompanied by his mangy hound, vanished into the crowd. 'He looks like trouble,' he agreed, and the men exchanged knowing looks.

The heavy Bactrian camels were unsuitable for the hot, dry conditions ahead, and their cargoes of silk, lapis lazuli and precious spices, brought in stages from as far away as Afghanistan, were reloaded onto the backs of the single humped dromedaries, animals thought more suited to long periods on more arid terrain.

The merchants who owned the dromedaries were working with the attendants in making final adjustments to their precious cargoes, to be sold at a good profit when they reached the insatiable buyers of Egypt. Some would travel the entire route, transferring their goods to fresh animals several times. Others had written contracts with middle-men, who guaranteed to get them the best possible price for their goods at the end of the long trail. A few, travelling with oxen or donkeys, were only going as far as the next large town and had attached themselves to the caravan for protection.

Still waiting to be loaded, and rolled up in stacked mountainous piles, were brightly decorated Anatolian carpets, woven with motives of animals both exotic and domestic. Last to be put on the camels' backs would be the heavy sacks of barley, a staple food on the journey for both men and beasts.

Among the many traders, Clytes noticed a wagon piled high with loaves and rolls of various grains. The baker was doing a good trade and it was only because of Clytes' long reach that he succeeded in purchasing enough buns to fill a small sack. He held one out to the dog, but it looked away. Puzzled, Clytes placed the bread on the ground, only to see it devoured in a lop-sided gulp. The animal looked wary, expecting to be hit, but Clytes only stroked its great head. 'I don't know which of us is in worst shape,' he murmured, as he put down another bun. 'I'll have to give you a name, boy. Something heroic, eh, to suit your size. One that will make people cautious. 'Fury'?' he suggested to the dog, after some deliberation. Hmm, perhaps not, he mused, looking at its sad, downcast eyes.

Eager shouting broke this one-sided conversation as riding towards him came the camel train master, being hailed by several merchants and caravan attendants, all vying for his urgent, last-minute attention. Clytes, sprawled on one of the barley sacks had been waiting patiently to talk with this man. He was determined to be part of the venture but knew he must first prove himself useful to the man in charge.

The self-assured attitude of the lanky Eleusinian gained the headman's keen interest instantly, and as soon as he'd dealt with the pressing concerns of the traders, he waved him over.

'You look as though you've been in a fight. Did you win?'

'The other man looks worse. He won't be killing any more bears for a while.'

'Babak? I'm impressed. You're lucky to be alive! Any encumbrances, outlander? Family?'

'Only the dog.'

'Camels take priority for food and water. He could end up as dog meat.'

'I'll take care of him.'

'Good breed. Jaws like iron.'

'Maybe.'

'How far are you going?'

'All the way.'

'On foot?'

'If necessary.'

'Do you have money?'

'Enough.'

'If we're attacked, will you fight?'

'I've never run from a fight.'

'I don't like troublemakers. Cause me any problems and I'll have you dealt with......understand?'

'I just want to get to Egypt.'

Further questioning revealed Clytes' astonishing fighting history which convinced the wily leader that the services of this battle-scared, seasoned warrior was an offer not easily passed up. Accompanying the caravan were the usual paid guards, who rode their own camels, but Masoud had travelled this route many times. He knew a man like Clytes could be useful. Anyway, the man had fought Babak and survived. Now that was a fight he'd have paid good coin to see.

The time for leaving had overrun due to a heavy downpour of rain in the early hours, making loading difficult, and now all was noise and activity as final loads were being carefully re-arranged by the practised caravaneers. An uneven load on a camel would be greeted by complaining howls from the animal, but total silence could mean the load was too heavy. To keep control of such a lengthy caravan the dromedaries were split into teams of ten, and when in motion they walked in single files linked together by ropes, tail to muzzle. Only men with experience of the particular peculiarities and needs of these beasts of burden were put in charge of the teams.

Within a few hours of fighting over a loaf of bread when his mental state was fuelled by an overwhelming sense of grievance and despair, Clytes was on his way south, taken on by Masoud as a security guard for the camel train. It was springtime. In Attica, the people were preparing themselves for the renewal of hostilities.

SIX

INTO THE EIGHTH YEAR of the war, following a successful run of campaigns and with no threat of a Spartan invasion, the Athenians were able to leave the confines of their city to safely plough and replant their fields. Also, travel was more reliable, and the Dionysian festivals were well attended.

Cleon's aggressive leadership, however, was not appreciated by all Athenians, and the playwright, Aristophanes, had once again used his coarse comic skills to mock the demagogue.

Having previously been taken to court by Cleon for supposedly bringing shame on Athens in front of foreign spectators at the City Dionysia, Aristophanes' newest play, 'The Knights' was performed at the earlier Lenaia festival. The weather being more inclement during the winter month of Gamelion, Cleon hoped that few foreigners would be able to travel to see it.

The comic actors, Leon and Panthas, were seated a long way from their glorious leader, who, following his recent military successes was entitled to a front row seat, but his violent gestures accompanied by a furious commotion witnessed amongst his friends assured the delighted pair that the play did not go down well with the strategos. Through the antics of the slaves in the household of the elderly character Demos, who represented the people of Athens, Aristophanes bombarded the audience with a blatant satirical criticism of Cleon. With this blistering farce, the playwright inflicted the promised revenge on his powerful enemy, but whether it was the serious underlying message; warning the demos to be aware of bribery and corruption by unworthy leaders; the wooing of the aristocrats with visions of another golden age, or the vulgar humour and sexual innuendo that appealed; 'The Knights' won first prize at the Lenaia.

'I wish Clytes had been here!' exclaimed Panthas, as the pair left the theatre, surrounded by a vociferous crowd all loudly discussing the play. 'He would have applauded Aristophanes for painting his own face to play the part of Cleon. No mask-maker dared make an image of him!'

'If Cleon's policies continue to bring results, the mob will continue to love him!' shouted Leon above the clamour. 'No play by Aristophanes will change that!'

'Didn't the chorus look splendid!' gushed Panthas. 'The efforts of our knights should be appreciated.'

'Yes, Aristophanes was clever to praise the cavalry,' agreed Leon. 'He will need them to protect his back! He pulled no punches!'

'Well, I still say we were first!' said Panthas, without malice.

'We were,' assented Leon. 'But Terches' little play will be lost in time. This play will last. It *was* funny!'

'All that farting!' chortled Panthas, while holding onto to Leon as they carefully negotiated the steps. 'My sides are still sore from laughing!'

With hopes of victory on the horizon, The City Dionysia, two months later, was enjoyed by people from near and far and the acting duo, between their own performances, attended several events. They met up with acquaintances not seen in the metropolis for some time, for fear of either catching the plague or becoming entrapped in the city during a Spartan attack. Fretting about the absence of their friend Clytes, they pestered everyone who knew the Eleusinian for any news of him, and by the time they finally encountered Theomenes who'd recently arrived from Mesembria in the company of his friend, Angelos, they were beside themselves with worry. The sad news as to what had happened at Pontus, only amplified their anxieties.

'Clytes is well able to take care of himself!' exclaimed Stephanos, frustratedly, when Theomenes and Angelos later paid their respects to his family at their humble abode. 'I learnt that during our adventures in Persia. You needn't worry about *him*.'

Stephanos had just been presented with Clytes' sword, and it swung in its shoulder scabbard as he swaggered around the small room. 'I always envied Clytes being given this sword by Diokles,' he said, truthfully, as he lovingly stroked the ornate gold pommel, 'but I accepted that he should have it......obviously. As a non-Plataean he couldn't have done more to help our cause.'

'As Diokles' son-in-law, Stephanos, I thought it should be passed to you,' said Theomenes. 'You held our group together during our adventure, and I can think of no-one more deserving.' Seeing the proud Plataean lost for words, he changed the subject. 'Any news of Glaucus? Is The Helmsman in the city? How's the ship 'Delias' holding up?'

'Last I heard, he was in Sicily with the fleet, waiting to invade,' replied Stephanos. 'The islanders are still in conflict with one another, so it's only a matter of time before their resistance is weak enough for us to take the entire island. If reinforcements are asked for, we could be meeting up with the big redhead before too long.'

'And 'the old girl'? How is the Delias?' pressed Theomenes.

'Well, the news is not good,' Stephanos answered, hesitantly. 'She sank......apparently!'

Theomenes and Angelos looked at one another incredulously. 'I gave him that ship for his wine enterprise!' exclaimed Theomenes. 'In gratitude for his efforts in rescuing The Shield. What happened?'

This could take some time,' said Stephanos, still strutting. 'I would value your opinions,' and he indicated to his friends to be seated. 'The tale he told me,' Stephanos went on, in a tone of disbelief, 'was that he was courting a lady of a certain age......but she had some wealth from investments in a local marble mine...... *apparently*. I was sceptical but he seemed to believe it all. Anyway, he was invited to join a hunting party with members of her family and accidently got shot in the arm.'

'What do you mean......*accidently*?' asked Angelos.

'Well, it's what happened later that got me suspicious,' answered Stephanos. 'As you know, Glaucus had a regular trade going between Thrace and Byzantium for his wine, but when they insisted that he couldn't steer the Delias because of his injury, which he admitted was only superficial, the family recommended someone to take his place so he wouldn't lose the shipment. I think Glaucus liked the idea of a few weeks being cared for by his ladylove and he agreed. That was the last he saw of the ship.'

'So, what's so suspicious?' asked Theomenes.

'He was told that the new helmsman wasn't up to the job, and the ship sank in the strong current of the Bosporus,' replied Stephanos. 'What do you think, Theo?'

'I think that it could be true,' answered Theomenes, candidly. 'Glaucus is the best helmsman in all Hellas. It's amazing he got the Delias as far as he did. She was an old ship.'

'Hmm,' responded Stephanos, still pacing the floor. 'Something doesn't seem right to me.'

'But Glaucus obviously believed the story,' spoke up Angelos.

'Yes, he would!' said Stephanos. 'That's my worry. He really does believe that the other helmsman wasn't as good as him. Even though the man was *in his own waters*?'

'What about the lady?' asked Theomenes.

'Oh, she wanted nothing more to do with him, of course,' Stephanos replied, with obvious disgust.

'Was Glaucus with Bion or Cassa?' asked Theomenes, with concern. 'Were they in the crew?'

'You know Glaucus always used local sailors with knowledge of the currents, Theo. But the family also picked the crew,' said Stephanos with emphasis.

'So, no friends lost then?' said Theomenes, relieved.

'You're missing my point, here!' replied Stephanos, in frustration. 'I think it was all a trick to relieve Glaucus of his ship. I don't think it is at the bottom of the Bosporus. I think they stole it, and the sad thing is, he left his axe on the ship.'

'Oh, not his axe!' exclaimed Theomenes. 'That is bad news. I think Glaucus would rather have lost a limb, than be parted from that weapon.'

Fearing being slashed by Stephanos, as he persisted in examining his newly acquired weapon to test its balance, Theomenes suggested they continue their discussion outside, and the men left the claustrophobic confines of the house to sit in the shared courtyard. Soon the walls reverberated with the sound of their differing opinions, especially when the conversation drifted to plans for the retaking of Plataea, and on hearing their lively debate, neighbours began to drift from their simple workshops, to join in.

'Our generals are overstretching themselves, in my opinion!' one old man was bold enough to state. 'Cleon should give serious consideration to Sparta's offer of peace,' but he was immediately shouted down by many voices. For the ordinary citizens of Athens, it seemed Cleon could do no wrong.

SEVEN

AFTER A PEACEFUL SPRING, farmers and their families left their makeshift accommodation in Athens, believing it was finally safe enough to return to their cherished homes and villages. In the city, meanwhile, their ten generals with overblown confidence, pored over plans for their next ambitious campaigns. Emboldened by the unexpected change of circumstances in the war, the democratic factions in Athens' neighbouring states of Megaris and Boeotia had been stimulated into action. With promises of help from Athens, the leaders of these parties now plotted with the generals to join the victorious Athenian League. Despite the roasting at the Lenaia Festival, Cleon, rightly or wrongly, had been given the credit for their good fortune at Pylos and his generalship was extended for another year.

On the island of Sicily, however, a totally different course of events was unfolding. The shark like presence of the encircling Athenian warships had galvanised the warring factions to make peace with one another, and embassies from all the Sicilian cities assembled to try to bring about a pacification. The commonsense of doing so was spelled out to them by a fierce democrat and natural orator by the name of Hermocrates from the city of Syracuse, who, with sound judgement, spoke earnestly to them.

'If I now address you, Sicilians, it is not because my city is the least in Sicily or the greatest sufferer by the war, but in order to state publicly what appears to me to be the best policy for the whole island.

We see the first power in Hellas watching our mistakes with the few ships that she has at present in our waters, and under the fair name of alliance speciously seeking to turn to account the natural hostility that exists between us. If we go to war, and call in to help us a people that are ready enough to carry their arms, even where they are not invited; and if we injure ourselves at our own expense, and at the same time serve as the pioneers of their dominion, we may expect, when they see us worn out, that they will one day come with a larger armament, and seek to bring all of us into subjection.

The quickest way to be rid of it is to make peace with each other; since the Athenians menace us not from their own country, but from that of those who invited them here. In this way instead of war issuing in war, peace quietly ends our quarrels; and the guests who come hither under fair pretences for bad ends, will have good reason for going away without having attained them.'

The Sicilians took his good advice and came to an understanding among themselves to end the hostilities, each keeping what they had. As a result, the three-year civil war between the city of Syracuse and Sicily's pro-Athenian towns ended, and the commanders of the Athenian forces, which had been sent to Sicily to support Greek settlements, accepted the fact that they hadn't the numbers to take the now unified island.

'Well, what a fiasco!' the helmsman, Glaucus, exclaimed angrily, to his friend Cassa. 'Three years of effort have been invested into subduing this island......and it ends like this!'

'It's unheard of!' replied the rowing master. 'Hermocrates must either be an exceptional orator or else he's used some means to persuade our generals.'

Glaucus, still tormented by the loss of his ship and subsequent wine business, answered gruffly, 'I could use some of that persuasion!'

The heavily populated island of Sicily was wealthy due to its strategic position on lucrative trade routes, and its rich volcanic soil produced an abundance of wheat, olives, almonds and fruit, so when the crews heard the news that their commanders had signed a peace treaty with the islanders and were returning the fleet to Athens, their eager hopes of some profitable looting, were immediately dashed.

Bion, one of the veteran rowers and a close comrade of both Glaucus and Cassa, was not one to stay silent and voiced what many in the crews were thinking. 'How can we return to Athens empty handed? We'll be mocked at best. Ostracised, most likely. They'll be expecting another Pylos!'

On their inglorious return to Athens, two of the generals were indeed exiled, and a third, Eurymedon, was fined for supposedly taking bribes to sail away with the fleet. Their pleas that they'd insufficient forces to subdue the whole island, were greeted with cries of 'shame!' from the angry citizens. Recent successes had given the Athenians a feeling of invincibility, and the populace now confused their hopes with their strengths.

With the taking of Sicily no longer a possibility, the generals looked closer to home for hope of a successful outcome. After their humiliation across the seas, they turned their sights on neighbouring Megara, anticipating a quick victory. With twice yearly invasions from Athens and constant attacks from their exiled oligarchs based in their seaport of Pegaea, the democratic government of Megara was under unrelenting pressure. Believing the citizens were close to wanting a return of rule by a powerful few rather than by the many, the democrats feared for their lives. In desperation they decided to join the Athenian alliance for protection. There was just one problem. Megara, even though democratic, was an ally of Sparta. How to proceed with their aims and not forfeit their lives to other Megarians, who were in favour of remaining in the Spartan alliance, would require a cunning plan.

For this they sought the help of the Athenian general Hippocrates, and the real hero of Pylos, general Demosthenes. Demosthenes, in turn, sought the help of the Plataeans, and in particular the remaining members of the now disbanded Shield Company. The scheme devised would require some audacity and most likely street-fighting, and he believed the exiled Plataeans would give a good account of themselves.

'I want to be first to enter the city!' Stephanos demanded, and he received no objections from the Plataeans gathered around him. They were discussing the forthcoming campaign at the house of Hypatos, Theomenes' uncle, and the city Stephanos was referring to was not Megara but his own beloved birthplace over the border in Boeotia. 'Those Theban murderers will finally get their just rewards!' he said, fiercely.

'We've waited a long time for this,' spoke Theomenes, seriously, as he looked around the crowded room. 'But we cannot do it without Athenian support. Before they help us to re-take our city, we must first add our weight to assisting those Megarians who now want to ally themselves with Athens.'

'Can they be trusted to hold their nerve though?' asked one of the older men present. 'How many times have they welcomed back their oligarchs? More than I can remember.'

'The more resolute democrats have been rehearsing their stratagem for weeks now,' spoke up Stephanos. 'So far, the Spartan supporters haven't suspected anything. Once we are through the city gates, it will be soon over. The citadel will be ours.'

'The ruse sounds feasible enough,' remarked Erastos, a veteran of The Shield Company. 'I just don't trust Megarians......as friends or foes.'

'Demosthenes has asked for our help and we mustn't disappoint him,' insisted Stephanos. 'I was one of the sixty men chosen to fight beside him on the beach at Pylos. I've had personal experience of his tactics. If *he* believes the plan will work, then *I* believe the plan will work.'

'First Megara, then Plataea!' shouted Angelos, eagerly, and the room erupted.

EIGHT

EACH NIGHT SINCE CLYTES had started his journey south, he'd been woken by the dog's low whining. There was always some noise or activity after dark, either from the hobbled camels grumbling as they lay down after grazing, the snoring of his travelling companions, or the quiet banter of the night guards as they sat around their fires. 'It's alright, boy,' Clytes would say, wrapping himself more tightly in his blanket. 'Nothing to be afraid of.'

On the fifth night, it wasn't the animal's whining that disturbed his sleep. It was the cold. He woke, shivering, and immediately noticed that the dog wasn't there. Thinking it had gone to relieve itself, he curled up in his blanket again and immediately fell back to sleep. In the morning there was still no sign of the dog. Clytes' first thought was that Masoud was involved in some way, remembering how dubious he'd seemed, about the care of the animal on the journey.

'My dog's missing,' said Clytes pointedly.

'What's that to do with me?' he answered, tetchily.

'I told you I'd be responsible for it,' said Clytes, sharply. 'You should have told me if there was a problem.'

'Look Clytes, I don't know what you're talking about,' replied Masoud. 'I've more important things to worry about.'

Clytes glowered down at the man for a moment, then believing what he'd been told, hurried back to his camping place, expecting the dog to be back.

'Those animals are loyal creatures, my friend,' remarked Hasim, one of the camel-pullers who camped close to Clytes. 'My father has one similar. It's like a member of the family. Had it long?'

With sudden clarity, Clytes replied, 'You think it's returned to its old master then?'

'I don't doubt it,' replied Hasim, knowingly.

'Damn!' exclaimed Clytes, and he gave a furious kick to a half-filled leather water bag, sending it flying through the air.

'Hey! You, there!' came an angry shout. Clytes looked in the direction of the outcry and saw an enormous black Arab dressed in long billowing robes, striding purposefully towards him. Almost blocked from view by his bulk was a heavily caparisoned camel, topped by a colourful tented howdah, and it was being led by a handler, in what Clytes considered, overly ostentatious dress. The tasseled curtain on the howdah parted slightly and a slender arm as dark as ebony, adorned with several gold bangles, extended from it. It held Clytes dripping water sack. A woman's voice called out imperiously. 'My mistress wants you to collect your missile,' the man in the flowing robes said to Clytes, with more than a hint of menace.

Curious, Clytes approached the carriage. Through an opening in the drapes drifted an intoxicating scent of perfume, and he waited for the curtains to open fully so he could get sight of the passenger within, but he was to be disappointed. His water sack was handed back to him through the gap without comment. Calling out to her attendants, the lady and her entourage moved slowly on down the line of the camel train towards its head. As he turned away, Clytes thought he heard the sound of female laughter.

'If you value your life, keep well away from that one!' remarked Hasim, his voice loaded with wisdom beyond his years. 'A cousin of mine tried to get a glimpse of her bathing. He's now begging on the streets of Mazaka. He had his eyes put out.'

'Thank you for the warning but there's no need,' responded Clytes. 'I'm not interested. But I am intrigued. Who is she?'

'Shamira of Tadmor. Her father is ruler of the lands around the oasis. He collects the king's taxes from the Euphrates to the Orontes, as well as taking a little extra for himself! We'll pass through the edge of his territory on the way to Damascus. His daughter has complete control over his shipments between Mazaka and the old city. More ruthless than any man! In fact, it's rumoured she is half-man,' said Hasim, winking knowingly at Clytes.

'What?!' queried Clytes.

'Yes, she has a dick as well as a cunt!' replied Hasim, laughing half-heartedly.

'You know that for a fact?' asked Clytes.

'Well, no,' Hasim answered, hesitantly. 'But it's common knowledge. Anybody who tries to find out ends up blind, castrated or dead!'

'I'm even less interested, now!' said Clytes, shaking his head in disbelief.

That day they made steady progress, the caravan moving at a man's walking pace, ever southwards. Clytes had made an effort to be helpful with the loading and unloading of the pack animals in one particular group and now knew the names and stories of several of his travelling companions. After chores were completed and food had been eaten, he would sit with them around their night fire to talk and sing. That night they were joined by an uncle of Hasim's, a regular camel-puller from a group near the end of the line. The talk drifted to what had happened to Clytes' canine companion.

'Strange you should mention a dog,' said the man. 'I heard such a barking before we camped last night. Probably encountered a predator. It was a long way off, but bloody persistent.'

'Shit!' cursed Clytes.

The following morning, before the sun was even fully up, he set off on foot to retrace the route of the camel train. He took with him some food and water - also bow and arrows. He had no idea what to expect. A mutilated carcass most likely. Killed by one of the big cats or perhaps a snake.

Walking at a brisk pace he reached the area of the previous night's campsite after midday but headed on further north, taking into account the details given to him by Hasim's relative. This was a well-worn route, and he came across several travellers. Questioning them as to whether barking had been heard in the vicinity, eventually led him to small hillock, topped by an old ruin. He kept calling out, 'hey!' all the while thinking, why didn't I give him a bloody name? Continuing his shouting as he searched the hill, he was finally greeted with a loud, deep bark.

The animal was lying in the shelter of a crumbling wall and growled softly as Clytes approached. Believing it was hurt, Clytes tried to calm it by speaking gently. 'Quiet now. It's alright,' he said, reaching out to stroke him. Then he saw Amir. The boy was curled up behind the dog and he wasn't moving. Clytes immediately thought he was dead, then, to his relief, Amir's eyes flickered open. Gently he raised him up. There was a gash on the side of his head which had obviously been licked clean, and because of the dog's administrations, there was mercifully little chance of infection.

For miles, Clytes carried the boy on his back, but eager to return to the caravan as quickly as possible, he gladly accepted the help of any traveller with transport willing to convey the boy south. The trio spent another night under the stars before finally catching up with the slow-moving line of camels, during which time Amir was able to relate to Clytes what had happened.

'I lost the money you gave me, master,' he confessed, miserably. 'Robbers took it from me. I think they thought they'd killed me,' he said, feeling for the gash on his temple. 'I couldn't follow the camel train anymore. I felt dizzy so I hid in the old building. I was so cold until Baz found me.'

'Baz? I thought it didn't have a name.'

'It's what I named him. In my head only, master. My uncle would have been angry if he knew. He didn't like giving animals names.'

'The dog belonged to Yazuv?!'

'Yes, master.'

'You followed me when I told you not to, Amir. I warned you it would be safer to stay with your uncle.'

'Don't send me back there, master!'

'Well, it seems Lykaon's not getting everything his way. The gods have intervened with a four-legged guardian!'

'Who's Lykaon?'

'Someone else who follows me, Amir. Anyway, my lad, what sort of a name is Baz?'

NINE

THEY TRAVELLED BY NIGHT with muffled oars. Destination? The tiny island of Minoa off the Megarian coast. Occupied by an Athenian garrison since its capture by general Nicias three years previously, the outpost effectively blockaded by sea, Megara's main port at Nisaea, which was occupied by a garrison from the Spartan alliance.

With the first part of the plan completed without detection, general Hippocrates proceeded under cover of darkness to lead his six hundred heavily armed hoplites across the narrow causeway to the mainland. Here, he met up with his co-commander, general Demosthenes, with the rest of the advance guard consisting of loyal Plataeans and a contingent of Athenian home guards. Being lightly armed they'd travelled overland and had hidden themselves close to the mile long walls between the port of Nisaea and the city of Megara, waiting for the dawn when they were to rush the gates. Hippocrates and his troops had concealed themselves in a ditch nearby, in a heightened state of alertness, ready to complete the attack.

Before sunrise, according to the pre-arranged plan, they waited in silence as a group of men, labouring under the weight of their task, approached along the road from the sea. They were hauling a wheeled cart, topped by a sculling boat and were heading for the large wooden gates giving access to the long walls. Every night for weeks, Megarian democrats had practiced this manoeuvre. On the pretense of carrying out covert night raids on the Athenians based on Minoa, the Spartan guards would open the wall gates to allow exit for the boat and its crew, and each morning before dawn, when the boat was brought back, the gates were reopened for them.

Shouts were heard from the guards on the wall, acknowledging the return of the boating party, as the Megarian oarsmen glanced around anxiously for any indication of the arrival of the expected Athenian advance guard. Relieved on hearing the pre-arranged signal called out close by, they prepared themselves for action. From the cart, one of the men retrieved a large axe. His comrades came equipped with recently sharpened knives.

As the gates swung open the group quickly pushed the cart into the gap, while the axe-man got to work in deftly removing one of the wheels. The wagon was now stuck in the opening, preventing the cursing guards from securing the walls. Before they realised what was happening, Demosthenes and the Plataeans were through. The Megarians immediately began killing the gate keepers while the Athenian general, accompanied by Stephanos and the rest of his comrades, sought out members of the wall guard. As the sun rose, those on the battlements became easy targets for arrows and slingshot, and Angelos' careful aim brought a quick death to many. With the gates now securely under their control, Hippocrates and his hoplites stormed through to continue the attack with spear and sword on the now alarmed garrison. Believing the whole of Megara had turned against them and were now in league with Athens, those still able, fled in confusion to the protection of fortified Nisaea.

The long walls were now held by Hippocrates and Demosthenes. The garrison - made up of different members of the Peloponnesian League - was too afraid to venture out. The next part of the plan was to take the citadel, and the Athenian forces headed towards the city gates where they expected their co-conspirators to be keeping to their part of the bargain, but instead of the gates being opened to give battle, at which time the pro-Athenian faction would turn on the pro-Spartan faction, they remained firmly closed. The plot had been discovered.

By this time, according to the pre-arranged plan, the main Athenian force had arrived on the scene. Four thousand fresh troops and six hundred cavalry had travelled overnight along the coast road from Eleusis, and they were expecting to be taking part in the capture of Megara. Stephanos struggled inadequately to explain to a recently arrived Theomenes, the reason why the gates of the city weren't being opened to them as promised by the Megarian democrats.

'Who's barring the city, then?'

'The Megarians.'

'Who controls the long walls?'

'We do.'

'And the port?'

'The Spartans, still.'

'Erastos was right. We should never have trusted the Megarians.'

With no help forthcoming from the trapped democrats inside the city, the generals had no choice but to turn their attentions to capturing the port of Nisaea, and with building equipment brought from Athens, the army worked day and night in blockading the settlement by land. After only two days of siege, the garrison capitulated. They'd run out of food since their supplies normally came daily from the city, and having had no contact with the inhabitants, it was assumed they were no longer their allies.

Little did they know that if they'd only held out for a few more days, they could have avoided being ransomed. The Spartan general, Brasidas, was in nearby Corinth, gathering an army for an attack on Thrace, but on hearing of the attack on the Megarians, he hurried to their aid with four thousand of his force. Discovering that the Athenians were down by the sea, he chose three hundred men to go with him to the city, where he expected to be made welcome, but the divided Megarians refused to open the gates to him. Assuming a battle would soon be taking place between the Athenians and the Spartans, they decided to watch from behind their walls and wait for the outcome.

Unable to get his own way but determined to keep the city under Spartan control, Brasidas returned to his troops and prepared to do battle with the Athenians the next day. With the coming of dawn, he discovered that messengers he'd sent to the Boeotians requesting their urgent assistance had been successful, and his army was increased by the arrival of their troops, who'd marched to the defence of Megara. In their party were over two thousand hoplites and six hundred cavalry making Brasidas' combined forces stronger than the Athenians by almost a thousand men.

By travelling over Mount Cithaeron during the night, the arrival of the Boeotian force was unknown to the Athenian generals, so when Demosthenes first gave his order to Stephanos and his Plataeans to carry out skirmishes on the enemy camp, he was unaware of the additional risk.

Lightly armed and taking with them members of the Athenian home guard, Stephanos and his men set off at first light, eventually splitting into smaller groups. Their purpose was to cause as much damage as possible to anything which would sustain the enemy. Farms were raided, food stores scattered and herds driven off. Any crops were trampled. When opportunities arose they harassed the patrolling sentries, and keeping low, moving stealthily through the underbrush, they took the guards by surprise. One unfortunate, who'd wandered off on a call of nature, was brought down by a slinger's careful aim, to be quickly despatched by Stephanos, using his recently acquired superior blade. While smoke curled up from the early morning campfires and the sound of men's voices began drifting across the plain, they continued undetected, until a single man's voice was heard, screaming out in alarm. This was soon followed by more agitated shouting, then a hand-to-hand fight for survival quickly ensued. With their presence now discovered, their signalman blew urgently on his trumpet, giving warning of the counterattack, which was quickly relayed back to the Athenians at the port of Nisaea. Some of the Plataeans managed to rejoin Stephanos, but many of the group became separated. It was now every man for himself.

'Cavalry!' shouted Stephanos, urgently, as a group of horsemen thundered across the plain towards them. With their distinctive armour, the Plataeans were in no doubt as to where the riders hailed from. 'Boeotians! Save yourselves!' he yelled.

'When did *they* arrive?' cursed Angelos, incredulously, who like Stephanos and others, was looking desperately for some vantage point. 'Demosthenes never mentioned cavalry!' Scrambling quickly up an incline they took up defensive positions with spears pointed outwards, as a cohort of riders sped by, hurling their lances in their direction. The archers and slingers with Stephanos, let fly with a barrage of missiles aimed primarily at the horses, causing more than one to throw its rider.

'Did you hear that?' one of the men from the home guard, shouted excitedly.

His comrade, frantically searching for suitable stones to refill his empty sling, yelled back, 'What was it?'

'A horn!'

'Whose?'

'Ours! I'd recognise Damon's signalling, anywhere.'

'You'd better be right!'

Over the plain, Boeotian horsemen were ruthlessly hunting down the rest of the scattered raiding party, but on hearing the Athenian clarion calls approaching from the direction of the port, they immediately ceased their activities. The sound of their own signals suddenly drowned out everything else, and they rode to obey the orders to reform.

Cheering was heard from the hillock, where Stephanos and his group were watching the dust cloud in the direction of Nisaea, getting closer, and it grew louder still on seeing Theomenes at the head of his cavalry unit. As he charged by, Stephanos raised his gleaming sword, and shouted out, 'Thebans, Theo! Remember Plataea!' With a grim wave, Theomenes hastily acknowledged his friend's rallying cry.

The opposing forces mustered around six hundred horsemen apiece, and the open Megarian plain provided adequate space for them to show off their skills. The war horses of Boeotia were renowned for their prowess on the battlefield, second only to those bred on the flat, fertile plains of Thessaly, and the Athenian horsemen watched in awe as the Boeotian riders, looking confident of victory, trotted on in close formation, their shields and javelins held ready for action. Showing off their wealth, many in the front ranks wore expensive body armour. Open helmets were decorated with brightly coloured horsehair plumes. Horses were elaborately bridled. Theomenes was well aware that even though their forces were equal in numbers, they were outmatched by the quality of horses and horsemanship of the Boeotians - but he'd learnt a thing or two during his time in the unit. Fellow cavalrymen, Makron and Astos, who'd initially caused Theomenes cruel humiliation in calling him a country bumkin, had, since his exploits in Persia looked to him for leadership. Also, his corps commander, Dadilos, was not averse to receiving advice from the Plataean hero.

'Wear them down, Dadilos!' Theomenes urged his leader. 'They've been travelling all night. They may look very fine, but that could be to their disadvantage!'

'Until the Megarians make up their minds as to whose side they're actually on,' replied Dadilos, gravely, 'don't take any risks.'

'Not if you want to live long enough to see your home-city again,' Makron advised. 'Save yourself and your horse for the invasion of Boeotia!'

The uncertainty of the Megarians caused both factions to be cautious of taking undue risks and few losses were suffered on either side, but the horsemen became scattered and grasping the initiative, Dadilos took Theomenes' advice and he ordered his lightly armed mounted archers to carry out hit-and-run attacks. Endeavouring to avoid the barrage of missiles, the more heavily encumbered Boeotians had to swerve their horses sharply, and they began to tire. Watching in growing frustration was their leader, and he left the mound where he'd been surveying the field and charged boldly down the incline, accompanied by the rest of his group of high-born cavalrymen.

Theomenes had been fighting furiously to get closer to this privileged party. He knew of the leading Theban, distinctively protected by an extravagant cuirass and a gleaming helmet topped with a flowing red plume and rejoiced at this chance encounter to bring him down. There was a long-time score to settle. Theomenes had been too young to protect his city of Plataea during the two-year siege, but his elder brother, Alexeis, had died in the attempt. In the three years since, the feeling of guilt had never left him. It was every Plataean's belief that the Spartans would have spared the besieged garrison, if certain prominent Thebans hadn't insisted on the death penalty. One such noble was on the battlefield and in Theomenes' sight.

Taking little account of warnings from his comrades, he shouted at the enemy commander in an attempt to distract him. 'Murdering bastard!' he yelled. 'Theban scum!' Realising he had the man's attention, he continued hurling insults by alluding to the nobleman's mother and her scandalous past, until the entire group, baying for blood, turned their horses towards him. Theomenes sought out the hillock where he'd last seen the Plataeans and bolted his horse towards it, hoping they'd still be there. Yelling loudly, he was relieved to see Stephanos, Angelos and the others, suddenly rise up from their hiding places with weapons raised, and like a beacon of hope, sunlight was glancing off the golden pommel of Stephanos' weapon.

'Now's our chance, men! For Plataea!' he shouted, as he leapt from his horse to join them. Taken by surprise, the Theban commander and the handful of men with him were brought down by a bombardment of projectiles, and once unhorsed the Plataeans were able to take their long-awaited revenge.

Although the skirmish caused insufficient casualties to change the course of events, it was the Athenians and their loyal allies who sang the victory song around the trophy set up with armour and weapons taken from their dead enemies. On top of the pile, Theomenes placed the fine Boeotian helmet with the flowing red plume, while around him, fellow Plataeans sang hymns for the souls of Phalinus and the rest of their martyred countrymen.

'It would have to be Brasidas, eh Stephanos!' Demosthenes, cursed, as he looked toward the enemy's gathering forces, and thinking back to his visit at the prison, Stephanos replied, resignedly, 'Yes, it would have to be him.' After their previous joint encounter with the Spartan general at Pylos, both men knew this battle could prove interesting. From the front ranks of their army, formed beneath the long walls, they watched as enemy forces moved down from the plain to gather in battle order opposite them and waited for the usual galvanising of the troops by the sounds of battle cries and the deployment of the flute players. But there was no riding along the front ranks by Brasidas. No stirring speeches from the Spartan general. All remained quiet.

Hippocrates sent a runner with a message to Demosthenes. 'What's he up to?'

Demosthenes sent a message back. 'He's playing to the Megarian audience, watching from the walls.'

Another message from Hippocrates arrived. 'Let him make the first move.'

Demosthenes answered. 'I agree. We've achieved our main objectives.'

Brasidas guessed correctly that the Athenians would be reluctant to do battle against his superior forces, without assurances from the Megarians, and he also was not inclined to risk valuable men unnecessarily which could jeopardise his campaign in Thrace. He'd shown the Megarians he was prepared to do battle for their city. His challenge had been refused. He hoped he'd done enough. The Athenian generals decided that the better part of valour was to accept what they'd achieved already. They still held the island of Minoa and they'd captured the long walls and the port of Nisaea which would cause further hardship to Megara. Believing they'd satisfied the honour of Athens, Hippocrates and Demosthenes re-focused their attentions on the forthcoming invasion of Boeotia and withdrew their forces from the field.

On seeing the Athenian army leave, Brasidas was accepted as the victor by the Megarians, and he and his troops were allowed into the city. The axe-man and other democrats who'd most closely conspired with the Athenians, accompanied the army back to Athens, but others of their persuasion, who made the fateful decision to stay, were later executed by the returning oligarchs.

TEN

WITHIN A VERY SHORT time of rejoining the camel train it became obvious to Clytes that his funds would not stretch to supporting Amir for the entire journey to Egypt. Now fully recovered, the youngster enthusiastically offered his help wherever it was needed, but it wasn't enough to ensure his place in the caravan, and Clytes often saw the boy being chased away by the more surly attendants.

'I need to teach you some tricks, Amir,' remarked Clytes, one evening. 'Baz, too. I hope the pair of you are quick learners.' There were several amateur entertainers among the camel train attendants, from musicians to acrobats and jugglers, but what occupied the spare time of the travellers most, was gambling. So, during the following weeks, whenever there was a spare moment, the diverse trio was seen wandering off from the encampment to practice what Clytes hoped would get all three of them to Egypt. Amir, he now accepted, would never go back to his uncle, and Baz, the camel coated guardian with the heart of a lion, he wanted to believe had been sent by the gods.

They limited the times as to when and where their improving skills were applied, for Clytes was careful not to draw undue attention to their activities, but gradually their fortunes improved, and a consistent earner was Baz. He could not be fooled in the three shells and hidden pea game. As the walnut shells were moved around, it looked to anyone watching, that the dog with the downcast eyes had no interest whatsoever in the actions of the player, but Clytes had patiently taught the animal to indicate to himself or to Amir, exactly which shell the pea was under, and even if it had been removed by cheating and was no longer in play.

Board games were where Clytes excelled. He had such a way of disarming his opponents by his supposedly casual banter or the precise timing of telling a hilarious joke, that his opposite number often lost while still laughing.

One of Amir's tasks, whilst offering his services throughout the moving caravan, was to listen out for any dice games being planned. That was where the big money could be won, especially when the travelling merchants arrived at the various towns along the route. Whenever Clytes thought he had enough to gamble with, he would often be found in this select group. When all else failed they resorted to acrobatics. With Amir balancing on Clytes' shoulders, the pair juggled with curved blades, cooking utensils, even discs of flat bread, and eventually Baz was included in their performances.

'Thank goodness you're light!' said Clytes, as he thrust down his foot on one end of a plank of wood balanced over a wobbling stack of camel saddles, hurling a supposedly blindfolded Amir spinning into the air, just as the great hound, dragging along a wide wreath of woven branches embedded with the occasional vicious blade raced towards them, arriving at the precise moment the boy fell to earth, feet first within the circle and mercifully unscathed. It was the first time they'd tried out this particular stunt in front of an audience and Amir stood bowing triumphantly. They were rewarded with shouts of approval from the people watching close by, and some even threw coins. Encouraged by this, Clytes placed Amir on his shoulders, and they continued their act with nimble moves of acrobatics. All was going well until Clytes noticed they were being watched by the occupant of the heavily decorated camel howdah which he knew belonged to fellow traveller, the Syrian noblewoman, Shamira. In an instant Amir tumbled to the ground, crying out in alarm. As Clytes clumsily attempted to raise him up he suddenly bristled as behind him he heard, not for the first time, the woman's stifled laughter. 'You need more practice!' he muttered to Amir, in exasperation.

That evening Clytes received an invitation, delivered by a servant of the dark-skinned lady. The acrobats were requested to give an evening performance before her tent when the caravan was due to replenish its water supplies at a river in three days' time. Clytes was immediately apprehensive. He believed their rudimentary act still needed work, so what could be the real reason for the invitation? It was an unusual situation for him to be in, and he was in a quandary as to how best to proceed. The lady was obviously well respected by Masoud, and her family held great power in the region, but the lurid stories he'd heard while sitting around the night fires made him cautious of any unnecessary contact. To ignore the request, however, could also bring unwanted trouble.

Due to the lack of light, Clytes thought that fire would aid them in their act and could also add some drama. Miraculously, the dog seemed impervious to the hazard and not for the first time Clytes thanked the deities on Mount Olympus for sending the creature to him. After their usual routine of acrobatics with added torches this time, Clytes theatrically poured oil over the circle of branches and set fire to it. He then sent the blazing wheel hurtling along the ground. At a given signal to the dog, Baz bounded after the wheel and fearlessly leapt through the narrow gap between the roaring flames.

Appreciation for the act seemed more muted than Clytes had hoped, but several men came over to take a look at the dog, remarking on its size and his lack of fear.

'He's wasted on tricks,' remarked one. 'You should put him into fights.'

Others thought likewise.

'He's not a fighting dog,' replied Clytes, firmly.

'Why not?' asked a man, suspiciously.

Clytes was reluctant to divulge the problems with his companion. Only he and Amir were aware of its slightly awkward gait, and the dog was useful as a guard dog only if people thought he had teeth that could bite.

'He's more useful to me as a guardian. Been with me since a pup,' he lied.

'Still, it's a waste!' boomed Habib, the monumental black bodyguard to the lady Shamira. 'Worth a lot of money......as a fighter!'

'He's not for fighting!' emphasised Clytes, bristling. 'But I am, ...if anyone's interested!'

'Oh, not again!' sighed a concerned Amir, conscious of how heavily his master was outnumbered.

Help was at hand. Shamira had been enjoying the performance from the shelter of her tent and seeing how events were unfolding, she called out to Habib to bring the acrobats to her ornate pavilion; to a section especially screened off for guests.

Clytes, glancing around, immediately wondered what her private quarters were like, if this was only for visitors. Staring up at him with gentle intelligence, their long legs stretched out nonchalantly on luxurious rugs, were two golden-haired hunting dogs. He was impressed. This lady travels in style, he thought. He judged it would take at least ten camels to carry her personal requirements alone. He was directed by a male attendant to sit on a large, colourfully decorated wool filled cushion, which he instantly found awkward because of his long legs. He tried folding them, tucking his feet together, and then, to his dismay, he suddenly fell backwards. It was not stifled this time. Shamira's laughter was unrestrained. Still laughing, she entered through a gap in the screen and indicated sharply to her servant to assist Clytes to stand, but by getting his feet tangled in a leopard skin rug, he almost fell again.

'It's my long legs,' he mumbled, incoherently, realising he was in the presence of the most beautiful woman he'd ever set eyes on.

Tall, statuesque almost, she walked towards Clytes with a grace belying her height - and obvious curves. Spellbound, he thought her eyes resembled deep, dark pools, sparkling in moonlight. Her soft dark skin shone invitingly in the light of the oil lamps, and he was conscious of the scent of jasmine oil emitting from her thickly braided, ebony black hair. When the screen had parted, he'd caught a glimpse of the paradise within. A ceiling of billowing red silk; wall hangings depicting arousing scenes of erotica; a sumptuous bed.

The boy and dog were accommodated outside the tent and provided with a smaller cushion each, but Baz had the same problem as his master. He flopped over the sides, his legs sticking out awkwardly but then became more interested in the smell of the item and began snuffling at the cushion, pushing it along with his nose as though it was an animal to be herded. It was Amir's turn to laugh. He felt happier than he'd ever been in his life and listening to the laughter coming from within the tent, it seemed that his master was getting along well with the rich lady. After being brought food and drink, the likes of which neither of them had tasted before, both boy and dog fell fast asleep, unaware of Clytes and the lady Shamira when they quietly left the tent.

The night ride was Clytes' suggestion. After being waited on like a prince by the lady's attendants, he didn't trust himself. She was so beautiful. But the images put into his head by his fellow travellers would not leave him. A cooling ride is what he needed to bring him to his senses, and to his relief, Shamira agreed. After ordering two horses to be prepared, she abruptly dismissed her groom and bodyguard. Did she witness the flicker of concern on the face of her riding partner? If she did, she didn't let it show.

The stars and moon, brilliantly bright, illuminated the landscape in a splendour of silver light, and Shamira, giving her magnificent white Arabian its head, galloped freely, the horse's tail flicking wildly as they twisted and turned around obstacles of rocks and trees. Clytes had never seen such boldness in a woman before. Not even Anthousa. He galloped after on his equally high-spirited, desert-bred animal, intoxicated by the cold night air and this exotic, exciting woman.

When they halted their sweating horses and drew near to one another, Clytes' resolve weakened. He reached over to her. The stories he'd heard? Just rumours, he told himself. He was surprised when she pulled at her horse's head and moved away from him.

'Can I ask you, why you wanted me to come tonight?'

'You make me laugh!'

'It's not intentional.'

'That's what makes me laugh.'

'Did your dead lovers also make you laugh?'

'They're no loss.'

'That's no consolation to me!'

'I think we'd better go back.'

Amir was still asleep. Deeply asleep. And alone. Clytes shook him until he drowsily smiled up at him. 'Amir! Where's Baz?'

Clytes felt the cushion to see if it was still warm. It wasn't, but he felt something else. Raising his hand he saw blood. The pair looked at one another with mutual dread.

'Did you have anything to do with this, Shamira?'

'To do with what? What are you accusing me of?'

'The boy has been drugged and the dog's gone! You planned this. With that bodyguard of yours, Habib!'

'You're mad!'

'Lend me your men, then. To find the dog.'

'I will do no such thing!'

'If I find Habib *is* responsible, I'll kill him!'

When it was light enough to detect the direction taken by the kidnappers, Clytes and Amir set off alone. The few drops of blood that were found, lead them in the direction of the river village where he assumed Baz would be sold on by Habib. The Eleusinian had won and lost money on many dog fights, and he tried not to imagine what could happen to the already maimed animal in one of those pits.

Walking purposefully onwards he looked skywards, and seeking Olympian guidance, cried out, 'Where is he?!' Increasing his pace, he tried, without success, to shake off the recurring belief that Lykaon's evil spirit was still following him and maliciously interfering in his life.

ELEVEN

FUELLED WITH BRAVADO AFTER their unexpected run-in with Brasidas at Megara, when the feared Spartan commander declined to do battle, Athens' generals turned their attentions to enemies on their other border -the Boeotians - and they thanked the gods that Brasidas could not foil their plans this time. Leading a motley army of helots and mercenaries he'd reportedly left the territory heading north on his original mission to assist king Perdiccas of Macedonia. During that same summer, Demosthenes set off for Naupactus in the Corinthian Gulf, with a fleet of forty triremes. His purpose? To gather enough democratic sympathisers to fulfil his own essential part in the forthcoming invasion of Boeotia, scheduled to take place in the late autumn.

Four hundred hoplites travelled with the fleet and in the group of the commander's closest companions, his presence on the flagship requested personally by the general, was Stephanos. The Plataean wasn't the only member of the dissolved Shield Company sailing with Demosthenes. Helming one of the great triremes was the larger-than-life redhead, Glaucus of Thessaly. Recently returned from the failed attempt to capture Sicily, he was once again looking for gains from conquest, either in the way of bonuses paid by their trierarch, or plunder if the opportunity arose, as were his old comrades, Cassa and Bion, also crewing in the fleet heading for Naupactus. Both had demanding families to support, especially Bion. He, more than any of them had revelled in the fame generated by the return of the Marathon shield and the attraction of so many women, was an opportunity he exploited to the full. Glaucus and Cassa tried their best to warn him, but it was too late. The arrows had already stuck. The love god Eros, frustrated at Bion's boastful and flagrant behaviour, chose for him a strikingly beautiful auburn-haired girl from the lower city, with a rapacious sexual appetite and a need for material wealth to match. To support his demanding Roxanne, the broad-shouldered, thick-necked oarsman toiled like a slave to earn his place as a thranite on the upper rowing deck, and when his thoughts turned to what she could be up to in his absence, his hands often bled.

The plot to conquer Boeotia was an ambitious one, requiring precise co-ordination. Demosthenes was to travel by sea to the west coast and Hippocrates was to travel overland to the east coast. A date was agreed so that the attacks would be carried out simultaneously, hopefully splitting the Boeotian armed forces which would give the democrats their chance to take control. As in Megaris, the two generals had been scheming with the more than willing dissidents wanting to break from Theban dominance, but this time they were optimistic that their bold, two-pronged offensive would put such fear into the Boeotians that resistance from *all* factions would be thought futile. Under Cleon's lucky star, the Athenians felt confident of quickly annexing the territory on their northern border, blocking once and for all the route used by Sparta to attack Athens' allies in the far north. After autumn crops had been safely gathered in, if all went according to plan, it could all be over before the full onslaught of winter and with little loss of life.

In the weeks preceding the campaign many sacrifices were carried out throughout the city, in an attempt to influence events, and in the Plataean contingent, excitement at the prospect of recovering their own city was at its height. One such ceremony was held at the palatial lodgings of Akaterina, widow of Phalinus of Plataea. Given refuge by Pericles, the now deceased, revered leader of Athens, Akaterina and her son had remained as guests of the aristocrat's much-loved mistress, Aspasia, and her young son, Pericles Junior.

The two women had become close friends through their shared grief at the loss of their illustrious consorts, and during the troubling times that followed, the first lady of Plataea continued to give support to Aspasia. Unable to legally marry due to a Periclean law which only allowed citizens born of Athenian parents to marry, following the death of Pericles, Aspasia became the consort of another Athenian general - Lysicles. All too soon, however, tragedy struck again. While in command of twelve ships sent to plunder Caria in Asia Minor, his army was attacked and Lysicles and many of his men were killed. Grieving once again and with a new-born baby to care for, Aspasia relied more than ever on the friendship of Akaterina, and the two strong women now focused on the upbringing of their respective offspring.

The survival of Plataea's first lady and that of her son, Akylas, had been a constant source of hope for the Plataeans during their years of exile, and many had been the comings and goings of her city's dignitaries and military personnel when grievances were expressed and numerous, unproductive plans argued over. Finally, with the threat of Spartan interference thought unlikely, Athens' generals felt confident enough to make a move, and an expectant gathering of Plataeans had crowded into the marble pillared antechamber fronting the villa. Leaping onto a small stone plinth, the ten-year-old future Shield Guardian, stood proudly before the eager and clamorous guests, then with a steady sweet voice and surprising maturity, he boldly addressed the determined faces of his fellow countrymen.

'My mother and I cannot convey how much we owe to the lady Aspasia, who welcomed us into her home when I was just three years of age. Her house has a well-deserved reputation as a place of eloquence and learning and being acquainted with so many illustrious artists and thinkers has been an experience unparalleled.' He stumbled a little over the last word and glanced anxiously towards a wooden screen, where out of sight, he knew his mother and Aspasia were watching him. More importantly, he hoped that his hero, the flamboyant, charismatic nobleman, Alcibiades, would be listening, somewhere, also. With renewed confidence, he carried on. 'But we cannot understate our feelings of elation with regard to the imminent invasion of Boeotia. To finally return to our homeland has been a long-held dream by all of us assembled here.' At this point, as he'd been coached, he took a quick gulp of air. 'I know every man's face,' he stated with boyish passion, his palms spread upwards, sweeping the crowd. 'I know every man's story. Our pride has suffered. Our patience has been strained, but we have endured, for just this moment.' Pausing briefly for effect, he looked to the heavens, then accompanied by wild cheering, he shouted; 'Praise the gods! We are going home!'

To chants of 'Long live Plataea!' the boy was enthusiastically lifted from his pedestal and carried on the shoulders of two eager young men into an elaborately decorated andron, where food and wine had been laid out for them.

'He sounded just like his father!' remarked Theomenes to his companions, as he and others poured through the ornate doorway, following in the wake of their city's blonde mascot. 'Phalinus' spirit lives on!' responded a choked and misty eyed Plataean elder. Observations which were repeated many times in the numerous speeches held that day.

From behind the fretted screen and unseen by the visitors, Akaterina and Aspasia gave a mutual sigh of relief.

'You instructed him well, Aspasia! He spoke clearly and with such confidence.'

'It was a subject matter close to his heart, Akaterina. The passion was all his. I only honed the rhetoric. I taught Pericles to spread his hands like that. The crowds adored him!'

Now that there was a real possibility of returning home, the problem of how best to raise her son when the protection of Aspasia came to an end, caused concern for Akaterina, and she decided it was time she sought a new husband. Until Akylas came of age to reclaim his father's land and property, he needed a guardian. Her protectress was renowned for her intellect, and in the matters of love and marriage was particularly sought out by individuals looking for a suitable partner.

'There's another reason I need to find a husband, Aspasia,' confided Akaterina. 'I'm concerned about the time Akylas is spending in the company of Alcibiades when he comes here. I don't want him influenced by Alcibiades and his friends until he's old enough to decide for himself. His father's death left a void hard to fill and Alcibiades is......well......so overpowering and persuasive. I think Akylas looks up to him......too much.'

'Alcibiades does have some of Phalinus' qualities, Akaterina, but he is no father figure. I should know. Pericles took him in as a boy after his father was killed in battle, and he was living here when I came to live with Pericles. He stayed with us until he started his national service, which was not long before you and Akylas joined us. He was always trouble......and morally? Well, what can I say? Totally corrupt. Even Socrates couldn't get him to change his ways, and he has always admired Socrates. I'm surprised he hasn't made a pass at you, Akaterina. No-one is safe from him when he decides to take a lover......male or female. This will always be his home and he will always be welcome, but now you have broached the subject, I share your concern. Akylas needs a guiding father figure, before Alcibiades ruins the boy. It will be my greatest pleasure to help you in this matter. We shall start our search immediately,' and looking close to home, the two women from their hiding place, peered through the apertures in the screen towards the open doorway of the andron and the crowded room beyond.

'Did Alcibiades hear me, mother?' asked Akylas, eagerly, when reunited with the two women.

Knowing how much her son had wanted the handsome aristocrat to be there, she tried to soften his disappointment. 'He must have had something very important to do, my darling, to have missed your speech.'

Aspasia, well used to such disappointments, was not so gentle. 'Never rely on Alcibiades, Akylas.'

TWELVE

BELIEVING THERE WOULDN'T BE much time to save the dog, Clytes and the boy immediately began making enquiries around the village. Most people were wary and reluctant to get involved, but they finally found a woman, visibly in need of a coin, who passed on some useful information. She denied any knowledge of either Habib or Baz, but she told them there was a regular dog fight held in a town about five miles away, where every month, people came from all across the territory. 'The next big fight must be soon,' she told them. 'Some locals have left already with their dogs.' Clytes knew the type; bold fierce animals, used to fighting off wolves or even bears, in the protection of their flocks. The pair set off immediately, following the river as directed by the villager, hoping their instincts were correct.

They found the town without difficulty and the situation was worse than Clytes expected. The individual wooden crates they passed by, were occupied by an assortment of dogs. But there were also a few iron cages, containing bears. In his not-too-distant past, Clytes would be feeling a sense of anticipation at the forthcoming fights, hoping he'd be coming away a little richer, but this time it was different. The deafening sound of barking filled him with dread.

'We split up, Amir,' said Clytes, urgently. 'If one of us finds him, we meet up by that inn over there. Try not to let Baz see you! Until I can work out what to do, I'd prefer that people didn't know of our involvement.'

'I'll do my best, master!' replied the boy, as he walked away through the town, trying not to look too conspicuous.

Clytes noted the scars on the regular fighting dogs, some wearing their viciously spiked collars and felt the nervousness of the recently acquired ones. He purposefully pushed his way through the groups of men inspecting the cages, everyone looking for that one dog that could make them some quick money, as he would have done once. Some dogs were demented with rage and jumped up at the bars of their cages, growling; teeth bared. Their names were noted by the betting men. Others were cowed, visibly shaking. Some got prodded to gain a reaction, and if there was none, they were discounted.

Clytes peered into crate after crate, his emotions reeling between dread and hope, for several dogs looked much like Baz, but none matched him for size. Then he heard it - loud, ferocious barking, coming from somewhere ahead of him. He recognised the sound instantly and almost ran in its direction, thrusting aside anyone in his path.

The dog was the centre of attention. It shook the crate violently, half mad with anger and fear; foam dripping from its fangs, while groups of men crowded around, roaring to give encouragement. But it wasn't them that Baz was distressed about. Amir was on the ground being kicked by two men, but compared to Clytes, they were not so big, and before anyone could intervene, he was able to grasp them both by the hair. 'Pick on someone your own size!' he growled, before giving them both a hard kick.

Amir came by his side. 'I'm sorry master, but Baz saw me before I saw him. He started howling. I tried to calm him but I was dragged away. No-one would believe me......that he's *my* dog!'

'It's too late now,' replied Clytes, half smiling.

'Now, who owns the dog?' he asked, looking around at the suddenly quiet and expectant crowd.

'I think it's him, master,' Amir answered, pointing at a large, oily faced Syrian, sitting on an ornate and cushioned, wooden chair. He was sandwiched between two attendants. One wore a heavy leather money belt. The other sat at a small table containing writing equipment.

'Ah, you're the money!' exclaimed Clytes. 'Well, I have something to tell you, friend. The winnings you are expecting won't happen. The dog is no good! I should know. I owned it last.'

'And your reason for being here, is?'

'I want the dog back.'

Laughter.

'I'm prepared to pay.'

'Show him the takings.'

'Not as much as that.'

'I thought not.'

'We need to talk......privately.'

The two men moved away from the noisy, crowded street and halted by an alleyway, which was quieter.

'Well, what's the problem with the dog?'

'He can't fight. He has no grip with his jaw. It's damaged.'

'You saw the crowds. They only see his size. He put on a good show there. I think he can take care of himself.'

'He'll be mutilated!' You'll lose whatever you paid for him.'

'The man who sold him to me was in a hurry. I didn't pay so much. I took a gamble.'

'Big man. Arab. Long flowing robes.'

'That's the man.'

'Hmm.'

'Unless you can match what's being bet on him, friend, the fight goes on.'

'I can't.'

'Have a wager. He might win!'

'He won't.'

'Well even if the dog's killed in the fight, I've more than covered my costs already, and the bets are still coming in. Whatever the outcome, I'll do alright.'

'Can you do one thing? Can you give him a protective collar?'

'If he's as useless as you say then I want to make as much money as I can from this one fight. Without the collar people will be impressed. He could arouse more interest. They will think he's fearless. Invincible!'

'I won't forget this!'

'Look, stranger, I bought the dog in good faith! If he's still alive at the end of the fight, I'll let you buy him back. That's the best I can do.'

THIRTEEN

TO CLYTES' CONSTERNATION, THE man with the oily skin built up Baz's fighting abilities to such an extent, that no-one dared match their dog against him. For the challenge to be fair, they argued, there was only one animal that could be tested against the great hound. A bear. Clytes again asked for Baz to be fitted with an iron spiked collar. He vehemently pointed out, that the bear would be fitted with such a device, so why not the dog.

Again, his request was refused.

The Syrian had never taken so much money for a fight before, and fearing that Clytes would attempt a rescue, or that the owner of the opposition would tamper with the dog, guards were posted, with instructions to stay there until the time of the contest.

'Can't you think of a plan, master?' asked Amir, desperately. 'A distraction or something, so we can save him?'

'What do you think I've been doing, lad! I don't want him torn to pieces, any more than you do!'

The desolate pair sat as near to the dog's crate as possible, to give some comfort to their canine friend but far enough away to be out of earshot of the guards. Clytes went through the ideas he'd been having, with Amir, but on hearing each one, the boy looked doubtful, shaking his young head in disbelief.

'How can you spear the bear without us being killed for it? And if you spear Baz before the bear attacks him, we'd be killed for that too! Other desperate suggestions put forward by Clytes he also discounted.

The owner of the bear, together with his helpers, finally arrived to remove the great beast from its cage. With cruel stabbings and loud shouts and with small hounds snapping at its feet, the animal was forced in chains towards the fighting pit.

Clytes, head in hands, cursed the ever-lingering memory of Lykaon, and did the only thing left to do. He prayed to all the gods on Olympus.

'Master? Look up!' cried Amir, suddenly. 'Look, master!'

Clytes lifted his head and shading his eyes, looked up at the sun.

'I've seen this phenomenon before, Amir!' shouted Clytes, jubilantly, as he grabbed hold of the boy. 'Come on, lad, we don't have much time!'

As the sky darkened, the noise of howling wolves could be heard in the distance and this set the dogs off, to bark incessantly. The bear broke free from its captors and pandemonium ensued as in semi-darkness the men attempted to recapture it, but they were hampered in their efforts by the loose dogs, freed from their kennels by Clytes and Amir. They were running everywhere and panicked by the situation, attacked anything in their path, including their keepers.

For four and a half minutes, a cloak descended over the sounds of screams and mayhem, and when the moon had finally passed over the sun, and sunlight returned to the chaotic scene, Clytes, Amir and Baz were nowhere to be seen.

FOURTEEN

HASIM AND SOME OF the other caravan attendants were genuinely relieved to see the trio's return, but Masoud's reaction was much cooler. With a tirade of expletives, which he appeared to relish, he vented his anger on Clytes for his total lack of commitment to the protection of the caravan.

'And if that dog goes missing again,' he added, in frustration, 'it'll be because I've killed the useless animal! It's been nothing but trouble. If it wasn't for the fact that a certain lady finds you amusing, I'd have you chased off!'

Clytes immediately went to seek out Shamira's tent.

'Where's Habib?'

'You'll find him at the waste pit.'

'You know what I have to do. Say your farewells to him now.'

'There's no need.'

He found what remained of Habib, in a cooking pot. The severed head had obviously been attacked by flies for some days, but despite the empty eye sockets it was still recognisable. Clytes also noticed there wasn't a tongue.

'You've done my work for me,' said Clytes, on his return to Shamira. 'Why? I didn't take you for such an ardent dog lover.'

'Habib was my personal bodyguard. He left my service without permission, and he paid the price. You will take his place.'

'You make it sound as though I have no choice!'

'Do you want to stay with the caravan or not? Masoud will do as I say.'

'After what happened to Habib, I'd like to think about it!'

'You are in my debt, Hellene.'

'Habib was a eunuch. I'm no eunuch!'

'Your duties will be to protect my person. Your services in any other regard will not be required.'

Clytes wasn't sure if he felt insulted or relieved.

When Amir heard the news, he was ecstatic. 'Master, you will have your own camel! We might sleep in a tent!'

'At what cost?' replied Clytes, and he suddenly shivered. He thought he felt a cold finger moving slowly down his spine.

'If she likes you, master, then I like her.'

'Keep away from her as much as possible, Amir! Do you hear me? You could upset her......accidently. The lady's not quite what she seems.'

Despite his reservations, Clytes approached the role of camel riding bodyguard as though he was the main lead in a theatrical production, quickly realising that chaperoning the high-powered noblewoman gave him an opportunity to perform on a much larger personal stage than he'd previously been used to. Hasim and others seemed subdued at his elevation, but he shrugged off their concerns about his female employer. She genuinely seemed to like him. Anyway, he could take care of himself.

At night he continued to enjoy their rides together. By day she taught him how to hunt with her hawk and her sleek, fast desert hounds. Amazed, he would watch them working in unison, when the white falcon would hover, signalling to the hounds if prey was discovered, and the dogs would then race at incredible speed to bring them down. Nothing could outrun them, not even the fleet-footed gazelles. Recklessly, he even took part in the noisy, chaotic camel races, to please her. She laughingly told him that his mother must have been frightened by a camel while carrying him - due to his long legs. At the various trading posts on the route, he was impressed at how she handled herself in haggling with often wily and greedy merchants. Accompanied by her agents, rarely would she allow them to pay more than she intended, and on selling, only her asking price was acceptable. There was almost no product in which Shamira didn't trade, and there was always another town, eager for her quality goods. Her working camels carried ingots of gold, silver, tin and copper; amber, pearls, rubies and emeralds; spices, honey, olive oil, rose oil, frankincense and myrrh; carpets, cotton, wool and fine linen; bronze mirrors, jewellery and glass, and last but not least, purple dye.

Clytes saw more money change hands, than he'd ever seen in his life, and he noticed that the lady liked to spend it. Not just on herself but also on her retinue. As her bodyguard, he was told that he must look the part, and he soon resembled a leaner version of Habib. With his long flowing robes and brightly coloured turban, he appeared taller than ever. The look of glowing admiration on Shamira's face, however, was enough to stifle any complaints from Clytes.

He accompanied Shamira everywhere and took his lead from her as to what was required of him, depending on the situation. Sometimes he was instructed to appear imposing, at other times, dutiful and distant. On several social occasions he was allowed to sit next to her, almost as a consort would. When she traded with local tribes they were wined and dined in expansive tents and entertained with wild dancing and displays of reckless bravery by the young men. In the towns they were often invited to lavish villas, surrounded by verdant, irrigated gardens, where the dancing girls and acrobatic acts were of a more refined nature. He never encountered any trouble and confessed to Amir that he could get used to such a life. It was the best part he'd ever played, and he suspected that Habib had not been favoured with such treatment.

The caravan had been travelling for over three weeks when it arrived at the city of the eight hills: the great trading city of Khalibon by the wide river Belos. On the outskirts, several large inns with spacious courtyards had been purposefully built, to give rest to travellers and their animals. Masoud and his camel-pullers were more than ready to make use of the amenities. Here, in safe surroundings, they had ready access to food and washing facilities and time to treat any ailments. It was also a chance to meet up with old friends passing through.

It was at Khalibon that Shamira took a lover.

Rameen, an obnoxious, boastful individual, who seemed to flaunt his obvious physical attributes, was a guest of Farad, one of the local gold merchants, whose sumptuous mansion they visited in order to do some trade. During the lavish meal, where guests were comfortably seated around several low tables, Clytes couldn't help but notice the mutual attraction between Shamira and the young trader who was watching her from across the room, and he

openly expressed his displeasure when asked to leave his place at
the dining table he shared with Shamira and Farad, in order for
the young man to sit next to his employer.

'This is business,' she told him, firmly.

The gold merchant jumped up from the richly upholstered sofa
he was reclining on, spluttering with rage.

'How dare you behave in such a manner toward your mistress!'
he shouted, pointing at Clytes. 'I'll have you whipped for such
behaviour!' and he indicated to his attendants to restrain him.

'There's no need.' said Shamira, intervening quickly. 'I will
have him dealt with myself!'

Exchanging looks of obvious disapproval with Shamira, Clytes
was forcibly escorted outside where he stationed himself with the
merchant's house guards, waiting, fuming, until he was needed
again. Later, he was dismayed even further when he discovered
that the dubious young trader had attached himself to the camel
train and would be travelling with his own pack animals as far
as Damascus. Hasim was worried that Clytes might cause trouble
and he purposefully sought him out at his quarters in the vast
caravansary.

'Don't interfere or it could go badly for you and the boy,' he
warned him. 'This is the first time I've known her employ someone
like you. Her close attendants are usually eunuchs......chosen by
her family. I'm concerned for your safety, Clytes.'

'It's my job to protect her, and she sends me away! If that poor
excuse for a man causes her any harm, I'll......!'

'I've seen how men get drawn to her, Clytes......and I've seen
what happens to them!'

'Why warn me? Worry about him!'

After so many weeks of close contact, Clytes was annoyed at
being so abruptly removed from the lifestyle he'd been enjoying.
Who was this young man so easily taken into her confidence?
But Hasim told him that this was not an uncommon occurrence.
Shamira often took a lover during her travels. Sometimes more
than one, and always questionable individuals.

'I was worried that it would be you, my tall friend!'

Clytes laughed at Hasim's honesty. 'I've told you already. I'm not interested. But where do these stories come from? People show her nothing but respect. Apart from Habib, and he deserved it, I've not seen any sign of malice.'

'Clytes, you're too close to her. She's dangerous. Beautiful, but dangerous.'

'She's the most beautiful woman I've ever set eyes on......and I've seen a few.'

Since the arrival of the new lover, Clytes saw very little of his employer. Concerned about his change in circumstances and the possibility that his place on the camel train could be at risk, he ignored Hasim's advice and went to seek her out.

Masoud's caravan was staying for a week at Khalibon as part of a regularly held enormous trade fair, attended by hundreds of merchants. During the daylight hours they noisily shouted out their wares, and when the sun went down, they rekindled friendships around large communal campfires where they enjoyed feasting and diversions of all kinds.

Approaching Masoud's encampment he looked around for Shamira's open pavilion where he expected to find her watching the entertainment. A fire-eater was performing in front of her tent, and he could clearly see her reclining on animal furs, propped up with large wool filled cushions. Lying sprawled at her feet were her golden-haired hounds, and she was not alone.

A look of concern briefly crossed Shamira's face as Clytes approached.

'Your presence is not required. Please go now.'

'I'm supposed to be protecting you!'

'Leave us!'

Masoud, expecting trouble, came over with two of his men to offer Shamira assistance.

'Do as the lady says, Clytes!'

Feeling a mixture of disgust and confusion, Clytes reluctantly left the encampment and eventually met up with friends from the caravan, who were enthusiastically participating in the nighttime revelry. The town was not only seething with traders, but buyers also, many of whom he couldn't fail to notice were beautiful women, drawn by the immense variety of merchandise on offer. Some were there in order to ply their own trade. Avoiding any further contact with Shamira's entourage, he accepted what the lively, overflowing city had to offer and his period of self-inflicted celibacy came to an end.

His first encounter was with a lithe, double-jointed acrobat, who was able to achieve positions he'd previously thought were physically impossible. He wasn't sure if it was due to his prior abstention or her incredible skills as a contortionist, that he climaxed so strongly, but for a while he felt unable to move. The likeable young woman wasn't expecting any payment, but Clytes insisted. Lying, panting, on a carpet they'd taken down from a clothesline, they stared up at the stars from the flat roof of a house, seemingly unoccupied because of the revelries.

'I'm grateful! I was ready to thump somebody!'

'We could do it again......before you leave.'

'My dear, I would like to continue living!'

His second sexual encounter was with the wife of Farad the gold merchant, at whose house Shamira had first met her lover, Rameen. Recognising him in the town, she drew aside the screen of her horse-drawn conveyance to call him over to her.

'I've been looking for you.'

'Have you?'

'Are you still angry with my husband, for how he humiliated you?'

'Thank you for reminding me!'

'Well, are you?'

'I'd be lying if I said I wasn't.'

'He's away on business tonight,' she whispered, encouragingly. 'If you want to get your revenge, visit me at my house this evening.'

The experience was less energetic than with the acrobat but much more comfortable. Wearing a diaphanous silk gown, the lady emerged fresh from bathing in rose water, and the sweet aroma made him think of a perfumed garden. He carried her first, and at her insistence, to the vast marital bed overlooked by the bejewelled eyes of a pair of solid gold eagles. As she lay back on down filled pillows, their bodies cooled by sheets of the finest linen, Clytes thought that it was like making love on a cloud, especially after his recent exploits on the flat roof.

Fumbling with silken ribbons, he removed her superfluous flimsy garment, then leaned back to admire the lady's pampered body, glowing invitingly in the soft lights of the oil lamps. Slowly, he kissed every part of her, and she responded with shrieks of delight.

'Aren't you worried about the servants?'

'Don't stop!'

'Won't they tell your husband?!'

In response, she cupped his mouth firmly with her hand. 'Don't talk......and don't rush it,' she entreated, as he entered her. 'I want to remember tonight!'

'Then stop wiggling your arse about, woman!'

When later, he carried her, naked, into the dining area, she laughed, mischievously.

'Yes, do it again here!' she told him, as he sat her on the edge of a long serving table, and she wrapped her legs tightly around him.

He was rougher than he'd intended to be, due entirely to the embarrassing memories of the last time he'd been in the room, but the lady made no complaints as the table shook. He lifted her by the buttocks, with his member still inside her, and with no little satisfaction, sat himself down on the expensively upholstered ottoman which he knew was her husband's personal seat. The lady's perfumed hair tumbled about him as she straddled him vigorously, still emitting unrestrained cries of passion.

Groaning, he questioned her again. 'Why are you taking this risk?'

'I also want revenge on my husband, Clytes!'

'Oh?'

'Rameen was *my* lover! Now, because of some lucrative deal with my husband, Shamira has him!'

They came as one, all passion spent, each fuelled by their own sense of grievance.

After a week of trading and feasting, the caravan departed the city, and the bragging young trader came along too - instigated by Farad in order to separate his wife from her lover. In exchange for her assistance in his predicament Shamira believed her father would be impressed with the advantageous new trading terms she'd managed to extract from the gold merchant, and with a handsome new lover as a diversion, she continued her journey more than satisfied with her part of the bargain.

Clytes and Hasim, together with the boy and the dog were watching from afar as Shamira's slow-moving howdah swayed on down the line. Riding at her side, on what had been Clytes' camel, was her new companion. Hasim shook his head. 'He won't make it to Damascus my friend. You'll see.'

FIFTEEN

TWO DAYS AFTER LEAVING Khalibon, Hasim sought out Clytes.

'Keep a lookout for bandits now we've left the town,' he warned him.

'I've not seen anything suspicious.'

'You won't. But they're there. They'll be watching us.'

'I wish I still had a camel! When's the most dangerous time?'

'Any time. Preparing to camp before the animals are unloaded, or at a river crossing or oasis when people are distracted. The rear of the train is most vulnerable but nothing of great value is ever put there, mainly the practical needs of the caravan. If they feel bold enough though, they could try an attack anywhere along the line, if they know there's gold.'

'Shamira?'

'Shamira's camels are well protected, Clytes. Take your orders from Masoud from now on......and keep your distance from the woman. We are nearing her father's territory.'

On the third day after leaving Khalibon as they progressed steadily south-westward, the caravan entered a landscape scattered with low hills, and Masoud, knowing bandits operated in this area, instructed his guards to be watchful.

'What can I do?' Clytes asked the caravaneer. 'I should be protecting Shamira.'

'She left at first light with Rameen, Clytes. They've gone hunting.'

'At a time like this? What in Hades is she thinking? You should have stopped the idiots!'

'I've only just been informed, Clytes. The lady does as she pleases. She knows the risks. She knows this territory as well as I do. I'm sending some men to higher ground. You'd better go with them......and take the dog with you. If you see anything suspicious, get him to bark. Loudly!'

Clytes emulated the others clambering up the scattering of rocky outcrops aligning the route, with Baz leaping awkwardly alongside him, and as the guards silently watched for any movement other than that of the slow-moving camel train below them, Clytes scanned the skies, looking keenly for the lady's hawk. From the summit of a cave riddled precipice, he shielded his eyes from the blazing sun, searching for any sign in the landscape which indicated the whereabouts of the errant hunters. The dog's sudden growling alerted him to distant shouting and looking in that direction, he saw the guards clambering quickly back down the slopes, firing arrows as they ran. Galloping towards the rear of the caravan, threatening to attack the baggage animals, was a band of black garbed horsemen, and people were running along the line with whatever weapons they had, to fend them off. From his high vantage point, Clytes took one final look around him for sight of Shamira and her companion, without success, but he did notice something else below him, the swift movement of a second group of horsemen charging from behind one of the many hills. It was proceeding rapidly towards the head of the caravan. Encouraging Baz to bark loudly, he scrambled down the incline, yelling as he went.

'It's a trick, Masoud. To the van! They're going for the gold!'

Hasim's fears were being realised.

Alerted to the ruse, Masoud urgently changed his orders, and members of his camel riding escort were quickly diverted to defend the wealth being carried in the caravan. The marauders came screaming and yelling from behind a low hill, with curved swords raised, racing wildly up and down the line. The camels, disturbed by the sudden activity, began pulling on their ropes, causing mayhem for their handlers as loads began toppling to the ground. The bandits seemed to know exactly which camels to target and Shamira's gold was in jeopardy. Clytes, dodging around the animals' long legs, waited as one of the riders sped towards him. Yelling at Baz, the dog instinctively leapt at the galloping horse, felling its rider instantly, then the fearless colossus held him down, his huge open jaws poised over the terrified man's jugular. Clytes quickly despatched the raider, then taking the man's weapons, he grabbed the reins of the loose horse and mounting easily, began a ferocious attack on the other raiders, causing many to flee. Baz proved to be an excellent defender, and snapping threateningly at the legs of the horses, he caused more than one to throw its rider. The double-pronged attack was thwarted but not without some losses. During the fracas, one of Shamira's loaded camels had been successfully freed from the line and was led away by the fleeing group of surviving raiders, accompanied by their frenzied shouts of jubilation.

While order was being restored and wounds were being attended to, the two hunters returned, to receive stares of incredulity and suspicion. At a heated discussion later that day, Shamira defended herself by stating that one of her own shipments had been taken, and Rameen also vehemently denied any involvement. In a private conversation with Masoud, Clytes voiced his own suspicions.

'If I were a gambling man......'

'Which you are.'

'Which I am. My bet would be on the wife of Farad, the gold-merchant at Khalibon. I have some knowledge of the lady, Masoud. She bears an unconcealed grudge against Shamira for taking her man. My bet would be on her for passing on information about the gold shipment.'

'Don't you think it's suspicious that Rameen went missing just at the time of the attack?'

'Coincidence?'

'I doubt Shamira's father will see it that way.'

'Have you met him?'

'Farnaka? More times than I would have liked!'

The needs of the ambushed caravan drew Masoud away, and Clytes was left wondering just what kind of man the ruler of Tadmor was.

SIXTEEN

A WELCOMING PARTY WAS AWAITING the arrival of the caravan, when ten days after the attack it finally reached the shores of the north flowing Orontes River. It had been sent by Farnaka, Shamira's father, along the desert road from his oasis at Tadmor. From within Shamira's tent, angry words could clearly be heard between the ruler's envoys and Rameen, while the sound of Masoud's loud protestations caused apprehensive discussions around the campfires that night. The travellers knew that nothing escaped the ruler's many spies, and they were now wondering what would happen to their caravan leader, since Farnaka had obviously been informed about the loss of his gold.

The following morning, a tortured and mutilated body was discovered. It was Rameen, and like Habib, his tongue had been burned away. He'd also been castrated.

'I'd hazard a guess it wasn't him,' ventured Clytes to Hasim. 'I didn't like the man, but I wouldn't have wished this on him. Do *you* think he betrayed us?'

'Does it matter? He would have died anyway.'

'You keep saying that!'

'I've told you. He knew too much. About her and, you know......!'

'I'm not convinced about that either!'

The caravan rested by the river for two days, during which time, Farnaka's men exchanged the gold and merchandise destined for the palace at Tadmor, for goods brought from Mesopotamia via the oasis route. Their pleas for Shamira to return with them, as ordered by her father, fell on deaf ears. She genuinely seemed to be grieving over the death of Rameen, since for the whole two days she was not seen by anyone, other than her own servants - until she sent for Clytes.

'I'm sorry about Rameen,' was the first thing he said, on entering her tent. It was a lie, but he thought she would appreciate his concern.

'Don't be,' was her surprising response.

'So, you think he was responsible, then?'

'Don't question me, Clytes.'

'Why did you send for me?'

'I need you to stay with me until my father's men have left for Tadmor. I want to continue with the camel train as far as Damascus. There is work still to do, which cannot be left in the hands of my agents.'

'Are you afraid of your father, Shamira? Are you worried that he'll blame you for the loss?'

'I am not afraid of my father, Clytes, and stop questioning me about my personal life! The gold will be found. My father will see to that. The thieves will pay dearly for attacking his camels!'

As she turned away, Shamira's dark lashes fluttered. Tears, thought Clytes? He surprised himself at his strong feeling of relief that the preening Rameen would no longer be constantly at her side, and he excused his altered reasoning by assuming that

69

Shamira believed him guilty. Perhaps the man was responsible for the attack after all. Perhaps he did deserve his brutal end. Farnaka's men left for Tadmor, without their ruler's daughter returning with them, and the caravan proceeded on its journey.

The second encounter with bandits unnerved Clytes more than the first, because on this occasion a group of young boys were taken as hostages, and one of them was Amir. They'd been enjoying some free time swimming in the river and had unthinkingly drifted out of sight of the encampment. To get the youngsters back involved some frantic negotiations, since time was money for the caravan, and it did not want to be held up for long; something the robbers were well aware of. Their leader was a shifty looking individual, with few teeth and even less compassion, speaking with the oily ease of someone accustomed to a life of scheming and corruption. Ill-equipped to attack the passing camel-trains, his motley band of followers eked out a sporadic living by hostage-taking when the opportunity arose and judging by their desperate demeanor, Clytes suspected they were quite capable of murder. The boys were held captive on the other side of the river and the terms were that they would be escorted mid-river in a boat, if another vessel carrying the agreed merchandise was brought in exchange.

'We're not greedy,' the toothless man slyly informed them. 'We don't want to attract trouble but think seriously about what your boys are worth to you. We know what we can get for them in a slave market,' he added, with a gaping grin. We'll be back in the morning. Have your answer ready.'

Speedily gathered to discuss their next move, were the anxious men who'd had children taken, Clytes included.

'We can't let the bastards get away with this!' one of the men exclaimed, angrily.

'Pay them what they want!' spoke up a desperate father. I'm not having my boy sold into slavery!'

'Give in to that scum and they'll do it again,' argued Clytes.

As for the rest of the men concerned; including merchants, camel-pullers and a cook, they were not interested in sorting out the local kidnapping problem; they just wanted an acceptable price quickly agreed upon, but this was proving difficult because of the disparity in their individual wealth. Emotions were running high and Clytes believed violence could erupt at any moment.

He spoke up again. 'They're low-life and obviously not well organised. They appear to have no weapons of any worth. If you give them what they want, word will travel that you are weak, and when you use this route again, you'll encounter further attacks, but from more formidable men. I would not do anything to jeopardise Amir's safety, or any of your boys, but if I can devise a plan, will you at least listen to it?'

Masoud was consulted and he supported Clytes in his reasoning for a plan to rescue the boys. He had enough trouble with bandits as it was, without attracting more, and if word got out that his camel-train was fiercely protected, it could only be to the good. Clytes had proven to him that he was a worthy fighter. He suspected that the other guards were a little in awe of him.

The plan counted on greed, blinding the kidnappers to what was actually happening under their very noses, and as Clytes drew diagrams in the earth, Masoud and his armed guards were soon nodding in eager agreement as they became fully conversant with the ruse. Two boats were to be hired, as near in likeness as possible, and both were to bear the same name, so the owner's reluctant permission was needed to temporarily repaint the sign on one of the vessels. The merchants were then asked to choose what should be placed in the boat to be exchanged for the children. This caused further heated debate, as Clytes kept asking for more to be offered. His reassurances that they would get their wealth back was not believed by all. Nevertheless, Clytes was finally satisfied with the value of the goods brought forward, and they were spread out on thick, colourful rugs for the toothless man to inspect, when he returned the following day, alone.

'He obviously doesn't want his companions to know what's being traded,' whispered Clytes to Masoud. That makes it easier for us.'

'I'm pleased to see that you value your children highly!' said the man, unable to suppress his delight, as he greedily viewed the quantity and variety of merchandise laid out before him.

'We are eager to continue our journey and want no further delay,' said one of the merchants, his voice struggling to remain steady. 'This will all be yours when we get back our children...... but not before. Are you satisfied?'

'You can have your boys back,' replied the man, eagerly, now in a hurry to leave with his ill-gotten gains. 'When I give the signal, my men will place them in a boat and the exchange will take place.'

'Roll up the carpets,' ordered Masoud, and the robber watched with barely concealed avarice as eight weighty rugs were carefully folded over and carried into the waiting vessel.

Lying unnoticed nearby was the beached second boat, covered completely with a sailcloth. It contained Masoud's armed men, each one hidden in a heavy rug. They lay waiting for the sound of a fracas which would alert them to the boat switch. The diversion had been rehearsed during the long, anxious night when Clytes had given the portly cook the benefit of his acting experience. At his signal, the cook, armed with a large cleaver, ran towards the kidnapper, crying out angrily.

'If you've hurt my boy, I swear by all the gods, that I'll hunt you down and cleave you from your toothless head to your shrivelled balls!'

As rehearsed, some of the men rushed to hold him back, but he pushed them away, his fat arms flaying wildly, and like a bull he charged at the man again.

'I want proof that he hasn't been harmed, before I give you one obol!' he roared, still waving the heavy cleaver.

'If anything happens to me, you'll never see him again!' squealed the man, trying to hide behind Clytes and Masoud. 'Keep him away from me!'

'Hold him!' yelled Masoud, and the group of merchants, as pre-arranged, grabbed hold of the cook and dragged him away, still shouting.

'Let's get this done!' Masoud cried out.

In different circumstances Clytes would have accused them all of over-acting.

A flaming torch was brought from the camp in order to send the signal across the river, and Masoud, Clytes and the kidnapper, hurried towards the shore.

'We're not leaving until we see your boat setting off,' said Clytes menacingly. 'And no tricks!'

'I want this over with as much as you do,' said the man, glancing greedily at the rolls of carpet lying in the prow of the boat, and he waved the lighted torch at intervals until he saw a similar signal from the other side. 'They're coming!'

Pushing the boat out into the current, the three men each took up a pair of oars and started rowing towards the centre of the river. Masoud, who knew every youngster in the caravan, turned his head to watch as the boats drew closer together. 'Are you all safe?' he shouted.

'Yes, Masoud!' Amir called back. 'We're all here!' and he waved excitedly when he saw Clytes was also at the oars. As the distance narrowed, one of the four men guarding the children, threw a rope to be caught by his leader and the vessels were hauled together.

'Now, my friends!' said the kidnapper, speaking triumphantly to Clytes and Masoud. 'I have another proposition. Why don't we re-negotiate the terms of this transaction? I think you could persuade the merchants to be a little more generous, eh?' He indicated to his men to hold back the children, and some cried out in fear.

'Amir!' shouted Clytes, urgently. 'Jump! All of you. Into the water!'

'You're outnumbered!' cried out the robber, incredulously, standing with his toothless mouth agape.

'I don't think so!' replied Clytes, grinning, and emerging from the carpet rolls, scrambled Masoud's men. The caravaneer quickly despatched the robber with a ruthlessness Clytes had previously believed unthinkable of the man, while his men ferociously took care of the others.

Shouts from the children alerted the men to their immediate plight. Although they'd avoided the slaughter by jumping into the river, they were now in danger of being swept away by the strong current. Taking up the oars, the men managed to turn the boat and they began pulling with all their might to catch up with them, but it was not fast enough for Clytes. When he saw the cook's young son sink beneath the waters, he dived over the side, swimming powerfully to where he'd last seen the boy. Three times he surfaced, gulping for air, before he finally emerged holding the drowning child, and handed him, half-conscious, into the arms of Masoud. The other children, including Amir, managed to grab hold of the oars and were pulled quickly to safety.

'I thought you'd drowned, master!' cried a sobbing and frightened Amir, when Clytes was finally dragged back onboard, and he clung to him tightly.

'Me? I can swim like a dolphin!' Clytes boasted, theatrically, making Amir's tears turn to giggles in an instant.

SEVENTEEN

THE ROAD TO DAMASCUS, which became increasingly lush and green as they approached the old city, attracted many thieves, and the camel train continued to be pestered by opportunists and also beggars, until they arrived at their destination. Once he'd seen to the affairs of the caravan, Masoud sought out Clytes to thank him for his invaluable assistance on the route. He found him with Amir and Baz close to the hostelry which would be their home for the next two weeks. All three were sprawled on the grassy verge of a trickling stream, the man and the boy with their feet dangling in the refreshingly cool water.

He stooped to fondle the dog's ears, failing to notice the friends amused shared grin.

As he left, he glanced back. He felt eased in mind; relieved that he'd not had to kill Clytes, as he had Habib and Rameen.

EIGHTEEN

SURROUNDED BY EVERY LUXURY the wealthy city of Damascus could provide, Shamira, absorbed in thought, paced the marble floor of her expansive villa, stepping on exquisitely beautiful inlays of myriad flowers, closely watched by her hunting dogs as they lay stretched out on the appreciatively cool surface. Also watching but not wanting to interrupt, was a male attendant bearing a silver tray piled high with tiny bundles of papyrus, each one tied up with a tasseled, colourful string. Owned by her father, the palatial accommodation, set by luxuriant water gardens where goldfish swam and peacocks preened, was sequestered behind high stone walls - her usual place of abode when reaching the terminus of her trading journey. Somewhere she could entertain her guests, also lovers, in privacy. Knowing the caravan would be moving on towards Egypt without her, she realised that while the time allowed in Damascus, this would be her last chance to make her true feelings known to Clytes, hence the rejection of her father's wishes that she return to Tadmor, but, she wondered, was her decision a wise one? Ever since Clytes had joined the camel train at Mazaka she'd felt drawn to him and experienced emotions that were entirely new to her, but did Clytes feel the same way?

Her thoughts were interrupted when one of the scrolls toppled to the floor and she asked, sharply, 'What is it?'

'Many invites, mistress!'

'So soon?' she answered, without enthusiasm, but accepting that business came first and that there was still much to do on behalf of her family, she went to open the requests and invitations recently arrived from affluent families in the city, all eager to negotiate with her before their rivals could.

After so many months journeying along dusty roads, the city was a welcoming green paradise for the travellers. Fed by two rivers and numerous springs, the area was fertile all year round, with flower-filled meadows, orchards of apricots, and woods of poplar, walnut and myrtle. Making the most of their idyllic surroundings were Clytes and his two companions, who were bathing in one of the many spring-fed pools situated around the city. Amir and Baz scrambled up to a rock platform, taking delight in jumping together into the cool water, causing an enormous splash.

'Are you trying to kill me, Amir!' shouted Clytes, only just avoiding being crushed.

'It's great fun, master! You try!' and at Amir's insistence all three of them leapt recklessly into the pool, the man and the boy yelling joyously.

Later, when they lay naked in the sun to dry themselves, with the great hound moved some distance away to shake itself vigorously, Clytes felt a shadow fall over him and he looked up to find Masoud staring down at him.

'Get dressed, Clytes. Shamira wants to see you. I know the way,' he added, somewhat resignedly.

Approaching the villa, Clytes couldn't help but give out a whistle of appreciation. 'The lady lives in some style, Masoud. Her family must be rich indeed!'

'Rich and ruthless, my friend. I'll leave you to go in yourself. I've already spoken with the lady.'

While being taken to Shamira by a handsomely dressed servant, Clytes looked around the interior. Fine ornaments of gold and silver adorned exquisitely designed furniture, and statues in marble and bronze lined the corridor to her quarters. Suddenly conscious of his appearance, he tugged at his damp clothing and tried to smooth down his tangled hair.

'Your hair's wet,' Shamira remarked, as he approached.

'I came straight here. Masoud seemed concerned.'

'It's none of his business! Where were you bathing?'

'By the tall rock. The boy enjoyed jumping from it.'

'I don't think I know the place. Perhaps you could show me?'

'I could? But was there something......?'

'Yes, Clytes. You won't be in the city for much longer, but while you are here, I need you to accompany me when I make my transactions.'

'If you're looking for a replacement for Rameen, Shamira, you can look elsewhere!'

'I disobeyed my father, Clytes, by not going back to Tadmor, simply because I want to make it up to him for the loss of the gold. I can negotiate much better than my father's agents, but I need someone with me. I know I can trust you. I need you.'

'When do we start?'

'Tonight......and please don't come dressed like that! I've been invited to the governor's house!'

With access to her extensive wardrobe of beautiful garments and also her vast collection of elaborate hair adornments, jewellery and exotic perfumes, Shamira was able to create the impression she wanted, that evening, and was gratified to see the look of admiration in Clytes' eyes. She thought her bodyguard came a little overdressed for his part, however, with his tasseled cummerbund and embroidered shoes, and forcing back an amused smile, assumed he'd done it on purpose to make a point.

The evening went well with many contacts being made and Clytes was again impressed at how much respect Shamira seemed to enjoy. He watched her as she moved about the room, looking stunningly beautiful in a red silk gown, heavily embroidered with rich gold thread, and at the eminent guests who respectfully stepped aside to allow her passage to converse with others. He would be leaving her company soon, probably never to see her again, and he was sad at the thought. The lady was obviously showing interest in him and he certainly wanted her, but what about the rumours? What about the warnings from Hasim?

Later that evening, the die was cast.

In the moonlight, the rock pool shimmered invitingly and with Shamira's trusted servants ordered to keep away any unwanted attention, she unashamedly removed her clothing and slid into the water.

'Join me Clytes!' she called out, then she swam, unhurriedly, to the far side of the pool, her long dark hair spreading out around her. As she turned and started to swim back towards him, Clytes, naked, stood watching her, hesitating. Then, slowly, like the goddess Aphrodite rising from the sea, she started to walk from the pool towards him, the moonlight reflected on her dark, wet skin. As the water became shallower, he remembered Hasim's warning, but he couldn't take his eyes away.

As she stepped out of the pool, he surveyed her naked body and gasped, with obvious relief.

'Oh, Clytes, I'm surprised at you!' Shamira responded, laughing. 'I thought only fools believed the stories being spread about me.'

'But where do they come from? Who started the rumours?'

'Does it matter? Come! The water's lovely!'

Supported by the water, he lifted her up, and her long legs entwined tightly around him. She clung to him passionately, showering him with murmurs of love and he kissed her hard and longingly in response, before sweeping her up into his arms and carrying her to the bank. Their love making was the most intense he'd ever experienced. It was as though he were under the spell of an enchantress and nothing else in the world existed. When he climaxed, it was though he'd fallen into oblivion, and so powerful was their mutual passion, even death held no fears for him.

Guarded by Shamira's servants, the pool became 'their pool' and they returned to it often to make love and she would scream with delight while holding hands with Clytes as they jumped together from the rock. Shamira held nothing back in her lovemaking. Her desire for Clytes was all encompassing. He moved into her villa, and she lavished him with gifts, with compliments, with love.

One night she said to him, 'I want to open up to you, Clytes. Tell you everything. But if I do, I'm afraid you'll leave me.'

'We've both had a past,' he murmured. 'It's enough that you want to tell me things. Keep your secrets......and I'll keep mine.'

'You'll stay?'

'I'm not going anywhere.'

Rumours of their relationship quickly spread throughout the caravan, and it was not long before Masoud sought out Clytes.

'I like you Clytes, and that's why I'm warning you. Do not see Shamira again or things will go badly for you. The caravan will be moving on in a few days. Please the gods, you will be travelling with it!'

'And if I'm not?'

'Remember Rameen? It's your choice.'

That night, Clytes broached the subject of Masoud's warning with Shamira.

'If you have nothing to hide, why are you so hard on your ex-lovers?'

'It's my father's doing. He thinks the rumours will keep men away from me. He gets jealous.'

'Jealous enough to have them killed?'

'He doesn't want me to love anyone else. Someone who could come between us.'

'What kind of father goes to such extremes for the love of his daughter?'

'He loved my mother very much. She was from Nubia on the river Nile and very beautiful. She was my father's favourite. I was twelve years old when she died. People tell me I look a lot like her. My father favours me, Clytes, because of the love he had for my mother.'

Shamira looked up at him and opened her mouth to speak again, but unable to meet his gaze, she lowered her long dark lashes. Clytes studied her face, drinking in her loveliness - uncomprehending.

Suddenly, he asked, 'Are you trying to tell me something?' Shamira maintained her silence and turned her face away. 'What is it?' he asked, concerned.

'Don't look at me like that!' cried Shamira, pushing him away.

The truth dawned on Clytes. 'You share his bed!' he said, astounded. 'In return for sexual favours, he's given you control. Is that it?!'

'What can other men offer me, Clytes? Why be someone's subservient wife, when I can have anything I want, go anywhere I want. Everyone fears my father! I have the ultimate protection.'

Clytes leaped from the bed and paced the floor, struggling to understand how he could have been so unsuspecting. He turned on her, angrily.

'But you can't have any man you want!' he shouted. 'Low life! Enemies of your father! Men you don't care what happens to them. What a pair you are. What about having your own family; children......or is that something else you've neglected to tell me?'

'None lived.'

'By all the gods, what does that mean?! That your father disposes of those problems too? I don't know whether to pity you or despise you! I want to believe that you've been manipulated by your father.' He pleaded with her. 'You do see that this isn't right? You could break free.'

'I *am* free. I have respect. How many women can do as I do? My brothers do as *I* say! It's my choice.'

'Is it your choice? The respect you speak of is induced by fear. Fear of your father!'

'You are safe, Clytes. Please don't leave me! My father will believe you are no threat to him. I can take other lovers. I can convince him you are an amusement only.'

'Thank you!'

'You said you loved me!'

'Not that much!'

His mind in turmoil, Clytes left the villa and as soon as it was daylight, he went to find Masoud.

'Did you kill Rameen? Habib?'

'Of course.'

'The things that happened to her ex-lovers; you were responsible for that too?'

'It's complicated, Clytes.'

'Did you know about Shamira and her father?'

'I guessed.'

'I respected you.'

'It's not easy, Clytes, having to deal with Shamira's needs as well as the demands of her father. How do you think I'm able to travel through these lands? Besides the legal taxes, there are bribes to be paid, threats to be endured, and private arrangements are always expected by such people as Farnaka. I protect her Clytes. Better than you ever could.'

'Is that what you call it, Masoud? Protection? More like exploitation......for your own lucrative ends! Have you informed Farnaka's spies about me?!'

'I had no choice, Clytes. Shamira knows my arrangement with her father. I warned her but she still took the risk. It has worked well enough *and* to her satisfaction. Until you arrived!'

'Perhaps the lady now wishes for change?'

'She won't give up the life she has.'

'We'll see!'

'I'll do what I can to protect you, Clytes. I owe you that...... at risk to my own life, I might add, but my advice is to leave Damascus, immediately.'

All too soon, news circulated that Farnaka himself had arrived in the city, accompanied by a party of his bodyguards. Ever since his daughter had not returned to Tadmor, his spies had been trying to find out the reason why, and they quickly found out about Rameen's replacement. As soon as Farnaka arrived at his villa, he immediately questioned his daughter, but getting no satisfaction, he sent for Masoud.

'I thought him no threat, my lord. He entertained her, yes, but I saw nothing inappropriate between them. The caravan is moving on in a few days' time and this man is eager to get to Egypt. He is interested in nothing else!'

People of the caravan were questioned but such was their desire to shield Clytes, that they failed to mention how fierce a fighter he was and the heroic part he'd played in protecting their camel train, and they spoke only of how he entertained them with his acrobatic tricks; of the young boy he'd adopted and about the great dog that went everywhere with them. Shamira's servants also, as fearful of their mistress as they were of her father, pleaded ignorance and managed to avoid more harsh interrogation.

Shamira's pleas came from a desperate place, knowing what punishment her father would extract if he knew the truth. She flattered him excessively, telling him there was no one else holding the key to her heart. The man he spoke of was an entertainer only. He amused her. The reason she'd travelled on to Damascus, she explained, was to impress her father and she showed him all the contracts she'd agreed on his behalf. Farnaka had never heard his daughter plead for the life of anyone before and when he doubted her explanation, he was taken aback at her response. She was more like himself than he'd realised and just as ruthless it seemed. When her pleadings failed to bring the result she wanted, she implied she would disclose his treatment of her to his sons. This revelation immediately made him uneasy. They were weak, yes, but they could still rise up the people against him. Shamira, he calculated, would prefer the situation to remain as it was. He knew his daughter enjoyed the power she had. Why take the risk of upsetting her over this matter? The following day, Masoud was again sent for, expecting to be ordered to kill Clytes, but Shamira's threats had had their affect. The punishment would still be harsh, but Clytes could live.

'Don't think about releasing the dog, Clytes,' warned Masoud, grimly. 'Either the dog's body is taken to Farnaka or Amir's. His men are holding the boy right now.'

'I can't bury him?'

'Sorry, Clytes.'

'Fuck you, Masoud! It's you I should be burying!'

'I'll come with you,' Hasim offered.

'I'd prefer to do this alone.'

'Here, Clytes,' said the cook. 'It will be quick. I've sharpened it. Cut deeply. And take this. It will distract him,' and into Clytes' hand he pressed a chunk of goat meat.

In a quiet spot he held the dog close while talking softly, repeating, 'it's alright, boy. It's alright. I'm here.' He stroked his great head while waiting calmly for the blood to drain from the severed jugular vein, then, ashen faced, he laid him down and stroked him for the last time. Shaking with grief and anger, he returned to Masoud.

'It's done, you bastard! Now, let me see the boy!'

'You'll see him at the port.'

'The port?'

'You're to be put onboard a ship. It's that, or.........'

'If you've hurt him, Masoud......!'

Restrained by shackles and under the watchful eyes of Farnaka's men, Clytes was taken to the shores of the Mediterranean, where he was relieved to be reunited with Amir. As they stood on the jetty, Clytes looked in vain for sight of Shamira.

'Did you hear laughter?' he asked, Amir.

'No master. Why would anyone laugh?'

'Only another sadistic bastard!'

Before boarding the waiting vessel, Amir was held back by Masoud.

'Farnaka's orders, Clytes. Amir must remain here. If you don't leave, I have orders to kill him. He will stay with the caravan, Clytes. He's well-liked by the men. I'll take care of him.'

'To become a paid assassin like yourself, Masoud! I don't think so!'

'You don't have a choice!'

'You're a fucking son of a bitch, Masoud!' yelled Clytes, and he threw himself on the caravaneer, grappling him to the ground. With his hands around his neck, he squeezed Masoud's throat so tightly he would have choked him, if Farnaka's men hadn't fallen upon him with cudgels. He was dragged onto the boat, barely conscious, where the captain of the Phoenician merchant ship, together with members of his crew, quickly tied Clytes' hands to the guardrail. As the rowers pushed off from the shore, Amir, who was being held back by Farnaka's men, shouted desperately, 'Master! Master! I want to come with you!'

But Shamira *was* there. Mingling with the multitude of people at the bustling harbour, she observed with sadness as the boy was denied access to the boat and the inevitable fight between Clytes and Masoud which followed. As Clytes was carried onboard she continued to watch anxiously and sighed with relief when she saw that he still lived. Concealed behind the drapes of her camel howdah, wrapped in Clytes' cloak, she waited until the boat was out of sight, then holding the garment to her face, she inhaled deeply and wept.

A few days later the caravan moved on - with a new master. After Shamira and her father had left for the natural splendour of their oasis, Masoud's body was found floating in the rockpool. Everyone assumed it was Farnaka's doing, all except Hasim and Amir, who believed the most likely culprit was Shamira.

NINETEEN

S LUMPED ON THE DECK of the ship, Clytes gradually came to his senses and realising what had happened, he shouted at the captain to release him. 'Put me ashore, captain! I have unfinished business, there!' he demanded.

'Hey! I give the orders here!' the Phoenician retorted. 'I've a family in Tyre and I want to see them still alive when I return. If Masoud tells me to take you far from here, then that's where you're going!'

'There's a boy left behind,' explained Clytes, angrily. 'He's being held against his will!'

'You're staying here. If you show your face there again, my family's dead for sure!'

'Well, if that's your concern, what's to stop you just throwing me over the side?'

'Because of a certain lady's interest, that's what! You're to be put ashore, *alive*, when we reach our final destination, and until then, I'll guard you as though my own life depended upon it...... which it does.'

'Where are we heading?'

'Sicily. That's why Masoud chose my vessel, and that's where we'll part company. Pray to the gods, the winds are favourable. The sooner I can wash my hands of you the better. We'll be joining a convoy when we reach Cyprus, and because of the delay you've caused, we'll now be sailing through the night!'

Situated at the prow of the merchant ship was a small stone altar dedicated to the Phoenician god Melqart, thought by sailors to be their protector, and before any long journey, which was always fraught with danger, a simple ceremony was performed when a libation of wine was poured over the altar and prayers intoned. Before setting forth, the entire crew, including Clytes knelt before the shrine, while a priest called upon the god to protect the sixteen souls onboard.

Until the ship was taken up by its great sail, a limited number of rowers propelled the cargo ship, and untied from the rail, Clytes was forcibly lashed to the rowing bench. Angry, almost to the point of murdering someone, he watched as the shoreline receded, but finding no means of escaping from his predicament, he furiously gripped the oar.

'You'll be released from your bonds while out at sea,' explained captain Tadeus, 'but when near land you'll be restrained, understand?' He looked upwards with satisfaction as the large square sail suddenly filled with wind, and the carved horsehead at the prow, leaped forward with the force of it. 'I'm not taking any chances with you,' he added, determinedly. 'Now help the men secure the cargo. You'll be working your passage.'

Tadeus' varied shipload consisted of scented cedar logs from local forests, rolls of expensive purple dyed cloths and embroideries from Tyre, and a consignment of exotic food seasonings from the east; cinnamon, turmeric, saffron, ginger and pepper. Providing protective coverings for the vulnerable sacks of spices and the more delicate items, were heavy Anatolian carpets, acquired from the merchant, Shamira of Tadmor. Also, due to being delayed while waiting for Clytes' arrival, enormous rolls of papyrus from nearby Byblos had been added to the cargo; taken onboard just before sailing.

'Akbar sailed without them,' explained the port official to Tadeus. 'Probably in a hurry to return to his woman in Citium. Can you take them? You'll meet up with him when you join the convoy.'

'I'll take them,' the captain had agreed, by adding his mark to the altered export order. 'But lover-boy owes me a favour!'

Even though the captain knew this coast like the back of his hand, night travel was always hazardous, especially in such a strong wind, and keeping the precious merchandise free from seawater contamination in a heaving sea was a major concern. The experienced crew, trying to make up for lost time, worked hard to maintain a steady speed, without losing control of the straining sail or overtaxing the steering gear.

Trying to sleep that night at the end of his shift, lying on the swaying deck, Clytes was tormented by memories of the life he'd been so cruelly torn from, and grieving at the killing of Baz, his thoughts turned to The Wolf of Thebes. You may have taken everything from me, Lykaon, he cursed, inwardly, but the gods have spared me yet, and for as long as I live, may Hades hear me, I'll damn your black soul! That night it was bright with stars, and by adjusting the sail, the strong wind which had blown westerly all day, continued to carry them northward. Welcoming the continuing divine gift, Tadeus' sail crew, utilising as much of the gusts as possible, controlled the ship like a runaway racehorse, while the helmsman Ahumm, manning his station at the stern steered the way, hugging the coast up towards Cyprus. Still believing the gods were allowing Lykaon's spirit to torment him due to his arrogant determination in wanting to kill the Theban, Clytes dejectedly looked up at the heavens, unheedful of the sound of the waves crashing against the boat and the crack of the billowing sail flapping above him. As he stared at the dazzling cosmos, his eyes became fixed on a stream of stars as they shot across the sky. He prayed to the goddess Hera, 'the queen of heaven' to watch over Amir, now believing that the boy was better off without him, then finally fell into a fitful sleep to dream of swimming with Shamira in a star-filled rock pool, which suddenly changed into a terrifying whirlpool, and in a lovers embrace they were dragged down, down, down. He woke with a start when cold seawater washed over him, and reeling from the intensity of the dream, he struggled to stand upright on the heaving deck, to be confronted by an equally unsteady Tadeus.

'The papyrus has broken loose!' he yelled through the wind. 'Help the men secure it! Then he turned to the crew struggling with the violently flapping canvas. 'Shorten the sail!' he ordered.

Broken free from their restraining ropes, the heavy rolls bounced and careered dangerously across the flooded deck, while the men in near total darkness, frantically tried to grab hold of them. The loose cables, picked up by the wind, whipped through the air, one striking Clytes viciously across his back. He was thrown forward on the slippery boards and only just avoided being hit by a large bolt of papyrus hurtling towards him. Another crew member, unaware of the coming danger, took the full force of the blow, and he was pitched instantly over the side.

'Man overboard!' yelled a comrade, frantically. 'It's Umar!' But in the darkness and with a swelling sea, everyone knew there was little hope of recovery. Although the ship had slowed with the sail more narrowly furled, they continued to be buffeted by high waves, and no sign could be seen of their lost crew member.

'Throw them over the side!' yelled the Phoenician, in desperation. It's not possible to save them all. If Umar's still alive, he might be able to cling to one!'

With the loose bolts heaved overboard, the remaining stacks of papyrus were able to be successfully secured, but as waves continued to crash over the prow, Tadeus decided to lengthen the sail again. Going faster might smooth out the pounding the round-hulled freighter was getting from the high swells. The carved horse's head at the prow, rose and fell, and as the ship's timbers groaned and shrieked with the increased stress, it was as though the vessel had become the god Melqart's sea-monster, the great winged hippocampus, galloping furiously through his watery kingdom.

Guided by Polaris and trusting his experienced crew, Tadeus let the force drive them onwards, but the nearer they got to Cyprus, the stronger the west wind blew. His hope was to reach safety at the Phoenician held town of Citium on the southern coast of Cyprus, where protected from the winds the convoy would be sheltering, but despite their best efforts the ship was blown off course, driven past the long pointing finger of the island, avoiding the nearby Cleides Islands - onwards, towards the coast of Anatolia.

Unable to rendezvous in Cyprus and afraid of being wrecked if he attempted to make a landing, the captain had no choice but to carry on alone towards the island of Rhodes, some three hundred miles to the west, in the hope that the rest of the convoy would follow in due course. Along the southern coast of Anatolia, the sea current ran westward, and together with the slight wind which blew off the land, the merchant ship was able to proceed slowly, working against the prevailing oncoming wind. As a third weary day dawned, the captain bellowed to Clytes, 'Take your turn at the helm!'

To relieve the exhausted helmsman in his task of holding steady the twin paddles, the crew had worked in relays to help Ahumm steer the ship, but as Clytes fought his way to the stern, holding fast to the handrail, he saw something in the distance. Besides the concern for keeping the cargo dry, there was another threat to its welfare. Pirates were a major problem for commercial traffic, and a lone merchant ship, close to the shore, without the protection of an armed convoy, was a gift for raiders.

'We have company!' yelled Clytes, as three small sails were spotted, silhouetted against the morning light, following in their wake and approaching fast.

'Raiders!' shouted Tadeus. 'We'll try and outrun them. Pull in the rowboat!'

With great difficulty the small rowing craft, used for transporting crew and goods to shore, but now filled with ropes and tackle, was laboriously hauled on board. Without its drag, the ship immediately moved faster in the water, but still the vessels chasing them, unimpeded by weight of cargo, were getting closer.

'Throw the tackle overboard!' Tadeus ordered, resignedly, 'and the spare cables!'

Also heaved over the side went anything deemed dispensable; the tents and bedding, heavy cooking pots, bundles of dried cedar wood for their fires, and all their provisions, save for some dried fish, a sack of barley and the precious flasks of wine and water.

'They're still gaining on us, captain!' shouted Clytes, watching intently from the stern.

'We'll have to sacrifice more cargo to lighten the load!' Tadeus conceded, grimly. 'Get to it! Start with the papyrus!'

Without constantly manoeuvring the sail to catch what wind there was blowing off the land, their progress could be impeded to such an extent that they'd face inevitable capture, but to outrun them, just how much cargo would need to be sacrificed? Wild yelling could be heard coming from the following crafts, and when Clytes looked back, he saw one of the small craft had been overturned. It had been hit by the discarded papyrus. Cheers erupted from the Phoenicians, when they realised their good fortune, but the euphoria was short lived. One of the remaining raiding boats had succeeded in sailing alongside and an iron grappling hook landed heavily on the deck. Although the pirate ship was a lot smaller, it gradually slowed the merchant ship to such an extent that it changed course and began heading dangerously towards the shores of Cilicia, while the other marauding craft, filled with screaming brigands, believing they'd been triumphant, followed closely on their tail. It wasn't only the merchandise in peril, but also the lives of all on board. If captured alive, then a slave market beckoned. Clytes expected they'd soon be boarded and overpowered, since the remaining brigands still outnumbered Tadeus' crew.

'Cut the rope!' bellowed the captain as his ship was being forced off course, and members of the crew who'd been unable to detach the hook embedded in the deck, and which was being held there with great force, struggled to slice through the thick cable. The freighter was drawn so close to the enemy vessel that one of the marauders was able to clamber aboard, intent on stopping the cable from being severed. The man, of immense build, enraged at the loss of one of their vessels, wielded his great axe murderously and screamed for vengeance. Clytes, fearful for his fellow companions, indicated urgently to the helmsman to retake his rudder. Just as the leviathan raised his weapon to strike, Clytes jumped onto his back, taking him by surprise, and pinning him to the deck he repeatedly pounded the man's great head on the boards. Tadeus, afraid his unlooked-for passenger would be killed, putting the lives of his own family in jeopardy, yelled for his men to go to Clytes' aid. Their concerted efforts forcibly disarmed their attacker, and still struggling, they heaved his considerable bulk over the side. Leaving the men still trying to disengage the cable, Clytes picked up the man's fallen weapon, tucking it into his corded belt, then putting his own fears aside, he recklessly leapt onto the deck of the assailing craft. Overpowering the man nearest to him, he pressed the blade to his throat. Many years previously he'd lived a similar life to these sea robbers, and he knew they would want to avoid a fight. Opportunism without risk to themselves was their aim, and now events had turned against them. 'You've lost one boat *and* your comrades!' shouted Clytes. 'Unless you want to lose another, release the cable!'

Their leader at the stern, holding fast to an ornate carved canopy, resentfully accepted Clytes' reasoning and now thoroughly discouraged following the unforeseen demise of his most powerful crew member, he bellowed to his men to stand down. With the tow rope released Clytes quickly grabbed the rope ladder of the merchant vessel and climbed back onboard where Tadeus and his men were full of praise for his actions, and the captain relieved that Clytes still lived, ceased to roar at him, even allowing him to keep the weapon he'd taken from the drowned raider. When he later took his well-earned rest from duties, trying to get some sleep on what remained of the papyrus, Clytes had time to think about what had happened. Relief at breaking free from the sea robbers was mixed with a feeling of dread, for the worse for wear pirate boat he'd boarded was undoubtedly the 'Delias' and the weapon, now in Tadeus' safe keeping until he was safely deposited on Sicily, was surely Glaucus' double-headed axe. He knew his old friend would never have given up his boat without a fight and with enormous sadness he feared the worst. Bereft at the thought and believing the gods had not yet finished punishing him, he no longer cared about his own future and threw himself into helping the men of the freighter in getting their ship to the island of Rhodes, where a welcome rest was sorely needed before they could proceed on their journey to Sicily.

As they cleared the coast of Anatolia, the wind known by sailors as the Etesian, changed course so sharply from west to north-west, that Tadeus was forced to lower the sail entirely or risk being driven south across the Aegean. The steering gears also were lashed to the sides of the boat to prevent them from being shattered in the squall, but thrashing about on the deck was the rowboat, and Clytes called out, urgently.

'The lifeboat, captain!' 'It's breaking up the timbers!'

'Tie it more securely!'

'It's making the ship unstable!'

'Cut it loose then! Lower it over the side. It may help to slow us down.'

The crew members involved in the task, tied themselves to anything solid and managed to lift the boat over the stern, but as it hit the water the craft immediately overturned and was swept away with such force its tethering rope instantly jerked free.

Ahumm, the helmsman, who'd lashed himself to the sternpost, exclaimed, 'Well that was clever! How will we get ashore now? I can't swim!'

91

'Why ever not?' answered Clytes, incredulously, who was roped next to him.

'Better to drown quickly, than to float around for days without hope. Look at what happened to Umar!'

'Anybody else who can't swim?' shouted Clytes.

At least five others confessed to having no skill, Tadeus being one of them.

'I'll get you ashore!' volunteered Clytes.

'Deploy the sea-anchor!' shouted Tadeus, in desperation, as the ship continued to be driven perilously onward, and a leather bucket which was attached to the freighter by a long chain, was thrown overboard. This, the captain hoped, would cause enough drag on the stern to keep the ship on a steady course Without sail or steering, with some roped to the guardrails and others to the masthead, the crew prepared themselves to ride out the force of the wind, praying fervently to their god Melqart to get them safely to land, but their ship was now at the mercy of the powerful Etesian, and the island of Rhodes was left far behind as they were driven relentlessly southwards towards the distant shore of Egypt.

After eight long days and nights without rest since setting off on their voyage, the wind unexpectedly ceased. Far from land, with the sun high in the sky, their vessel suddenly became becalmed on a sea as smooth as a looking glass, reflecting the cloudless blue sky above. Chunks of flotsam floated by, of broken timbers and wreckage of a lost cargo; olive oil, going by the slimy surface of the sea all around them. Suddenly, one of the crew shouted out that he could see something ahead of them and protruding from the surface of the water was the hull of a large, upturned merchant ship. But, of survivors, there was no sign. On the steady deck, Tadeus called his crew together to pray for the souls of the unknown mariners, knowing how close they'd come to being capsized themselves, and Clytes moved them all with the rich tone of his beautiful singing voice. Exhausted by their experiences, but relieved at their deliverance, the seamen knelt in front of the stone altar and singing with raised voices, gave thanks to the great god of the sea.

As their chanting ceased, sounds of shouting came to them carried across the water from some distance away where the indistinct outlines of two or three ships could be seen, and obviously in distress going by their urgent calls for help. Egyptian merchant vessels, Tadeus suggested to his men, obviously becalmed as they were, and he debated as to whether they should row to their assistance, but as he watched he saw the reason for their cries of terror. Emerging from behind one of the stationary vessels appeared the shark-like presence of a mighty trireme, the rhythmic dipping of its many oars catching the sunlight.

'Gods, help us!' cried Tadeus. 'Athenians! Those poor buggers are sitting ducks. They don't stand a chance.'

Clytes rushed to the rail to watch.

'Don't think about a rescue,' said the captain to him, sharply. 'It's plunder they're after. Unless you've a rich family willing to pay your ransom, you're likely to be sold with the rest of us.'

Listening to the screams coming from the defenceless freighters, Clytes looked around at the trusting, hard-working seamen he'd journeyed with. He'd welcomed being part of their confined world; their struggle to survive and protect their cargo had forced his own morbid thoughts to dwindle in the mind. He decided not to mention Theomenes and other friends from his past who would confirm his credentials. They were as dead to him now as Glaucus undoubtedly was, and he gravely informed the captain that he knew of no-one who could vouch for him.

'They've got their hands full right now, but they'll have seen us, alright!' acknowledged Tadeus. 'Our only hope is to get out of sight.'

They'd had nothing to eat except a bite of dried fish and few handfuls of barley, since throwing their provisions overboard and were weak with hunger and lack of sleep, but with no sign of the wind returning they'd no choice but to take to the oars. Clytes joined the others and began to row, and under a burning sun, across a placid sea, they pulled until their lungs felt as though they were on fire and their arm muscles became cramped with pain, in a desperate effort to put as much distance as possible between their vessel and the scene of violence and mayhem they'd witnessed all too close to them.

Accepted as undisputed masters of the seas, Athenian warships were on constant patrol and since plunder from piracy had become a much-needed addition to Athens' strained coffers, any merchant ship without armed support was thought fair game. With the cessation of the wind, the Athenian trierarch was having a good day. His ship's incredible rowing capacity of one hundred and seventy men, meant the becalmed Egyptian traders were sitting targets, and they were quickly and ruthlessly overpowered. Placing some of his own men in control of the commandeered vessels, the trierarch then set his sights on the slow-moving Phoenician trader seen in the distance. Confident of capture, the piper was ordered to strike up a steady rhythm, and the remaining rowers, singing a song of victory, gave chase.

TWENTY

WHEN TADEUS SAW THE trireme ploughing through the water towards him, its many oars rising and falling with absolute precision, he despaired. Since a boy accompanying his father, he'd sailed these seas, and like many generations of sea-going Phoenicians before him, he had intimate knowledge of the winds and currents and the positioning of the sun and stars and considered himself a master seaman. Without convoy protection he'd survived a pirate attack and brought their ship safely through a powerful Etesian, but he knew when he was beaten. Even if he dispensed with his entire cargo his men could not outrow a trireme. Kneeling on the deck he prayed fervently to Melqart for his intervention while his crew, emitting groans of exertion interspersed with sporadic invocations, continued to pull strenuously. They were perspiring profusely, some complaining of an aching head, others of a tightness in the chest, as the air had suddenly become heavy and oppressive. To the south the sky had begun to darken dramatically and realising what this signified, the occupants of the merchant ship instantly forgot about the trireme. 'Sandstorm!' yelled Tadeus, jumping to his feet, and all too quickly, roaring towards them came a choking orange wall of wind-blown sand. Brought from the distant Sahara Desert by the heartless sorokos wind, the sea began to churn with angry foam, tossing the ship violently, and visibility through a thick yellow dust was reduced to just a few feet.

The heat hit them like the sudden opening of a vast oven, sapping every last vestige of strength from the men as they tried to shield themselves from the stinging sand being driven into their eyes and mouths. Collapsing on the deck, their garments soaked in dust-covered sweat, they gasped for air with an unquenchable thirst burning their throats. Tadeus and Clytes managed to drag themselves to the rail, expecting the Athenian warship to come looming out of the soup-like haze at any moment. They knew it was there as indistinct cries could be heard coming from the enemy vessel since it too had been struck by the sorokos. Tadeus instructed his men to remain still and not to make a sound, as shrouded by the cloak of the sandstorm, they waited in an agony of suspense. Sounds of the trireme gradually grew fainter and fainter, and after what seemed like hours on a constantly rolling deck, uncertain as to where the enemy ship was, they held their breath for a second time as the menacing, rhythmic splashing of the oars was heard once again. The Athenians hadn't given up hunting their prey, and terrifying, fierce cries emitted from the crew of the prowling trireme. All were now silently praying as their vessel was tossed about like a leaf in the wake of the trireme's powerful, but mercifully unseen passing. Hiram, the youngest crew member, unable to endure the tension, clutched at his stomach and vomited over his nearest shipmate.

Again, they waited, expecting to be rammed at any moment, until the Phoenician captain, believing that their assailants were now out of range, gave the order for the sail to be unfurled. A pale sun had momentarily become visible through the gloom and taking his bearings from this brief glimpse, he instructed his helmsman accordingly. In the suffocating heat any task no matter how small, felt Herculean, and the sail crew began grumbling amongst themselves. The ship could drift for evermore for all they cared. All they wanted to do was to lie down. Due to the unbearable heat, they were unable to concentrate, and their grumbling turned into a fierce argument as to which one of them wasn't giving it his best effort.

The canvas was finally dropped and the ship at long last moved speedily forward, but the strength of the wind brought no respite. It felt as though the very air was on fire. Clytes and the helmsman roped the twin rudders into a fixed position, not having the strength to hold them, and the rest of the men lay where they could, letting the sail carry them heedlessly onward through the sickly yellow seascape. With a burning thirst and his head feeling as though it was in a vice, young Hiram suddenly cried out and wildly scrambling over his prostate shipmates he made for the rail, intending to jump into the inviting, cool sea. Clytes had wondered which one of them would break first having previous knowledge of how crazed men became when the sorokos blew, and moving as quickly as his depleted strength allowed, he just managed to grab the boy before he fell. Slapping him hard he stopped his yelling at once only for it to be replaced by heaving sobs, but not one tear would be felt on his cheeks since they were dried instantly by the searing wind. The effort exhausted Clytes and he collapsed onto the sand covered deck, panting for air. His throat hurt as though filled with broken glass but knowing how precariously low their wine and water containers were, he suffered in silence.

Unbeknown to him, Tadeus was watching, glowering. The pressure he felt in his head was almost unbearable and throbbing painfully as though there was an iron band around it. Hiram's wild attempt to jump overboard had unsettled him, and he started to believe that his journey was plagued with unusual bad luck. There'd been difficulties from the outset, he realised, and he brooded over the loss of Umar, an experienced and well-respected seaman. There must be a reason for their setbacks, he fumed, not wanting to put any blame on himself, and in the dim light his eyes searched out Clytes who was lying prone near the stern. The crazed notion came to him that he was the source of their misfortune. Yes, he decided, it wasn't poor seamanship - the Hellene was the cause of their bad luck.

When a starless night fell, the hot dry wind continued to blow, and the heat was just as fearsome, and with all their flasks now drained dry their only hope was to find land quickly. Above them flapped the remnants of what had once been their sail, for the canvas torn by the sand-filled wind was now hanging in shreds, and there was no other since they'd dispensed with all spare tackle in order to shake of the sea-robbers. Tossed about rudderless on a choppy sea in total darkness, the ship slowly began to spin. Clytes thought he was the only one conscious of it, the rest of the crew having succumbed to the exhausting heat, until he became aware that Tadeus had crawled along the deck and was near him.

'It's your fault!' the exhausted man hissed in the darkness. 'Ever since you boarded my ship, we've had trouble!'

Ahumm, the helmsman, who was also lying close to the stern, stirred wearily.

'What's going on, captain?' he asked, through parched lips.

'The Hellene, Clytes! He's brought all this bad luck!'

'What?' exclaimed Clytes, suddenly realising Tadeus was talking about *him*. 'It was me who saved you from the pirate attack.'

'It was to save your own skin!'

'You're not thinking straight, Tadeus!'

'We missed the convoy waiting for you!'

'Then blame Masoud!'

'I'm going to kill you for what you've done!'

'Hold on there captain!' argued Ahumm, struggling to raise himself. 'He's worked as hard as any of us.'

'He got rid of the rowboat, knowing that many of us can't swim, just so he could escape by swimming ashore. Can't you see that?' Tadeus croaked, before being racked by a fit of debilitating coughing.

'It's the heat!' came a choking voice, as another crew member became aware of the disturbance. 'It will turn us *all* mad.'

In the dark, with the vessel turning and turning out of control, the men were too exhausted to move, and the captain's ravings went ignored. Worn out by his own exertions he sank into a sweat-soaked stupor where he lay. But Clytes was uneasy. Plagued by his own morbid beliefs, he wasn't surprised that the captain thought he was a bringer of bad luck. Uncertain as to how events would unfold, he ensured he'd tied himself securely to the sternpost and tried to remain alert. He knew that tempers flared during such storms, long held jealousies erupted, and even murders were committed - when the madness inducing sorokos blew.

As suddenly as it came the sandstorm passed and a fresh wind sprung up from the north. The change in the atmosphere was phenomenal, and the men struggled to their feet as though rising from the dead to gratefully gulp in the life-giving air, Tadeus included. To Clytes' relief the man seemed to have no recollection of what had transpired between them, and Ahumm, gripping him by the shoulder gave welcome reassurances that he'd no intention of reminding the captain of his momentary lapse into madness. With the passing of the storm, it was as though the stars had been blasted by the sand, and they sparkled with such brilliancy they looked close enough to touch. It was possible to see far into the distance, and Hiram was sent up to the 'crow's nest' at the top of the mast to take a look around. He saw no sight of land, but there was also no sign of the trireme. Tadeus immediately looked to the heavens and murmuring prayers of gratitude to the deities of the cosmos, took his bearings from the position of the North Star. Satisfied as to their location, he spoke to his crew.

'We're a long way from Rhodes, men, but if my calculations are correct, we are by Melqart's mercy, very close to the island of Crete!'

They all looked upwards at their tattered sail.

'Yes, it means we'll have to use the oars, but if we take it in turns, by sunrise I think we'll get sight of its eastern shore.'

Progress was painfully slow but putting trust in his knowledge he eventually sent Absalon, the eldest member of the crew and most in need of a rest from rowing, to take soundings. At intervals a lead weight attached to a line was thrown over the side. Eventually, he was able to shout, '20 fathoms!' Later, his rasping cry became '15 fathoms!' Then, on the horizon, a dark outline was seen. 'Land ahead!' he managed to shout, jubilantly. Thanking Melqart and also their own captain for their salvation, the men collapsed over their oars with exhaustion and being too weary to move, remained where they were, to wait impatiently with parched lips and growling bellies, for the dawn. Finally, the sun began to rise in the east, the starlight gradually faded, and the sky changed to a luminous pale gold.

'We've more company!' shouted Absalon at the prow. 'Dolphins!' and the remainder of their eventful journey to the safety of the elongated island of Crete was blessed by an extraordinary display of what the Hellenes believed were the leaping messengers of their sea god Poseidon, joyously showing them the way.

As their vessel drew closer to the land, the sailors on the merchant ship were joyful - all but one: Clytes. He recognised this coastline and memories of what he'd experienced there, even after more than a decade had passed, were still vivid. The harsh grey rock formations stretched steeply along the coastline, and Tadeus climbed onto the rail, holding fast to the horse-head prow, searching keenly for sight of a landing place he would recognise. Mercifully, the wind had dropped sufficiently for the ship to approach land safely, but he was aware that his men were exhausted and sorely in need of rest. Travelling any further to find a deep harbour with help at hand was out of the question. Any landing place would have to do.

Crete, known by locals as 'the big island', stretched for over one hundred and sixty miles, but the anchorage Tadeus was looking for was on its easternmost edge. He again sent Hiram to the top of the mast to get a better view from the cup-shaped 'crow's nest' and let out a groan of relief when the boy's excited cry came back, 'I can see it!' The men, with hands blistered and bleeding, began to pull with what was left of their strength towards a large, protected bay dotted with small boats. Due to the cessation of the strong winds, fishing vessels had begun setting out, and Tadeus called out to one of them to ask if they would assist in getting his crew ashore. The Phoenician gave no indication to Clytes that he'd any recollection of his momentary madness, but he did remember - some of it, and he felt immense relief that he hadn't killed the Hellene, not while there was still a chance he could fulfill his promise to Masoud. His fears that his unwelcome passenger would escape while swimming ashore remained, however, and he was grateful for the fisherman's aid. Anchors were lowered fore and aft, and half the crew were left onboard to guard the moored ship, while the rest, including a restrained Clytes, were ferried to the beach.

'There's no need for the manacles!' Clytes objected, strongly. 'I've no intention of going back to Damascus. Your family's safe!'

'We all need rest,' replied the captain, wearily. 'I need to know where you are while I'm asleep.'

'Your concern is touching!'

'It's a necessary precaution, Clytes......until I get you to Sicily.'

As he was made to follow the others towards the meagre comfort of a nearby fishing 'village', he stumbled awkwardly across the stone strewn beach, the shingle crunching beneath his feet bringing memories flooding back. Many years previously, when just out of military service, he'd regularly sailed these coasts. Following the deaths of members of his close family, caused by Lykaon the Theban, he'd been left with family debts to repay, and being unconcerned about the consequences of his actions, the grieving twenty-year-old had sought a life of recklessness and danger and joined a group of marauders operating in Cretan waters.

The myths of this island fascinated all Hellenes, and remnants of its once great Minoan past were to be found everywhere on the island, but that was long ago, and the Dorian inhabitants of Crete now lead a very reduced existence. During the continuing war between Athens and Sparta, Crete was able to remain neutral due to its remote location, but Athens was always wary of the historic Dorian connection between Crete and Sparta and took great care to keep the islanders constrained. Consequently, there was no surplus production on the island because there were no means of getting it to outside markets, squeezed as they were by Athens' control of the Aegean. Olive cultivation, goat keeping and fishing was carried out for local consumption only, but supplementing those basic occupations was a lucrative slave market, and of course, piracy.

TWENTY-ONE

'WHERE WERE YOU HEADING, then?' asked one of the fishermen, as Absalon and Hiram, began loading provisions onto the small fishing craft, destined for the crew left guarding the merchant vessel.

'Sicily, by our god's mercy,' replied Absalon.

'What's your cargo?' the man queried, casually.

'Cedar!' responded Hiram, innocently.

'Be quiet, Hiram!' spoke Absalon, sharply, then addressing the fisherman who was trying to look intent on his rowing, 'What's it to you?' he barked

'Just making conversation, friend,' he replied. 'Didn't mean anything by it.'

'Well, keep your curiosity to yourself! And that goes for anybody else asking questions!'

The eldest and youngest members of the crew had been sent by Tadeus to relieve two of their shipmates, to take over their shifts in maintaining a constant watch for any unusual activity near their vessel. The captain expected that news of their arrival was already spreading quickly and that it would eventually attract unwanted attention. It was a question of when they'd be targeted, not if. While a replacement sail and a suitable rowboat were being acquired, giving his men the opportunity to rest, he would remain vigilant. Tired as he was, he was more than eager to be on his way.

The fishermen's 'village' consisted of a cluster of worm-eaten upturned boats, no longer seaworthy, and the wreckage of others patched together to form makeshift but serviceable shelters. The main village, close to the ruins of an ancient temple, where the women and children lived safe from attack, was at the other end of a five-mile long, steep sided valley named 'The Gorge of the Dead', due to the numerous burials found in the cave tombs lining the walls - thousand-year-old relics of the island's great Minoan past.

To cook and care for the weary crew, women were brought from the upper village. They were a welcome sight for the seamen, as were Tadeus' mariners for the local females, being on such a remote part of the island, and it soon became evident to the captain that his men were being made more welcome than he'd have wished.

'Might as well make the most of the time, eh captain?' called out Ashmun, one of the sail crew. He was being served a meagre but welcome bowl of goat and vegetable stew by one of the women, and by the way she was 'giving him the eye' that wasn't all he expected to be served. 'The ship needs some attention, and so do we,' he added, chuckling, as his female companion began to slowly move her fingers through his sand-encrusted hair.

Clytes lay close by, chained to a large boulder, and he watched the activity with some apprehension. He was witnessing a scene all too familiar. His thoughts were interrupted when a woman sat down near him, and placing a bowl of food into his hands, spoke quietly.

'It is you, isn't it? It is Clytes?'

'Lyra?!'

'Yes, it's me! By all the gods, Clytes, I never expected to see you here again.'

'I never expected to be back here again!'

'Why the chains? What's happening?'

'Long story.'

CHAPTER TWENTY-ONE

'Where are you being taken? Is it serious?'

'Nothing for you to be concerned about. A misplaced love affair. I came between a father and his daughter, and I'm being taken to Sicily for my sins!'

'Ha! 'The angry poet'! You haven't changed.'

'Angry poet?'

'It's what we used to call you. You were so full of hate when you were here......angry all the time. But the women......they all adored you! They all wanted to heal your hurt......including me.'

'I don't have many good memories of being here, but your kindness, I've never forgotten, Lyra.'

'Is that all you remember?'

'I remember everything, including things I'd sooner forget.'

'But not us?'

'No, Lyra, not that. How's your brother? How's young Cato?'

'He's well. He'll be back from fishing later this evening. He's not so young, now! Twenty-four!'

'You're married, I expect?'

'I married Marcus.'

'Good choice!'

'I never expected to see you again.'

'Yes, you told me that already. I'm happy for you......really!'

'I'm not the girl I was.'

'You don't look any different to me, Lyra, but how did you recognise *me*?'

'Oh Clytes! You were my first! Now, eat. I'll make sure I'm the one to look after you. I'll bring you more wine soon. There's plenty being brought from the village. From what I've overheard, you're all to remain here.'

'I don't think our captain would have it any other way. He's worried the ship will be attacked.'

'He's right to be worried, Clytes.'

'Still carrying on the old trade, then?'

'What else can we do? The Athenians have done their best to make us destitute. Marcus and Cato will get you freed soon, Clytes. They will be so pleased to see you!'

When Lyra went to attend to others, Clytes was left in a dilemma as to whether he should warn Tadeus. Meeting up with Lyra and Marcus again could lead to his freedom, but at what cost? He didn't want to see any lives lost. They were all a lot younger when they came to his aid the last time, and he owed them much. Lyra was only sixteen, he remembered, and Marcus was not much older. Cato was a boy of thirteen or so. He was angry then. Lyra was right there. The Theban, Lykaon, had robbed him of his family and he hated the whole world. He was a willing participant in attacking any ship that looked assailable, not caring about the danger to his own life, but then the Egyptians caught him.

Just as was happening now, the women diverted the landing crew of the Egyptian grain ship which had been blown off course from its original destination of Athens, while the menfolk attacked what they assumed was the lightly guarded merchant vessel. But there was also a contingent of paying passengers making this particular voyage, and they were not prepared to give up their wealth without a fight.

Unbeknown to Clytes, feelings of jealousy were running high in the mind of their group leader, Manousos, ever since he'd become aware that the men preferred taking their orders from the young, bold Eleusinian, and the Cretan's chance to be rid of Clytes came with the arrival of the Egyptian vessel. As usual, Clytes was first to board, screaming maniacally and wielding a sword he'd captured during a previous raid. Expensively equipped, however, the passengers proved formidable adversaries and Clytes was beaten to his knees. Seeing Clytes fall, gave Manousos the opportunity he'd been waiting for and yelling to his men that Clytes had been killed, he ordered the attack to be aborted. As they watched later from the shoreline, however, it soon became evident that Manousos had been mistaken.

As a warning to others considering an assault on their ship, Clytes, still very much alive, was bound by his wrists and ankles, then weighted down by a heavy iron chain he was thrown overboard. By means of ropes and pulleys he was dragged under the keel of the ship to be hoisted up on the opposite side, coughing and spluttering. Made to dangle from the sail's yardarm, while exuberant cheers emitted from passengers and crew, he was then given time to recover from the pounding he'd received when his head repeatedly struck the ship's hull, before being plunged into the depths once again.

This terrifying ordeal was endured twice more, during which time his comrades stood watching in helpless horror from the shoreline, and with tensions running high, young Marcus accused Manousos of deliberately lying about Clytes' demise. A fight broke out, when Manousos attacked Marcus with a knife, and in the fracas, Manousos was killed. Desperately seeking a way to help Clytes, Marcus asked which of the young men who were with them on the beach was the best sponge diver, and young Cato came forward, boasting he could hold his breath the longest. A fishing boat was immediately launched, and as the small boat sailed innocently out to sea, Cato, with his sponge knife strapped to his thigh, slipped over the side, unnoticed. The boy was accustomed to being in deep water and found no problem in swimming beneath the surface until he reached the Egyptian ship. Pressed to the side of the vessel, he waited anxiously until Clytes was again plunged into the sea, then he dived under the keel after him. Bleeding profusely and barely conscious, Clytes was aware enough to realise that help had arrived. Once freed, the pair shot to the surface, gasping for air, and quickly concealing themselves behind a moored fishing boat, they waited out of sight until the sun went down when they were able to swim safely back to shore.

Clytes remembered the enormous cave away from the village where he was hidden for days, until the Egyptians finally sailed away believing he'd come loose from his bonds and had either drowned, or his blood had attracted a predator. Cato's sister, Lyra, had come with food and wine, while he recovered from his trauma. It was his first true love affair and certainly hers, but eventually, the pull of getting revenge for the loss of his family gnawed away at any thought of staying with Lyra, and he returned to Athenian territory to await the reappearance of the murderer, Lykaon, who'd been sentenced to a term in exile for his crime.

It was the present that concerned him now. As he'd been lying, watching, with his back against the rock, more wine had arrived, and with their half-empty bellies the crew members on shore had become more and more inebriated. The remainder of the crew left guarding the ship amounted to only seven men, one who was too young to put up much of a fight and another too old. He believed he knew the character of Tadeus, and he reasoned that the man who'd brought his cargo this far, would not just hand it over now. He feared for the consequences.

TWENTY-TWO

THE WEATHER CALMED SIGNIFICANTLY after the passing of the sandstorm with just a fresh breeze blowing and making the most of the opportunity to venture further out to sea, the fishing fleet was late in returning. No attempt had been made to capture the merchant ship, despite the fact that some of Tadeus' crew members were lying comatose at the boat village. Marcus was out with the fleet, and nothing would be done without his authority. Clytes, although still restrained, had been moved from the beach and was now accommodated in more comfortable conditions in one of the 'houses'. The Phoenician captain was getting anxious, however. There seemed to be no attempt being made to supply him with the ship's equipment he badly needed to continue his voyage. As he felt the welcoming breeze against his face, he grew restless to be on his way, but the only member of his ship's complement, still as watchful as he was, he'd noticed, was Clytes.

As the sun began to set, the watchers; some eager, others not so, kept a lookout for the returning boats, but it was not just the local fishing vessels that were seen approaching at the day's end. There were large ships too, following them in. Coming across the Cretan fishing fleet had been fortuitous for them, they told

Marcus. Having survived the sandstorm, they were, like Tadeus, in need of urgent supplies and they willingly let him guide them to the large inlet where he'd assured them of a warm welcome. Before nightfall the beach was awash with sailors, and in the bay, captains of battered merchant ships from Libya, Egypt and elsewhere, were vying with one another for a place to drop anchor.

Braziers were set alight at intervals along the shore, as were rushlights and quickly prepared cooking fires. Marcus and the rest of the fishing crew had never obtained such good prices for their timely catch, and hard bartering went on throughout the night, as needy merchantmen exchanged part of their luxury cargo for essentials. As news spread, a procession of flaming torches emerged from the gorge, when people arrived from the upper village, bringing yet more wine and whatever they had spare to trade, and with the women came the music and the dancing, creating a party-like atmosphere on the beach. Clytes, looking through the rudimentary doorway of his 'prison', chuckled with some relief. He felt there was no longer any threat of violence, and he likened the gathering to the aftermath of a wild Dionysian festival. Essentially outnumbered in terms of mean fighting power, the villagers forgo their plans to attack Tadeus' merchant ship and consoled themselves with getting the best deals they could for the provisions required by the travellers. What followed was a busy and lucrative period of trading and time for Clytes to become reacquainted with Marcus and Cato.

Since Tadeus' discovery that Clytes had friends on the island, he was guarded day and night, but so eager were the Cretans to hear of his exploits and also to learn of how the war was progressing, that they still sat with him for hours, mouths agape, hanging on his every word. Within days, his private audience with friends had swelled to a regular crowd as news spread of a storyteller being in their midst, and revelling in the attention, with a few embellishments and also some selected omissions, Clytes theatrically recounted the more colourful events of his life since he'd last been on the island.

'I'm glad you got your revenge on Lykaon!' Marcus exclaimed. 'You rid the world of an evil man, Clytes.'

'Don't wish too hard for something, Marcus. If you get it, there's usually a price to pay.'

'The Fates decided when that man should die,' spoke up Cato. 'You were their means to that end. Just as I was fated to save you from drowning!'

'The Fates must be enjoying a good laugh in my case, then. My life's hardly been one of distinction.'

'It's not over yet,' suggested Marcus.

When the ships had been refitted and the winds became favourable once more, the rested crews were eager to be on their respective ways, and Tadeus joined forces with other merchants who were taking their goods to Sicily and Italy. Clytes was also eager to leave the island. He had no wish to return to the life he'd had there, and he felt awkward seeing Marcus and Lyra together, especially as Lyra still seemed to have feelings for him. He was sure he hadn't imagined it when she kept wanting to be alone with him.

They came to see him off, to wish him good luck, and to tell him they would be sacrificing a goat for the safe journey of the convoy. He told them he'd appreciate their prayers. He was filled with renewed hope since the storytelling and the sooner he reached Sicily and regained his freedom, the better. Seeing the animated faces of his audience and feeling the excitement his words generated had stirred in him a desire to return to the theatre, and a whole new audience awaited him on Sicily.

As the departing ships with their newly repaired sails billowing in the strengthening wind, headed out to sea, a vivacious young girl, tall for a ten-year old, stood waving from the beach, surrounded by her group of friends.

'Did you tell him, Lyra?'

'No, I didn't. Why complicate things now. She knows *you* as her father.'

'A dull one, in comparison, don't you think?'

'Look at the situation he was in though, Marcus. And you heard his stories. The last thing a man like Clytes would want, is responsibility. It would mortify him to learn he's a father!'

'It's for the best, Lyra.'

TWENTY-THREE

DESPITE THE PRAYERS OF Clytes' friends on Crete, the convoy's journey to Sicily was not without incident. An earthquake struck on their fifth day out at sea, and it was felt through the hull of Tadeus' ship with such force, they thought they'd struck a submerged island. It caused a tidal wave fifty miles long which travelled at speed towards Sicily, passing the convoy within minutes. They narrowly missed colliding with one another and afraid there may be a series of such surges which *could* cause a collision, the ships split up and Tadeus found himself alone again. He was relieved to be in deep water and not in harbour. He'd experienced such an alarming phenomenon before and knew that when the waves hit land, it could be devastating. They had sufficient provisions onboard having re-stocked on Crete, and the seasoned mariner made the decision to delay their journey until he was sure there were no aftershocks. When they finally approached the coast of Sicily it was immediately evident that he'd made the right decision.

The south-eastern coast had taken the brunt of the tsunami and the first harbour they arrived at was strewn with the wreckage of boats and vegetation. Amongst the debris they recognised the remains of at least two of the merchant ships which had been in the convoy from Crete and obviously had arrived too soon. Even inland they saw evidence of destruction from repeated high waves striking the southern shore. Tadeus' ship eerily passed through a lifeless sea of debris, before dropping anchor and lowering the rowboat.

Clytes wondered what sort of future awaited him as he looked at the devastation and in frustration, he turned on Tadeus angrily when the order was given to have his wrists placed in irons.

'What's the point now, Tadeus? We're here! You've done what Masoud asked of you!'

'Until I've registered your arrival with someone in authority, you will remain in my custody, Clytes. I want to do this as quickly as possible, so no tricks!'

Clytes was furious. 'I'm not part of your bloody cargo, Tadeus! I don't need to be signed for!'

'You obviously don't know Masoud as well as I do. I've seen him torture men and smile while doing it. You'll do things my way!'

The islanders looked on warily as the newcomers reached the shore, and one of the men pointed angrily at seeing a passenger alight in chains, fuelling their fears even more. Grieving at their losses, the men wanted to kill the fettered individual instantly, believing he was the one who'd brought the bad luck to them, and an angry mob approached the rowboat as it was pulled up onto the beach.

Tadeus tried to explain about Clytes being of no danger to them and about his own family under threat in Damascus. All he wanted was to deliver his passenger to someone in authority, he argued, but they were adamant. 'Look about you!' one of them yelled. 'Where are *our* families?' The situation was desperate and people were looking for a scapegoat. They were forced to defend themselves as they edged their way back to the rowboat.

'That was unnerving, to say the least!' exclaimed Clytes. 'It would mess up your plans if I was to be killed before you acquired your fucking delivery note!'

Leaving the desolation behind them they sailed further up the coast, seeing evidence of destruction, but less so, until the wind carried them out into the Ionian Sea, around the headland called by sailors, 'the pig's snout', until with some relief they finally set eyes on the relatively untouched enormous bay of the renowned cultural trading city of Syracuse glowing welcomingly in the sun. Tadeus accepted that unless he wanted to attract more unwanted attention, he would finally have to give Clytes his freedom, and he resignedly ordered for him to be released from his shackles.

'This is my final destination Clytes, and it is where we will definitely part company......just as soon as I have my letter!'

'How long will you be staying?'

'It will take a week or more to unload and a few more weeks to reload with grain. Our next voyage is to Carthage where we'll spend the winter.'

'I wish you an uneventful journey, captain!'

CHAPTER TWENTY-THREE

'It's always eventful.'

For more than forty years Syracuse had been a democracy, governed on similar lines to Athens, and with Clytes' compliance, it was with the chief magistrate of Syracuse that Tadeus requested a meeting. After explaining to him his situation regarding Clytes, the Eleusinian was called into the dignitary's office.

'The waves have brought you to my city at an opportune time, Clytes of Eleusis. For three years we have been menaced by the Athenian fleet, but no more. You have arrived at a time of peace on the island.'

'What happened?'

'We Sicilians are no longer fighting amongst ourselves, and Athens can no longer divide and rule. The generals sailed back to their homeland not a month since, achieving nothing!'

'I have no interest in what's happening in Athens.'

'The war with Sparta still goes on. If you do not return soon, you may be ostracised for desertion.'

'I'll take my chances.'

'If you wish to stay, what can you do? What are your skills?'

'I'm an actor.'

'Can you prove it? We have a fine theatre here, and Syracusans love their theatre.'

'*Be sober in thought! Be slow in belief! These are the sinews of wisdom.*'

'You know of our Epicharmus? I'm impressed.'

Encouraged, Clytes quoted more from Epicharmus.

'*The chickpea is a food which, by stimulating the flow of the digestive juices, facilitates digestion.*'

The official then tried, unsuccessfully, to stifle his laughter, as Clytes mimicked the actions of a rustic labourer continually farting from a surfeit of chickpeas.

'Aeschylus?' asked the archon, wiping away his tears.

'*Nor does night conceal men's deeds of ill, but whatsoe'er thou dost, think that some God beholds it.*'

The official began to enjoy the renditions and wished for more.

'Do you know Sophocles' play, 'Oedipus the King'?' he asked eagerly.

Clytes, drawing on his own experiences of grief, slipped character from comic to dramatic with ease and became the blind tortured King of Thebes.

'I care not for thy counsel or thy praise
For with what eyes could I have e'er beheld
My honoured father in the shades below,
Or my unhappy mother, both destroyed
By me? This punishment is worse than death,
And so it should be. Sweet had been the sight
Of my dear children - them I could have wished
To gaze upon; but I must never see
Or them, or this fair city, or the palace
Where I was born. Deprived of every bliss
By my own lips, which doomed to banishment
The murderer of Laius, and expelled
The impious wretch, by gods and men accursed:
Could I behold them after this? Oh no!
Would I could now with equal ease remove
My hearing too, be deaf as well as blind,
And from another entrance shut out woe! ....'

'Enough!' cried the magistrate, deeply moved, dabbing furiously at his wet cheeks. 'You are what you say you are. I am sure we can make use of your talents.'

Tadeus acquired his precious letter, signed and sealed by the magistrate, confirming that he'd delivered Clytes of Eleusis safely to the city of Syracuse on the island of Sicily. He was also thankful to still have his cargo almost intact and spent the following weeks in fulfilling his obligations. For Akbar's remaining papyrus rolls he negotiated his own price, since there'd been no word from any of the ships in the Cyprian convoy. It was assumed they'd been dispersed or had sunk in the storm.

Clytes arrived on the island just weeks after the Athenian fleet had returned to Athens, taking with it disgruntled crew members, Glaucus, Cassa and Bion. After the partial victory in

Megara the state was now preparing to invade Boeotia, and on the list of recruits posted in Eleusis of those men required to enroll for military service, were the names of Clytes and his cousins, Adelphos, Arkadios and Audas. While men crowded round to see whose names were on the register, Clytes, on the other side of the Ionian Sea, who in his absence had been promoted to captain, was giving forth his opinions to an eager group of Syracusans as to which of the playwrights; Aeschylus, Sophocles or Euripides, he considered the better tragedian. The chief magistrate had brought him to see the city's impressive theatre set into the southern slopes of the Temenite Hill and had allowed him to test the acoustics. He was in his natural element and his voice rang out pure and true. As he listened to the raucous feet stomping coming from Tadeus and the rest of the crew and the enthusiastic applause from the magistrate and his associates, he grinned, then he bowed flamboyantly toward Hermocrates, when the respected Syracusan statesman rose to his feet, clapping enthusiastically. He'd missed the exhilaration of performing in front of an audience. It was his first love and the most enduring. For the first time since learning of Anthousa's death, he felt relief from his morbid forebodings.

TWENTY-FOUR

A BARRAGE OF JAVELINS AND arrows rained down heavily onto the beach, forcing the soldiers to shelter behind their shields. Unable to proceed any further, trumpets blared out the signal for retreat as captains in the vanguard yelled out to their men, 'Return to the ships!' Struggling to maintain order, with the sand slipping beneath their feet, the men cautiously backed away from the unexpected onslaught to the relative safety of the sea, as from within their midst their commander could be heard shouting, frustratedly, 'Abort!'

At the helm of his flagship, Demosthenes watched the receding coastline in dismay as the rowers, pulling hard, headed the fleet back into the Corinthian Gulf. Raucous jeering accompanied their strenuous efforts, coming from the densely manned ramparts of the recently fortified city of Siphae on the western coast of Boeotia - the first Boeotian city Demosthenes had expected to fall willingly into his hands.

Removing his helmet and wiping the sweat from his brow, he addressed the handful of hardened fighters gathered around him. 'We've been betrayed, men! I fear the oligarchs have discovered the plot. The democrats do not have control, as we'd hoped.'

'Even though we've arrived earlier than planned, we are still too late!' exclaimed Stephanos, who was standing closest to Demosthenes.

The general's clenched fist pounded the rail. 'We delayed too long!'

'What now commander?' the Plataean queried. 'Another landing place?'

'The element of surprise has gone, Stephanos! Look at the height of those mountains. We'd be cut to pieces within half a mile. You saw their strength of arms. The whole of Boeotia has risen up against us!'

'But what of Hippocrates, general?' asked another of his companions. 'Without our diversion, he'll have the entire Boeotian army to contend with!'

Demosthenes answered, but without conviction. 'The Boeotian strength appears to be gathered on the western coast, ready to apprehend our forces. If Hippocrates is successful in his eastern offensive, we can only hope that the rest of the democrats will rise up to assist him as promised.'

'Is that likely?' interrupted Stephanos. 'I know these people. If Siphae hasn't turned, then I doubt if any other city will have the courage.'

'I fear you could be right,' answered the general, resignedly. 'If there was any chance of the plan succeeding, we needed to catch the enemy unawares. In that we have obviously failed.'

'Let's hope there's time to warn the commander,' spoke Stephanos again, his anxious thoughts now on his friends and fellow countrymen in the Plataean contingent.

He was bitterly disheartened at the unsuccessful outcome of so many months of preparation, and he sent a prayer to the gods, for them to favour the efforts of Hippocrates. Very soon, the general would be marching unsuspectedly from Athens with the flower of Athenian soldiery, towards Delium on Boeotia's eastern shore, where he expected to be joined by a successful Demosthenes and his army of recruited allies, arriving overland from Siphae. Within the Athenian army would be every Plataean able to bear arms, upholding the honour of their cherished city and how Stephanos now wished he could be marching with them.

Throughout the fleet frustrations were running high, and on the 'Aquila', fifth ship in the line, Bion became an easy target for the men to vent their feelings of failure. 'Your Roxanne won't be happy when you return home empty-handed, Bion!' shouted one of the thranites from across the rowing aisle. Straining at the oar the thickset rower continued to put his broad shoulders to the task and tried his best to ignore the whistles and taunts now erupting from his comrades. 'Didn't you promise her enough gold to encircle that pretty little neck of hers?'

'Mention my wife again,' snarled Bion, 'and something will encircle your neck, Phronius!'

'Ignore them, Bion,' said Chromis seated behind him. 'They're just giving vent. They know you can be easily goaded!'

'It's a bloody disaster!' groaned Bion. 'I thought our beloved leaders had a strategy!'

'Yeah,' responded Chromis, 'we've spent months getting this army together, and they're not here for the sight-seeing. By all the gods, Bion, what's Demosthenes' plan now?'

Chromis felt a sharp smack to the back of his head. 'Quiet down there!' bellowed Cassa, who was pacing the central gangway just above them. 'You lot do your job,' barked the rowing master, 'and let the general do his. Listen out, men, he's increasing the pace.' The piper blew faster, forcing the crew to focus on their rhythm, and without the distraction of Bion and his marital affairs; to also reflect on their own lost expectations.

Disillusioned by the turn of events, the grumbling spread throughout the fleet. The combined forces included thousands of recruits gathered from Arcanania and Agrae, and they'd been promised rich pickings in a campaign which was to be over as quickly as it started - and with little risk of any serious conflict - or so they'd been led to believe. They were expected to give support to the rebelling democrats, provide safe havens for the dissidents, and when the entire country fell under their control, return home - with some loot.

In order to give vent to their frustrations and allow them an opportunity to acquire some plunder, Demosthenes boldly diverted the fleet to the opposite shore of the Corinthian Gulf; to a town which had never been attacked throughout the war. A rich city, eleven miles from Corinth. A supplier of men and ships to Athens' enemies. Pro-Spartan Sicyon.

Again, it was not the outcome he expected. There was no element of surprise, which the commander relied upon. Seeing forty Athenian warships bearing down on them, galvanised the entire undiminished strength of the Sicyonians to such an extent, that after a thwarted attempt to take the city, it was the Athenians who bore away their dead. Demoralised at his failure to carry out his orders in Boeotia and at the loss of his men at Sicyon, Demosthenes took no further part in the campaign and returned to Naupactus. Now, all he could do was pray that his co-commander Hippocrates had more success.

It was Stephanos' opinion that Demosthenes had drawn the short straw again, as at Megara, but this time there was no successful coordination. Immediately after that conflict, the general had sailed a fleet of forty ships around the Peloponnese, to spend months in gathering men to support Athens' invasion of Boeotia, while Hippocrates, the thirty-five-year-old nephew of the great Pericles, had been given the opportunity to take all the glory as commander of the main army.

Although unwavering in his admiration of Demosthenes, Stephanos seethed at this lack of action. He expected humiliation at best for their commander on his return to Athens. There might even be a trial. He and many other of the hoplites now fervently wished they were with Hippocrates. Socrates would be there. Also, Laches. As would many high-born citizens of Athens. He imagined them crossing the Asopus, envisaged the strongly marching columns of hoplites in full panoply on their way to Delium and he prayed for the safe keeping of Theomenes who'd be in the same cavalry unit as the rising star of Athens' nobility, Alcibiades, also a nephew of Pericles. Nothing could salve his conscience at not being part of the invasion, and he gripped his sword's gold finial tightly at the thought of the eventual deliverance of Plataea without him. As soon as they touched land he paid handsomely towards the sacrifices in thanksgiving for their deliverance, but also for the gods to favour Hippocrates - to give him victory!

TWENTY-FIVE

RUMOURS THAT DEMOSTHENES HAD been repulsed at Siphae, filtered across the border to Athens, brought by fleeing dissident Boeotians, and the people became hesitant about proceeding with the attack on their neighbours without the additional strength of the allied army in the west. Cleon, on the other hand, would not be deterred. It was his reasoning that if they could install a garrison in just one strong fortification in Boeotia, it would provide a rallying point for any democrats wanting to rebel. This successful stronghold, he asserted, would give encouragement to other towns to take the risk.

But the decision as to whether or not to continue the campaign had to be first put to the people, and Cleon used his oratory skills to good effect in convincing the populace of the necessity for the attack. Thousands of citizens dutifully assembled on the slopes of the Athens' Pnyx Hill to hear the result of the vote.

'You, the people, have spoken!' Cleon called out loudly to the amassed crowd. 'We march on Delium!' A roar of approval rose up at his announcement. The speeches had made their impression and now all were in agreement - the Boeotians had been a thorn in their side for far too long.

Hippocrates, who was still receiving last minute urgent requests for help from Boeotian collaborators, joined the Athenian leader on the rostrum to speak eagerly to the crowds. 'We have had a set-back, citizens,' admitted the dynamic commander, 'and I can understand your concerns, but we can still achieve our objective. We will fulfill our promise to the democrats who are wanting to join us, and we'll put an end, once and for all, to Boeotia's alliance with Sparta! We may not have the numbers we'd anticipated, but we are more than enough to put the fear of Hades into our treacherous neighbours. With or without Demosthenes, we *will* achieve victory!'

The people had been hearing talk of the attack on Boeotia since the summer, and now that autumn crops had been successfully harvested, they just wanted to get on with it. They would fortify Apollo's temple at Delium to give encouragement to the rebelling democratic faction and leave a strong garrison there as an act of good faith, but if no-one came to support them, the main army would then withdraw.

This new development, however, did not satisfy everyone. The Plataeans, who at long last were expecting to reoccupy their plateau, were angry.

'We've assisted the Athenians in every major conflict!' exclaimed Theomenes to his comrades as they stood listening to the speeches on the hillside. 'We've fought alongside them, willingly, whenever our men were needed, believing that one day they would help us to regain our city.'

'Something must have gone seriously wrong for Stephanos to be delayed,' spoke up Angelos. 'He was determined to lead the vanguard into Plataea.'

'Well, we'll be rejoining our units tomorrow,' replied Theomenes. 'Let's hope Cleon's plan does work and the democrats *do* rise up, or it will all have been a waste of time and effort on our part!'

'You're a lucky bastard though!' said Pyrus, a humble archer in the same unit as Angelos, and an admirer from afar of Athens' glorious son, the handsome but dissolute aristocratic nephew of Pericles. 'You'll be riding with Alcibiades! Have you spoken with him yet?' he asked, in awe.

'Not yet!' replied Theomenes. 'He has such a devoted following, it's impossible to get near the man!'

The prominent Temple to Apollo at Delium was thought the most suitable site to be fortified, being just over the border and only a few days march from Athens. Situated by the sea on the east coast, it was conveniently close to the Euboean Gulf, where a fleet of Athens' triremes would be ready to give support if needed.

Scouts were sent ahead of the marching columns to look out for any sign of the enemy, but they repeatedly came back with nothing to report, for wasn't the enemy on the western coast, keeping a lookout for Demosthenes' forty triremes? On the third day, the army arrived at the undefended sacred site, and the labourers began work immediately to change the peaceful sanctuary of Apollo into a fortress.

First a great ditch was dug around the temple and its precincts, and the earth from it was used to form a rampart into which wooden stakes were driven. More strength was added when nearby houses were demolished and the rubble, together with wood cut from precinct vines, was thrown in. Finally, wooden towers were constructed, providing even further height to the fortifications. The work was carried out with the utmost expediency, for soon after they'd occupied the temple, collaborators began arriving to give warning that the Boeotian boeotarchs, outraged at the sacrilege, were gathering an army at Tanagra, just a few miles from Delium. With Demosthenes no longer a threat, men were arriving from all over the territory.

Hippocrates urgently gathered his captains. 'The work is almost done here, men, and we've still not heard anything from Demosthenes. Nor is there anything to indicate that the country is in a state of rebellion. It's possible, of course, that other parts of the country are in the hands of the democrats, but if that isn't the case, then we're not going to get any further help. If you have any thoughts, I'd like to hear them......and quickly!'

'I think there's still time for the democrats to rise up,' said one.

'We've not seen any sign of the enemy,' spoke up another.

'I say, we stay and finish the job!' shouted Theomenes.

The general consensus seemed to be that it was too soon to give up on the enterprise, and after further discussion, Hippocrates raised his hand for silence.

'I propose we take the army back over the border and make camp there until we have more information. The rest is up to the democrats. If the Boeotian generals believe we are returning to Athens, they won't attack. Inform your units! We move at mid-day!'

Five days after entering Boeotia, the Athenian army left the protection of the sanctuary-made-fortress and moved back over the river Asopus - out of enemy territory. The large corps of unarmed labourers, Hippocrates sent back to Athens, while he remained at Delium with the garrison. He was still negotiating with the collaborators and receiving vital updates on the strength of the opposing forces gathering close by.

In the Boeotian camp at Tanagra, it was just as Hippocrates predicted. On receiving information from their scouting parties that the Athenian army was in retreat, the Boeotian generals decided it was no longer necessary to risk a pitched battle. All the generals, except one. Eleven military leaders represented the various cities of Boeotia; one from each, apart from Thebes, which had two. Pagondas, a sixty-year-old veteran Theban commander, argued strenuously against the other generals, and when he received no support from them, he tried reasoning directly with the soldiers.

'Boeotians, the idea that we ought not to give battle to the Athenians, unless we came up with them in Boeotia, is one which should never have entered into the head of any of us, your generals. It was to annoy Boeotia that they crossed the frontier and built a fort in our country; and they are therefore, I imagine, our enemies wherever we may come up with them, and from whithersoever they may have come to act as enemies do. And if anyone has taken up with the idea in question for reasons of safety, it is high time for him to change his mind. The party attacked, whose own country is in danger, can scarcely discuss what is prudent with the calmness of men who are in full enjoyment of what they have got, and are thinking of attacking a neighbour in order to get more. It is your national habit, in your country or out of it, to oppose the same resistance to a foreign invader; and when that invader is Athenian, and lives upon your frontier besides, it is doubly imperative to do so. As between neighbours generally, freedom means simply a determination to hold one's own; and with neighbours like these, who are trying to enslave near and far alike, there is nothing for it but to fight it out to the last.'

This and more did Pagondas say to the men gathered at Tanagra, and such was their supportive response, that his fellow military leaders were persuaded to change their minds.

It was now late in the day and fearing the Athenians would move on to safety before nightfall, Pagondas ordered an immediate attack. He halted his army where an intervening hill prevented the Athenian army from seeing the full extent of his numbers and then set out his battle formation. The Athenians, taken by surprise, immediately despatched a rider to Hippocrates, who was still at the Temple of Apollo.

'They've crossed the Asopus, commander!' Your captains want to know your orders!'

Hippocrates knew that if they attempted to flee, the powerful Boeotian cavalry would cut his men down like scythes moving through a wheatfield.

'Stand and fight! Line up for battle! They're my orders!'

Leaving three hundred cavalry to guard the temple, Hippocrates hurried to rejoin his army, only to find the opposing forces were already in line, and they'd taken control of the hill.

Shouting out encouragement, he passed quickly along the Athenian front ranks, but before he could even reach the end of the line and finish his speech, the Boeotians had struck up their battle hymn, and the Athenians were forced to shelter under their shields as a thundering hail of javelins began crashing down on them. Accompanied by trumpet blasts and battle cries, the heavily armed Boeotians then streamed down the hill towards the Athenian lines. Yelling their own rallying cries, the Attic hoplites boldly ran up the slopes to meet them, despite their captains roaring out orders to let the Boeotians come to them, and their advice of 'don't waste your strength!' went unheard in the eagerness to engage. Shield clashed violently against shield as the opposing sides obstinately pushed against each other in a desperate struggle for supremacy.

The armies of Hippocrates and Pagondas each included seven thousand heavily armed hoplites, but there the similarity ended. The Athenian army, weakened by plague and invasions, faced an enemy relatively unscathed by such calamities. Whereas Pagondas had one thousand cavalry, Hippocrates had only six hundred. Five hundred peltasts were in the Boeotian ranks. In the Athenian army, there were none. While Pagondas had ten thousand lightly armed troops, Hippocrates had barely any. The thousands of poorly armed labourers which had accompanied the army to Delium, were now on their way back to Athens. Only a few stragglers had become hurriedly incorporated into the ranks.

With Hippocrates and the captains roaring them on, the Athenians successfully pushed their way up the centre of the hillside, and the combined forces of the Boeotian alliance retreated before their onslaught. Occupying the slopes on the right, however, was a contingent of Thespians, and they did not run, but bravely stood their ground. Without support, it was an act which sealed their fate as they eventually became surrounded by Athens' finest fighting men. It was a ferocious confrontation, and in the heat of the battle the Athenians became disorientated. As they encircled their adversaries, they met their own men coming the other way and mistook them for the foe. Tragically, friend killed friend and even family members attacked one other, before realising their horrific blunder. In their grief, they annihilated the Thespians.

On the left flank there was much stronger resistance. Unbeknown to Hippocrates, Pagondas had formed his phalanx entirely of fellow Thebans, with three hundred of his oath-sworn bravest and best in the van, and instead of being eight ranks deep, as was usual, he had twenty-five and mostly hidden over the rise of the hill.

A loud reverberating cry rose up from the packed ranks of the Theban hoplites, as with spears levelled above their oval shields, they charged down the hillside in a dense mass of bronze and iron. In the Athenian force, besides carrying their fighting long spears, the men were also equipped with two throwing javelins, and as the orders rasped out, dulling their fear, a wave of these destructive weapons poured onto the ranks of the careering Thebans. Yet still they came on, scrambling over the wounded, and there was a terrible clash as the two lines of infantry met.

The Athenians in the van took the shock of the collision on their shields, to lunge with spear or sword in a wildly desperate effort. The lines of the Attic troops bent under the fierce onslaught, eventually falling back against the relentless surging mass of a much superior force. On witnessing the slaughter of their comrades, fear began to spread throughout the Athenian lines, and many threw aside their encumbering weapons. The men on the left flank began fleeing for their lives.

Pagondas was now able to concentrate on what was happening elsewhere and on learning of the Thespian defeat, he immediately despatched five hundred of his yet untried cavalry to stem the tide. The centre and right flanks had been successful in forcing the Boeotians into retreat, but when they saw hundreds of fresh horsemen charging towards them from behind the hill, they thought it was the vanguard of another army come to join forces with the Boeotians. Exhausted and also grief stricken, due to the loss of so many esteemed Athenians at their own hands, their resolve weakened. The men of the centre and right flanks were now also in full flight.

Pagondas' next act was to release his thousand strong cavalry: the best cavalry in all Hellas.

The order 'head for the hills!' was heard, shouted above the melee by the remaining Athenian captains, but also, 'return to the temple!' and 'try for the ships, men!'

It had become a rout.

Theomenes, and what remained of his cohort of cavalry, did their best to protect fleeing comrades who were on foot. On seeing Angelos and Pyrus being chased by Boeotian spearmen, he shouted urgently, 'To me, Angelos!' The two foot-soldiers had been part of a small contingent of lightly armed troops protecting the rearguard of the army of labourers on their return to Athens, but they'd lingered too long and become embroiled in the conflict. With no heavy weapons to defend themselves with, they were defenceless against the rampaging Boeotian cavalry and expected to be cut down at any moment. Overwhelmed with relief they ran to Theomenes. 'Stay with me!' he exhorted, as he urged his horse forward, away from the soldiers advancing towards them. The trio adopted a brave front; Theomenes with his protective shield and drawn sword, and the archers on either side of him, with strained bows speedily replenished with arrows. All around them men were being cut down, as they fled in panic, and Theomenes was hard pressed to defend his friends. 'Get his weapons!' he shouted urgently, when coming across a body that had not yet been stripped, and he moved his horse between Angelos and a group of enemy foot soldiers, who looked determined to intercept.

A javelin hit the stallion in the flank, and the suddenness caused the horse to throw its rider. Angelos was now exposed as he ran to retrieve the weapons of a dead Athenian, and an arrow struck him forcibly in the back, pitching him forward. 'Oh God! Angelos!' Theomenes cried out, who was now on the ground and fiercely deflecting missiles with his cavalry shield. A division of peltasts and archers was moving, unwavering, through the body strewn landscape towards them.

The shocked stallion struggled to get to its feet and stood quivering as Theomenes broke off the protruding javelin shaft.

'Angelos is gone!' exclaimed a distressed Pyrus. 'He's hit his head!' Putting their own lives in danger they struggled to lift their prone comrade, but as the shouts of their enemies grew louder, they were forced to admit defeat in trying to retrieve Angelos' body. Theomenes grabbed Pyrus by the shoulder, yelling, 'It's no use! We'll have to leave him!' Quickly remounting, he hoisted up the archer to sit behind him, and in desperation, forced the wounded animal into a gallop, heading towards the distant mountain of Parnes, north of Athens - and safety. But the blood loss ultimately took its toll. The stallion slowed to a walk, then collapsed. The two men were still very much in danger with the Boeotian cavalry on the rampage, and using the dead horse as cover, they concealed themselves as best they could while watching in horror as fellow comrades were hunted down like animals, the painful vision of Angelos, an arrow protruding from his back, seared into their minds.

The utterance, 'I know that grey!' was suddenly heard by the two men and recognising the high-born Athenian accent, they crawled out from their hiding place to look up at a resplendent horse and rider.

'Theomenes!' exclaimed an astonished Alcibiades. 'Thank the gods you live yet!'

The arrogant looking cavalryman seemed to be surrounded by an invisible protective shield, and the horrors faded away as Theomenes looked up at the god-like vision of the handsome aristocrat. Memories of Phalinus, the late Shield Guardian of Plataea, flooded back, giving him courage.

'Is that your late father's horse?' asked Alcibiades, with some concern.

'It is indeed, Astor, sire,' replied Theomenes, deeply affected. 'We have lost a great heart! He served me well in so many campaigns.'

'You still have Selene, I hear. Breed more Astors!' stated Alcibiades, positively, for all the world as though they were chatting socially in the Agora. 'Come! Join us! I will see us all safely back to Athens. Do or die!'

Theomenes gently removed Astor's bit and bridle and stroking his strong neck one last time, murmured, 'Godspeed fearless Astor! Eubalos will be waiting to welcome you!' Then he and an awe-struck Pyrus joined with Alcibiades' grim faced, illustrious companions, who'd also been rescued from Boeotian swords - for already under the providential protection of the fearless Alcibiades, was the wealthy aristocrat, Laches; faring badly since being unseated from his horse, and his close friend the renowned philosopher, Socrates, who'd been fighting bravely as a foot soldier.

Only the coming of night saved the Athenian army from being completely annihilated. Some, like Alcibiades and his party, made it to the safety of the Parnes mountain range. Others got as far as the fleet in the gulf where triremes were waiting to rescue them. Many fled back to the recently fortified temple of Apollo at Delium, where the marooned garrison of three hundred cavalry still held possession - but this was the worst of decisions.

TWENTY-SIX

I N THE FEW HOURS between mid-day and sundown on a late autumn day, the Athenian army was routed, overpowered by a stronger Theban led force, and it was the Boeotians who set up their war trophy of plunder taken from the dead. The Athenian casualties were many, and their bodies covered a wide area as men had attempted to flee the ferocious Boeotian cavalry. Apart from their weaponry and armour, personal items such as rings and amulets were also stripped from the corpses, also every item of reusable clothing and footwear, to be donated to the temples for the benefit of the poor. When everything of value had been collected, women and children rushed to the scene to scavenge for anything that was left.

Watching this horror was Angelos. When the arrow was pulled from his shoulder he woke from his stupor with a rush of agonising pain, but being too weak to cry out, it went unnoticed by the overburdened soldier, carrying more than his own weight in plundered weaponry, that he still lived. Ravens, the messengers of the dead, softly alighted close by and proceeded to peck out the eyes and tongues of his comrades, but he was powerless to chase them away without drawing attention to himself. Slumped over the body of a dead Athenian, he lay, with dried blood from a head wound sealing shut one of his eyelids and waited for the inevitable.

The carts returned and the collection of the bodies began. Angelos knew they would find him soon and witnessing the heinous desecration carried out to the corpses by the Boeotians, he couldn't help himself; he retched. It drew the focus of a group of peasants who were sorting through discarded clothes and sandals, in too poor a state to be dedicated to the gods. He felt rough hands turning him over and was surprised to see, not soldiers, but four women staring down at him.

'He's not one of ours. What do we do with him?' asked the youngest member of the group. 'If there's a ransom, we deserve some of it. We found him!'

'We could do with someone to help us on the farm,' ventured her shrewd, elderly mother, her back bent by hard work. 'Your father's getting too old.'

'You'll need to get him well first, Ava,' suggested her cousin, who was of a similar age. 'He's lost a lot of blood.'

'Can you speak?' asked Ava, pushing Angelos with her foot.

Too weak to respond, Angelos just stared back, blankly.

'Be quick, Ava!' urged her sister; the fourth member of the impoverished family group. 'The soldiers are moving nearer!'

Looking around to ensure they weren't being watched, the women quickly covered Angelos with rags then bundled him, awkwardly, onto their primitive hand cart.

After piling up the bodies of their enemies and leaving a guard over them, the Boeotians retired to their city of Tanagra to plan their strategy for the retaking of the temple at Delium, but first they sent a herald to Athens. On the road, the man was met by an Athenian herald coming the other way. He'd been sent to demand the return of their dead. The Boeotian told him that he would not be heard until he had first delivered *his* message.

He told the Athenians that they'd broken the law of all Hellenes in violating the temple of Apollo, in using the sacred water for their own personal use and destroying protected groves. If they wanted their dead back, they must first vacate the temple.

Having in mind the temples of Plataea, now in the hands of the Boeotians, the Athenians answered that the law of the Hellenes was that conquest of a country, whether more or less extensive, carried with it possession of the temples in that country. If the Athenians could have conquered more of Boeotia this would have been the case with them. As things stood, the piece of it which they had got, they would treat as their own, and not quit unless obliged.

With no evacuation of Delium expected, the Boeotians sent for reinforcements. Darters and slingers arrived from the Malian Gulf; two thousand heavy infantry from Corinth; the Peloponnesian garrison which had evacuated Nisaea, and some Megarians with them, all marched against Delium to attack the fortified temple. For two weeks the besieged men held out, waiting in vain for either the Boeotian democrats to rise up, or the arrival of Demosthenes and his allied army.

In the meantime, the bodies remained under Boeotian guard.

In an effort to finally bring the blockade to an end, the besiegers took drastic action.

They sawed in two and scooped out a great beam from end to end, and fitting it nicely together again like a pipe, hung by chains a cauldron at one extremity, with which communicated an iron tube projecting from the beam, which was itself in great part plated with iron. This they brought up from a distance upon carts to the part of the wall principally composed of vines and timber, and when it was near, inserted huge bellows into their end of the beam and blew with them. The blast passing closely confined into the cauldron, which was filled with lighted coals, sulphur and pitch, made a great blaze, and set fire to the wall, which soon became untenable for its defenders, who left it and fled; and in this way the fort was taken.

Of the defenders, some were killed in the blaze, and two hundred were made prisoners, but many who'd fled the battle were able to make it to the waiting ships, as were most in the cavalry detachment, including Makron and Dadilos, who'd ridden like the wind to safety.

Soon after the fall of Delium which took place seventeen days after the battle, the herald from Athens, who like others in the city had no knowledge of the numbers killed, came again to ask for the dead. This time his request was granted and over one thousand rotting corpses were returned to the Athenians, including that of their general, Hippocrates. Only five hundred on the Boeotian side had been killed - mainly the Thespians.

The women of Athens wailed hysterically at their tremendous loss, as loved ones were found amongst the barely recognisable corpses, and for weeks a thick blanket of smoke from the numerous funeral pyres hung over the desolate city. It was Theomenes who came to claim the body of Angelos. He knew no-one else would be coming, since the young Plataean had lost his family in a Theban raid some years before. Next to Clytes, he was his closest friend. With a cloth tied tightly across his nose and mouth, he walked down line after line, pulling back the covering on any corpse that looked the height and build of Angelos.

Claimed bodies were being taken away by loved ones, to be prepared for burial, and one such grieving family was that of Adelphos, cousin to Clytes of Eleusis. Comforted by her remaining sons, Arkadios and Audas, their mother Callidoras, shrieked like a mad woman and tore wildly at her hair, when she recognised the mutilated body of her eldest boy; the second of her sons to die during this war, her youngest, Alastor, having perished in the plague of Athens some five years previously. Overwhelmed by the numbers many were just placed on the ground, the tents being full, and the unclaimed bodies were a distressing sight. Some of the corpses weren't complete and severed limbs had been placed next to torsos, which may or may not have belonged. Teeth smashed into skulls, arrow strikes in eye sockets, shinbones severed by swords, showed all too clearly the brutality of war.

'I couldn't see him?' he told Pyrus, later. 'The bodies are in such a putrid state, I couldn't recognise him!'

'Do you think he was still alive?' said Pyrus, hesitantly.

'Oh God! Do you think we left him in the hands of the Thebans?'

'Maybe we should check the list of prisoners,' suggested Pyrus.

'You're right!' exclaimed Theomenes, suddenly filled with hope. 'He may have lived!'

But their search proved futile; the young Plataean was not on the list, and with renewed sadness they both went to the mortuary tents to look again at the unclaimed bodies. There were still several, none of which would have been recognised by their nearest and dearest.

'I think that's Angelos,' said Pyrus, hesitantly, as they looked down on the remains of what he believed had once been a tall, strong-limbed young man. They asked the attendant to turn the body over. 'There's the wound, Theomenes.'

'But, what of the other lacerations?' queried Theomenes. 'This man has severe leg injuries too.'

'Only the gods know what desecrations were carried out to the corpses,' replied Pyrus, shaking his head.

'I can't see another body of his build and colouring. It must be Angelos,' said Theomenes, sadly. 'We cannot deny him a decent funeral just because the Thebans mutilated his corpse.' He called over the attendant and claimed the body.

With Hippocrates dead and the city in deep mourning, Demosthenes found it easier than expected to defend his lack of action to Athens' leader, Cleon. He argued that because there was insufficient manpower to collect the harvests and at the same time fortify Delium, by the time the crops had been gathered in and the men were free to take part in the invasion, the whole of Boeotia was aware of the proposed uprising. He contended that even though he'd arrived early at Siphae, it was impossible to achieve anything. It was already too late. Despite the return of the general and the two hundred of Athens' foremost warriors, under his command, it was the worst of defeats, and the campaign put an end to Athenian hopes of ever being able to subdue their northern neighbours. Once again, Athens was enduring intense grief and loss of self-esteem, and every household was affected.

Stephanos arrived home to his wife, a changed man. For all Plataeans the failed invasion was a disaster, but for this proud soldier, the end of the dream came particularly hard. Night after night he angrily paced up and down their cramped accommodation, while Micca, desperately wanting to comfort her beloved husband, but knowing he was best left alone, lay listening in quiet torment, and tried to hide her own disappointment by weeping alone.

Life was also strained in Bion's household. He'd made bold promises to his wife Roxanne which he'd been unable to fulfill, and when she spurned his lovemaking, he feared the worst.

'Have you been faithful, while I've been away?'

'Why are you questioning me? I don't like it!'

'I've missed you. I love you, Roxanne!'

'If you loved me, you wouldn't let me live like this. Why did you marry me, if you couldn't provide for me?'

'Many women would be content with what you have. You just keep wanting more!'

'You told me you were a member of The Shield Company. You said you were famous and that we'd be rich!'

'I *was* with The Company, and proud of it!'

'You were never one of them. You made it all up. While you've been away my father found out what you're really like. *'Never do a Bion!'* That was you, wasn't it? The man who borrowed money because he thought he was going to be rich. Ha!'

'I've paid back that debt!'

'Bion, you're not a hero! You're a joke!'

'Your father provided no dowry for you, Roxanne. He would have given you away to anyone!'

'He thought you had prospects! You told him I would want for nothing. He knows I can do better than this. I'm leaving you, Bion. I'm getting a divorce!'

TWENTY-SEVEN

'**B**ION IS OUTSIDE, GLAUCUS. He looks agitated. Is he waiting for you?'

The Helmsman, wearily rose from his bed and went to the communal walkway outside his rented room. In the gloom he peered over the parapet to the courtyard below. The caretaker pointed to where rushlights intermittently illuminated the figure of man walking backwards and forwards.

'There he is, Glaucus. Something's up with him.'

'I'll go down,' replied the big man, shrugging his shoulders in puzzlement.

'Something wrong, my friend?'

'I won't come closer. Send me away if you have to. I've killed her, Glaucus!'

'What?'

'Roxanne! She's dead!'

'By all the gods, man, keep your voice down!'

'She was going to leave me!'

'Where did it happen?'

'I strangled her!'

'Calm down! Where is she?'

'At our house. I came straight to you. I couldn't take this to Cassa's door. He has a family to support.'

'And what about me? I could lose my helmsmanship, you idiot! Or worse!'

'I'm sorry Glaucus. I didn't know where else to go.'

'Are you sure she's dead?'

'Oh yes! I didn't mean to do it!'

CHAPTER TWENTY-SEVEN

'What about your housekeeper? Was she there?'

'She was. She ran away, screaming.'

'Then you haven't got much time.'

'What should I do, Glaucus? Confess?'

'You won't get much sympathy in court my friend. Roxanne may have been wayward, but she was a beauty and had many suitors. You caused a lot of jealousy when you married her.'

'You warned me she'd be trouble. I should never have married her!'

'Too late for that now. We need to get help, or we'll both be in serious trouble. Her father could have already rounded up a mob to find you. The first places they'll look, will be homes of family and friends. Eventually, they'll seek out members of The Shield Company......but hopefully, not yet. You can't stay here, though. We are known to be friends.'

'I'll go away, Glaucus. I should never have involved you.'

'Too late for that too!' replied the redhead, thinking quickly. 'The tomb to Cimon's horses! We've walked past it many a time. There are caves close by. Hide there until I come for you.'

'Will your caretaker say anything, do you think?'

'He won't say anything. He's a good friend.'

Stephanos was not asleep when Glaucus quietly knocked on his door and explained his nocturnal visit.

'How did you avoid the night patrol?'

'I had to take many detours, Stephanos. The rod-bearers are out in force, and I saw an angry crowd heading in the direction of Bion's mother's house, the poor soul. They're looking for him already.'

'The idiot! Her father held out for just such a fool as him. Someone presumed to have money, and so lovestruck he wouldn't insist on a dowry. He made too much of himself. They both thought he had prospects. He has little chance of a lenient sentence. It should be exile, but the father could whip up the jurors for the death penalty. He's not only lost his daughter, but his hopes of a comfortable old age, too.'

'I totally agree, Stephanos, but will you help? He was a great asset in helping me get the Delias to Pontus. He's not a bad man.'

'I'm not happy at his lack of control, Glaucus, but I'll help him if I can......if only for old times' sake.'

'Should we include Theomenes in this?'

'It's a risky business for anyone to get involved in, and the murder of a wife is particularly distasteful, but I think he'd expect to be informed.'

Glaucus nodded. 'I'll get back to my quarters, Stephanos. If anyone arrives looking for him, I'll try and mislead them.'

For both Stephanos and Theomenes, the diversion came as a welcome relief from their respective grieving; Stephanos at the failed attempt to retake Plataea, and for Theomenes, the loss of Angelos and his brave warhorse, Astor. Memories of the heady days of their adventures in hunting for The Shield, returned, and they were of one accord. If a member of their group preferred exile to most likely a death sentence, then they'd help him to escape.

'We need Clytes at a time like this, Stephanos,' suggested Theomenes, who'd been woken from a troubled sleep by a member of his uncle's household. 'His skills at disguise would be useful.'

'We need a plan and quickly, Theo. Nobody will get through the gates now, without being checked.'

'What about Clytes' actor friends? I wonder if they'd help.'

'Leon and Panthas? Is it fair to involve them? They're hardly used to danger!'

'I wouldn't say that. It takes a lot of guts to stand in front of twenty thousand spectators......especially if the play isn't to their liking!'

'We have to ask them tonight, Theo.'

'I know where they're living. My dreams of late have been rather bleak. I'd welcome a night stroll.'

'I'll come with you. Glaucus says the Scythian guards are out looking for him already. We don't have much time. Bion could be found as soon as people are abroad. He's hiding near the tomb to Cimon's racehorses.'

'I know the one. That's given me an idea. I'd like to put up a monument to Astor.'

'Why not? More worthy than many a politician, or even some generals I could mention.'

'A murderer!' squealed Panthas. 'I don't want to see him! I don't want him to look at me! He could infect me with his poison!'

'Listen to what Theomenes and Stephanos have to say,' said Leon, only a little less shaken than his overwrought friend. 'It is a dreadful crime. We agree on that. But, if they believe the man is worth helping, then we should try and overcome our abhorrence.'

'Thank you, Leon,' said Theomenes, gratefully. 'I'm sorry for putting this pressure on you both, but if Clytes was here, I know he would help this man. I need a disguise to get him through the city gates, before a full hunt gets underway, and I don't know who else to turn to.'

'Give us a few moments to talk this over, please,' said Leon, seriously, and with an arm placed around his anxious partner's shoulders, they began to talk in earnest. After much gesticulating and cries of alarm from Panthas - when he described, in lurid detail, the many ways they could be put to death for assisting a murderer - and soothing sounds coming from Leon, they finally came to a decision.

'We can help with costumes, but one man in disguise is at risk of being discovered and under torture there is the risk that we could all end up being implicated. A troupe of actors, on the other hand, would have a much better chance of leaving the city without being apprehended.'

'That sounds feasible, Leon,' said Stephanos, nodding encouragingly. 'On behalf of Bion, I thank you both. It's a brave thing that you're doing!'

To be praised by the courageous and handsome warrior, Stephanos, delighted Panthas greatly, and his flabby chest expanded to such an extent that Leon believed his companion had forgotten to breathe. He quickly gave him a slap on the back, causing instant deflation.

'We will do this to help someone from The Shield Company,' Leon declared, assertively, in an attempt to validate Stephanos' unexpected faith in them. 'We weren't involved in your adventure, Theomenes, but let no-one say that we wouldn't have had the courage......had we been asked.'

'We never doubted it, my friends,' Theomenes replied, graciously. 'Never doubted it.'

'But how can we organise *anything* in such a short time, Leon? I'm not giving away our ideas for this year's festivals!' grumbled Panthas.

'We can adapt something from last year's performances. What about the show we put on about Aristophanes' play, 'The Knights'? We can put together a small charade, if one of these bold fellows has armour we can borrow, to make it look more authentic.'

'I can help there,' offered Theomenes. 'When do you think we could be ready?' he asked, anxiously.

'If you can provide a horse and suitable armour for Bion, we can do the rest,' Leon answered, confidently, 'but he'll have to remain hidden for one more night. As soon as the sun is up, I will pay a visit to archon Isarchos. We'll need his permission.'

To bring some cheerfulness to a disheartened city, Leon was able to gain the ready approval of the chief magistrate, to take a small troupe around the streets of Athens and out into the surrounding countryside, to advertise the forthcoming Lenaia and Great Dionysia festivals. At such a dark time for the inhabitants, archon Isarchos welcomed the diversion of the approaching drama competitions, and he even agreed extra funding be provided so that Leon could proceed speedily.

Only Bion's co-conspirators were aware of the rower's involvement in the pageant, and for fear of contamination by his deed - or retaliation, his character was kept away from the other participants. Disguised from head to foot in Theomenes' rich armour and wielding a realistic looking spear, Bion looked convincing as 'the knight'. Riding a horse hired for the occasion, due to Theomenes being reluctant to involve any from his uncle's stables in the escapade, it also was transformed. With colourful trappings and an elaborate feathered headdress adapted from one of Panthas' costumes, the animal of dubious breeding became a warhorse.

Bion decided his best chance of escape was to get to the ports and secure a place on a cargo ship going as far away as possible, so the southern gate leading to the road between the Long Walls to Pireaus, was their focus. Hoping they could vacate the city before the law had a chance to track down their fugitive, Leon and Panthas set off with the troupe soon after sunrise.

Bion was fitted out in a closed helmet and full armour and being completely concealed, it hid his extreme nervousness. He rode slowly but purposefully, as Theomenes had strenuously emphasised, followed closely behind by his marching comrades and a mule-drawn cart full of 'captured prisoners', wailing their lot in the rear.

If they thought their early departure would not draw too much attention, they were wrong. Curiosity and the need for some entertainment, diverted people from their normal morning tasks, and soon 'the knight' had acquired a multitude of 'camp-followers', determined to have some fun.

Leon and Panthas, dressed as heavily padded soldiers, were positioned immediately behind the horse to stay close to Bion, and they marched with exaggerated waddling and panting at the head of a line of equally preposterous army characters. Whether tall and thin or short and fat, each man wore a similar appendage between his legs; not the wooden horse's head of the previous year, but a large carved phallus which protruded brazenly from his costume. As the men stomped by with shoulders back and chests boastfully expanded, it created a comical scene with their erect members all vigorously rising and falling to the rhythm of the piper. The unfortunate actor at the end of the line, who'd been chosen to have his ample arse bared, caused more hilarity when a dog decided to take a bite at it, and even Stephanos and Glaucus, watching with concern from the sidelines and prepared to cause a diversion, if necessary, couldn't help but laugh. But most attention was reserved for the wagon load of unfortunate 'prisoners' at the rear. Wearing grotesque face masks and mock Theban helmets, they knew what to expect from the waiting onlookers and braced themselves against the repeated onslaught of rotten apples and stinking food scraps pelted mercilessly at them.

'What a smell!' grimaced Leon, as they neared the southern gate. 'Is it the horse passing wind, or the rider?'

'I'm sorry Leon. It's me,' mumbled Panthas, apologetically.

The gateway finally loomed into view and the spear in Bion's hand visibly started to shake.

'Just keep moving!' Leon warned. 'We are nearly there!'

As they passed under the gateway, the guards leaning over the defense wall shouted out obscenities at the laughable scene moving beneath them, and unable to resist a final indignity, one man fitted a stale bread roll to his sling, and to cheers from his comrades, he succeeded in knocking off one of the 'Theban' helmets.

The spectators, having enjoyed their lighthearted diversion, drifted back to work and the troupe left the confines of the city, with Leon praying that Bion would not be tempted to look back. Believing the oarsman might lose his nerve, he continued to give him encouragement as they travelled along the busy carriageway leading to the sea. Finally, they reached a small roadside shrine to Demeter where Leon halted the column for a rest, for this was where Bion had agreed to exchange places with Theomenes.

'This is as far as we go,' said Theomenes, sadly, when they'd found a place to talk away from the others. 'I'll take over from here.'

Bion quickly removed his disguise and helped Theomenes on with his armour, while keeping a lookout to make sure they weren't being watched.

'Thank everyone for me,' said Bion, his voice unsteady.

Clasping him firmly by the hand, Theomenes thrust a heavy pouch of silver into Bion's palm. 'Small recompense, comrade. For as long as the memory of The Shield lives, your name will not be forgotten.'

'If only she'd......'

'You'd better go quickly!' stressed Theomenes, anxiously. 'They could be checking the ports. May the gods go with you!' and he grasped Bion in a strong embrace of comradeship.

With final garbled words of gratitude, Bion, with a heavy heart, strode off towards the Pireaus. The thought of being ostracised from everyone and everything he knew, scared him. He was already missing his friends. He hadn't said goodbye to his old friend Cassa - or even his own mother. He thought of her cooking and of the loving welcome she invariably had for him after a long absence; always so appreciative of anything he brought her. When he thought of the shame he'd now brought to her door, he stumbled, as stinging tears blurred his vision. In his confusion, he imagined he could hear the sound of Cassa's children running excitedly after him, and he looked back, expectantly, but there was no-one.

Standing alone on the road, struggling against the urge to go back, he watched in the distance at the smoke trails rising up from the multitude of Athens' hearths and furnaces, wondering which one might be from his mother's home, but as he stood, his thoughts in turmoil, the memory of his beautiful Roxanne; her lifeless body laid out tenderly on their loveless bed, drove everything else from his mind. 'You were right!' he groaned, despairingly. 'I am a fool!' and in a state of utter wretchedness, Bion turned his back on the city of his birth and hurried towards the ships - and the uncertain future of an exile.

TWENTY-EIGHT

'HIT HIM AGAIN, HUSBAND!' squawked the old woman. 'He can hear you, alright!'

'How can you be sure, wife? You found a right one, there. What good is he, if he can't understand what we want him to do?'

'He's feigning it, husband! Isn't he daughter? You said he turned to look when he heard you approaching, and he smiled.'

'He did, father, and got a kick for his insolence!'

Shackled to one of the wheels of the farmer's handcart, Angelos, bruised and hurting, lay very still. Initially, he was in such a weak state that he couldn't respond to their questioning, but as he recovered, he quickly realised that this was not like the household of Theomenes, where slaves were treated humanely. He was in the hands of a poor and callous family, obviously unaccustomed to possessing a slave. He had thought that the daughter might be more sympathetic and trying to imagine what Clytes would do in such a situation, he smiled at her. It was a mistake. Subsequently, he made the decision to resist all their attempts to get him to talk and to be as unresponsive as possible towards the vicious old couple who were expecting him to work for them. No Theban was going to make a slave out of *him*! But defiance turned to dread when the old farmer gave instructions to his daughter.

'He'll understand a good flogging! Go and get your cousin Oulixes. Tell him to bring his whip!'

Oulixes was astounded to learn that his elderly aunt had captured an enemy soldier, albeit an obviously traumatised one, and with memories of the invasion still very raw, he initially wanted to kill the prisoner. Pleadings from his uncle, however, to only flog their new acquisition, made him see an opportunity to improve his own household, and he did as he was asked, thinking to bide his time before taking Angelos for himself.

The Plataean had listened anxiously as the argument swayed one way, then the other, and when the death sentence was lifted, he suffered the subsequent fall of the whip with some relief, but the feeling was not to last.

After Oulixes had left, the family withdrew to discuss their situation.

'I don't see how we can claim a ransom for him, father, if we don't know who he is......and I could see that Oulixes wants him for himself.'

CHAPTER TWENTY-EIGHT

'I could see it too, daughter.'

'What do we do, husband?'

'He's been nothing but trouble. We sell him, wife, and as quickly as possible......before Oulixes comes back. We'll tell him he escaped!'

'Ah, here we have a strong young man!' a harsh voice called out. 'Help him up!' he shouted to an assistant, and Angelos, his hands tied behind his back, was forcibly dragged to his feet. He looked around horror-struck, to the sound of yelling and loud voices all around him. His plan to cause problems for his elderly captors had gone very wrong. They'd sold him to a trader, no-questions-asked, and he was now in a slave market.

'He doesn't look in good shape to me,' said a prosperous looking farmer, coming over to inspect the goods. 'He's had a bad beating. It could mean, he's trouble. What can he do?'

When Angelos didn't respond, he received a sharp blow to his already painful head.

'Tell the man what you can do!' prompted the slaver, angrily.

Angelos desperately wanted his hands to be freed. He visualised what he would do if they held a weapon! Boeotians had taken possession of his hometown; they'd stolen his father's farm and destroyed his family. He imagined what Theomenes would do in his situation. Defiantly, he raised his head and spat in the trader's face. The blow was harder this time and he sank back to his knees.

'This idiot's of no use to me,' responded the farmer, turning away. 'Not worth his bloody keep. What else have you got?'

Angrily, the trader called over his assistant. 'I'm not going to waste my time trying to find a buyer. Take him with the others going to Gamunk the Thracian. Make sure you get the going rate for hire.'

'You're dead meat now, you moron!' said the assistant, menacingly, to Angelos.

The Plataean glared back and inwardly cursed. Cretin!

For two miserable days in midwinter, the group of slaves for hire, chained together with heavy metal headcollars, were forced to walk barefoot towards their grim fate in the unforgiving iron ore mines of northern Boeotia. Some of the prisoners were branded on the forehead, meaning they were repeated runaways and were now either mentally defeated by life's experiences or plainly deranged. For Angelos there would be no chance of escape on the road north, and by the time he arrived at the mines, he looked in such poor shape that Gamunk the site manager, tried to bring down the hiring rate.

'But what good is he to me......in this state? He won't last!'

'His injuries are superficial. He's strong enough. Just obstinate.'

'Awkward bugger, eh?'

'Could have got a good price for him and a better future than this place, but he wouldn't co-operate.'

'Well, you know how it is here. Resistance only leads to an early death.'

'I've watched him. He doesn't seem ready to die.'

'Then he'd better do as he's told.'

'A word of advice. Don't let him fool you. He can hear alright. He just doesn't speak.'

'He's not here for his oratory skills.'

The landscape was like nothing Angelos had ever seen before, although he'd heard the stories of the brutal Hyettos mines on Boeotia's northern border. In all directions the surface of the earth was scarred with deeply gouged trenches, and ominously dark holes dotted the hillside where tunnels had been dug, following the rust red veins as they wove underground, all in an effort to extract the much-needed iron ore. Mountainous heaps of rubble scattered the site where at intervals high above the shivering slaves, guards stood, some paired with large snarling dogs. The cold air resounded to the sounds of hammering and of the whip-carrying supervisors shouting out their commands and threats, but apart from the noise and the sight of the back-breaking activity, it was the lack of eye contact that Angelos noticed. Each worker seemed so focused on the task in hand that even when their group arrived, clumsily climbing over piles of discarded rocks, no-one looked in their direction. Yet, he instinctively sensed their simmering mood - a conflicting mixture of hopelessness and rage.

'Bring them here!' an overseer shouted, stridently, gesturing furiously to attract their attention. 'Tunnel collapse! The rest of you carry on working!'

Immediately, Angelos and the other prisoners were herded, stumbling awkwardly, avoiding carts and wagons towards the opening of a tunnel, where a man's frantic shouts could just be heard.

'Unshackle them. I want it cleared,' instructed the overseer. 'This is a rich seam!'

The chains on his headcollar were detached from the others, and Angelos immediately looked about him, looking for any means of escape.

'You're not going anywhere!' snarled a guard. 'Get in there!'

Cautiously he moved into the choking gloom lit by meagre oil lamps, when a naked slave covered from head to foot in a pale grey dust; the only one to have avoided the collapse, grabbed him by the shoulder, muttering angrily.

'There are eight in there. Two are only boys! We knew the firing was too fierce!'

Angelos realised that it could well be him trapped in such a passage, and he quickly joined forces with the grimy veteran miner in trying to clear the obstruction. Because of his height and the low roof, it proved back-breakingly painful, and further discomfort was suffered due to his constantly watering eyes, caused by the reek of vinegar which had been used to cool and shatter the rock after first being heated by fire.

The rock fall was of limestone blocks, some too large to be moved without first being broken up. There was only room for three men at a time to hack with chisels and hammers at the fallen rock, with a relay of others to fill the wooden trays to be dragged to the entrance. It was hard work and slow, and the dust laden air was suffocating. Angelos deduced that unless there was ventilation somewhere down the tunnel, no-one would be coming out alive. Working in shifts the obstruction was eventually cleared and the broken, bloodied bodies were brought out. There were no survivors. Details from their tattoos were recorded to be passed on to their owners, but apart from that, there was no other acknowledgement that they'd once been someone's sons. Angelos, and some of the group he'd arrived with, were now allocated to work the dark stained tunnel they'd gruellingly succeeded in re-opening.

His accommodation that night was a hard earth floor, where he and the other slaves lay in rows shoulder to shoulder in order to fit into the cramped, foetid building, and a long chain was passed through all their headcollars - each end padlocked to a wall. Many of the occupants had injuries, Angelos noticed, but he saw no attention being given. The mine was worked night and day by over a thousand slaves during two alternating shifts of ten hours and only ending when the oil lamps ran down. At any one time there could be sixty slaves crammed into the one-storey building to grab what rest they could, and there were ten such buildings at the mining site. Many more were situated where the metal workers were housed. Here, night never fell and the stars never shone, due to the constant glow from the hungry smelting furnaces. The conditions were harsh. For some, they were inhuman. The following morning Angelos received his wrist tattoo, painfully inflicted with a hot blade and infilled with black ink, denoting the name of his slave-trader owner, and a number. The temporary pain endured as the incision was made into his flesh was nothing compared to the burning shame he felt whenever his fingers ran over the stigma.

Throughout his first week at the mine, Angelos stubbornly maintained the impression that he was mute, as he listened and watched keenly for any chance of escape, but then something happened which almost made him break his silence. He was sat with others in his gang, which included their leader, the survivor of the tunnel collapse, known as 'the goat' because of a bony nodule in the centre of his forehead. They were awaiting their first meal of the day; a bowl of thick gruel and coarse bread, when a commotion broke out nearby. One man, belligerent in attitude despite his circumstances, was clearly dissatisfied with his portion and had grabbed the ladle being used to dish out the food. The guards were there in an instant and the slave was dragged away.

'What will happen to him?' asked one of the gang members.

'A flogging,' answered 'the goat', nonchalantly. 'He'll be back.'

'Do you know him, then?'

'He's a survivor. Been here for years. That's one gang you don't want to be in.'

'Why, what's wrong with it?'

'Plataeans. The Boeotians hate them. They get less rations and the worst treatment than any other group here.'

Angelos, badly affected by what he just heard, almost broke his silence, but despite a deep yearning to be with his fellows, the thought of getting even worse treatment, stopped him from speaking out. He still had hopes of escaping the brutal mines and it occurred to him that being in the Plataean crew would lessen his chances.

'Enjoy your breakfast, lads,' said 'the goat', sarcastically, and nodding in the direction of the Plataeans, added, 'There are some here who would kill you for it!'

Filled with anger but also shame, Angelos put his head down and maintained his silence.

Although Plataea was situated in the territory of Boeotia, and its capital, Thebes, was only eight miles from it, there was a long-running animosity between the two cities. Almost a hundred years previously, the Plataeans refused to be threatened into joining the Boeotian League, harshly ruled over by dominating Thebes, and they sought protection from Athens, which was granted. Over the ensuing years Plataea repaid the Athenians by being a loyal ally and stood by them when Attica was twice threatened by the Persians. The Boeotians chose to be on the side of the invaders and shared in their defeat.

In more recent times their grievances stemmed from the Thebans' unprovoked attack on Plataea eight years previously, when one hundred and eighty of the invading Theban army were captured and subsequently executed by the Plataeans. The consequences resulted in war being declared between Athens and Sparta, with Thebes choosing the Spartan side. Plataea was put under siege and eventually forced to surrender, and in retaliation for the killing of their soldiers, Thebes demanded the cruel execution of two hundred and twenty-five of Plataea's defending garrison.

Throughout the whole Greek world, the war had brought many long-held grievances to the fore, but between Plataeans and Thebans, their mutual hatred was all consuming.

TWENTY-NINE

AFTER HIS SUCCESS AT Megara, when he managed to persuade the city to stay loyal to Sparta, Brasidas marched north with his untried soldiery of helots and mercenaries. After one surrender, the Spartans were fearful of a second, now that the stigma of being first had been removed. Consequently, there were no hardened spartiates in the column, Brasidas himself being the only warrior of merit. Half-funded by Perdiccas, king of Macedonia, to help him in his battles against his enemies, the Spartans took the opportunity to send Brasidas on a campaign, which if successful, could force Athens to release her prisoners. If not, well, no-one of worth would be lost. Not even Brasidas would be genuinely mourned, for jealousy was running freely through the veins of the elite, high-born families of Sparta. Many thought he had an un-Spartan way of doing things.

True to his character, when his army arrived at the borders of Athens' loyal ally, Thessaly, instead of waiting for permission to enter, he marched boldly on, risking an attack from their renowned cavalry, and before the Thessalians had made up their minds as to whether he was friend or foe, his column had left their open plains and was being made welcome in the lands of Perdiccas. Here, he met up with the king's Macedonian force with the intention of marching on Arrhabaeus, the rebellious ruler of Lyncestis. Wanting to avoid a confrontation with Perdiccas, however, Arrhabaeus asked Brasidas to mediate. Perdiccas was furious. He'd brought the Spartan to fight his enemies, not to talk to them, and when Brasidas refused to invade Lyncestis, he cut his funding from a half to one third.

If all was not going according to plan for Perdiccas, the collaboration went well for Brasidas, resulting in the successful capture of the important colony of Amphipolis, north of the Athenian held Chalcidice peninsular. It was a great loss to Athens, due to the source of timber in nearby forests and the vital array of goods, including gold and silver, which came to Attica from near and far via the Strymon bridge.

During a snowstorm Brasidas took the city by surprise, and while people were in fear and before reinforcements could arrive, he immediately offered the citizens such generous terms that they felt they could not refuse them. People who wanted to stay would retain their citizens' rights, but anyone who wanted to leave could take their property with them. By the time the Athenian general, Thucydides, sailed from the nearby island of Thasos with his seven triremes, it was all too late. Due to the quick thinking of Brasidas, the citizens of Amphipolis had changed their allegiance to Sparta.

Thucydides did arrive in time to secure, Eion, the seaport of Amphipolis, but he was blamed for the loss of such an important colony and found guilty of military incompetence. Exiled for twenty years, he was free to travel, enabling him to gather information from eyewitnesses of the war, and for the rest of his life he devoted his time to recording, as objectively as possible, a detailed history of the long-running conflict.

When news spread throughout the Chalcidice region of how generous the Spartan invader was who declared wherever he went that his sole intention was to liberate all Hellas from the greed of grasping Athens, other towns begged to be next to change their allegiance, believing the Spartans were finally acting with real energy. Reeling from their defeat in Boeotia, the Athenians responded as best they could, by sending garrisons to support their colonies, while Brasidas sent for reinforcements from Sparta. His request was ignored. Partly out of jealousy, but also because they were reluctant to escalate an expensive war in a territory so far from home. What they wanted was peace, or at least for their prisoners in Athens to be released. The taking of Amphipolis and the real possibility of other towns falling to Brasidas, was thought sufficient to secure a negotiation.

Freed from the constraints of his fellow countrymen, however, Brasidas, with his assorted army, was able to operate as he saw fit, which was unlike any other commander of his time, and one by one the towns of the area, suffering from the tyranny of Athens' ever-increasing demands for tribute, fell under his spell. Even the gods seemed to favour him. When the Athenians in the colonised city of Torone stood against him and tried to construct a tower on top of a house, the weight made the dwelling collapse with such a loud crash that the Athenians believed Brasidas was responsible, and they fled to their ships. The Spartan had been on the point of making an assault and had promised the first man who scaled the wall, the enormous sum of thirty silver minae. Deciding that it was divine intervention rather than human endeavour that had caused the Athenians to flee, he dedicated the money to the goddess Athena whose temple was close by. During the rest of the winter, he re-organised the places he'd already won over and devised plans for the taking of many more.

While the Spartan general was in his element in Thrace, the Athenians were grieving over the loss of their army in Boeotia, and so ended the eighth year of the war between Athens and Sparta.

THIRTY

AFTER THEIR DEVASTATING DEFEAT in Boeotia, the Athenians were anxious to put a stop to Brasidas' winning campaign in the Chalcidice, consequently the Athenian general,

Laches, supported by the peace-loving general, Nicias, was successful in putting forward a motion in the Athenian Assembly for an armistice with more than willing Sparta. Terms were agreed for an initial one-year truce, to commence in the spring of the ninth year of the war. While time allowed, Brasidas was intent on putting as much pressure on the Athenians as possible to force them to release the prisoners, and as news of his exploits spread throughout Athens, cries of 'Brasidas! Brasidas!' had become a regular cheer from the cells. Just as the spartiates had always believed, their daring commander was fighting hard to win them their freedom.

Before the armistice had begun, the town of Scione in the Pellene district, decided to come over to Brasidas, believing they had a shared heritage as descendants of the people of Pellene in the Peloponnese. The charismatic commander had impressed them greatly, and they imagined all Spartans must be like him. To accept their allegiance, Brasidas travelled in a small boat behind one of his triremes, thinking that if he was approached by a bigger boat than his, the trireme would protect him, and if an enemy trireme attacked his, they would ignore his small boat, enabling him to get to Scione, unscathed. Two days into the truce, Scione was accepted into the Spartan alliance. When knowledge of their treachery reached the Athenians, they were furious, and Cleon threatened to put all its citizens to death. Brasidas proclaimed that he would stand by them, no matter what, and he was given every mark of honour; crowned with a gold crown as liberator of Hellas and decked with garlands as though he were a famous athlete. Such was the faith in this dynamic Spartan, that Mende, rich in gold and silver and a healthy contributor to the coffers of the Delian League, was encouraged to revolt also, although in the full knowledge that an armistice was in force. Islands, and any land by the sea, were considered by Athenians to be theirs by right, due to their undisputed control of the seas, and Brasidas made preparations for the inevitable arrival of the Athenian fleet. Women and children, he sent to safety with commander Polydamidas together with eight hundred men to protect them.

Constrained by the truce, Brasidas was unable to continue his drive to win over any more Athenian colonies. The time had finally come when he had to repay Perdiccas for allowing his army into Thrace. He was part-funding the enterprise, after all. The king accepted nothing less than an attack on the rebellious Arrhabaeus, and Brasidas reluctantly joined his sponsor on the march to the highland territory of Lyncestis, reluctantly leaving the towns of Scione and Mende to their fates.

The joint commanders had a force between them of three thousand hoplites, one thousand cavalry and a great number of ancillaries, but the battle for Lyncestis did not go according to plan. Perdiccas was expecting reinforcements from his Illyrian allies, but when they eventually did turn up, it was to give support to his enemy, king Arrhabaeus. These tribesmen appeared so terrifying that fear spread through the ranks, causing Perdiccas and his men to flee in the night, and when Brasidas awoke the following morning, he discovered he'd been abandoned. Greatly outnumbered he feared his unhardened army of freed helots and mercenaries might run in panic and so he spoke to them stirringly, but also calmly, in a manner more like an Athenian than a blunt Spartan, concluding with these words:

'The present enemy might terrify an inexperienced imagination; they are formidable in outward bulk, their loud yelling is unbearable, and the brandishing of their weapons in the air has a threatening appearance. But when it comes to real fighting with an opponent who stands his ground, they are not what they seemed; they have no regular order that they should be ashamed of deserting their positions when hard pressed; flight and attack are with them equally honourable and afford no test of courage; their independent mode of fighting never leaving anyone who wants to run away without a fair excuse for so doing. In short, they think frightening you at a secure distance a surer game than meeting you hand to hand; otherwise they would have done the one and not the other. You can thus plainly see that the terrors with which they were at first invested are in fact trifling enough, though to the eye and ear very prominent. Stand your ground *therefore when they advance, and again wait your opportunity to retire in good order, and you will reach a place of safety all the sooner, and will know forever afterwards that rabble such as these, to those who sustain their first attack, do but show off their courage by threats of the terrible things that they are going to do, at a distance, but with those who give way to them are quick enough to display their heroism in pursuit when they can do so without danger.'*

Immediately following his address, Brasidas began to lead off his army, which he formed into a square, with light troops and baggage protected in the centre and his youngest fighters on the outside to fend off attacks. Together with three hundred chosen men, he placed himself at the rear of the retreating army, successfully turning about to fight whenever they were harassed by the enemy, then moving quickly forward when their attackers withdrew. Unable to break the tight formation, Arrhabaeus' men rushed ahead to block their escape at a narrow pass, but Brasidas, being aware of their intention, split up his three hundred hoplites who successfully fought to secure the high ground, allowing the main body of the army to make its way through. On reaching safety in the lands of Perdiccas, the soldiers came across abandoned yokes of oxen and fallen baggage, left behind by the Macedonian army in their night flight. So incensed were they at being deserted, that they slaughtered the animals and took the baggage for themselves.

Perdiccas now believed he had an enemy in his territory worse than the Athenians and decided never to trust Brasidas, or indeed any Spartan, ever again. Not for the first time the king of Macedonia changed sides and sued for peace with Athens.

THIRTY-ONE

JUST AS BRASIDAS FEARED, when he returned from upper Macedonia, he found the town of Mende had been retaken and Scione was under siege. During his absence, general Nicias had arrived with fifty ships to reclaim the Athenian colonies taken during the armistice. With a combined army of Athenians and locals, he eventually brought Mende back into the fold, partly due to the heavy-handedness of the Spartan commander Polydamidas, whom Brasidas had left in charge. When the democratic faction of Mende decided they did not want to fight the Athenians, the commander dragged the Speaker of the Assembly from his place with such force, he rendered the man unconscious. It seemed to the inhabitants of Mende that freedom from Athens only meant subservience to Sparta, and the people rose up against the Spartans and their collaborators. Scione, however, argued against the assertion that it had changed allegiance knowing a truce was in place and would not surrender to Nicias. A Spartan expeditionary force had at last been sent to aid Brasidas in his support for Scione, and the populace, fatefully, decided to hold out.

Unfortunately for them, the Spartan troops under the command of Ischagoras would not reach Thrace. To prove his loyalty to Athens, Nicias directed Perdiccas to use his influence with his friends in Thessaly, to stop the approaching soldiery in their tracks. Ischagoras and a few close companions were forced to take a ship up the coast, finally meeting up with Brasidas, and in typical Spartan fashion, undid all the goodwill Brasidas had earned, by taking command of Torone and Amphipolis, dashing their hopes for independence.

Unable to defeat the inhabitants of Scione, who were supported by the Spartans and their sympathisers who'd fled from Mende, Nicias built a confining wall which completely surrounded the town, and by the close of summer the construction was complete. Leaving a garrison to maintain the blockade, he took the main army back to Athens.

CHAPTER THIRTY-TWO

For the rest of the year the Spartans and the Athenians were constrained by the truce, but at the end of winter, Brasidas was forced to take desperate action. Knowing the one-year armistice was soon to end, he was fearful for the people under siege in Scione. The promised Spartan reinforcements had not materialised and he believed the threat by Cleon of Athens, to kill everyone in the city could soon be carried out. He made a bold attempt to draw off the garrison Nicias had left at Scione, by attacking nearby Athenian held Potidaea. Arriving at night, he personally succeeded in placing a ladder against the outer wall without being detected, but the offensive was discovered and the garrison sounded the alarm. Without the element of surprise, he was forced to lead off his army and to abort the attack.

Despite Brasidas' best efforts to rescue them, the Scionians were still under siege, trapped behind Nicias' walls, when the truce expired in the spring.

So ended the winter and the ninth year of the war.

THIRTY-TWO

ATHENIAN SPRING SUNSHINE WARMED the enclosed courtyard of Hypatos, where sprawled on several long couches, a group pf Plataeans were gathered for a hoped-for convivial evening of wine and entertainment, but the conversation had inevitably drifted towards what was on all their minds, the end of the ceasefire with Sparta.

'Cleon is pushing for command. He's determined to finish what Nicias started.'

'Yes, now he knows Perdiccas is on our side again and the Spartan reinforcements have been blocked. That's typical of the man!'

'He thinks he'll relive his glory days of Pylos, but Demosthenes deserved more credit for that victory.'

'He's an opportunist, not a strategist. He's no leader of men.'

'Against Brasidas! Who does he think he is? Miltiades?'

'Someone has to retake Amphipolis......and Scione.'

'Scione? Where's that?'

'Near Potidaea.'

'Never heard of it.'

'Pays six talents a year in tribute, apparently, but rebelled during the truce......with encouragement from Brasidas.'

'He went too far!'

'Cleon has threatened to put all Scionians to death.'

'He would!'

'They placed their faith in the Spartans. Always a foolish thing to do.'

'If Cleon has his way, they'll pay dearly for their treachery!'

The talk ceased abruptly when the servants arrived to take in the couches. The air was starting to cool, and food was ready to be served indoors.

'Have you decided which of Hypatos' horses you'll be replacing Astor with,' asked Stephanos, his hand placed on Theomenes' shoulder.

'There are two stallions in my uncle's stables right now which I'm considering. I'd like your opinion, later.'

'I'm no judge of horseflesh, Theo. In fact, I don't even like the smell of horses!'

'They probably don't like the smell of you, either!'

'Don't worry, I'll keep my opinions to myself. I expect your uncle's conversation will be about nothing else, this evening!'

'He still mentions the loss of Astor. I sometimes think he would have preferred the stallion to have survived rather than me!'

Stephanos was correct in thinking that his host would end up talking about horses, but it was worse than he imagined. As the evening wore on and the wine flowed generously, Hypatos became overcome with excitement about some news he wanted to impart to his guests. He clapped his hands loudly and beckoned to a servant to come to him, whispering into the youth's ear, and the obedient young man hurried away to fulfill his master's wishes. The guests were all smiling and murmuring amongst themselves, looking forward to the entertainment they assumed Hypatos had prepared for them.

Accompanied by excited clapping from Hypatos, instead of the expected musicians and female company, a middle-aged scribe, his fingers blackened with ink, was escorted into the andron. He carried a papyrus scroll, and Hypatos personally jumped up to provide a long bench for the scribe, so eager was he to show off the contents to his guests.

'Can you guess what it is?' he asked them, enthusiastically.

None dared speculate.

'I have finished my book, dear friends! In this, my sixtieth year, I have finally completed my comprehensive work. This good scribe has just compiled the very first copy of 'A Guide to Horse Breeding - with illustrations'! Find the page which relates to what constitutes a good horse', he told the slave, indicating eagerly to him to unfurl the scroll. 'This particular description is already mentioned in Simon of Athens' great work, but I have updated it somewhat. If you would like your own copy, by the way, my scribe will gladly make you one. Now, just listen to this!'

Theomenes, who was well aware of his uncle's exhaustive labour of love, couldn't help but smile at his enthusiasm, and with more fighting in the north soon to be upon them, not even Stephanos was in a mood to quell it. Brasidas! He wished he could quell his memory of *him*! Why, he thought, uneasily, was he plagued with the belief that their destinies were somehow intertwined?

THIRTY-THREE

TO THE DISMAY OF the Plataeans and also of many others in the ranks, Cleon succeeded in persuading the Assembly to give him command of the campaign in Thrace. With promises from Perdiccas that his army would join with the Athenians and news that other chiefs would also send a large force of Thracian mercenaries to his aid, at the onset of summer, when the armistice had expired, Cleon confidently set forth with twelve hundred hoplites, three hundred horse and a great number of allies. With thirty ships he arrived first at besieged Scione, and upon receiving information that Brasidas was not at Torone, he took some of Scione's heavy infantry from the garrison there and seized the opportunity to retake Torone. Leaving a force to guard the city, he then sailed to the port of Athenian held Eion, to wait for the promised additional forces to arrive, when he would make his move on Amphipolis. As time passed, however, and the reinforcements did not arrive, anxiety in the army increased.

'Why are we waiting, Stephanos?' asked Akios, a fellow Plataean. 'The men are getting anxious about Cleon's strategy. Does he actually have one?'

Having already warned Cleon about the grumbling in the ranks, Stephanos was reluctant to reveal his true concerns to the one hundred and twenty-eight Plataeans under his command. Since his meeting with Cleon, his doubts had increased that the general could outmanoeuvre Brasidas, and he knew that the last thing an army needed was a lack of confidence in their commander, especially going up against such a strong opponent.

'Reinforcements, Akios. He's waiting for Perdiccas.'

'But we all know there's an inferior force at Amphipolis!' argued his comrade. 'There can only be one reason why Cleon hasn't attacked already. He's afraid to face Brasidas.'

'That kind of talk is no good for the moral of the army! I don't want anyone in our unit adding to the unrest. Do you understand me?'

Akios nodded, although unconvinced.

The meeting between Stephanos and Cleon had not gone well, but the Plataean wasn't surprised at that. Ever since the Plataeans had taken the rescued Marathon shield directly to Delphi for safe keeping and denied Cleon the glory of displaying it in Athens, the relationship between them had been strained. Cleon was not the kind of man to forget an insult, and he never missed an opportunity to remind them of their 'error'.

'I will move on Amphipolis when I'm good and ready!' he'd screamed at Stephanos. 'The men will thank me for the wait. With additional forces we can storm the city and avoid a pitched battle.' Then, determined to belittle Stephanos, he added, sarcastically, 'My plan should please your Plataeans. They're good street fighters, are they not?'

To the frustration of the army, Cleon continued to wait for the reinforcements, but as accusations of cowardice increased, he decided to provide the men with some activity. Orders went out to prepare as though for a parade. Horses were groomed, helmets and armour polished, leatherwork was oiled and plumes were combed. In an effort to quell the rumours that he was afraid to face his Spartan opposite number, he marched his freshly groomed men upriver and to the very walls of Amphipolis; not to give battle, but to take a look at the lie of the land from where he would make his later assault. He believed that Brasidas would not bring out his inferior force against the flower of Athenian soldiery, so was not surprised to find the walls of the city unmanned and no sign of an occupation force.

Unbeknown to the general, however, Brasidas was watching his every move from a nearby hill, and he rushed back into the city to inform his fellow commander, Clearidas, to prepare for battle. Concerned that his motley collection of ill-equipped allies would be in awe of the gleaming array of soldiery parading so brazenly in front of the city, he decided to confide in them his plan of action, while also reminding them of their common Dorian birthright of courage and valour.

'I imagine it is the poor opinion that he has of us, and the fact that he has no idea of anyone coming out to engage him, that has made the enemy march up to the place and carelessly look about him as he is doing, without noticing us. But the most successful soldier will always be the man who most happily detects a blunder like this.

I, with the men under my command will, if possible, take them by surprise and fall upon their centre, and, do you, Clearidas, afterwards when you see me already upon them, and, as is likely, dealing terror among them, take with you the Amphipolitans and the rest of the allies, and suddenly open the gates and dash at them, and hasten to engage as quickly as you can.

'*Show yourself a brave man, as a Spartan should; and do you, allies, follow him like men, and remember that zeal, honour and obedience mark the good soldier, and that this day will make you either free men and allies of Sparta, or slaves of Athens. Even if you escape without personal loss of liberty or life, your bondage will be on harsher terms than before, and you will also hinder the liberation of the rest of the Hellenes. No cowardice then on your part, seeing the greatness of the issues at stake, and I will show that what I preach to others I can practise myself.*'

What Brasidas lacked in strength of arms, he made up for in seizing the opportunity that Cleon's carelessness had provided, and behind the city gates, troops and cavalry lined up, awaiting the signal. Cleon, who'd been under the impression that Brasidas would be reluctant to bring out his poorly equipped force against fully armed, seasoned hoplites, now panicked when the unexpected movement of a great number of horses and soldiers' feet, was seen under the gates. He'd not expected to fight, and believing they were about to break out and attack him, he sounded an immediate retreat.

The men in the left wing who were closest to the safety of Eion moved out first, but the manoeuvre was not quick enough for Cleon and he joined the retreat in person, disastrously wheeling about his right wing in the process and exposing its unarmed side to the enemy. Seizing the moment, Brasidas, with one hundred and fifty heavily armed troops, stormed out from gates in the walled fortifications, while Clearidas and his force, charged out through the city's main gates. Attacked on both sides, the Athenians were thrown into total confusion, and Cleon, having no intention of standing and fighting, fled for his life. His progress was hindered, however, by his ostentatious armour, and he was overtaken by a lightly armed peltast. Brought down by the targeteer's careful aim, the controversial leader of Athens was killed outright.

Theomenes, in full cavalry regalia and surrounded by his equally splendid comrades in the cohort, had been on the right flank when he heard the order to retreat being sounded again and again, but engagement with the enemy had become inevitable when hundreds of yelling Spartans and their allies poured out from the city, cutting off their escape back to Eion. Attacked by local horsemen, his men fought valiantly to break through as missiles flew all around them. Slashing at assailants to the right and left of him, Theomenes feared the worst for Stephanos and the rest of the Plataeans who were in the centre of the line, and by the sounds of screams and mayhem coming from that direction, they were in the thick of the fighting.

Even though Spartan commanders wore no distinctive regalia, Stephanos recognised Brasidas immediately from his first encounter with the man at Pylos. His memory of him yelling at his men to drive the ships onto the shore had never left him, and he was certain that this was the same man, urging his followers in the attack.

'You are Dorians! You were born with courage! Down with the tyranny of Athens!'

'Brasidas!'

The seasoned warrior, his long hair beneath his helmet, matted with blood and sweat, bore a terrifying aspect as he swung around to face Stephanos. Wounded and in obvious pain, he resembled a proud beast, ready to strike out at any adversary that approached him.

'You chose a bad time to recognise me, Athenian!'

'Plataean!'

'Same difference!'

'Not to me!'

Roaring, in an effort to overcome his pain, Brasidas lunged at Stephanos, but the Plataean skillfully deflected the surprisingly forceful thrust with his shield, while at the same time, striking out with his sword at an attacking soldier who'd come to his leader's aid.

159

'You carry a fine weapon......Plataean! I look forward to relieving you of it!'

'You'll feel its quality soon enough......Spartan!'

Stephanos was supported by fellow Plataeans; his most trusted and experienced fighters, and it became a desperate fight for survival as the blades and shields of Brasidas' men clashed mercilessly against their own. Seemingly oblivious to his wounds, the Spartan leader continued to rally his men as they relentlessly attacked the Athenian force. All spears were gone in the initial fighting. This was now bloody hand to hand combat, when death could come quickly and vigilance was all. But the loss of blood ultimately took its toll on the Spartan commander, and in the midst of the carnage he collapsed, moaning, to the ground. Quickly, his comrades rushed to encircle their beloved leader, and forming a defensive shield around him, they put up a courageous fight to protect him, some paying with their lives.

'Let them go!' shouted Stephanos, suddenly, above the din, and he ordered his men to hold back. Amidst the chaos and turmoil of battle, he'd come face to face with the courageous Spartan general and compared him to his own commander. Would that Cleon's hoplites had loved him as much! The Spartan was mortally wounded, he could see that, but he wouldn't watch him being butchered. Brasidas' closest comrades hurriedly lifted their commander, bleeding from several wounds, and carefully placing him on his shield, they carried the injured warrior from the field.

Defiant still, the Spartan looked around for Stephanos and seeing the blood splattered Plataean watching him, grim-faced, he struggled to call out to him. 'If you live to get back to Athens, Plataean, give my regards to commander Styphon. Tell him I'll be seeing him again soon......in Sparta!' As he watched his dying enemy being taken from the battle, his face grimaced in pain, Stephanos almost hoped he would.

The loss of the Spartan commander created no relief for the remaining embattled Athenians. Driven by Clearidas and the Spartan's allied forces, survivors of the Athenian right wing sought safety on a nearby hill, where they courageously repelled the attacks several times, until missiles thrown from afar by the allied cavalry and peltasts, decimated their numbers and their ranks finally broke. Fleeing from the hill in disarray, it was now every man for himself, as both cavalry and infantry of the Athenian army fought desperately to return to Eion, and safety.

One such foot soldier was Socrates, who yet again, found himself fleeing for his life from a battle. He was spotted by a member of Theomenes' cohort, as he staggered with exertion up a mountain path, and the horseman pulled him to safety. As they rode, the cavalryman felt compelled to ask the philosopher how he coped with life as a soldier and witnessing the atrocities men did to one another. 'I deal with the horrors of war, young man, by living my life to the full, and I try and look for the good in the world, such as you stopping to help me now!'

Another horse fleeing south and carrying two riders, was 'Celer', a stallion from Hypatos' stables. Theomenes, with a small group of riders had come to the rescue of a severely wounded Stephanos, who was being supported on either side by fellow comrades and desperately trying to avoid a barrage of missiles being thrown from a band of enemy horsemen. The Athenian riders were hard pressed to drive them off, but eventually they succeeded in giving the Plataeans time to raise Stephanos onto the horse.

When the Athenian losses became known later, even Socrates found it hard to remain philosophical. Six hundred souls, many being from Athens' finest families, perished at Amphipolis and only seven Spartans, but with Cleon and Brasidas amongst the dead, the war's two most aggressive leaders had been removed from the scene, and Nicias was finally able to persuade the Athenian Assembly to sue for a long peace with Sparta.

Brasidas, having lived long enough to learn of his great victory and believing he'd done enough to free his comrades in Athens, was buried with full military honours in a publicly funded tomb in the agora at Amphipolis. All statuary of Hagnon, the original Athenian founder of the city, was removed and replaced with that of the Spartan general, and from then on, the people of

Amphipolis claimed Brasidas as their city's founder. So proud were they of his memory, annual games and ceremonies were carried out in his name.

THIRTY-FOUR

THE FIFTY-YEAR PEACE TREATY between Nicias of Athens and Pleistoanax of Sparta, brought no peace for the Plataeans. Signed, ten years almost to the day since the war began with the Theban attack on their city, hopes of returning were dashed once again when Sparta's major allies; Boeotia, Megara and Corinth, refused to accept the terms.

Part of the agreement was that each party should restore the conquests acquired during the ten-year conflict, but problems arose immediately when Sparta could not persuade the Boeotians to give back Plataea. They argued that Plataea had not been acquired by force, but that the city had been given up to them voluntarily. In retaliation, Athens angered the Megarians by arguing in a similar fashion regarding the port of Nisaea; that the Spartan garrison there had not been taken by force but had surrendered voluntarily. The Corinthians, who wished the war to continue, justified their refusal by stating it would be a betrayal of their allies in the Chalcidice, to sign a treaty with Athens. And then there was the problem of Amphipolis. Following Brasidas' lead, Clearidas supported the citizens in their desire for independence, and he refused to hand over the city to the Athenians. He also denied his fellow Spartans having control, by returning with the army that had accompanied Brasidas, back to Sparta. The consequence of not being given Amphipolis, was Athens deciding to hold onto Pylos. Always afraid of a helot revolt, this act infuriated the Spartans since they considered Athenian held Pylos a constant attraction for fleeing slaves.

CHAPTER THIRTY-FIVE

The start of the Peace of Nicias, coincided with the ending of a thirty-year peace treaty between Sparta and her powerful democratic neighbour and longtime enemy, Argos. Having remained neutral during the ten-year war, their army and coffers were still intact. Having gained nothing from the terms of the peace accord, various states now sought to form an alliance with powerful Argos, in an attempt to create a new league, able to stand up to Sparta *and* Athens.

Watching these shifting alliances was the ambitious young aristocrat, Alcibiades. When the Spartans would not accept him as a signatory to the peace treaty due to him being under the age of thirty, and chose his political enemy, Nicias, instead, the hot-headed twenty-nine-year-old felt humiliated. He argued that his family had, in the past, promoted Sparta's interests in Athens, even giving him a Spartan name, and that he personally had ensured the safety and well-being of the spartiate prisoners. Knowing the Spartans were demoralised having failed to 'free Hellas from the tyranny of Athens', he now set his sights on weakening their hold on the Peloponnese and did his utmost to whip up anti-Spartan feeling in Athens.

THIRTY-FIVE

WHILE ALCIBIADES WAS SEEKING to forge his reputation as a statesman like his uncle before him, the Plataeans sought to forge a new life for themselves, far from Athens.

The sad fate of the people under siege at Scione, did not change after the demise of warmonger, Cleon. The Athenians were so incensed at the betrayal of the Scionians to Brasidas, that when the siege was finally brought to an end, in the year following the signing of the peace treaty, they carried out a deed of such brutality it would be a stain on Athens' reputation for years to come. Implementing Cleon's deadly threat, all males able to bear arms were taken to Athens, where they were publicly humiliated before being executed, and the women and children they forced into slavery. Scione was then offered to the stateless Plataeans, who'd suffered a similar fate at the hands of the Spartans.

Some Plataeans were not convinced of Athens' motives for her generosity, however, and there were arguments for and against the move. Akios, a soldier in Stephanos's command, and Pyrus the archer, seemed to sum up the main concerns amongst their fellow countrymen.

'This is not what we fought for,' said Akios. It's not Plataea! We are not welcome in Athens, and that's the truth of it. We're a constant reminder to them of our valour and their lack of it! They want rid of us.'

'I think it's a generous offer,' Pyrus responded. Gratitude for our loyalty.'

'Yes, our bloody loyalty. They're using us! They just want us to protect their interests in the Chalcidice.'

'Well, who better to help guard the peninsular?'

'They've executed the inhabitants! We're hardly going to be made welcome in the area.'

'The Spartans killed our people at Plataea! It's just retribution.'

'It's on an exposed headland......and a long way from Athens' protection.'

'There's the fleet at Potidaea.'

When every alternative had been discussed, one final question remained.

'Do we have a choice?' asked another Plataean present. 'It's either a mediocre life in Athens or the chance of something better in Scione.'

There was no final consensus, but when brave Erastos spoke up, many wanted to believe as he did.

'We'll have our own lands to farm again......and there's peace at last!'

At the beginning of the war, the treasuries which were safeguarded on the acropolis in Athens on behalf of the Delian

League, held the enormous sum of over six thousand talents - and one hundred and eighty poleis contributed to the fund. At the time of the signing of the Fifty-Year Peace Treaty, an increased four hundred poleis were contributing to the fund, but such had been the crippling expenditure of the war, the treasuries were almost empty. Sparta also, was impoverished.

Hoping against hope that the peace treaty would hold, the Plataeans made preparations to move to Scione by the sea.

THIRTY-SIX

D EEPLY SCARRED BUT NOW fully recovered from the wounds he'd taken at Amphipolis, Stephanos just had time to say goodbye to Styphon and the other Spartan prisoners, before moving his family north. The Spartans were also leaving the city. In fulfilment of Athens' part of the peace treaty, they were being returned to their homeland.

'It's true about the rumours then, that the Plataeans are leaving Athens,' said Styphon, sounding surprised. 'I trust all goes well for you and your family, Stephanos.'

'I'd prefer to be going home......as you are.'

'I told you Brasidas would not desert us,' answered the spartiate. 'He made the ultimate sacrifice to gain our freedoms.'

'He was a brave man, Styphon. The bravest I ever encountered,' said Stephanos.

'As are you, Plataean! Clearidas is in the city. He's returning to Sparta with us, together with Brasidas' army. He told us all about what happened at Amphipolis. Brasidas lived long enough to learn of his victory because of you, and he knew it would lead to this. We shall be forever in your debt.'

'I doubt if our paths will cross again, Spartan......*if* the peace treaty holds.'

'Not in battle my friend, please the gods!'

'Well, if ever you come by Scione......?'

'Ha-ha! I might take you up on that!'

Throughout the city many such farewells were taking place, and at his uncle's house, Theomenes was making final arrangements with Hypatos. The wealthy landowner was keen to invest further in the gold mines in the Chalcidice area, and he'd put his nephew in full charge of all his future business transactions in the area.

'Mydon has managed my interests admirably from Mesembria, but this opportunity to operate from Scione could widen our area of investments substantially. You have made contacts all along the coast, from your journeys to and from the Black Sea. When you get settled, make enquiries as to how we can acquire a mining contract, like Thucydides. He's in exile up there. Try and speak with him. And one more thing. Isn't it time you married Amara?'

'I've asked her already, uncle. More than once.'

'I understand. I apologise for intruding.'

'I'm afraid she'll never overcome the appalling things that happened to her, after the fall of Plataea.'

'Living a secluded life on Mesembria is one thing, but you will all be starting a new life soon with growing prospects and especially now her cousin's boy is your legitimate heir. If only for the sake of propriety, ask her again, Theo.'

'I will, uncle.'

Saying goodbye to helmsman Glaucus and the actors Leon and Panthas, was an emotional occasion for both Stephanos and Theomenes, and firm promises were made to meet up again at the Great Dionysia, in the following spring.

'Perhaps we'll see the return of our friend, Clytes!' Panthas had suggested, hopefully.

At the Piraeus, emotions also ran high, when the time finally came for Akaterina and her son to board their ship and to take their leave of Aspasia. It was not the leaving any of them had envisaged. Plataea was not that far away and regular visits would have been possible, but the distance between Athens and Scione meant contact would be infrequent between their two families, and young Akylas was bereft. Aspasia was like a second mother to him, and he'd thrived under her tutelage. Travelling with them was Akaterina's new husband; a marriage long delayed due to the unexpected defeat in Boeotia, when all hopes were dashed of returning home, but finally arranged with Aspasia's help. Although good friends, the two women were entirely different in character. Whereas Aspasia was a woman of exceptional intellect, wise in the ways of the world and able to thrive in the predominately male domain of philosophy and learning, Akaterina was conscious of being a figurehead for her overthrown city-state, and that it was expected of her to adhere to local custom. In selecting a consort, therefore, her choice had been limited to someone from her late husband's family. Initially, there'd been five individuals worthy of consideration, but eventually, after a long process of elimination, Sebastianos was chosen, the forty-three-year-old cousin of Phalinus; a childless widower and only surviving son of Ektor. Seriously wounded in the Theban attack on their city, he'd been evacuated to Athens before the siege, together with others who were deemed unfit for action, but his subsequent bravery as a member of The Shield Company, when he'd given support to his uncle, Androdamos, until his untimely death, had since made him a hero in the eyes of his fellow countrymen. But not in the eyes of Akylas, unfortunately. To the thirteen-year-old, he was too serious-minded and too slight of stature to ever replace his illustrious father. The last memory he had of him was from the age of three, riding on his broad shoulders during the spring festival which had brought about his tragic death. He remembered the scented flowers being thrown and some settling into his father's wheat coloured hair - the rapturous cheering - the beaming faces as he was proudly carried through the streets of Plataea. He felt so special - so loved. Alcibiades understood. The man had actually wept on saying goodbye to his 'golden angel' - and had promised to write.

The ships bringing the anxious Plataeans to the most western of the three fingers of the Chalcidice peninsular, carried all the precious belongings they possessed. Situated prominently on the summit of a steep south-facing hill, on the southernmost tip of the Pallene headland, Scione looked down the length of the Aegean Sea, where on myriad, busy waterways, ships of all sizes carried every kind of trade goods imaginable. Steering their way through the crisscrossing streams of traffic, they finally caught sight of the city which was to be their new home. Throughout the summer, teams of builders had been making the city habitable after the siege, ready for the new occupants, but many were seeing the city for the first time. With initial fears allayed and spirits uplifted, eager shouts could be heard coming from the men on the upper rowing deck and also from some of the women who were leaning precariously over the guardrails.

'Look at those shoals!' one man was heard to shout. 'These waters are teaming! I'm going to get myself a fishing boat.'

'You? A fisherman?' responded his rowing companion, laughing good-humouredly. 'Your mother told my wife that you have such an aversion to getting wet, she has to throw a bucket of water over you when you sleep!'

But the enthusiasm to start anew, was infectious.

'Olive groves!' cried an ancient, as they drew closer to the shore. 'Just like my old farm at Plataea.'

Luscinia, wife of shoemaker Kalos, who'd initially been apprehensive about the move, pointed out the abundance of fruit trees. 'I'll be able to keep bees again!' she shouted, excitedly. 'It is good to be out of that stinking city.'

The reason why Scione had become available to them quickly dwindled in the minds of the Plataeans, the war and the plague having numbed them to other people's misfortunes. Never having fully accepted life in the overcrowded metropolis, they were now determined to make the most of their comparative freedom, and the new opportunities opening up to them.

According to order of status, as had been accepted back in their home city, the Plataeans settled themselves into their new accommodation. Relatives of the late Phalinus and of their deceased commander Eupompides, were allocated the higher most villas, as was Theomenes for his family. Stephanos and Micca were delighted with the house they were provided with, being two-storey with a small walled courtyard and a roof terrace overlooking the sea, whereas Pyrus the archer and others of his standing, rented the smaller, huddled houses at the base of the hill, but still within the city's fortifications. Autumn was arriving and they looked forward to gathering in their first harvests; preparing for their first winter on the headland and making plans for the future.

With his villa now fully furnished and ready for occupation, Theomenes deemed the time was right to bring Amara and her household to Scione, before the seas were closed to traffic for the winter. For over four years, Theomenes' responsibilities had been split between his duties in Athens and his care of Amara and her household. Now, with a permanent home and prospects for every Plataean to make a good living, it was time to introduce Agapetos, who was getting close to his fourth birthday, to the countrymen and women of the boy's late mother, Marissa. He also decided to take his uncle's advice and to ask Amara, again, to marry him, even though he was painfully aware that any intimacy between them remained unlikely.

THIRTY-SEVEN

THE INITIAL EXCITEMENT AT leaving Athens and farming their own land again, soon turned to anxiety for the Plataeans, when due to an uncommonly long period of low rainfall and cool temperatures, they found the usually fertile land around Scione had become parched and dry. Manual watering had not been carried out by the previous inhabitants due to the two-year siege and their subsequent brutal treatment by the Athenians, consequently the fruit trees they'd come to harvest had borne poor crops which dropped too early. Even the olive trees had suffered. Heading into their first winter the storage sheds held less than expected, and three families of cheese makers, who'd been earning a good living in Athens, decided to go back there - never to return.

Living on such an exposed headland posed a security problem the Plataeans were unused to, and as they weren't the only ones suffering from a poor harvest, opportunist piracy became rife along the coast that winter as desperation forced people onto the water. When an unguarded warehouse situated just inside the city walls was raided, they realised they must adapt quickly to their new environment or starve.

Seven miles away along the coast, the city of Mende, which had also tried to break away from Athenian domination at the same time as Scione but changed its mind in time to be spared the Scionians' fate, had also been attacked, by a band of sea-robbers prepared to brave the winter swells, and all along the coast, towns which were not as defensively fortunate as Scione suffered a similar fate. A combined party of anxious citizens travelled to Potidaea to ask the garrison commander for assistance, but he refused to send out ships in adverse weather just to apprehend petty thieves, and they were sent away disappointed. Although the Plataeans were initially unwelcome in the area, their reputation for being worthy fighters overcame the reticence of their neighbours, and very soon aggrieved men from various towns on the peninsular began arriving at the gates of Scione, seeking their help.

Stephanos sympathised with them regarding the Athenian garrison. 'Don't hold your breath waiting for help from that quarter,' he told them, advisedly. 'We made that mistake.'

'Bad weather will drive them back to their own shores, soon,' spoke up Sebastianos. 'We're not seafarers. What help could we provide?'

The Mendean spokesman, by the name of Diondas, sensing their reticence, argued, 'You're safe behind your newly restored walls, but some of the other towns are not so well defended. We are all suffering reduced crops this year. The grape harvest has been devastated. We can't afford to lose a bean to these bastards! Are you with us or not?'

Stephanos and Sebastianos, moved by their plight, decided to talk it over with the rest of their fellows. If the Athenian garrison at Potidaea would not come to their aid, then the men of the Pallene had to protect the promontory themselves, and like it or not, they were now part of their community. Realising they had an obligation to help in any way they could, Stephanos returned quickly with an answer. 'We're with you,' he told Diondas, 'but we'll need to meet with representatives of the other towns affected. We need to discuss our strategy.'

'There's no guarantee they'll *all* agree,' the Mendean answered, hesitantly. 'Some are suspicious of you 'interlopers'.'

Curiosity, if nothing else, brought local leaders to the table. The heroic tale of retrieving the famed Plataean relic had grown with the passing years and to meet with some of the actual personages involved was draw enough.

The raiders, the Plataeans discovered, had crossed the Thermaic Gulf from mainland Macedonia, avoiding Potidaea to target southern towns on the peninsula's western most promontory. What hadn't been discovered was where they must be hiding in the region between raids, and treachery was suspected.

'Simmias can't be trusted!' spoke up a heavily bearded carpenter from Aege. 'And he hasn't come to the meeting.'

'He's weak and influenced by his son. A no-good son of a bitch!' answered Diondas, and others complained vehemently in agreement. 'If we're looking for where these bastards could be hiding, then my bet's on him!'

'Where is his place?' asked Theomenes.

'The other side of the peninsular. There's a salt-water lagoon with a narrow passage to the sea. It's surrounded by pine-forest. A perfect hideaway.'

'Then that's where we look first. But no hasty judgements.'

The following day, events took a turn for the worst for Theomenes and his initial request for caution changed to one for immediate action.

'Have you seen Amara and Mydon?' he asked Admetus, anxiously.'

'They went for a walk along the beach this morning, with Agapetos,' the old man answered. 'But they should be back by now.' When he saw the colour drain from Theomenes' face, he added quickly. 'I'll come with you!'

They found the mule, Cyclops, standing alone on the strand, his big white hide was smeared with blood. He was staring out to sea and visibly trembling.

Theomenes fell to his knees and cried out in a rage. 'They've taken them Admetus! They were safe on Mesembria. I should never have brought them here!'

Admetus placed both his hands on Theomenes' shoulders. 'They're alive, Theo. They wouldn't take dead bodies......and they won't want extra mouths to feed at a time like this. They'll want ransoms,' he said, reassuringly. 'All we can do is wait, my boy. I don't think it will be long.'

'Amara has been so well, Admetus. This will break her, surely!'

When word spread of the abductions, Theomenes was persuaded to believe that the kidnappers were still on the promontory. 'The winds have been too strong for a boat to get back to the mainland,' Diondas assured him. 'They have to be holed up here, somewhere.'

'Well, I don't want to wait for a ransom demand!' declared Theomenes, angrily. 'I say we pay this Simmias a visit. At the very least, he may know something.'

'We'll show you the way, willingly,' the Mendean replied. 'It would be good to see him put in his place......and that son of his!'

As soon as enough men, twenty in all, were equipped and ready to march, they set off through the dense pine forest and over the ridge, the backbone which ran the length of the Pallene, until they could see the eastern coast stretched out before them, and in the distance, the marble peak of Mount Athos rising from the sea. Diondas guided them south, following meandering goat tracks down the hillside, until they looked down on a large settlement situated by the side of a lagoon.

'What did I tell you! They don't look like local fishing boats to me,' he said, pointing at a number of sizeable vessels moored in the inlet. 'Well, they're ours now. I'll send one of the men to Aege, just along the coast. They'll bring what boats they can to block the inlet. Which one of you is the fastest runner?' he asked, turning to his fellow Mendeans, and a young man by the name of Sanes volunteered for the task.

'Tell them to come quickly!' said Diondas, as Sanes handed him his spear. 'You can count on me!' he replied, eagerly, before speeding off through the trees.

'I'm immensely grateful to you, Diondas,' spoke up Theomenes, 'in bringing us this far, but I don't expect anything more from you or your men in regard to the captured Plataeans. That is up to us,' and he looked around at Stephanos and the other armed men who'd come with him.

The Mendean looked astonished. 'You're not leaving us out of this! We all have grievances with Simmias. If the woman and child are here, then you can count on our full support.' The others nodded in full agreement. Theomenes grasped Diondas' hands, gratefully, then signalling for the men to follow him, they moved silently through the trees until they reached the animal pens at the edge of the town. Everything seemed eerily quiet, and their presence went undetected until they finally arrived at a scene which stopped them in their tracks. Surrounding a low roofed building near the marketplace, seemed to be every member of the community, all watching intently as a man crawled carefully along the roof.

Their sudden appearance caused panic in the crowd, and as every man seemed to be equipped with a weapon, they were drawn in an instant.

Diondas immediately called out to them. 'We want to speak with Simmias! There are more of us waiting in the trees,' he lied, 'so I don't advise any heroics.'

A man of mature years stepped from the crowd and came forward. 'Diondas? What's all this?'

'We've seen the ships, Simmias, so it will do no good to lie.'

'It's been a bad year, Diondas!' he pleaded.

'It's been bad for all of us! Where's Bojan?'

The man nodded in the direction of the surrounded building. 'In there!'

'What's going on?'

'My boy's being held hostage. I don't even know if he's alive or dead!' the old man exclaimed, and he signalled to the man on the roof to come down. 'He's my only son, Diondas.'

'Yes, and you've been far too lenient with him. He's a menace! You'd better tell us what's happening.'

'Bojan went out with one of the boats from the mainland...... just to see what they could find,' he said, shrugging guiltily. 'He came back with a woman and her child. I told him it would bring trouble!'

'Amara!' exclaimed Theomenes. 'Where's the woman?' he shouted.

'In there!'

'The boy?'

'In there too......and the lame one who was with them. Her brother?'

Before anyone could stop him, Theomenes pushed his way through the crowd, with Simmias following closely behind, the old man ordering the people to let them through.

'Mydon! Are you in there?' yelled Theomenes, hammering on the door. 'It's Theo! Open the door, Mydon. It's me!'

After an anxious wait, Mydon's distressed voice came back. 'I don't trust them, Theo!'

'I've come with support, Mydon. Is Amara alright?' he asked urgently.

A wooden bar could be heard slowly being dragged aside, and the heavy door suddenly swung open. Theomenes rushed inside, together with Simmias and some of the men from the village who'd forced their way through the doorway with him.

When Simmias saw the splattered blood, he immediately cried out, 'What have you done to my boy?!'

'Don't let them come any further, Theo!' Mydon, shouted. He was lying on a pallet, with one arm bound in a bloody rag, and what looked like a dead man was lying on the floor at his feet. Mydon's heavy leather boot was pressing down on the man's throat. 'He's not dead, but get them out of here, or I'll willingly break his neck!'

'He means it, Simmias,' said Theomenes, forcefully, as the distraught father tried to reach his son. 'If you want your son back alive, you'd better leave this to me.'

The men reluctantly backed away, encouraging their leader to go with them, and Theomenes quickly barricaded the door again. Amara was standing behind the door, her hands covered in blood. He hardly recognised her. He went to console her, but she quickly moved away from him, going instead to what looked like a bundle of clothes in the corner. It was when Theomenes saw the second body. The man had been castrated.

'Oh God!' he groaned, horrified, when he realised the blood on Amara's hands was not her own. 'Did you do this? I'm so sorry! I should have protected you! Is Agapetos safe?'

When he got no response, he turned to Mydon, and indicating the man at his feet, asked urgently, 'Tell me this is Simmias' son, and not the other one?!'

'He's our way out of here,' answered Mydon, grimly, 'otherwise I would have let Amara deal with him too!'

Theomenes spun around to look at Amara, hoping to give her some support, but was immediately struck by her chillingly calm demeanour. The bundle in the corner was her own cloak which she'd wrapped tightly around Agapetos to keep him from witnessing the dreadful scenes that had taken place, and after carefully wiping the blood from her hands, she began comforting the boy, smoothing his hair gently and talking to him calmly.

'Is he alright?' asked Theomenes, again. Amara stared directly at him, and a cold shiver ran down his spine at her strange look. 'You are Nicander's son,' she murmured to the boy. 'A Spartan's son. You are not afraid of anything!' Theomenes felt he was being deliberately shut out.

'We need to start negotiating,' he said, turning again to Mydon, 'while there's still something to barter with. I want to kill him, but, unfortunately, we need him. Are you sure he's still alive?'

'He's alive......just.'

'He doesn't look in such good shape to me,' admitted Theomenes, then he shouted for Stephanos and Diondas to come to the door, relating to them the situation and telling them to find and secure the stolen produce - and quickly.

'You heard the man!' said Stephanos turning to Simmias. 'Take us to where you've hidden the stores, and no tricks......then maybe you'll get your son back......intact!'

Word soon spread throughout the Pallene about the successful return of their precious harvest and in particular the Plataeans' part in it, and they were feted and praised for their efforts. For Theomenes, however, the elation at having rescued his family was to be short lived.

'I've decided to take Agapetos back to his homeland, Theo,' said Amara to him one day, soon after their return to Scione. 'I hope you won't stop me.'

'Homeland? What homeland? Plataea?'

'Sparta, Theo.'

'You can't! It's not what your cousin wanted!'

'Marissa gave birth to a daughter in Sparta. Agapetos has a sister there. He has family there. Nicander's family.'

'I've made him my heir! If you want him to have a sibling, we could give him one......you and I!'

'Oh Theo, please don't ask me again to marry you. I live only for Agapetos and the boy needs to know his family. What future can we Plataeans offer him now? We are stateless wanderers!'

'He'll be taken from you. He'll be made to attend the agoge.'

'He's Nicander's son, Theo. It's his birth-right.'

'Is this because I wasn't there for you? Is this my punishment?'

'You can't wrap me in wool, Theo. My mind became clear in that room. I defended myself and Agapetos......and Mydon also. Me!'

'It is because I wasn't there!'

'I want Agapetos to reach his full potential. I want him to grow up strong......and never to be afraid.'

'I don't want you to go.'

'I've made up my mind. Please allow me to do this. There is peace now with Sparta. As soon as the seas are open again, unless you stop me, I will be leaving Scione for Sparta.'

'I'm coming with you!'

'Mydon will go with me.'

'You've discussed this with Mydon......before me?'

'Mydon is a free man, Theo.'

'He has responsibilities here. My uncle's investments need him.'

'Hypatos has put you in charge now. There's still plenty of time for Mydon to transfer all that's necessary into your name. I thought it was fair to let you know my decision as soon as possible.'

'I should never have brought you here. You were doing so well on the island. I've let you down.'

'Times change. I've changed.'

'You're not leaving. I intend to make a good life for us here. I'll stop your allowance!'

'I have the gold jewellery that Imbros left for me, from his work on the Acropolis, and Mydon, thanks to you and your uncle, has savings.

'Will you come back when the boy takes up his education?'

'What the future holds for me, I cannot see. I just know that this is the right thing for Agapetos.'

From Stephanos, Theomenes received little comfort.

'I did everything I could to make her and the boy feel safe.'

'No-one could have done more.'

'She was happy, until this happened. I'll kill that Bojan the first chance I get!'

'From what I've heard, you're not alone in that regard.'

'I've spoken at length with Mydon. He received his wound trying to fight off the robbers on the beach, and he believes they would have killed him, there and then, if it hadn't been for Amara's quick thinking. She told them he was her brother, and a ransom would be paid. He was frantic when he realized Bojan and his accomplice were intent on raping Amara in front of the child. He hadn't the strength to take them both on, but he says Amara was magnificent; terrifying, even!'

'Ha! They wouldn't have known what hit them!' laughed Stephanos, harshly. 'The bastards thought they'd captured a submissive well-bred lady and a defenceless cripple. How wrong could they be?!'

'Well, Mydon now says that if Amara wants to go to Sparta, he wants to accompany her.'

'In Agapetos' case, I think she's right. Many wealthy families send their sons to Sparta for education. Plataeans are dispersing, Theo. We're giving up on the hope of ever returning to our birthplace.'

'I never thought I would hear that from you, Stephanos!'

'I'm being realistic......for once.'

'You have your family. A fine boy......and now another child on the way. If Amara and Agapetos go......and Mydon also, I'll be left with Admetus and Cyclops!'

Stephanos let out a chuckle which Theomenes took in good part, and he even laughed himself, although half-heartedly.

'Will you let her go?'

'What happened with those bastards has certainly hardened her thinking. She's very determined.'

'Now *you're* being realistic.'

'What can I do, Stephanos? As a friend, advise me.'

'You could humour her? She's been through a terrifying ordeal, bringing back all that happened before. She's hurt and angry and she's taking it out on you, naturally.'

'You think I should pretend to approve her decision, then maybe she will calm down and change her mind?'

'Well, fighting and arguing with her hasn't worked.'

Stephanos' advice, although well intentioned, had no effect whatsoever on Amara's decision, and late the following spring, she and her entourage set sail for Sparta.

'Thanks to your advice, Stephanos, I've now committed myself to funding the child's education!' said Theomenes, in feigned disgust, as he stood between his friend and Admetus watching the rise and fall of the oars taking his family on their long journey to the Peloponnese. After a period of silence between them, while the heavy-hearted trio waved continuously until the ship was out of sight, he suddenly said determinedly, 'I've always wanted to see Sparta. If there's any hint in Mydon's messages, that things are not turning out the way Amara had hoped......'

Admetus was inspired by the idea. 'I just might come with you. It would be useful research for my 'Histories'!'

Also watching the ship leave were other members of the Plataean fraternity, including Sebastianos and his recently adopted son, Akylas. It had become evident to those who cared about the family that the pair were not bonding as well as Akaterina had hoped, and an argument between them could clearly be heard.

'I want to stay with Theomenes!' the boy was shouting. 'I don't want to go yet. I'm fourteen! You treat me like a child!'

'You're due at the running track. Your trainer will be waiting for you.'

'You can't tell me what to *do*!' answered Akylas, deliberately shouting in order to gain Theomenes' attention.

'You will go when I say so,' Sebastianos responded, firmly.

'I hate you!' shouted Akylas. 'Alcibiades says you're a nobody!'

The harsh slap was heard by everyone there and an audible gasp rose up in response. Some felt sorry for Akylas, son of Phalinus and their 'golden boy' - a living link to their more glorious past when Plataeans had fought and won at Marathon. Others felt sympathy for Sebastianos, someone who would never receive the love and respect that had been showered upon their brutally murdered Shield Guardian.

'Alcibiades has poisoned the boy's mind against Sebastianos,' remarked Admetus, sadly. 'A cruel thing to do in my opinion.'

Not wanting to interfere in what was a personal family matter, people began to disperse, and Theomenes, seeing how uncomfortable Sebastianos' looked, went quickly to thank him for coming to say goodbye to Amara and Agapetos.

'My, how you've grown!' he said, turning to look at a flushed and noticeably angry Akylas. 'You're quite the young man now and a credit to your mother.'

Theomenes took Sebastianos by the hand, squeezing it firmly. 'I would take it as an honour if you would call at my house soon. We could reminisce about when you and I charged those Persian hordes and Stephanos was jealous because your tally was higher than his!'

'Ha! I remember! He wanted to claim that crazed Scythian as *his* killing.'

'The one with that stinking cloak of flayed skins? No, it was definitely your sword that took off his head. Do you still have that monstrous curved blade?'

'I do!'

'I'd like to see it again. Does it still have the blood?'

'Sadly not.'

'What was your head count......I forget?'

'Sixteen!'

'Sixteen, to my mere twelve. Well, I look forward to your visit, Sebastianos. Don't forget to bring the sword!'

'Please give your mother my regards,' he said kindly to Akylas. 'I know she will miss Amara's company almost as much as I will.'

Akylas, now looking paler, answered politely, 'I'll give her your message, sir. Thank you.'

As Sebastianos and Akylas set off quietly, Stephanos and Admetus agreed to accompany Theomenes back to his grand villa on the hill.'

'That was a fine thing you did, Theo,' remarked Admetus. 'The boy doesn't appreciate how hard Sebastianos is trying to be a good father to him.'

'He spent too much time with Alcibiades to appreciate the decent qualities in *any* man!' Stephanos added, hotly. 'Does he still send letters to the boy?'

'He does,' replied Theomenes. 'Presents too, so Amara told me. Akaterina is not happy about it, naturally.'

'It's a good thing he's far away from that man's influence!' Admetus commented, with feeling.

After months of having Amara and Agapetos living at the villa, immediately upon entering, the friends were struck at how depressingly silent and empty it now seemed.

THIRTY-EIGHT

A S PART OF THE Peace Treaty, Boeotia was required to return all prisoners taken in recent conflicts, and this included those captured during the Battle of Delium, four years previously. Some of the more troublesome individuals, who'd been made captive when the Temple of Apollo was retaken, had been sent to the same iron ore mine where Angelos was still enslaved, and news of the releases soon spread throughout the site. Many of the prisoners of war were in a wretched state, and one man fell on his knees and sobbed in front of his interrogator, so thankful was he to be recognised as the person entered on the papyrus scroll. One by one, as their names and histories were checked against the records, men had their head collars removed and were able to leave the brutal conditions they'd endured since their failed attempt to subdue Boeotia. As Angelos became aware of these events, his mind was thrown into turmoil. He'd fought at Delium. His name should be on the list. But he'd not spoken in all the time he'd been at the mines, and he sought desperately to think of a way to make the envoys, who'd been sent from Athens, aware of his plight.

The released prisoners were considered too weak to begin their journey back to Athens immediately and were allowed time to regain their strength, and during the days the envoys waited for their comrades to recover sufficiently, Angelos anguished over the fact that he must be included in the recorded details of men either captured or missing. Resigned for a long time to the fact that there was no means of escape from the mines, he was now afraid he would miss this unique opportunity to be set free. Early one morning while being prodded to his allotted workplace, he seized his opportunity when he saw one of the envoys leave his tent to hail the attention of Gamunk, the site-manager. Ever since he'd heard of the arrival of the envoys, whenever he'd been unobserved, Angelos had croakingly exercised his vocal cords and with great effort he shouted out in a rasping voice, 'Long live Athens! Long live Athens! Long live Athens!' He was hit forcibly by a guard, and he fell to the ground. Curling into a ball to avoid being kicked, he continued to shout, hoping the Athenian would hear him. The figures of Gamunk and the envoy suddenly loomed over him.

'What's all the commotion?' Gamunk demanded.

'Delium! Prisoner!' rasped Angelos.

The envoy looked down at him with keen interest.

'Don't let him fool you,' barked Gamunk. 'They'll tell any tale to get out of here.'

'Name? asked the envoy, unfurling his document.

'Angelos.'

'Father?'

'Voukolos.'

'Birthplace?'

'Plataea. Farm. Asopus.'

'I have no-one of that name, written here.'

'Plataea! Phalinus! Shield Guardian!' Angelos croaked, desperately.

'You're not on my list,' repeated the Athenian, shaking his head. 'But he was intrigued by the mention of the famous shield and decided to check the records of *all* the prisoners being returned to Athens.

'He's a madman,' insisted the site manager, angrily, when the envoy returned with more scrolls. 'He's never been right in the head. It's the first time I've heard the bastard speak!'

'He's not mad to want to be out of this place,' remarked the envoy, looking sympathetically at Angelos' overworked scarred body.

As every list was carefully checked, Angelos waited anxiously, but the result wasn't what he expected.

'There's no Angelos of Plataea mentioned amongst the prisoners to be released into my care, not from any part of Boeotia. Nor is any such person mentioned among the missing.'

'You have all the men you're entitled to take from me......apart from the two that unfortunately didn't survive. Whether they're able to walk or not, I want you all off my site today,' said Gamunk vehemently. 'You're unsettling my workforce.'

'Old women! Slave market!' croaked Angelos, in his last, urgent attempt to relate his story.

'I told you,' said Gamunk, smirking. 'Not right in the head.'

Angelos watched despairingly as the Athenian, after casting him a look of annoyance, strode off quickly to attend to his duties. Then Gamunk turned on him, laughing cruelly.

'Plataean, eh? Son of that troublemaker Voukolos? Well, whether you are or you aren't, you've just talked yourself into trouble. Assign him to the Plataean crew,' he barked to one of the guards. 'Give him half their normal rations until I tell you otherwise. He'll pay for trying to make a fool out of me!'

Gamunk was Thracian, and like many of his countrymen, his extensive knowledge of mine-working had secured him lucrative employment outside his home state, but he was well aware of how serious the consequences could be for him if he didn't follow his Boeotian employers' orders, particularly in relation to any Plataeans falling into his hands. He'd killed more of their kind by overwork and starvation, than any other group, but their obstinance in not appearing sufficiently cowered, grated on him intensely, especially the unbreakable fortitude of their leader. Their resilience was making him look weak. As he watched Angelos being led away, he remembered being told an old saying about Plataeans being 'plucky', and it worried him that this 'pluckiness' could bring about his own downfall.

If Angelos thought he would be made welcome by his fellow countrymen, he was mistaken. They were unusually suspicious when he was suddenly thrust into their midst, and he overheard the broad-shouldered individual with the scarred back; the man he'd often seen being taken away for punishment, warn the crew to stay clear of him until he'd been questioned. Consequently, he was still treated as an outsider, and he slipped back into his silent, mute world; all burning questions relating to his father being suppressed for the time being.

The brutal treatment in 'the goat's' crew was nothing compared to the relentless cruelty meted out to the Plataeans. Twenty of his fellow countrymen worked the night shift in the deepest tunnel at the Hyettos mine, and after just one week labouring alongside them, Angelos didn't expect to live for much longer. On his second week on starvation rations, his gaunt features didn't stir when the guards unblocked the doors, flooding their dark, fetid quarters with flaring torchlight, as another night of torment commenced to the usual cacophony of barking dogs and men. It was when the Plataeans' attitude towards him, changed. Before the guards could become aware of his senseless state, their apparent leader caused such a disturbance, that by the time order was restored, Angelos had been shaken into wakefulness by his fellows. While he staggered with them to their allotted seam, he saw the outspoken Plataean being dragged off to receive yet another flogging.

To supplement Angelos' meagre rations that day, the rest of the team shared a portion of the very little they had, and when their leader returned from his punishment, Angelos was coherent enough to answer the man's initial questioning. Bleeding welts on the Plataean's broad back told the story of his recent beating, adding yet more livid scars to his already tortured flesh, but despite being in pain, the man was thorough. By the time the interrogation was over, which was spread over the following days, Angelos had almost fully regained his voice. It was the telling of his exploits with Theomenes of Hysiae, in returning the Marathon shield, that finally won the Plataeans over. Especially their leader. His name was Iairos, or Strong-Arm, as he was known to his fellows, due to his past skills with the javelin. He knew the family of Theomenes well and sorely wished he'd been involved in his adventures.

'How long have you been here?' Angelos queried, finally turning the tables in asking the questions.

'Six years. Since the escape from Plataea during the siege.'

'Do you know anything about my father, Voukolos?'

'He was here. We tried to escape together but were caught. It wasn't my first attempt, hence the brand on my forehead. He didn't survive the punishment. He died......about three years ago. I'm sorry.'

'He was here? Oh God! And I didn't know. I could have been with him. I could have saved him!'

'He wasn't a physically strong man, Angelos. He would have died in this miserable place......one way or another.'

'I'm ashamed. My stubbornness stopped us from being reunited.'

'It would have given him no joy to see you here. He assumed that after the Thebans captured him, you'd all sought protection behind Plataea's walls. To hear of his mother's killing and what happened to your brother and sister would have only brought him more grief.'

'How have *you* survived? How do you keep going?'

'Hatred. Also hope.'

'Hope? Hope of what?'

'There's always hope.'

Gradually, Angelos was introduced to the rest of the gang; men who'd farmed close to the Boeotian border and were captured like his father; two friends of Iairos who'd escaped with him at the break-out from Plataea, and stories from the others told of each unfortunate circumstance which had led to them being at the mine. When he finally recognised someone or remembered the man's family, he felt ashamed of the wasted years he'd stubbornly kept his distance, but the men seemed to bear no grudges, such was the understanding they all had of the need to survive.

It was another week before Iairos felt confident enough to show Angelos the tunnel.

'It was your father's idea, but it was taking too long to dig, and his health finally gave out. The main tunnel runs deep and has poor air. Only Plataeans are made to work this seam at night, so we've managed to keep it secret.'

Angelos looked into the blackness of a narrow burrow, just large enough to crawl into, and revealed only when a slab of limestone which blended seamlessly into the tunnel wall, was removed. 'If you hadn't shown me, I'd never have known it was there. Where does it go?'

'West. The worked tunnel goes north, into the hillside, following the iron ore. Voukolos reasoned that if searches were made, they'd concentrate on the eastern side......coastward. He was right. They've never thought to look for escape attempts going further inland. The day shift is worked by wretched individuals, near the end of their working lives. They're too far gone to think of escaping. They'd never find it.'

'How long have you been digging?'

'Five years.'

'Five years?!'

'Keep your voice down. Sound travels along these tunnels.'

'But I could have been helping.'

'Your father didn't escape by it Angelos, but if the gods have mercy, then you will.'

'I owe my father that. You can count on my efforts, Iairos.'

'We'd welcome your help. We've lost three men this year. Gamunk intends to work us all to death......in his own sadistic time!'

A whistling signal from a member of their gang made the Plataeans hurriedly replace the boulder, just before the strident shouting from an overseer, accompanied by the sound of a cracking whip, came down the tunnel. Miciadas was a free-born Theban, and the chief supervisor charged with controlling the Plataean workforce, and he didn't hold back in causing misery at every opportunity.

'What are you arse-holes doing down there? What's the fucking hold-up?!'

Iairos placed his hand on Angelos' shoulder and quietly murmured, 'All of the supervisors hate our guts but watch out for this one. He's a particularly mean bastard!'

CHAPTER THIRTY-NINE

With those few words, Angelos finally felt he'd been accepted.

It soon became apparent to him how they'd managed to keep the tunnel hidden. The Plataeans trusted no-one and that included the knowledgeable slave inspectors who carried out regular surveys of the quality of the rock, before choosing where it was worthy of extraction. At least they didn't stay long, so bad was the air. They were a group apart, having no dealings with any of the other gangs and suffered their deprivations stoically. Iairos was able to coach Angelos on how best to bear the lashings which were meted out to him on the least excuse, since Gamunk had become aware of his background, and as with Iairos, each beating only fuelled his hatred and his determination to stay alive. The escape tunnel was progressing, giving the Plataeans hope, and like the metal they helped to forge, the beatings only made their spirit more resilient.

THIRTY-NINE

THE PLATAEANS COULDN'T QUITE believe Euthymios when he crawled out backwards from the narrow escape tunnel, and whispered, ecstatically, 'There's a cave!'

'What could you see?!'

'Starlight!'

'Is it flooded?'

'No. Stalacites are hanging from the roof, but it looks completely dry. We've done it, Iairos. We've made it!'

As soon as the opportunity arose, early one morning near the end of their shift, Iairos went quickly to check out Euthymios' findings. He came back elated.

'You can't see the mine from the cave exit. It's perfect.'

Over the following days their plan of escape was honed, until every man knew just what to do, and Iairos watched his men keenly, checking for any change in demeanor that could give unwanted indications to the guards of their altered circumstances. They chose a night with a good moon having decided to make a break for it at the beginning of their night shift, while tools were still sharp, oil lamps were full and wine and water carriers recently replenished.

'We're not going without you, Iairos!'

'Angelos, look at my back. Look at my forehead! I'd be caught as a fugitive and sent back in no time. Go! Go now! Before you put everyone's life in danger.'

The rest of the Plataeans, nineteen in all, had already crawled their way down the tunnel, ushered on urgently by Iairos. Now it was Angelos' turn.

'Not without you!'

'For your father's sake.'

'You're coming too.'

'Who will block the entrance?!'

The two men, the last to leave, had struggled to rest the stone slab in the opening while trying to squeeze past it into the tunnel, but it had proved to be impossible.

'We lift it from the inside,' insisted Angelos, desperately, but this too defeated them.

'It can't be done, Angelos. It will be discovered and all our efforts will have been in vain. Go! Let me do this. Think of the others, man!'

Before Angelos could protest further, Iairos had leaped from the tunnel, and it was plunged into darkness as he heaved the stone into place. That was the last Angelos saw of him - grim-faced and resolute.

With the aid of his oil lamp, Iairos checked every edge of the stone slab, and satisfied that it couldn't be detected, he proceeded further into the hillside, following the main tunnel. The flame dimmed dramatically due to the poor air, but his eyes had become accustomed to darkness, and he could see well enough for his purpose. He quickly felt the slender stone pillars which had been left unworked to support the roof and taking the tools from his belt he began to hack at their weakest points. Dust and rubble fell all about him, but he kept on pounding until the columns shattered and a large ceiling slab crashed to the ground. It was followed by others. Then he ran for his life, meeting the overseer, Miciadas, coming down the tunnel towards him.

'What the fuck's going on, scum?' the man yelled.

'Retribution arsehole!' shouted Iairos, and before the Theban knew what was happening, he staggered backwards against the wall, struck by a hammer blow from Iairos.

'You'll all die for this!' screamed the Theban, clutching at his bleeding head.

'Your threats mean nothing now, you bastard! Oh, I've waited a long time for this. May your soul be forever tormented in Tartarus, for all the innocent men you've killed here!'

The rock fall grew heavier and Iairos left the Theban to his fate. He burst from the exit, surrounded by billowing clouds of dust, as roaring down the tunnel behind him came the sound of crashing stone.

'Where's Miciadas?' immediately asked one of the guards.

'He was just behind me!' Iairos answered innocently, and with feigned surprise, added, 'he must have got trapped!'

The remains of Miciadas were retrieved, but Gamunk refused to reopen the rest of the tunnel. It was too deep, he said, and the seam was running out anyway. 'The owners don't think it's worth risking any more lives......just to bring out the bodies of Plataeans,' he told Iairos, callously and with obvious satisfaction.

Iairos yelled at him and threatened to kill him, which he thought appropriate considering his men had supposedly been left to die in the rock fall. He was beaten for his colourful verbal lambasting, but not too severely. The Thracian's Plataean problem had been resolved, and for the time being he only had one to torment. He could afford to take his time in killing this one. Iairos had proven to be the toughest individual he'd ever had to deal with; the man appeared indestructible - but Gamunk knew that every man had his limit - and now he was alone.

Iairos was immediately assigned to 'the goat's' tunnel, where it was immediately apparent his arrival was not welcome. The last thing the crew leader wanted was this known troublemaker bringing them unwanted attention, and a clash of personalities was evident from the start. But Iairos's consuming thoughts were not about his difficulties in adapting to a new crew, or with Gamunk; they were with his fellow countrymen and their desperate flight to freedom. He also had hope. When helping in the retrieval of Miciadas' body, he was relieved to see that the escape tunnel had not been covered by the rock fall.

FORTY

THE PLATAEANS WERE DISTRAUGHT when Angelos related to them what had happened with Iairos and they began to panic, and even when Angelos explained that the tunnel would have been exposed without Iairos's sacrifice, it still took some time for them to calm down and focus. Finally, they accepted that they must stick to the plan, not just for their own sakes but his also, as they all believed he would be paying a heavy price for their escape. But first they had to be freed from their shackles. Each man had brought with him his tools and they began working on releasing each other's neck collars. For this purpose, the cave was ideal, being far from any habitation, and not one man left until they were all freed. Before setting off on their perilous journeys, the men gathered together and knelt in prayer. Firstly, to thank the almighty gods for granting them their freedom, and secondly, for the deities to protect Iairos, who had sacrificed everything for the love of his fellows - to give him the strength to endure Gamunk's inevitable punishment.

The men split up into ones and twos, and where necessary a stronger man supported a weaker one, believing that way at least, some would avoid recapture, and Angelos and Euthymios decided to team up together. They all knew the dangers, but after what they'd endured at the mines, they were resolute. The mountain range where the mine was situated was close to Boeotia's northern border with Locris and this was where Angelos and Euthymios decided to head for. They would hunt what they could and steal if an opportunity presented itself, but they swore they'd never put their trust in another living soul, unless it was a Plataean. As each man stood at the cave entrance, he looked to the heavens, then taking bearings from the starlit cosmos, one by one they vanished into the mountain vegetation, unaware that due to Iairos's quick thinking, no-one was looking for them.

FORTY-ONE

TO STOP HIMSELF CONSTANTLY thinking about Amara, Theomenes decided to seek ways of furthering his uncle's investments in the Thracian gold mines. It being an Olympic year meant transport and accommodation would be difficult to find as competitors and visitors from all points of the compass converged on Elis for the Games, but in the autumn, he finally took Hypatos' advice, and set off to find the exiled Athenian historian, and lately a strategos of Athens, Thucydides, who had mining rights in gold mines in the area. Admetus insisted on going with him, not wanting to miss the opportunity of meeting up with the great chronicler. They eventually tracked the man down, living in comfortable circumstances with his rich Thracian wife on their family estate, where their every need was catered for by a large number of household slaves.

Recently returned from the Games, Thucydides was delighted to have an audience to regale with his recent experiences, especially when he learned that the Plataeans had not attended due to being occupied with their move to Scione.

'You missed some drama! The Spartans were banned from entering. They'd marched their hoplites into Elis earlier in the year, in retaliation for its alliance with Argos......and then they refused to pay the fine for violating the Olympian truce! But the eminent spartiate, Lichas, was not to be deterred. He entered his chariot in the name of a Theban family, and it won, naturally.

Wanting to prove it was he and not the Boeotians who had the winning horses, he rushed onto the course and tied the victory ribbon on the charioteer, himself. He was arrested by the umpires and dragged away to be publicly flogged!'

'Lichas, flogged?' gasped Admetus.

'That would not have pleased the Spartans!' exclaimed Theomenes.

'We expected them to storm the Games at any moment! An armed guard had to be mobilised. It was all very tense, to say the least.'

Desirous of news from any quarter, the pair were welcomed as honoured guests at his lavish home, and long nights were spent in discussion, while the two historians exchanged their views on the state of affairs between Athens and Sparta. One person seemed to dominate the great chronicler's thoughts.

'Alcibiades will be a difficult man to control,' said Thucydides, shaking his head at memories of a man he considered too self-centred and vain to be a force for good. 'Peace does not sit well with such an individual.'

'He's a persuasive speaker, I believe,' said Admetus. 'He speaks well at the Ecclesia, apparently, but how could he not......being brought up in Aspasia's household.'

'He believes he wears the mantle of Pericles, but he is *not* the statesman his uncle was. He is exceedingly ambitious and knows no allegiance to anyone except himself. He has been made strategos, so I learned at the Games. He will want to strut on a far larger stage than the Ecclesia, believe me! Nicias will be no match for that man's deviousness.'

'We can only watch events and write down what we perceive,' replied the older man, sagely. 'Perhaps our words will be read by men when we are long gone and warn them of how nations can be too easily driven to war.'

'On that hopeful thought, Admetus, I think we should retire. The servants have fallen asleep. I have so enjoyed your company these past days. The details you have given me regarding the events at Plataea have been fascinating. The fact that the men took off one sandal so as not be bogged down in the mire......and the counting of the bricks to ensure the correct height for the ladders. Perhaps you could stay on here, while Theomenes busies himself with his uncle's interests? There is so much you could still tell me.'

'I would like that very much, but Theomenes is having some difficulty in obtaining a permit to mine here. 'We may be returning to Scione very soon.'

'You're a wily old fox!' laughed Thucydides. 'Alright then. In return for all you can tell me about the attack and siege of Plataea, and I want every detail mind, I will ask my wife's family to assist Theomenes in obtaining a contract. Do we have an agreement?'

'There is much to tell, you, Thucydides. Apart from my own experiences, I have taken notes from many eye-witnesses.'

'Good man! I can see I have a worthy rival in you, Admetus!'

Over the coming days, Plataea's chronicler unhurriedly released detailed information to his host, which was eagerly written down for posterity by Thucydides' scribes, and in return, Theomenes finally obtained what his uncle most desired; permission to open a gold mine.

'Have you ever been to a mine, Theomenes?' asked Thucydides, one day.

'Never. My uncle's assistant, Mydon, handled his affairs in Thrace......until the war ceased with Sparta. Now there is peace, apart from periodic garrison duty, I am redundant, so he has given me the task of developing his interests here.'

'I will take you to one. It will open your eyes as to the price being paid for our greed.'

The inspections were indeed a revelation to Theomenes, on seeing how readily the mine owners, without malice aforethought, worked men into an early grave. The prize was the gold and the workers merely the tools to extract it; to be casually discarded when no longer of use. He was relieved to finally sign the highly sought-after contract on behalf of his uncle; then leaving it to others to find a suitable seam to mine, the pair made arrangements to return to Scione before the weather worsened, making travel disagreeable.

'I look forward to seeing you and Admetus again soon, Theomenes. It has been an illuminating experience for me, to hear of how the Plataeans tried to defend their city.'

'Brave but futile!'

'I intend to put every detail told to me by Admetus, into my chronicles. They'll make engrossing reading!'

Later that day, on speaking with Admetus, Theomenes was interested to know just what the old man had told the attentive chronicler.

'Did you tell him everything?'

'I did not!' answered Admetus, indignantly. 'I am writing my own account of what happened. It is far more interesting than Thucydides' dry objective approach.'

'But that is how you like to record events.'

'Not since what happened during the attack. My writing is far more subjective now. I knew the people who died. I have copious notes taken from survivors. And I've followed your life, Theo,...... with interest.'

'I look forward to reading about it!'

'All in good time, my boy. A fitting chapter would be to visit Amara and Agapetos in Sparta. To see how their lives have moved on......in the peace.'

'I mentioned that very subject to Thucydides......about going to Sparta. Apparently, he wants to go there to continue his research and would like to accompany us.'

'Can't I be allowed to write anything, without having to share it with him?'

'I won't ask any more of you, old friend. We have what we came for. Well done, by the way......'wily old fox'!'

FORTY-TWO

A FTER A SUCCESSFUL BUSINESS venture in Thrace, Theomenes and Admetus finally returned to Scione in the late autumn to find the city in a state of rejoicing. Fifteen of the Plataeans who'd escaped from the Boeotian mines, having learned during their flight of the exodus of their countrymen from Athens, had, with luck and determination, successfully found their way to the Pallene peninsular, and one of them was Angelos. Emaciated and sickly, many were being cared for by their overjoyed relatives, but being without family, Angelos was recuperating with Stephanos and his wife Micca. On hearing the incredible news, Theomenes rushed to their accommodation, and immediately upon entering, Stephanos discreetly made his exit and shaking his head, concernedly, left him alone with Angelos so they could talk privately. Gradually, as an aged and worn Angelos, revealed what had happened to him since the disastrous battle at Delium, Theomenes became more and more agitated, especially as he'd recently witnessed the brutality of a working mine, and feeling enormous guilt at what Angelos must have endured, he burst out, 'But I thought you were dead! I paid for your funeral! Pyrus and I both thought you were dead. I would never have left you, otherwise,' he asserted. 'I think of you as a brother, Angelos! Tell me, what can I do to make amends? Anything! Just tell me.'

'I ask for only one thing from you,' replied Angelos, evenly. 'I've already related to Stephanos as to how we managed to escape. It was down to one man. He's most likely been killed for what he did, but if by some miracle he still lives, I want you to pay whatever price is demanded by the mine owners, to get him out of that place.'

'A Plataean? What's his name?'

'Iairos. Also known as 'Strong-Arm'. He served in the same unit with your brother, Alexeis.'

'Yes, Theo! I remember Strong-Arm!' exclaimed Stephanos, who'd been listening, anxiously by the doorway, and burst back into the room. 'It was partly down to his javelin throwing that I managed to get through the blockade. The man still lives!'

'If you can call it living,' said Angelos.

'I'll pay whatever it takes,' Theomenes agreed in earnest, 'as I would have done for you, Angelos......had I known. Now that hostilities have ceased with the Boeotians, I can leave for the Hyettos mines whenever you say.'

'Now, would not be soon enough.'

Theomenes understood that in order for Angelos to start forgiving him he must first bring Iairos safely home and having had only a few hours rest since journeying from Thrace, he was driven by guilt and remorse to set off the following morning for Boeotia, travelling with the only captain - in return for an inordinate fee - prepared to take his ship south in poor sailing conditions. Stephanos, Sebastianos and Pyrus, went with him, all praying that their heroic countryman was still alive.

The journey was plagued with difficulties, and as they entered the Euboean Straits, Theomenes instructed the captain to steer his ship for the nearest safe harbour. After experiencing the man's poor seamanship and the near loss of his vessel, he didn't trust him to negotiate the ship any further. With forty miles to travel on foot, it caused the foursome extreme anxiety at the thought that they may be too late - until, cold, dirty and weary, having taken little rest, they finally arrived at the mines.

Unconcerned as to how they must appear, Theomenes approached a man seemingly in some authority and immediately demanded to be taken to Gamunk, the site manager.

'He's not here.'

'Where is he? I need to speak with him, urgently.'

'You're out of luck. He's dead.'

'How?'

'Had his throat cut by the Thebans.'

'Well, in that case, I need to speak with his replacement.'

'That would be me, until the new man arrives from Thrace.'

'I'm here to secure the release of one of your workers. I'll make it worth your while.'

CHAPTER FORTY-TWO

'Which one?'

'Iairos, a Plataean. He's been here for years.'

'You're out of luck, again. He's not here, either.'

Theomenes feared the worst. 'Dead?' he asked faintly.

'He's the reason why Gamunk was executed. We had a tunnel collapse and the Plataean crew was believed to have been killed in the fall, but when that troublemaker, Iairos, went missing, a search was made. We found a tunnel near the seam where they'd been working. Must have taken them years to dig! The mine owners realised that every Plataean must have escaped, and Gamunk paid the price for his lack of diligence.'

'What are you saying? The Plataean, Iairos, has escaped?'

'Well, he's not here!'

'I will pay you well for him, in whatever state he's in. Even if he's at the point of death,' Theomenes pleaded. 'I will not hold you to account.'

'You must want him very badly, and I would willingly take up your offer, but, unfortunately for me, he's not here.'

Theomenes took some silver coins from a small pouch. 'Here, take this,' he proffered. 'I want to see the tunnel you speak of.'

'This is not my day. Soon after it was discovered, we fired it.'

'We're not leaving without him!' Theomenes, cried out in desperation.

Stephanos placed a calming hand on his shoulder. 'We have to believe him, Theo. Why would the man deny himself a small fortune? Even if he is afraid of the site owners, men lose their lives here every day. He could just tell them he'd died.'

'Do you all agree, then?' he asked the others. 'That Iairos has escaped?'

'What else can we think?' answered Pyrus.

'When we return to Scione, I propose we erect a statue to him,' suggested Sebastianos. 'The man deserves to be honoured.'

'I like that idea,' agreed Stephanos. I hope he lives to see it!'

'I don't think a statue will satisfy Angelos though,' said a dejected Theomenes.

FORTY-THREE

DESPITE FIERCE OPPOSITION TO the treaty, from factions in both Sparta and Athens, the two super-powers wished the peace to hold, and each continued to turn a blind eye to the other's acts of aggression, but after only one year, the fifty-year treaty was starting to fray.

Sparta, still desperate to get back Pylos, signed a peace agreement with the Boeotians, part of the terms being that Boeotia gave back to Athens the captured fort of Panactum which was on their shared border, in the hope that this would sufficiently placate the Athenians. The Boeotians did as they were asked and also returned all Athenian prisoners held on their soil, but to the consternation of the Spartans, the Boeotians, vindictively, first razed the fortress to the ground. The Athenians were furious at the destruction and about the treaty Sparta had signed with the Boeotians, which was strictly against the terms of their own peace treaty and refused to give back Pylos. A delegation from Sparta was sent immediately to Athens, to plead their cause.

They first met with the Senate, explaining that they'd come with full powers to arrange all unsettled disputes between them, and being men in favour of the peace treaty, they were able to convince the Senate, of Sparta's honourable intentions in going into the alliance with Boeotia. On hearing how well they were received, Alcibiades feared they would also persuade the people, who'd be gathered to hear them speak at the Assembly the following day. He seized his opportunity. Meeting with the Spartans in secret, he impressed them so greatly, he was able to trick them into renouncing their diplomatic powers and to allow him to speak to the people on their behalf. When they stated in front of the Assembly that they did not in fact have full authority, and that Alcibiades would, therefore, plead their cause, the people were outraged, the Senate felt they'd been lied to, as this was a direct contradiction to what they'd been told the day before, and Nicias, who'd worked hard to maintain the peace, was made to look a fool. Alcibiades, on the other hand, looked the hero of the hour for supposedly revealing Sparta's trickery, and soon after, on turning thirty, he was made a general.

With Sparta's allies in disarray, but still unable to actually form a league due to their own distrusts, Alcibiades urged Athens to create an alliance with democratic Argos - and with any other states in the Peloponnese willing to join with them. Since his success at throwing doubt on Sparta's trustworthiness at the Assembly, his plans to shatter Spartan dominance in the Peloponnese finally began to bear fruit. When Sparta refused to break its alliance with Boeotia, the Athenians felt betrayed, and with passions running high they took Alcibiades' advice and concluded an alliance with the democratic state of Argos, together with her allies, Elis and Mantinea.

Due to Alcibiades' persistence and cunning, Athens finally had a powerful foothold in the Peloponnese, and just as Brasidas had previously operated in Thrace, the glory-seeking general now set his sights on bringing more states over to his side. At the first opportunity, showing utter contempt for Sparta, he boldly marched into the peninsular at the head of an armed troop and passed here and there as he pleased, under the full protection of Argos and her allies. For a time, he was successful, and others joined the alliance, encouraged by promises from Alcibiades that the might of Athens' army would unite with them against Sparta. In Athens, however, Nicias thought Alcibiades' hostile manoeuvres under the noses of the Spartans could lead to the breakup of his hard-won peace treaty, and when Tegea, a powerful ally of Sparta and of strategic importance to the state, was threatened by Alcibiades, his fears became reality. If Tegea fell, the Spartans would be trapped within their home state and subjugation would soon follow. Feeling they'd been humiliated enough, Agis, son of the warrior king Archidamus, finally took decisive action and amassed the finest Hellenic army ever assembled in the war to that time. Athens was forced to make a decision; either to keep the peace with Sparta and therefore abandon Argos, Elis and Mantinea, or face the consequences of open war in a land battle in Sparta's own backyard. Persuaded by a confident Alcibiades, Athens, surprisingly, chose to stand by her newly acquired democratic allies, but due to caution shown by Nicias and Laches, who argued for a more defensive strategy - only up to a point.

The warring factions finally met at Mantinea, where the combined forces from Argos, Mantinea and Athens took up a strong defensive position on the ridge of a steep hill. Three thousand Eleans had intended to be there but were delayed by their attack on Lepreum, a contested border town with Sparta, intending to cause further harm to their powerful neighbour. When king Agis arrived at Mantinea, he initially ordered an attack on the hill, but realising it was unassailable, he immediately withdrew his men. This gave the impression to the democratic alliance that the king was unsure, and when they became aware that the Spartans were attempting to block the local waterways which could flood the territory of Mantinea, they confidently descended from the hill in full battle order, taking the Spartans by surprise. The shock to king Agis was only temporary, however, and he was quickly able to rally his disciplined troops. His tactics had worked. The enemy was now on the plain where he wanted them.

On the Argos side were eight thousand men, of which one thousand were hoplites from the Athenian alliance under Laches' command and three hundred cavalry commanded by general Nicostratus - all that Alcibiades could persuade Athens' generals to send. Acting as an advisor only on this occasion, having been denied a generalship due to opposition from Nicias and others of a less hawkish disposition, he continued to press his fellow countrymen to send more support.

On the Spartan side were nine thousand troops, which included three thousand five hundred Spartans, and such was the dire situation they felt they were in, never before had so many warriors from the incomparable spartiate class taken to the field together.

Watching these events from a safe distance, with a mixture of awe and trepidation, were Thucydides and Admetus, who were visiting the Peloponnese with Theomenes. Grouped together with other non-combatants who'd gathered to watch the events unfold, the two historians looked down from their high vantage point onto the gradually filling, Mantinean plain. Theomenes, who was in Sparta to persuade Amara to return to Scione, missed the opportunity to join his friends, having become embroiled in a prolonged argument with the family of six-year-old Agapetos.

'What a spectacle!' exclaimed Thucydides. 'Never in my life, have I seen so many Spartan elite lined up for battle. Brasidas' veterans are there too. They mean business!'

'I feel like a twelve-year-old boy again,' gushed Admetus, 'watching the Persians fight on the plains of Plataea. I've never forgotten that spectacle. But this is also something to behold!'

Tens of thousands of burnished shields and breast plates, in line after line, glinted in the sun before them and fiercely gripped spear shafts topped with lethal leaf-shaped blades, forested the plain. Dyed horsehair plumes created a sea of waving colour, and beneath the gleaming helmets, every spartiate's hair had been oiled and braided by his own personal helot. The onlookers on the hill strained their eyes to watch, pointing out excitedly when a particular faction was recognised.

'It's started!' one man shouted. 'The trumpets are calling the men to prayer.'

'It will be a sorry day, whatever the outcome,' said another.

Solemnly, they listened to the stirring rise and fall of invocations being intoned as each soldier made peace with his past and prepared himself for death, then all too soon the air reverberated to the sound of erupting cheers roaring from thousands of throats, as the commanders stirred their troops into action. *The Mantineans were reminded that they were going to fight for their country and to avoid returning to the experience of servitude after having tasted that of empire; the Argives, that they would contend for their ancient supremacy, to regain their once equal share of Peloponnese of which they had been so long deprived, and to punish an enemy and a neighbour for a thousand wrongs; the Athenians, of the glory of gaining the honours of the day with so many and brave allies in arms, and that a victory over the Spartans in Peloponnese would cement and extend their empire, and would besides preserve Attica from all invasions in future.*

The Spartans meanwhile, man to man, and with their war songs in the ranks, exhorted each brave comrade to remember what he had learnt before; well aware that the long training of action was of more saving virtue than any brief verbal exhortation, though never so well delivered.

Then the steady rhythm of the flute players rose up as they led out the Spartans on their disciplined, slow march into battle, in sharp contrast to the trumpet blares of the Athenians and her allies, who advanced with haste and fury.

Thucydides, a commander himself not so long before, immediately pointed out to Admetus that both right wings were drifting to the right, as exposed soldiers sought protection behind their comrades' shields. 'It's a common problem......but look! If the Spartans don't close ranks, it will leave a gap!'

Just as Thucydides expected, as soon as the allies were aware of the divide opening up, they succeeded in breaking through the line, forcing the Spartans back as far as their supply wagons, and killing some of the older men on guard. It was then that the rest of the spartiates, especially the chosen three hundred surrounding their king, showed themselves superior in courage, and they rounded on the Argives and the Athenians with great strength, instantly routing them, the greater number not even waiting to strike a blow, but giving way the moment that they came on, some even being trodden under foot in their fear of being overtaken by their assailants. Those they didn't strike down, the Spartans magnanimously allowed to flee from the field, to hide, ignominiously, in the nearby woods.

The battle had been fierce with much at stake on both sides, but the strength of Spartan discipline conquered the weaker Argive coalition, and at the end of the day it was king Agis who claimed a decisive victory.

'I see no glory in war,' said Admetus, shakily, as he looked down on the mayhem. 'The sole purpose is murder!'

'It was a vainglorious enterprise by Alcibiades, and this disaster is solely attributable to him, Admetus!' exclaimed Thucydides, angrily. 'The Spartans were fighting so close to home they were able to commit their entire army......and their discipline was something to behold. Would that I could have led such men! What a fiasco! Where was our leadership?!'

'Our commanders just weren't up to the task,' answered Admetus, sadly.

'If Laches and Nicostratus haven't been killed in the fighting, I trust they'll do the only honourable thing left to them!'

By a single battle, with the loss of three hundred men, the Spartans regained control of the peninsular, boosted their moral and considerably increased their prestige abroad. There'd be no more talk of the Spartans having lost their nerve. Argos was made to sign another peace treaty with Sparta, and Elis and Mantinea were brought back into the Peloponnesian League.

Despite his bravado and scheming, Alcibiades' dream of creating a powerful democratic alliance to counter Spartan power, had come crashing down. When a total of eleven hundred men, including two hundred Athenians together with their generals, Laches and Nicostratus, were lost at Mantinea, he expected to be held responsible for the disaster, and he unscrupulously turned to his rival, Nicias, for support. Nicias, as different in character to Alcibiades as any man could be, also feared he'd be blamed, and he was persuaded by the silver-tongued manipulator to save his own skin by offering up that of another. When the rabble-rousing politician, Hyperbolus, tried to provoke the people to ostracise either Nicias or Alcibiades, in order for some stability in strategy to be achieved, such was the strength of following for the two men, their joint votes went against Hyperbolus, and he, himself, was ostracised.

Undaunted by his failings in the Peloponnese, Alcibiades continued with his exorbitant and debauched lifestyle. Still in the prime of life, he caused both male and female hearts to flutter as he paraded his beauty around the agora, his excessively long, purple edged robes trailing the ground behind him. The more senior Athenians were shocked and disgusted at his outrageous behaviour, fearing his scornful and overbearing demeanor likened him to a despot, but love him or hate him, it seemed his fellow countrymen couldn't live without him. Mesmerised by his charisma and good looks, they were drawn recklessly along with him - on his daring, unstoppable pursuit of fame and fortune.

FORTY-FOUR

AFTER A GAP OF two years, while Theomenes re-established himself in Scione and waited in vain for Amara to return, he and Admetus had finally travelled to Sparta, but when they arrived, it was not the best of times. Not only because of Sparta's fight for survival at Mantinea, but also because Agapetos' family was in deep mourning. Only weeks before Theomenes' arrival, Eireni, Nicander's daughter by Marissa, a previously healthy, energetic child of twelve years and as adventurous as any boy had died from complications arising from an infected bee sting. The only granddaughter of Nicander's parents, her death was sorely grieved over, and emotions were running high. Until that time, Amara, with support from Mydon, had shared the upbringing of young Agapetos with Kora, Nicander's remarried widow, but the family were now demanding change. They were determined that the boy should be solely brought up by them, and the women, especially Kora and Nicander's mother, Aglea, were most vociferous on the matter. They were both adamant that there was no longer any need for Amara to remain in Sparta.

'Don't take your grief out on him, or me!' argued Amara. 'I am also grieving for Eireni. Agapetos misses her too. He needs me to help him through this!'

'I've already explained why, Amara. He needs to be disciplined!' exclaimed the formidable matriarch, in frustration. 'We have only one year left to prepare him for the agoge and a life of service to the state. There have been six wasted years already!'

'They have hardly been wasted!' answered Amara, her temper rising. 'His tutor thinks he is advanced for his age.'

'It is his lack of discipline which requires attention,' responded Aglea, forcefully. 'He answers me back when I tell him to do something. He says, *my mother* would not like the way I speak to him. Having you stay here will only cause friction and conflict.'

'I will leave when he is taken into the agoge, but not before. He needs me until then and I will not abandon him.'

'His family do not want you to stay,' Kora interrupted, angrily. '*I* do not want it. We are entirely different in our upbringings. You could not possibly prepare the boy to the standard required.'

'I am not leaving. Whatever *is* required, I want to be involved.'

'We are grateful for your care of Agapetos,' said the grandmother, without conviction, 'but his family have rights. Agapetos belongs to a very powerful family. We will go to any lengths to claim the boy!'

Theomenes became involved in this family conflict, only reluctantly, initially thinking that it would fulfill his desires if Amara returned with him to Scione, but on speaking with family members at their request, when they impressed upon him that Amara must leave with him, his ire rose to such a degree that he found himself defending her decision to remain.

The menfolk were absent. The entire male population, except for some helots, having been called to arms, and the remaining womenfolk were not as Theomenes was used to. Strong, educated and far more independent than their Athenian counterparts, he found them extremely difficult to converse with without losing his temper. However, after insult after insult was hurled at him, and particularly those in respect of Mydon and Amara, he ended up responding in kind to the blistering language of Kora and her mother-in-law.

'Mydon, I would defend with my life! You only see his disability. It will not make Agapetos 'soft' as you seem to be implying, to have him involved in his life until he starts his schooling. There is much that Agapetos can still learn from him, as to what constitutes being a man. As for Amara, and I make no apologies for my lapse in manners, you know fuck all of the strengths of this woman! If anyone can prepare the child for the harshness of what life has in store, she can. Look beyond her upbringing. Talk to her!'

Taken aback at Theomenes' outburst, Kora became defensive. 'We are at war, and we do not yet know what the outcome will be. I hope for you and your friends' sakes that we are victorious. Outsiders will not be welcome, if we lose.'

Ignoring her threats, Theomenes continued. 'I'm not finished yet, Aglea. You may or may not know it, but I have legal guardianship of Agapetos. *I* know he is Nicander's son: *you* know he is Nicander's son, you only have to look at him, but can you prove it?'

'What are you implying?'

'Amara wishes to remain with the boy for only one more year, and I'm prepared to bend to her wishes, since it means so much to her, but if you deny her, I will have the boy returned to Scione, as is my legal right.'

'We will apply to the law!'

'The courts could take years! Think about it. I'm sure you'll come to the right decision.'

When the army returned, there was both rejoicing and mourning and no time for any further discussion regarding the future of Agapetos, but one day Amara came to Theomenes after being at the house of the boy's grandparents, with her eyes bright and a smile on her lips.

'I am staying, Theo! I can't thank you enough for talking to her. Whatever you said has changed the family's attitude entirely. I know it is not what you hoped for, but I promise I will return as soon as Agapetos takes up his education.'

'I only want you to be happy.'

'The agoge is what's best for him, Theo. Already he has suffered the loss of both his parents and now his sister. I want him to be strong. He needs to belong.'

As soon as arrangements were made for travel, Theomenes and Admetus set off on their long journey back to the Chalcidice, leaving Mydon with instructions to maintain the threat that Theomenes would reclaim the boy if the family made life difficult for any one of them. Also remaining in Sparta was Thucydides, who was intent on furthering his extensive research.

'You missed seeing history, Theo,' remarked Admetus, as they rode towards the coast, 'and for what? We are going home without them.'

'Amara can be very persuasive!'

'Ha! She can wind you around her fingers as easily as spinning yarn!'

'Anyway, old man, we have plenty of time. You can tell me all about what you and Thucydides witnessed.'

'We witnessed the end of Alcibiades, Theo, that's what we witnessed. The people will surely blame him for the disaster.'

FORTY-FIVE

WHILE THE ATHENIANS WERE distracted by happenings in Sparta, Dium, on the eastern prong of the Chalcidice peninsular took the opportunity to revolt from the Delian League, and in the summer following the defeat at Mantinea, Nicias, who believed the area was of more importance to Athens than Sparta, due to its strategic position in protecting vital trade routes, was sent north to recover it, fearing others could also be tempted to change allegiance. For the Plataeans at Scione they accepted it was payback time, for it was general Nicias who'd forced the Scionians into surrendering their city, and with knowledge they'd acquired in the time they'd been living in the Chalcidice, they were confident of playing a crucial part in the campaign.

Having been notified of the imminent arrival of the fleet, all men of fighting age eagerly gathered together in the agora to hear instructions from their leaders. Sebastianos was overall commander, with Stephanos acting as second-in-command, and following their stirring speeches, the men were in full readiness to do their duty. When the cheering had died down, Stephanos found himself confronted by an over-excited Akylas. Now at the age of seventeen, he demanded to be allowed to take part in the action.

'Your step-father is the person to speak to, Akylas.'

'I've pleaded with him! He says, no!'

'I won't go over his head on this. He will decide.'

Furious at not getting the answer he wanted, in a rage Akylas continued to harass Stephanos, and halting by the statue to Iairos, which Theomenes had paid for in order to placate Angelos - the hero having still not shown his face - the young man stood his ground.

'I will be starting my two-year tour of duty soon, and I want to take the Theban sword as part of my equipment. Alcibiades says it should be mine by rights!'

'By what rights? What part did *you* play in defending Plataea? You were three!'

'My father gave his life defending our city. If he'd lived, he would have been entitled to the sword.'

'The people decided who should have it, and they chose Clytes of Eleusis. Until I know for certain that he's dead, I will guard it with *my* life!'

'But Alcibiades......'

'Alcibiades! Alcibiades! What has *he* got to do with anything? This is a Plataean matter!'

'He says there is no Plataea! My destiny lies elsewhere now. Alcibiades wants to introduce me to important people......people who are interested in helping me.'

'In return for what?'

'What do you mean?'

'You've inherited your father's good looks, Akylas, but sadly, not his good sense. You must know Alcibiades' reputation......the debauched company he keeps?'

'He thinks of me as a son!'

'He has fucked his own daughter, so the rumours say!'

CHAPTER FORTY-FIVE

'Do you want me to tell him that you refused to give it to me?'

'You can tell him to go fuck himself!'

Afraid of what he might do, Stephanos stormed off, and Theomenes, who'd witnessed the confrontation, hurried after him.

'Perhaps he *is* entitled to the sword, Theo. But not because Alcibiades says so. What do you think?'

'He has to earn it first, Stephanos. As Clytes did. As you did. The Eleusinian may still be alive. Until we know different, the weapon remains yours.'

In order to deter a large force being sent from Athens, and also to deflect hostile attention away from himself, Perdiccas, the wily king of Macedonia initially offered Nicias the help of his forces, but unbeknown to the Athenians, he'd already entered into an alliance with the Spartans. When Nicias arrived at the Chalcidice with insufficient strength of arms, he discovered too late of Perdiccas' treachery. A coordinated effort with the Macedonians was vital if Nicias was to succeed in his venture, and being unable to proceed as he'd wished, he sailed the fleet back to Athens, where plans would be made to reap revenge on the Macedonian king.

On board one of the ships was a stowaway. Akylas.

'He's gone to Alcibiades!' cried out Akaterina, as she shakily handed Akylas' note to her husband. 'He says you've driven him away!'

'I tried to protect him because of *you*! If he'd been my son by blood, I probably would have allowed him to see some action. It was you who said he would get himself killed trying to impress that confounded man! I'll fetch him back.'

'It's no use, Sebastianos! His letter is clear enough. He will only run away again.'

'Write a letter to Aspasia. Tell her what's happened. She will let you know if there's anything you need worry about.'

'I will do that now,' and she clapped her hands loudly to attract the attention of her house staff.

'I'll arrange a courier. The sooner she knows about this, the sooner your mind will be eased.'

'I know Aspasia cares very much about Akylas, but she is also protective of Alcibiades, and he has such a power of persuasion.'

'Sparta is eager to keep the peace treaty. The worst that can happen to the boy will come from frequenting too many whore houses and taverns.'

'As a caring mother, Sebastianos, that brings me no ease of mind. Aspasia's acceptance of such things is much broader than mine!'

'He would have left us soon, anyway, Akaterina, in order to begin his military service.'

'But it shouldn't have been like this! He's so vulnerable, still. He hasn't grown a beard yet.'

'I should have been firmer with him.'

'It was an impossible task, Sebastianos. I realise that now, with Alcibiades constantly reminding him of his former life in Athens, Scione will never satisfy him. It is hard to be the mother of such a son. My only child!'

'We will make sacrifices to the gods to keep him safe,' said Sebastianos, sympathetically, and when the servant arrived with writing materials, the young man hesitated on entering, seeing his master and mistress in a tender embrace, as Akaterina finally gave way to despairing sobs of loss.

At Theomenes' house, another message was being read. It was from Mydon in Sparta. Knowing Agapetos was soon to be accepted into his boarding school, Theomenes read it eagerly expecting it to be about travel arrangements, but there was no such news. Amara and Agapetos were well, Mydon wrote; nothing for him to worry about, but there'd be a delay in their returning to Scione.

FORTY-SIX

THE SUBJUGATED RACE OF Messenians, forced into slavery by their Spartan neighbours, suffered a grim and wretched existence under their abusive control, and for the slaves in the household of Agapetos' grandparents it was no exception. A helot revolt had brought about the premature death of their noble son, Nicander, and the state-owned helots allocated to their family were never allowed to forget it. One day when Mydon was visiting with Agapetos, he heard shouting and thinking the youngster was in trouble, he followed the noise of the commotion. But it wasn't the boy. A female helot was being held down by the boy's grandmother, and she was screaming at a male slave, to fetch a whip. The matriarch, red-faced and angry to the point of hysteria, shouted out to Mydon.

'Come here and hold her!'

Ever since his arrival in Sparta, Aglea had spoken to him harshly, barely missing an opportunity to refer to his lameness, but he managed to hold his peace for Amara's sake. 'What's the problem?' he asked, while glancing at the young woman who was bent, cruelly, over a chair.

'I've just caught her spying on you; probably intent on stealing!'

'No harm's been done. It was most likely the boy she wanted to watch. The women here are very fond of him.'

'Oh, take her to the kitchens, Vachos!' Aglea instructed her slave, harshly, 'and make her work without food today. And never enter this part of the house again!' she shouted after her.

As the woman was being led away, Mydon was impressed at how calm she'd remained throughout her ordeal. Not at all the cowed reaction he'd witnessed in other helots. He waited, hoping she would look up, and as if knowing he was watching, she rewarded him with the briefest of glances from her beautiful, expressive eyes. In that fleeting instant, Mydon felt that their very souls had touched - as if he knew her intimately - and she him. He felt light-headed, as though he'd drunk too much neat wine.

'I sense resentment, Mydon, as to how I run my household,' said Aglea, facing him, angrily, breaking the spell. 'Spartan women need to be strong. Our *men* are doing what all men should do......maintaining their fitness in readiness to defend the state!'

Mydon heard her only vaguely. He was still thinking about those eyes.

'It must be hard, Aglea,' he answered, finally.

She looked at him scathingly from head to foot, 'We are born to it, and *we* give birth to warriors!'

Agapetos ran into the room at that moment, followed closely behind by his Plataean nanny, who blanched on nearly colliding with the boy's grandmother. 'How many times have I told you not to run in the house!' she shouted at the boy. 'You must learn to obey! Your sister never disobeyed me.' She raised her hand to strike him, but Mydon instinctively caught hold of her arm before she could do so.

'It must be hard coping with grief without the support of your husband,' he said, sympathetically.

'Let go of my arm!' Aglea screamed at him, 'and leave my house this instant!'

'Say goodbye to your grandmother,' Mydon said, with emphasis. 'And, don't forget your manners, Agapetos.'

'I don't ever want to come back here!' he shouted, stamping his foot in a temper.

'Obedience! Loyalty! Endurance!' recited Aglea, firmly. 'First and foremost is obedience!'

'Your grandmother is only thinking of you,' said Mydon, bending down to look him in the eye. 'You will try harder to obey her *next* time.'

'Thank your grandma for your hospitality,' the boy answered, dutifully, determinedly fighting back his tears of hurt and anger.

After leaving the house Mydon dismissed the nanny, and thinking it would calm the boy down, he took Agapetos on a walk around the estate. Agapetos especially liked to visit the animal pens and to collect hens' eggs, which he was allowed to take back to Amara, but on this occasion Mydon lead him to the kitchen garden.

'Let's see what we can find for your mother, Agapetos. Some honey, perhaps?'

The seven-year-old, without the constraints of his grand-mother, instantly ran in the direction of the clay beehives which were situated in a small orchard at the far side of the vegetable garden. To protect the crops from animals, the area was fenced off and one of the entrance gates was close to the outdoor bread ovens. As he approached the hot smoking domes, Mydon searched for sight of the woman, but could see no-one of her memorable, shapely form; only the usual pair of middle-aged women busied with bread making and a stooped old man hoeing between the rows of vegetables. Without knowing her name, he was reluctant to make enquiries which could cause her more trouble, so he continued on towards the orchard.

On their return, Agapetos had forgotten all about his earlier confrontation, and he was in a cheery mood as he clutched his jug of freshly gathered honeycomb provided by the apiarist. The matronly women baking bread, were so charmed by his excited chatter that one of them called out to him.

'Agapetos! Would you like a bun to go with your honey, my cherub?'

Delighted, the boy went over to receive his treat, leaving Mydon free to wander towards the open kitchen door. He started as he caught sight of her. She was busy sweeping the earth floor, and when his shadow fell over where she was working, she glanced up. It was as though she was expecting him, and she smiled. The coarse unshapely garment she was wearing failed to hide her natural beauty, and Mydon thought his heart would burst out of his chest, it was beating so fast.

'What's your name?' he asked her, which, due to the faintness in his head, sounded as though someone else was speaking.

'Iola.'

'I'm Mydon.'

'I know.'

'Have we met before?'

'That depends on what you believe.'

'We need to talk.'

'It will be difficult.'

'I'll find a way.'

Before they were discovered, Mydon returned to collect Agapetos, and as if in a dream, walked back to the house he was sharing with Amara. He was suddenly conscious of his limp; not the consequences of a birth defect as Aglea often insinuated, but due to losing all the toes on his right foot from the plague of Athens. Subsequent gruelling travels in search of Plataea's stolen relic had resulted in an infection, causing further disability, while overuse of his left leg had brought about painful bone damage. He had a rolling gait which caused him embarrassment, but never more so than at that moment.

'Iola!' he murmured, as he walked through what seemed a changed landscape. Was the sky more blue? Was the tinkling chatter of the goldfinches, suddenly more sweet? He was desperate to see her again, but how could he without drawing Aglea's unwanted attention? He needed a woman's thoughts on his dilemma. He would talk to Amara.

'She is a slave owned by the state, Mydon,' was Amara's immediate thought. 'They cannot be bought or sold. Her life is harsh enough as it is, but you could bring about her death if Aglea ever suspected Iola was flirting with her guests.'

'No, it was nothing like that! There was a connection. We both felt it, I'm sure.'

'When the arrows of Eros strike, minds and limbs go weak. I remember the first time I set eyes on Imbros......and he felt the same way about me. Something irreversible happened that day.'

'I must see her again!'

'If the gods intend for it to happen, Mydon, they will find a way.'

'Do you believe the gods determine our lives, Amara?'

'Don't you?'

'I try to be guided by my conscience. Is that from the gods?'

'Is something worrying you?'

'Am I putting my own desires before her safety?'

'Don't do anything foolhardy. The Spartans accept no interference in the way they control their helots. They believe it is justified.'

'I can't stop thinking about her. Do you think she's put a spell on me?'

'You have obviously never been in love before.'

'I'm not sure I like it.'

'Oh, my poor Mydon......no other pain comes close!'

The lover did not have long to wait for helpful intervention from Mount Olympus. It was early summer and the great annual festival of Hyacinthia, in honour of Apollo, was due to be held at the village of Amyklai, where an enormous, gilded statue of the youthful sun god looked down over a field of billowing tents awaiting the worshippers. All military duties were suspended during the festival, and everyone was welcome to join in the events, even helots and foreigners. Thucydides was still in Sparta, enjoying the famed hospitality of the spartiate, Lichas. Still beavering away on his research, he was particularly eager to experience this important Spartan festival. Like every other woman in Sparta, Aglea and Kora had been busy for weeks, organising food for the banquet and preparing specially woven chitons which would be donated to the god during the festivities. The family would be prominent participants. They would be making sacrifices for the soul of Eireni, and for the protection of Agapetos - for the sun god to make him strong. Amara was to accompany the two women over the three-day festival, wanting it to be a happy occasion for her and the boy. This would be their last summer together, since the day was fast approaching when he'd be taken into the care of the agoge. Mydon excused himself from attending that day, by complaining of crippling pain. Aglea was relieved. It embarrassed her to be in the company of any male who did not embody the Spartan ideal.

'Do be careful, Mydon!' Amara had pleaded with him. 'If anything should happen to you!'

After a tortured night without sleep he replied, feverishly, 'She'll be expecting me, I know it! This could be my only chance.'

While the populace was worshipping at Amyklai, Mydon hurried to see Iola. He went straight to the kitchens where he expected she'd be working, but there was no sign of her. Enquiring as to her whereabouts he was led, nervously, by an elderly woman to the women's sleeping quarters - to a pallet in a dingy outbuilding. Iola didn't stir when he entered.

'Iola?' he murmured.

She opened her eyes and held out her hand to him, which he took, asking, anxiously, 'What's wrong? Are you ill?'

She pulled aside the coarse blanket to reveal the bloodied scars of the whip.

'Why did they do this?!' he exclaimed. Is this Vachos' doing?'

'I thought you'd be at the festival, and I pleaded to be allowed to go. Other Messenians will be there. But only Vachos from this household. I should have realised.'

'My dear! You suffered this because you wanted to see me?'

'I'm so glad you're here!'

'How do you bear it so calmly?' asked Mydon, shaking his head at the thought of what she must have endured.

'I know how to cope with it now.'

'What do you mean?'

'You won't believe me.'

'I'll believe anything you tell me.'

'You won't think I'm crazed?'

'I won't think you're crazed.'

After a long pause, Iola spoke again.

'The first time it happened I was scared, but now I can control it.'

'What can you control?'

'This is not my first placement. I have served in other households before this one. Since I was a child.'

'I understand.'

'I was abused. Often.'

'I'm listening.'

'He was hurting me. I couldn't fight him off. The pain got worse and I thought I would pass out. Then, I found myself sitting across the room, just looking at what was happening to me. I felt no pain. Nothing, really.'

'And this has happened again?'

'I can do it at will. Sometimes, when I'm being beaten, I float to the ceiling and watch myself down below. It's as though it's happening to someone else. Do you think I'm crazed?'

'I want to tell you something now,' said Mydon, squeezing her hand tightly in his eagerness to talk. 'I've never told this to anyone, and you can tell me if *I'm* crazed. Some years ago, I was in a life-or-death situation when I fell from my horse in the middle of a battle. I was terrified. Suddenly, everything seemed to slow down, and I saw my entire life flash before my eyes. My entire life! I'm a free man now but I was born into slavery and sold on when young, so I had no memory of my mother......until that moment. But I saw her! I felt her love!'

'I believe you.'

'Do you think we were meant to meet one another?'

'I felt protected the first moment I set eyes on you.'

'I wish I'd seen you first!'

Their intimacy was interrupted abruptly when the old woman returned with bread and drink for the invalid.

'She must get what rest she can while the family are away,' she insisted. 'There'll be none when they return.'

'Can I count on your silence?'

'What more harm can they do to me now?' she answered, wearily.

'I'll be back tomorrow......with better food!'

'Vachos has gone with them, but he'll be back to see that we're not slacking. You don't want to be caught here.'

'Is he not also a helot?'

'He is, but he thinks he'll be spared the whip if he spies on the rest of us.'

'I'll be careful.'

He returned quickly to Iola. 'Whatever it takes, my love, we will be together......and free!'

Tears swelled up in her eyes and she gripped his hand to place it on her wet cheek. 'There is a better existence Mydon. We see this life as though through a veil. I've never had a fear of dying, but now I want to live, so much!'

'Don't dwell on that other world, my dearest!' he said, leaning over to kiss her gently on the lips. 'You must trust me!'

'Take care of her,' he told the old woman, as he left. 'I'll make sure no harm comes to you because of this.'

Her rheumy eyes watched him walk out of sight, then she shook her head and mumbled, 'What nonsense men talk!'

The first day of the festival was a solemn occasion, given over to mourning the death of Hyacinthus, the young prince of Sparta, whom his lover, Apollo, had accidently killed in a game of discus throwing. It was a day of fasting, without pomp, and sacrifices were offered for the dead. The second day was one of celebration for the hero being brought back to life by Apollo and consisted of feasting on roasted goat meat and enjoying music and dancing. There were horse races, choir competitions and a procession of prettily decorated wicker carts, where girls and young women paraded in their finery. On the third day, more prayers were offered up to Apollo and Hyacinthus, special cakes were eaten, and the garments woven especially for this occasion were donated to the sun god's temple. With their ever-present fear of divine punishment, it was important for all Spartans to attend this festival, and even if their warriors had taken the field against an enemy, they always returned home on the approach of the Hyacinthia.

Apart from the events at Amyklai, activity at the homes of Aglea and Kora was hectic as they catered for friends and relatives during the Hyacinthia, and Mydon had only snatched opportunities to talk with Iola alone. When visiting with Amara and Agapetos, it was an agony for him to be so close but unable to go and see her. Finally, as life started to return to normal, Mydon took the first chance he could to visit the kitchens. There was no sign of her. He was frantic and he rushed to the outhouse where he thought she might be recovering from another beating. Vachos was there.

'Looking for someone?' he asked, sarcastically.

'Where's Iola?!'

'What's it to do with you?'

'I want to know where she is, you bastard. I'll beat it out of you, if I have to!'

'Ha! You can hardly stand!'

Before Vachos could prepare himself, Mydon had brought him to his knees in a choking grapple, his strong arms tightening around the man's throat. As Vachos weakened, Mydon released his grip a little, and asked if he was now prepared to talk. Vachos declined and was rewarded with a harsh painful twist to his neck. Unable to stand, he was at Mydon's mercy, and he believed he was about to kill him. He tried nodding his head and felt the grip loosening.

'Just tell me where she's gone.'

'Don't tell the mistress I told you!'

''I won't. Now, where is she?'

'She's dead.'

'No!' Mydon yelled, as he let go his grip. The room suddenly began to sway, and he felt as though the floor was coming up to meet him. 'I don't believe you!'

'I saw you both together. You should have kept away from her.'

'And you told Aglea, didn't you?!'

'Do you want to know what happened or not?' asked Vachos, staring murderously and rubbing at his sore throat.

'Did you kill her?!'

'I'll tell you what happened if you'll listen.'

'The truth! Everything!'

'I was instructed to take Iola into the mountains, to a site where criminals and prisoners are thrown into the Ceadas ravine. Spartans believe they'll be absolved from guilt that way since it's up to the gods to decide who lives or dies. No-one survives. I wanted to have her before I carried out the deed, and at first she fought me, but then she went limp......and let me do whatever I wanted!'

Mydon groaned and covered his ears.

'Are you sure you want to hear everything?' mocked the helot.

'You forced yourself on her!'

'She was willing!'

'You dirty, fucking bastard! What kind of a monster are you? So, you *did* kill her!'

'In the end, I didn't have to.'

'What do you mean?!'

'She jumped!'

In an agony of despair Mydon slid to the floor, his body trembling at the dreadful vision filling his mind. His beautiful Iola was dead because of the interest he'd shown in her. Amara was right. I should have listened to her! he agonised. It was a little while before, cold and shivering, he stirred himself, to find the helot gone. Wandering, in a frenzy, completely unaware of time or what he was doing, he eventually returned to Amara's house and startled her by his appearance.

'This is worse than I could ever have imagined, Mydon!' she exclaimed, on hearing his garbled, dreadful story. 'This family is, indeed, monstrous!'

'I'm going to see Aglea!' stated Mydon, fiercely. 'She can't be allowed to get away with this. Then I'm going to kill that pig, Vachos!'

'I'm coming with you.'

'I don't want you getting involved, Amara!'

I cannot leave Agapetos in the hands of these people, Mydon, without knowing exactly what happened. You can't stop me.'

Aglea was instantly defensive when confronted by their searching questions about Iola, replying that it was up to her what happened to the household slaves.

'But what you've done is inhuman, Aglea!' shouted Mydon. 'You're the cause of her death!'

'Are you talking about Iola?'

CHAPTER FORTY-SIX

'Yes, Iola! She didn't need to be pushed by the way......she jumped!'

'Jumped?'

'The Ceadas ravine!'

'Who told you this?'

'Vachos, of course!'

'Wait here,' said Aglea, and she hurried from the room, only to return with a terrified looking Vachos, who was trying desperately to explain his actions.

'You have over-reached yourself!' she told him angrily.

'I've only ever tried to please you!' he pleaded.

'You have pleased yourself, and I'm to blame for giving you too much authority. Now leave me, until I can decide on a suitable punishment!'

'He said he was acting under your instructions,' said Amara, relieved that Aglea was not involved.

'Iola accused Vachos of raping her,' said Aglea, by way of explanation for the fraught situation, 'and of trying to force her into an unwanted marriage with him. The friction was causing problems in my household, so I had her placed with a relative of mine. His wife has just given birth to a healthy baby boy and is in need of extra help.'

'What's this?' exclaimed Mydon, ecstatically. 'She's alive?!'

'Yes, she's alive. I'm not the ogress you think I am, Mydon. Vachos told me about your visits to the woman. He obviously could not control his jealousy when he tried to convince you that she was dead '

'Where is she?'

'I cannot tell you that. Iola is state property. The gods willing, you will be going back to your own lands soon, and you will forget all about her. Now excuse me. I have a household to run.'

When Aglea called for Vachos later that day, she received no response. At first, she thought he'd run away, since he now knew his future was an uncertain one, but the other helots in the household who'd suffered because of him, knew exactly where he was, since it was they who'd willingly shown Mydon and Amara

221

to his hiding place. When Aglea saw him, she almost gagged. Whatever punishment she'd had in mind, it was of no consequence now. From his shattered hands it was evident he'd never hold a whip again, and he was also no longer a threat to her female help.

FORTY-SEVEN

'**B**UT HOW CAN ANYTHING come of it, Mydon?' asked Amara, gently. 'Shouldn't you forget about her now?'

'I can't forget her. I have to find her!'

'Well, you can't ask anyone from Aglea's household. They have been made to suffer enough over what happened to Vachos.'

'Who else would know?'

'Kora, obviously, but we can expect no help from her.'

'We could ask Thucydides to help. He's still a guest at Lichas' house. That household must know every one of Aglea's extended family. All we need to know is which one of them has had a baby recently.'

'You intend for Thucydides to question Lichas' family? Are you mad?'

'I was dying Amara; sinking into an abyss, until I heard Aglea say she was still alive. It was as though someone physically dragged me back into the light. Nothing else matters but to be with her.'

'But Thucydides may not want to be involved. He could warn them.'

'It's a risk I'll have to take. I don't have much time. As soon as Agapetos leaves us, it will be expected that I return to Scione with you. If I remain here, they'll know why, and Iola could be moved again......or worse. When we leave Sparta, she must leave with us.'

'What a romantic you have turned out to be, Mydon!'

'I no longer feel alone, Amara. I want to spend the rest of my life protecting her.'

'I have known that feeling. So, what do you intend to do? This is not like rescuing a shield.'

'Thucydides is due to visit Aglea's house this week, to say goodbye to Agapetos. I'll find an opportunity to talk to him then.'

Leading up to Agapetos' leaving was a distressing time for Amara, as friends and relations came to congratulate the family and to wish the boy well, but hard though it was, she'd not altered her views on what she thought was best for her cousin's son. On graduation he would belong to a brotherhood without equal, protected by his peers throughout his life. The Spartans, in her opinion, did not risk the lives of their warriors unnecessarily: the purpose of the spartiate was to remain strong in order to defend his homeland, and what other homeland did he now have, but Sparta?

While the family was distracted by other guests, Mydon took his chance to follow Thucydides, when he saw the historian leave the house to take a walk in the sunshine with the boy. He watched the pair as they ambled along a pathway towards the orchard, the middle-aged man and the seven-year-old chatting amicably, until he saw Agapetos break away and run towards an old olive tree.

'Be careful, Agapetos!' Thucydides called out, as the boy began climbing higher and higher. 'You can't start school with broken bones!'

As Mydon drew nearer, he could see that Thucydides was looking anxious and he hurried towards the tree just as a loud crack was heard and a large branch crashed to the ground. Agapetos was left dangling from the broken stump, and he looked about to fall. Quickly, Mydon dragged the expensive linen cloak from the surprised historian's back, thrusting one end of it into his unsteady hands. As the robe was pulled taut between them, Agapetos let out a yell and fell heavily into their arms.

Once safely on the ground, he tried hard to recover his composure, and glaring up fiercely at the two men, he pleaded with them, 'Please don't tell my grandmother!'

The relieved pair responded quickly in unison. 'We won't!'

'You arrived at an opportune moment!' exclaimed Thucydides. 'My thanks to you, Mydon!'

'He's forever getting into scrapes,' Mydon admitted, ruffling Agapetos' dark head, brusquely. 'He knows no fear. He'll give his teachers much trouble, I fear.'

'A potential leader of men, eh?' said Thucydides, looking favourably at the boy. 'And it could all have ended here. It was fortunate you came along when you did.'

'To tell you the truth, Thucydides, I was following you.'

'Why? To keep an eye on the boy?'

'Another matter, entirely.'

'I'm in your debt, Mydon. Tell me. I'm intrigued.'

'I need your help to find someone. A woman. A helot.'

Surprising Thucydides with his request, Mydon thought it best to explain his predicament as quickly as possible.

'I know some of the details of your trial, which is why I'm putting my trust in you. I am also a non-believer......in the traditional sense.'

'I was accused of impiety as well as other things, that is true,' answered Thucydides, 'but I would not say I am a non-believer. Why do you need *my* help, particularly?'

As succinctly as possible, Mydon related what had transpired between himself and Iola.

'Did you see or hear any of our gods, when your life was shown to you?'

'I did not.'

'But there was something?'

'Oh yes! A powerful connection. Not of this world.'

'And this woman, Iola, you say she has been given certain gifts?'

'If you talk to her, Thucydides, you will feel the truth of what she says.'

'I attended the Hyacinthia, recently,' Thucydides replied, sagely. 'I witnessed for myself how fanatically religious the Spartans are. It is dangerous to deny the gods, especially here.'

'I understand that fully. I've never spoken to anyone about my beliefs, except to Iola, and now to you. It's urgent that I find her. They'll show her no mercy if they find out about her 'gifts'.'

'In truth, I've had similar conversations with the philosopher Socrates regarding his daimon, his 'internal oracle', as he calls it, while endlessly pacing the agora together in Athens. I've no doubt that he also would be most interested to hear of your experiences.'

'Will you help me to find her?'

'I cannot promise. I was fortunate to be only sentenced with exile, and I would not want anything to hinder my research now, but if I learn anything, without putting my life or anyone else's in jeopardy, then I will get the information to you.'

'One more thing,' added Mydon, quietly. 'Amara is the most formidable of women, but I would not want her life put at risk unnecessarily. She is entirely ignorant of my beliefs, and also of Iola's. She knows only that I love this woman.'

'Your secrets are safe with me. Not all the information I gather, gets written down!'

Before Thucydides left that day, he presented his expensively embroidered cloak to the family of Agapetos, knowing it would never be accepted as a garment to be worn, since Spartans abhorred anything ostentatious. 'Will you accept this as a gift to Apollo,' he asked them, politely, 'in the hope that the god will watch over the lad during his training?'

'It is a very expensive garment!' said Aglea, coming forward eagerly to claim it. 'The god will undoubtedly appreciate the sacrifice you are making, Thucydides.'

'It is indeed a most precious item,' the historian replied, and he gave a sly wink to Agapetos. As he was leaving the room, he saw Mydon was looking at him quizzically.

'Old habits, Mydon,' Thucydides whispered. 'They're hard to break. Why take chances with powerful forces? *Something* saved the boy!'

The poignant, unforgettable day of Agapetos' leaving, came and went - but there was still no word from Thucydides. While Mydon fretted, Amara wept. Forever seared into her memory would be the sight of the child she'd reared, being firmly lead away from her, dwarfed between two tall, imposing figures in their long blood red cloaks.

FORTY-EIGHT

NEARLY TWO WEEKS WENT by after Agapetos leaving, with no indication from Amara that she was preparing to return home, but the delay was attributed to her distress at having to say goodbye to the boy, and no immediate suspicions were raised, but anxious that Mydon would do something foolish if Thucydides didn't send word soon as to Iola's whereabouts, Amara was relieved when one day the man arrived in person, looking solemn.

'I have come with bad news, I'm afraid. Have you heard? The child, the helot Iola went to care for is sickening and not expected to live.'

'We have little contact with the family now,' said Amara, resignedly. 'I am very sorry to hear about the child.'

'This is the worst news!' exclaimed Mydon. 'The family will blame her, I'm sure of it. Have you found out where she is, Thucydides?'

'She is at Pitane, the settlement near the Eurotas ford. Lichas lives in the same village. It's a fashionable district, as you probably know. It will be difficult to go unnoticed there.'

'Then what can we do?' asked Mydon, helplessly.

'That's why I'm here, instead of sending a message,' Thucydides answered, authoritatively. 'I have been invited to attend a ceremony, together with Lichas' family. They're making sacrifices to the gods for the child's recovery. If there is no improvement the boy will be exposed to the elements. The family believe the gods will then decide if he lives or dies. It's the Spartan way. I'm making a contribution to the temple, myself. It's the least I can do.'

'But what about Iola?'

'If I find an opportunity, I can speak with her, but what would you want me to tell her?'

'Tell her to get out of there!' Mydon exclaimed. 'Tell her I'll be waiting for her!'

CHAPTER FORTY-EIGHT

'I can't just tell the woman to run, man! Do you have somewhere in mind?'

'When are the sacrifices to be made?'

'Over the next three days. I'm attending tomorrow. I came as quickly as I could.'

'I'll go there tonight then and hide by the river, south of the ford, but tell her I'll wait there for days if necessary. She may not be able to get away immediately. Tell her she *must* choose the right moment.'

'I'll do what I can. But perhaps you will also get invites.'

'We won't,' replied Amara, bluntly. 'We are no longer needed. But why are you getting involved?' she asked, curiously. 'It could make life difficult for you in Sparta.'

'I have always admired you Plataeans,......especially now.'

'Why now?'

'We are fellow exiles, are we not?' he said, smiling favourably at her, and he placed his hand over hers, squeezing it firmly. 'I know something of what happened to you, brave lady. I am completely at your service. Whatever I can do to help, you only have to ask.'

At the sudden reminder of past horrors, Amara brusquely pulled her hand away.

Supplied with enough food and drink for three days and taking one of Amara's cloaks, Mydon set off to find a suitable hiding place by the banks of the Eurotas, as close to the settlement as he dared, but far enough away from the busy river crossing so as not to draw unwanted attention. With his bundle safely concealed in the trees, he then positioned himself to keep watch on the riverside pathway leading from the village. He lost count of the times he started, thinking, in his eagerness that Iola was coming towards him, but on the evening of the second day as the sun was about to set, he had no doubts. It was her! She was hesitantly looking about and glancing back towards the village as she hurried on, unknowingly, towards the spot where he was hiding. He checked that no-one else was in sight then burst from the trees to pull her from the path. They were together at last.

'The baby may be dying, Mydon. ' she burst out crying. 'I've been so frightened!'

'You are safe now, my dearest!' he asserted, kissing away her tears, and clinging to one another passionately, they laughed shakily from sheer joy and relief. 'We have plans already in place to leave immediately you escaped from the house,' explained Mydon, hurriedly. 'Here, put this cloak on. You're shivering. We must walk in the dark to Amara's house, to be ready to leave for the coast as soon as the sun is up. It's all arranged! Hurry now!'

It was Thucydides they had to thank for the travel arrangements. He decided he'd stayed long enough in Sparta, explaining he was becoming homesick for his wife and family, back in Thrace. He suggested that Iola travel with Mydon, together with Amara's two Plataean women, while he and Amara journey together, back to their respective homelands, supported by his own slaves. Amara was initially cautious of this suggestion but realising that it would not take long before the family suspected Mydon for Iola's disappearance, she accepted the arrangement, and as soon as it was dawn, the plan was put into motion.

Fortunately, Iola was not like many helot women and with a few suggestions from Mydon, who knew every nuance of Amara's mannerisms and demeanour, he was able to instruct his beautiful Iola, dressed in Amara's clothes, on how to pass as a lady.

Mydon was relying on the fact that in order to discourage hoarding, the Spartans did not mint their own coins, using instead cumbersome iron bars as a form of currency, but in order to do trade, coinage from the rest of Hellas was readily accepted. Choosing a Corinthian vessel sailing out of the port of Gythium, the captain gratefully took the bag of silver coins offered by Mydon, and without hindrance or awkward questions, the respectable looking party of four left the Peloponnese.

When Iola went missing, an immediate search was made for the helot by the necessary authorities, but when Aglea discovered that Amara and Mydon had suddenly left Sparta she suspected what had happened. When there were no reported sightings of the runaway Iola, she decided not to pursue the matter further. Why risk complications? She had Agapetos. What was a troublesome slave compared to that?

The overland journey back to their old lives began enjoyably for both Thucydides and Amara. Mostly they were welcomed into the homes of local dignitaries as honoured guests, but when that was not possible they stayed at a hostelry, and it was always of the finest. Amara found Thucydides to be an intelligent and entertaining companion, and he appreciated her beauty and the way she'd courageously adapted to the situation. They behaved as tourists at historical sites, where Thucydides was most knowledgeable, afterwards wining and dining well. Misreading Amara's relaxed attitude after a particularly good meal, Thucydides leaned over to kiss her and was surprised by her reaction.

'I didn't mean to insult you!' he exclaimed, touching his reddening cheek. 'I apologise!'

'You gave me no warning!'

'You're a beautiful woman, Amara. You can't blame me for trying.'

'I'm sorry for slapping you like that. I am grateful to you. Being in your company; seeing so many new places, has stopped me from dwelling on sadder matters.'

'Let's forget all about it!'

On the next occasion, believing that this time, Amara was giving him encouragement, he felt for one of her breasts through her clothing and when he fondled her nipple, he noticed that she didn't immediately push his hand away. Aroused by the memory, that night he knocked on the door of the private room he'd taken for her at the hostelry and, naked, entered when he heard her call out.

'I'll leave if you want me to.'

By way of invitation, Amara moved aside her coverlet. As their bare flesh met, she fiercely pulled him down to kiss her, and then moved his head down to her breasts. He worked one nipple then the other with his tongue, and encouraged by Amara's low moans, he pushed her legs apart. It had been a long time since Amara had willingly been with a man, not since her husband, Imbros, and now her suppressed emotions were finally being released. For a man in his forties, Thucydides had kept himself in good physical shape, and gripping his erect penis Amara guided it inside her, bracing herself to receive his forceful thrusts. She climaxed again and again, her entire body convulsed by waves of pleasure, while her lover, wanting to satisfy her, maintained his powerful rhythm until he could hold no longer. Collapsing heavily beside her, he laughed, exclaiming, 'now that was a good fuck!'

Amara was shaking, and she began to sob, quietly.

'If I've hurt you, I'm sorry. It's been a while since......'

'No, you didn't hurt me. I was just remembering. Long ago, now.'

'I don't want to make you sad. I've enjoyed our journey together.'

'So have I.'

'We still have more time to enjoy, my dear.'

Amara began to tremble again, and Thucydides, placing his arm about her, held her close until she fell asleep.

In the night, Amara woke suddenly from a terrifying nightmare, to find herself being strangled by a powerful force. A heavy arm was crushing her throat and in panic she groped around for any kind of weapon from the bedside table. Her fingers closed around an ornate silver wine jug and using all her strength she smashed it again and again on the arm of her attacker. There was a loud cry of pain and as the pressure was released, she leapt from the bed, calling out frantically for help.

Thucydides' servants, who'd been sleeping outside in the corridor, ran into the room, one of them carrying a lighted oil lamp and holding it aloft, he cried out in shock at what he saw. His master was bleeding heavily from deep gashes in his arm, and the bedclothes were covered in blood.

Amara looked aghast at what she'd done and rushed to the bed. 'I'm so sorry!' she gushed. 'I was having a nightmare! I thought......!'

One of the servants hurried to fetch dressings and while his companion held the light, Thucydides' wounds were attended to. When satisfied that the bleeding had been stopped, he ordered them to leave, and as soon as he was alone with Amara, he shouted at her, angrily.

'What the fuck was that about?!'

'I felt I was being strangled,' Amara tried to explain. 'How is your arm?' she asked, apologetically.

'It has suffered worse injuries. Though never in bed, that I recall!'

'It's my fault. I gave you encouragement, and I shouldn't have.'

'I couldn't help but notice that you've been branded, Amara. Does it have anything to do with your nightmare?'

'Please don't ask me to talk about it.'

'But I'd like to help, if I can.'

'I'm sorry Thucydides. This was a mistake.'

During the rest of their travels, which now took a more direct route, the incident was never referred to again, and when they broke their journey at the next large town, Thucydides made a point of seeking out a jeweller and buying an expensive pair of gold ear-rings for his wife.

FORTY-NINE

THE EVENTUAL RETURN OF Amara and Mydon to their community in Scione was greeted with great joy, especially by Theomenes, and to welcome the delightful Iola into his extended family was an unexpected and happy surprise. So grateful was he to Mydon for his care of Amara that he insisted his friend's wedding be an occasion to remember and lavish preparations were quickly got underway, fuelling a mood of hope and optimism amongst the Plataeans. He was mystified, therefore, when Amara asked to speak with him, looking downcast.

'Theo, there is something I need to tell you,' she said, seriously. 'I think you ought to sit down first.'

'You look worried, Amara. What is it? Tell me?'

'There is no easy way of saying this, and I know you will be hurt. I'm expecting Thucydides' child, Theo.'

'I don't understand you. What?! Did I hear you right?'

'I don't understand either. Why is it happening to me now? I'm thirty-three!'

'You're telling me you're pregnant?'

'I am Theo. I know you're not going to be happy.'

'Are you sure?! Thucydides?'

'It was only the one time, Theo! Yes, I'm certain. I've missed two bleedings.

'I'm shocked Amara!'

'I knew you would be.'

'I can't tell you how this makes me feel. But you've always wanted your own child. Why aren't you happy? Don't you want to have the baby?'

'I do!'

'So, what's the problem?' he asked, curtly.

'He will want to claim it, Theo. He will say I am unfit to be a mother.'

'You'd better tell me everything.'

When Amara had finished, the solemn pair sat quietly for a while, pondering the situation, then Theomenes rose to his feet and burst angrily from the room, torn between wanting to lash out at Amara and consoling her. He'd thought that perhaps Thucydides had forced himself on her, but when he heard Amara's recap, he realised she had been more than willing. He felt betrayed. After all he'd done for her, waiting, waiting, like a fool, for her to heal. And with Thucydides, he fumed! He's old! What had kept him from raging at her, was the revelation that during the time she was held captive by the monster Lykaon; during intercourse, the Theban had frequently choked her until she passed out - hence the nightmare. Unwilling to reveal Amara's indiscretion to his friends, and face either pity from Stephanos or shame for Amara from

Admetus, he raged at the gods instead, for seemingly mocking him in this way. When feeling calmer, he sought her out, but he still could not quell his wounded pride.

'You've got yourself into a fine mess!' he retorted, as he paced up and down, his resentment pushing him to hurt Amara also. 'Of course Thucydides will try and claim the child......'

'I have decided Theo,' she interrupted him, quickly. 'It's not too late. There are herbs......'

'You didn't let me finish!' he said, sharply. 'He will claim the child, but only if he believes it to be his.'

Amara, anxious and confused since telling Theomenes her news, suddenly looked at him, hopefully, 'What do you mean?'

'If you really want to have this baby, Amara, I will ask you again. Will you marry me? We can make people believe the child is mine. Thucydides need never know.'

'You would do that, Theo?'

'This is not the way I hoped things would be, obviously, but I want you to be safe, Amara. I think having this child will bring you the stability you need.'

'My dear, dear friend!'

'Is that *still* all I am to you?!'

'I love you more than anyone, Theo. You must know that by now. What happened with Thucydides was a mistake. A release from the tension in Sparta and having to leave Agapetos behind. I don't know the woman you'll be marrying. I can't promise you anything. Are you absolutely sure you want to do this?'

'No, I'm not absolutely sure. Not now. But what other option is there, Amara? Tell me?'

'We'll make it work, Theo. We are a formidable pair, you and I.'

'Then we tell no-one about what happened between you and Thucydides. Certainly not my uncle, nor even our closest friends.'

'I agree. And thank you, Theo.'

'We will let it be known, that encouraged by Mydon's marriage to Iola, you have finally agreed to be my wife. I think our friends will accept that.'

'We could have a double ceremony. It will look less hurried.'

'We've experienced so much, you and I, since our carefree lives in Plataea, haven't we, Amara?' he said, thoughtfully.

'We have, Theo, but whatever the future has in store for us, we will face it together, won't we? All three of us,' she added, putting her hand on her still flat belly.

Hesitantly, he placed his hand over hers and repeated quietly, as though swearing a sacred oath, 'The three of us. Whatever the future brings.'

Admetus and the rest of their close friends were delighted to hear there'd be a double wedding, and the fact that Theomenes and Amara seemed somewhat subdued about the event, compared to the obvious joy seen in Mydon and Iola, was put down to nerves, which some found amusing, considering their long relationship. Hypatos was immediately sent word about the coming nuptials, with instructions that he come quickly, and overjoyed at the news, he set forth from Athens on the first suitable sailing, bringing with him the fastest stallion in his stables - a much-awaited wedding gift for his nephew.

Someone else eagerly awaiting his arrival was Akaterina. She knew that Hypatos would have access to all the gossip flowing around the Athenian agora regarding Alcibiades. Hopefully, not of her son, also. But as she dreaded, the news he brought was not to her liking. She and Sebastianos were not deceived by Hypatos' initial vague answers about Akylas, and he was finally forced to reveal more than he intended as to the rumours he'd heard about the young man. Alcibiades' lifestyle was showing no sign of maturing. In fact, he seemed more ambitious and outrageous than ever, and Akylas' name was often reported alongside his in tales of wild parties, involving shockingly, the mocking of traditional beliefs. He held back from telling them that Akylas had taken to speaking with a lisp, in trying to copy the speech impediment of his hero. In Alcibiades' case, it was found somewhat charming by his admirers, but with Akylas, it brought derision.

'Shame! Shame!' cried, Akaterina, when hearing of the pair's exploits. 'Thank the gods, Phalinus is not alive to witness his son's disgrace!'

The wedding gift from Hypatos to his nephew was admired by all, but especially so by Angelos, who'd been taken under the wing of a renowned horse-breeder from Leuctra after the fall of Plataea and considered himself skilled in evaluating a horse's qualities. He asked Theomenes if he could ride him and on his excited return, he shouted out, 'He's a natural! Goes like the wind!'

'Is he good enough, though, do you think?' asked Hypatos, expectantly, who together with Theomenes, had watched the skilled rider put the horse through its paces.

'There's more speed in him yet,' Angelos breathlessly answered. 'With more training and a good rider, I'd say, yes! Absolutely!'

'I thought so,' said Hypatos, proudly, going over to stroke its shining black withers. 'Since I witnessed him being born, I've had high hopes for this one! I named him Arete without hesitation.'

'He is poetry in motion, Hypatos,' said Angelos, looking with admiration at the stallion. 'Can I train him, Theo?' he asked, hopefully. 'We've time to get him entered.'

Still living under a cloud of guilt for abandoning Angelos at the battle of Delium, Theomenes was only too pleased to agree. Finally, there was something he could do to repay his friend. Being the trainer of a horse good enough to be entered into the Olympic Games had been greeted with far more enthusiasm than the running of the fishing boat he'd bought for him after his escape from the mines.

That winter the Plataeans were again obliged to assist Nicias, when in retaliation for Perdiccas signing a treaty with Sparta, the Athenian general arrived with ships to blockade the southern Macedonian coast. However, the halting of timber shipments hurt Athens as much as it did the Macedonians and new arrangements were eventually agreed. It had always been thought that Nicias was too lenient with the Spartans; that when drawing up the Peace Treaty, he should have insisted upon Amphipolis being handed over. With no threat from Sparta, he now set his sights on retaking the strategic city, but without help from the Macedonians, the venture was a failure and Amphipolis still managed to maintain her independence.

Life for the Plataeans at Scione resumed, and so ended the fifteenth year of the war.

FIFTY

THE SIXTEENTH YEAR OF the war was an Olympic year and although the peace was holding, battles for supremacy on the playing fields of Olympia were as fierce as ever. That year, the Games were made memorable due to one event - the four-horse chariot race. Alcibiades, striving to out-do his political rival, Nicias, and the pious general's lavish expenditure on public events, entered seven state-of-the-art, streamlined chariots. A number never entered before, by king or commoner.

Memories of the ceremonies on the island of Delos the previous year, funded by Nicias from his investments in the Lavrion silver mines, remained vividly in the minds of all who'd been there, and even those who weren't, felt as though they had been, so colourful were the descriptions. A new temple to Apollo was consecrated and it was a matter of record how splendid and worthy of the god his lavish outlays at Delos were. The choirs sent from the various cities to sing the god's praises were wont to put in at the island in a haphazard fashion, and the throng of worshippers when meeting them from the ships would bid them to sing, not with the decorum due, but while they were still disembarking and struggling to put on their vestments. But when Nicias conducted this festal embassy, he landed first on the neighbouring island of Rheneia with his choir, sacrificial animals and enough equipment to create a boat bridge between the two islands. During the night, the required number of vessels, brought with him from Athens, were decorated with gildings, tapestries and colourful garlands, so that on the following morning Nicias was able to lead his festal procession, with his choir arrayed in lavish splendour, singing as they marched, across the bridge to Delos. After the sacrifices and the choral contests and the banquets were over, he erected a bronze palm-tree as an offering to the god and consecrated to his service a tract of land which he bought at the price of ten thousand drachmas.

But it was not for Alcibiades to fund charitable causes fuelled by superstition. For him, prestige and promoting the immortal memory of his illustrious family was all that mattered. He wished to project status and power, hence the unheard-of expense of entering twenty-eight incomparable horses to the Games.

The five days of the Games began with a magnificent procession by all the competitors, including the horses and chariots of the equestrian events. Led by the judges in their purple robes, they travelled a day and a night along The Sacred Way from the city of Elis - where all athletes had undergone a month's final training - to the Olympic site, a distance of over thirty miles. Along the route, at the Fountain of Piera, the procession halted to sacrifice a pig, and the judges were ritually sprinkled with the animal's blood before being purified in the sacred spring. It was during this ceremony that Theomenes caught up with fellow Plataean, Akylas, when he finally found the young man alone and out of earshot of Alcibiades.

'I hear that you intend entering the category for boys, Akylas. Why?!' he asked him, angrily.

'Because I want to win!'

'At eighteen, you're too old......and you know it. Is Alcibiades encouraging you to do this?'

'What of it?' If I win, I win for Plataea. He says winning is all that matters!'

'Well, he would say that. It's cheating, Akylas, and when you are found out you could be whipped. You'll bring shame on Plataea, not glory!'

'Why should I be found out? Can you see any beard?!'

'The judges are not stupid! You've been assigned to the Athenian garrison. They'll make checks. Sebastianos hired one of the best trainers in all Hellas, for you in Scione, and no doubt Alcibiades has helped in a similar fashion since. You have every chance of winning in the men's race......unless your recent questionable lifestyle has got you worried? Have you kept up your training?'

'None of your business!'

'I'm warning you, Akylas. Either you change categories or word gets back to the judges. I will not allow you to bring shame on your father's memory!'

Arrival at the Olympic site was greeted by rapturous cheers from thousands of eagerly awaiting spectators as well as merchants and practitioners of every kind of trade and profession. People strained to catch sight of their sporting heroes, pushing and shoving to get a better view, and when sight was made of Alcibiades, leading his seven magnificent chariots, a roar of appreciation rose up like the surge of an ocean tidal wave. The officials struggled to keep back the crowds as people continued to heave forward alarmingly, and there was risk of a crush of bodies as they strained to see the athletes as they moved their way slowly to the Bouleuterion. Here they were classified into age groups to ensure fair competition and made to swear an oath in front of a statue of Zeus that they would abide by the rules. Faced with no choice, Akylas admitted his error and entered his name in the men's race for eighteen- year-olds and above.

The first day of the ceremonies was dedicated to the gods, when competitors and their families made sacrifices at their chosen altar in the sacred grove - and prayed for victory. Hypatos took no chances and made generous offerings to both Zeus and Apollo.

On the second day were the horse and chariot races, held at the Hippodrome arena, a wide, flat open space where the starting and turning points were designated by a pole. The first event of the day was the fastest and most perilous of all - the four-horse chariot race (the tethrippon). Twelve times around the track, covering almost nine miles, roared on by over ten thousand spectators. To secure the inside track was essential and collisions were inevitable, as the charioteers fought to be first at the turning point, causing carts to be flipped dramatically. Death or life-threatening injuries were common consequences.

For Alcibiades it was a triumph of self-promotion when his chariots, led by the most brave and fearless horses in all Hellas, roared past the post to take first, second and fourth places. Rather unjustly for the winning charioteer, who like the horses, only had a red woollen band tied around his head as reward for risking life and limb, it was the owner who received all the glory, and Alcibiades revelled in the tumultuous acclaim.

For Akylas also, it was a momentous time in his young life. He'd recently returned from Argos in the Peloponnese, where he was thrilled to have accompanied his hero, Alcibiades, as they'd sailed with twenty ships to again give support to the democrats and having secured a position in the Athenian garrison at the start of his national service, the young Plataean thought himself superior to his now considered lesser mortals. His striking good looks drew many admiring glances, which he used to his advantage and being regularly in Alcibiades' company only inflated his feeling of self-worth. Watching his mentor being carried triumphantly through the cheering crowds on the shoulders of adoring admirers, brought back memories of being carried on his father's shoulders at Plataea. He brooded, angrily, that he could have experienced that adoration again, if he hadn't been forced by Theomenes to compete against 'The Sicilian', who was the acknowledged favourite to win the men's stadion.

The next event of the day was the horse-race (the kele). Run on the same track as the chariots but for six laps, not twelve. Following the required month of prior training for all competitors, by the time Theomenes and Hypatos arrived at Elis it was evident that Angelos outshone all the other riders by a mile, including young Marcion, the Plataean, Angelos had been training all year. Angelos had a way with horses which had to be seen to be believed, and during the long walk to Olympia, Theomenes came to a decision.

'I'm too old though, Theo. Don't you think?'

'Twenty-eight's not old, not when there's a rapport with the horse such as you have. I've seen older riders than you in training. You are our best hope, Angelos, trust me. You qualify. You've done more preparation than Marcion!'

And so it came to be. When they reached the Olympic site, Angelos put his name down for the kele, and subsequent to Hypatos' lavish offerings to the gods, he and the stallion survived the heats without injury. Riding bareback with only a whip and an iron horse bit to control the speeding animal, good communication by the seat bones was essential - as was a good grip from muscular thighs. In Angelos' case, his long legs were an asset, giving him more reassurance on the turns. As the race progressed, blood could be seen coming from some of the horses' mouths, from bits cruelly fitted with barbs, and the flanks also were streaked from overuse of the whip. Theomenes would have no such device put into Arete's mouth. Angelos trusted the stallion's natural ability and his own voice for encouragement. All he had to do was hold on. The final stretch was a blur as he flew past the roaring crowds, and as one by one he left the other horses behind, the course opened up to him alone. He gripped tight, loosened the reins and let Arete have his head. They flew past the winning post with no other horses near them.

Afterwards he told Hypatos and Theomenes that he was so distracted by the deafening cheering and the showering of rose petals and scented myrtle, that he couldn't remember the red woollen ribbon being tied about his head, but he did remember making sure that Arete's was tied securely.

'Thank you, Theo, for having faith in me,' he'd said with obvious emotion.

'Thank Alcibiades!' replied a laughing Theomenes, thumping his friend enthusiastically on the back.

'What did he have to do with it?'

'Winning is all! I felt badly about replacing Marcion at the last moment, but you were the obvious choice. It had been staring me in the face and I hadn't realised it until I spoke with Akylas.'

'But you made him change categories, Theo.'

'Akylas suffers from an overblown sense of superiority and believes the rules don't apply to him. He could have brought shame on his family name. You, on the other hand, are too modest my friend!'

'Good news to be sent back to Scione, eh Theo?'

'Yes, indeed! What a welcome we're going to get!' he shouted above the din, before they were abruptly separated from Hypatos by noisy spectators, who lifted them up high and carried them, chanting their names, through the jubilant crowds.

That night there was a lavish private banquet, the likes of which was rarely seen in Hellas. Alcibiades, to celebrate his great victory, gave an open invitation to everyone attending the Games to come to his party. He gave the impression that it was entirely funded by him, although in fact it was heavily sponsored by friends and allies of Athens. He claimed that whatever glory he achieved benefitted Athens also, promoting her greatness throughout all Hellas and the rest of the world, but many people weren't convinced and worried about just how far Alcibiades' ambitions would take him. The showpiece of the extravagant outlay was a vast pavilion of stunning Persian design, ornately decorated, and furnished with gold and silver vessels borrowed from the official Athenian delegation. When he was forced to return them for a state ceremony the following day, he let it be assumed that the plate had been borrowed from him.

The third day was dedicated to Zeus, when one hundred oxen, supplied by the host city of Elis, were slaughtered in his honour. On an altar of a mountain of ash, accumulated from previous games, they were then roasted - the smoke from the fat encased thigh bones being sent skywards to the gods - the rest to be kept as part of the great banquet at the end of the Games.

The fourth day's events included the foot races, the most important of which was the two-hundred-yard sprint (the stadion); the length of the running track. The winner of this event gave his name to the four-year Olympiad and was considered the champion of the entire Games. Akylas had succeeded through the competing heats, and the few Plataeans who'd travelled to the Games, but without knowledge of his decline in fitness, were now beside themselves with excitement at the thought of him being the victor.

From starting blocks the race began with a trumpet blast, with officials at the start and finish to ensure no one cheated. With hardly time to draw breath the competitors ran naked on packed earth, their strong muscular legs pounding the track, with head back and arms pumping fiercely. If there was a draw they had to race again, but on this occasion, there was a decisive winner - the Sicilian, Exagentus - just as Akylas had feared. He came a despondent second, admitting to himself that Theomenes was right. His partying lifestyle had cost him the olive crown. When he sought reassurance from Alcibiades, he received no comfort.

'I knew you wouldn't beat the Sicilian,' Alcibiades told him, frankly. 'Why do you think I advised you not to enter the men's race.'

'But I did come second!'

Alcibiades, piqued at the adoring attention the beautiful young man was attracting, snapped back at him.

'Nobody remembers who comes second!'

The final race of the Games was for warriors in full hoplite armour; a very popular event and watched keenly by Theomenes in order to remember every detail to take back with him to Scione. Sebastianos had been unable to attend the Games due to fulfilling his duties as garrison commander, and Stephanos was awaiting the birth of his fourth child with wife Micca.

On the fifth and last day of the festival, no athletic events took place. It was a time to celebrate the victories and to honour the athletes. The ceremonies were held at the Temple of Zeus where Phidias' enormous ivory and gold statue of the god was crowned with a golden wreath. He sat on his gilded throne, watching solemnly over the victors; athletes who'd travelled from all parts of the Greek speaking world, coming forward as their name and hometown was called out, to be crowned with their simple but highly prized circlets of the sacred wild olive.

The last night was one of feasting and singing as people relived the glorious achievements of the Games, and a mass of pavilions and tents was set up to hold banquets and parties held by each delegation. The tent of the Athenian delegation was only half the size of Alcibiades' private pavilion, which did not go unnoticed. Many wondered if his inordinate expenditure demonstrated the power of Athens or the foreboding dominance of Alcibiades.

When finally, the town of tents was being dismantled and people began returning homeward, it was both a time of triumph and sadness for Theomenes. He had been approached by many prospective buyers for the stallion, after its victory, and had refused them all, but as rider and trainer, Angelos had also been approached with offers. His gentle approach to horse training with simple assertive gestures and his way of communicating with his voice, had attracted a lot of attention from many wealthy stable owners or their representatives, who'd specifically come to the Games looking for good bloodstock to improve their stud. There were also talent scouts on the look-out for such as Angelos, and he had accepted an offer.

'Are you sure it's genuine, Angelos?' Theomenes had asked him. 'It seems unreal.'

'It's the chance of a lifetime, Theo. The satrap has over a hundred horses in his stables at Sardis, alone. I can't turn it down. I'm not a fisherman, Theo. My skills are with horses.'

'But Sardis! Have you forgotten what happened there? It's where we lost Imbros and Telios.'

'Our lives have changed, Theo. I have no farm at Plataea. I have a fishing boat at Scione. A place I have no allegiance to. You have family there. I don't.'

'You are family!'

'I'm going, Theo. What did you tell me, before the race? That I was too modest. Well, coming first past the post changed all that. I want to take this opportunity. I want to see how far I can go.'

'When you returned to us, I was overjoyed. I thought the gods had heard my prayers, but there was a part of you that never returned.'

'The mines, Theo. They nearly broke me.'

'You will be missed, my friend.'

Trying to control his emotions, Angelos blurted out, 'I wouldn't be surprised if I don't find Clytes in Lydia!'

'Ah, so that's the real reason for your decision,' laughed Theomenes, half-heartedly.

'Take care of Amara and little Charissa. I was sorry to have missed her birth, but I'll do my best to be in Scione for her first birthday.'

'Yes, the baby came early. But all went well.'

'Thank the gods! You've been blessed, Theo.'

And so the friends separated; Hypatos back to Athens; Theomenes to Scione, and Angelos to Sardis and the household of Tissaphernes, satrap of Lydia by command of King Darius II of Persia.

FIFTY-ONE

FEELING CONFIDENT THAT SPARTA still wanted to maintain the peace, and would not therefore interfere, in the same summer that the Olympic Games were held, Athens made the decision to bring neutral Melos, the only island in the Aegean not paying them tribute, into the Delian League. The islanders were given an ultimatum; join us or face destruction. The Melians refused to pay the high price demanded and what followed was one of the most barbaric episodes of the war. Concerned that Melos could encourage other islands to rebel and thereby weaken their dominance of the seas, Athens was determined to send out a warning. After lengthy fruitless discussions, the Athenians asserted that it was the natural order of things for the strong to dominate the weak, and the Melians would have to suffer the consequences. With only might on their side to justify their actions, commanders Cleomedes and Tisias sailed with a fleet of thirty-eight ships carrying three thousand, four hundred combatants and laid siege to the island.

For months the people of Melos held out, hoping in vain that fellow Dorians, the Spartans, would eventually come to their aid, but Athens ruled the seas, and it was not to be. In the following winter they were forced to capitulate and as happened at Scione, the men of arms-bearing age were executed, and the women and children sold into slavery. Although Alcibiades was not directly involved in the taking of Melos, he had voted in favour of Athens' ruthless action, and he later chose one of the enslaved women for himself, having a child by her.

Emboldened by his successes at Olympia and the now seemingly more hawkish attitude of the generals, Alcibiades was looking to further his lofty ambitions, and the opportunity arose when envoys arrived that same winter from Egesta on the north-west corner of Sicily. They were at war with their Dorian neighbours in Selinus who were being aided by the Syracusans, and since Athens had a formal treaty with the Egestians, it was expected that the Athenians meet their obligations. As an incentive, the Egestians even promised to fund the cost of the venture, adding that other Sicilian city-states were waiting eagerly to join with Athens against the Syracusans. Since the time of Pericles, the Athenians had looked towards Sicily and dreamed of conquering the island with its enviously abundant grain harvests, so as not to rely on unpredictable imports from the Black Sea region, and also to cut Sparta off from *its* grain supply. It was decided that a delegation return with the envoys to Egesta to verify the truth of the wealth there. They returned in the spring with sixty talents of silver; enough to fund sixty triremes for a month; stories of how well they'd been treated; details of the exorbitant wealth held in their temples and how at each and every household they'd dined at, there was a lavish display of gold and silver. Believing the promises of the Egestians, therefore, the decision to send a fleet to Sicily was put to the vote, with Alcibiades pushing for an invasion of the entire island and Nicias, fiercely opposing it. He argued that it would take a force of one hundred triremes and five thousand men, believing the people would think the price too high. His plan back-fired, spectacularly. The Athenians had become used to getting what they wanted, and buoyed up by speeches from Alcibiades, inspiring them with talk of the great things they could achieve, the people agreed to the extra expenditure. For Alcibiades, his vision went far beyond rescuing Egesta. Sicily was just the beginning. Next to fall could be Carthage, then Italy and the whole of the Mediterranean. Even the riches of Byzantium could be theirs.

All was going well until the night before the sailing, when it was discovered that the faces and genitalia of the Hermes statues, which were set about the city as good-luck markers, had been deliberately mutilated. The citizens were thrown into turmoil believing that whoever was responsible was intent on overthrowing their precious democracy, and they feared bad luck would now befall the expedition. Due to witnesses already accusing Alcibiades of making a mockery of the mysteries at Eleusis by drunkenly dressing as a priest and revealing to uninitiated companions, details of the sacred rites, fingers were pointed at him and his wild friends for causing the destruction during a night of revelry. He vehemently pleaded his innocence and asked to be tried immediately. His enemies, however, knowing the main source of his support was in the army, waited until he'd sailed with the fleet the following day, before levelling charges. The ordinary folk of Athens resented dissolute, immoral aristocrats casting doubts on their cherished beliefs and wanted retribution. One of Athens' two sacred messenger ships, the 'Salaminia', was sent to apprehend him.

To be part of such an enterprise was indeed exciting for all involved, and the men's spirits were high. The plague was a distant memory and due to the peace with Sparta, the coffers had become healthy once again. Never had such an expedition been gathered before, such was the draw of the prize - and the expectations of receiving a warm welcome from the islanders. The whole population, citizens and foreigners alike, had flocked to the Pireaus to see the magnificent sight, passing all belief, with the gilded and painted triremes lavishly furnished with new figureheads, looking more suitable for a religious parade than for war. When they rendezvoused with their allies at Corcyra, the fleet had grown to one hundred and thirty-four triremes, as well as one hundred and thirty supply ships; over five thousand troops; four hundred and eighty archers; eight hundred and twenty slingers and light troops, together with all the ships' crews and non-combatants. A mighty armada.

From Corcyra the fleet sailed to Rhegium on the southernmost tip of Italy and awaited news from the messenger ships sent on to Egesta to verify that funds for the enterprise were readily available. When they returned with the alarming news that Egesta did not in fact have the funding, Alcibiades and Lamachas were astounded, but Nicias had suspected this all along. With their plans now in disarray, Alcibiades, in an act of intimidation, left the bulk of the fleet in Italy and took the sixty fastest ships down the Sicilian coast. On reaching Syracuse, the foremost ten triremes rowed, unchallenged, into the Great Harbour, and a herald proclaimed to the citizens there, that the Athenians had come to restore freedom to their Sicilian friends and allies and should there by anyone in Syracuse in favour of this cause, now was the time to come out and join with them. After reconnoitring the city and harbours for use at a future time, they sailed back up the coast to Catana, forty miles north of Syracuse and persuaded the people there to open up their town to them.

The rest of the fleet was then brought across from Italy, and it was while the fleet was anchored at Catana, that the Salaminia caught up with Alcibiades. He was put under arrest and ordered to return with them to Athens to stand trial on charges of religious sacrilege.

On board his ship was Akylas, who due to Alcibiades' influence, had been released from his duties in the city garrison. 'You're not going to miss this!' he'd told him. 'Stick close by me, boy. I'll look out for you.'

Alcibiades informed the heralds that he would return with them to Athens and agreed to follow the Salaminia in his own ship, while some of the combatants on board were transferred to other vessels, including young Akylas.

'But I want to stay with you, Alcibiades,' he entreated. 'Why can't I come back with you to Athens?'

'I'm innocent of all charges. It won't take long for me to clear my name. I'll be back in a matter of weeks,' he said, reassuringly. 'You don't want to miss all the fun, do you?'

Feeling embarrassed for appearing weak, Akylas put a brave face on the matter and agreed to be transferred to the 'Thetis', a veteran warship of the fleet and helmed by Glaucus, the larger-than-life Thessalian, distinguishable by his flaming red hair and beard. Akylas never saw Alcibiades again. On the way back to Athens the Salaminia and Alcibiades' vessel stopped at Thuri in southern Italy, and fearing he'd be given the death sentence on his return, during the night, he and his crew jumped ship and sailed to the Peloponnese, seeking sanctuary in Sparta.

The Athenians took this as proof of his guilt, and he was convicted in absentia and condemned to death. His property was confiscated and a reward of one talent was promised to whoever succeeded in killing Alcibiades or any of the charged men who'd fled with him.

Glaucus thought he recognised the flaxen haired Akylas, immediately he set board on ship, because of the striking resemblance he had to his father, Phalinus of Plataea, and when some of the men began mocking the young man, with his effeminate good looks and irritating lisp, he felt compelled to go to his aid. It reminded him of the first time he'd helmed the Thetis, under the captaincy of fair-haired Iandros, who at only twenty years of age, was ribbed mercilessly by the crew and had been sorely in need of his guidance. The hardened commander, now at the age of thirty-six, was trierarch of one of the newer vessels elsewhere in the fleet.

'What's he to you?' asked Cassa.

'I first remember him from when he was just three years of age. Just before his father was killed. They didn't deserve to become stateless, Cassa. The Plataeans are good people.'

'What can you tell me of him?' Akylas asked, when Glaucus made himself known.

'I only saw him briefly, lad. He was an exceptionally brave man, your father, I know that. You look at lot like him.'

So I've been told.'

'You've a lot to live up to.'

There was no activity over the coming days and Glaucus was able to get to know Akylas a little better. It quickly became clear to him that the young man was used to getting his own way. Adored by his mother and the displaced Plataeans, and being brought up in Aspasia's cultured household, had only been compounded by having too close contact with Alcibiades. He seemed remarkably unprepared for what was to come - in Glaucus' opinion.

'Drop the lisp,' he told him, as gently as a man of his blunt character, was able. 'You're not in Alcibiades' crowd now. You'll have to gain the men's trust. It will not be enough to be the son of Phalinus when the fighting starts.'

'I thought the islanders wanted us here.'

'It appears we've been duped. The rumours are, there is no welcoming party.'

'The Egestians also lied about their supposed wealth!' interrupted Cassa, angrily. 'The sneaky bastards borrowed the gold and silver from wherever they could and just moved it from place to place to impress our envoys. They must have been stinking drunk to not notice it was the same fucking plate they were eating from!'

Before the campaign had even begun, word arrived of Alcibiades' defection and despondency quickly spread amongst the crews, for he was the one who'd persuaded them to come in the first place.

'How could he abandon me, Glaucus?' exclaimed Akylas, devastated at the news. 'He said I was like a son to him!'

'If you'd gone with him, you'd have a price on your head. He did you a favour by not taking you with him.'

'I don't see it that way. Why didn't he return to Athens and clear his name?'

'Only Alcibiades knows the answer to that, lad.'

When the fleet sailed from Athens, there were three commanders; Alcibiades, Nicias and Lamachas and three separate suggestions as to how to proceed. Alcibiades, as the expedition's leading protagonist, had proposed first winning over any allies on the island before attacking Selinus and then Syracuse. Nicias, its leading critic and an unwilling participant, wanted to give support to Egesta to force Selinus into a settlement and then sail the fleet back home - unless there was evidence of substantial support from other city-states. Lamachas, an experienced fifty-year old career soldier, proposed they sail directly to Syracuse and take the city by surprise. Only one plan could be followed and Lamachas, getting no support for his sound idea, was forced to vote in favour of Alcibiades' suggestion. But now there was no Alcibiades.

'What will happen now?' asked Akylas.

'Fucked if I know, lad!' answered Glaucus, gruffly.

FIFTY-TWO

'CLYTES! WAKE UP!' A woman's voice whispered, urgently. 'I can hear Hermocrates!' but before her bed partner could respond, the eminent Syracusan had burst into the actor's lodgings.

Being an ardent theatre goer, the city leader had been drawn to the talented performer the instant he arrived in Syracuse, and during the intervening years a strong friendship had formed between them. On most matters, Hermocrates would seek out Clytes to ask his advice and on this occasion, it was particularly urgent. Not waiting to be announced by the help, he rushed into the bedroom.

'Have you heard about the Athenian fleet, Clytes, moored at Rhegium? What do you think their intentions are? Do you know anything? ......Clytes!'

Clytes sat up slowly, waiting for his head to clear, then swung his long legs from the bed. 'Get the girl to bring me some bathing water, my dear,' he asked the embarrassed woman sharing his bed and who was trying to remain hidden under the coverlet. Cloaking herself in the only blanket, the woman eased herself from the bed and grabbing her clothes from a nearby chair, hurried from the room, trying to keep her face averted from the curious statesman.

'Wasn't that the magistrate's wife?'

'Not one word! I can't help it if middle-aged women keep throwing themselves at me.'

CHAPTER FIFTY-TWO

'What happened to Eunice?'

'Gone. What were her parting words? I was unreliable and heartless, and she found me hard to get close to. Hah! I can assure you, there was no problem there!'

For nine years, Clytes had been a resident of Syracuse, living a life of indulgence and pleasure in the dynamic, democratic city, run on lines not unlike those of Athens. His knowledge of the theatre was hugely appreciated, particularly by the city's most prominent statesman, Hermocrates, and his unorthodox behaviour was generally overlooked, due to his extensive oratory and acting skills. Being something of a celebrity and still unmarried, the forty-one year old was lusted after by every frustrated middle-aged woman in the city.

A female slave hesitated at the doorway and on overhearing Hermocrates railing about an invasion, almost dropped the bowl of water she was carrying. Clytes beckoned her in and seeing the terrified look in her eyes, said, reassuringly, 'You know how rumours grow in the telling, Hermocrates. Probably a trading convoy's been seen.'

'You don't think it's true then?'

'It wouldn't make sense,' Clytes replied, as he splashed his face repeatedly in the cold water.

'We have never been aggressive towards the Athenians!' spoke Hermocrates, passionately, as he struggled to understand. 'We admire their way of life. We've even tried to emulate it here.'

Clytes rubbed vigorously at his wet hair which only made him feel worse, so he went to lie down again. 'I like what you're doing here,' he mumbled, indistinctly. 'It's a great city. I like living h......'

'We'll talk again when you are more communicative!' said the Syracusan, frustratedly, realising that Clytes, slumped naked on the bed, had closed his eyes and was no longer listening to him.

He was having the same problem with his fellow citizens, until Alcibiades rowed his triremes into the Great Harbour and the rumours became hard fact. Not knowing how to react, the stunned townspeople waited for them to leave before heading down to the water's edge, excitedly relating what they'd witnessed and retelling, fearfully, what had been called out by the herald.

'Now perhaps I'll be taken seriously!' Hermocrates declared loudly to Clytes. 'We've been sat on our arses for far too long, because no one wanted to believe the rumours!'

Clytes listened in dismay to the people all around him clamouring for action. He too had been reluctant to believe the stories of an invasion, but now he was forced to accept that his comfortable life in Syracuse was most definitely at an end. What were his people thinking of? Sailing so far from home with Sparta still undefeated, was sheer folly!

FIFTY-THREE

WITHOUT ALCIBIADES, NICIAS WAS able to follow through with his original plan to collect what he could from the Egestians and to sail around the island in a show of strength to encourage any wavering cities to come over to their side. If Akylas had wondered what war was like, he soon found out. On the way to Egesta, the young man was involved in the taking of the small, undefended seaport of Hyccara and enslaving all the unfortunate inhabitants. They were herded, terrified, onto the ships, where they took up the spaces previously reserved for the combatants. A group of young men jumped overboard and tried to swim back to shore, cheered on by their townspeople but they became trapped by the rowers' oars and mercilessly beaten. Akylas watched in horror as the waters turned red and listened grimly as cheers turned to mothers wailing, when their sons failed to resurface. The soldiers, Akylas included, then had to walk across the island, towards the looming cone of Mount Etna and its active volcano in the distance, back to Catana, and it was during the march that the young Plataean realised he was not the only one feeling afraid. Many of the troops were not much older than he was and also untried. They'd expected to be welcomed as saviours by the islanders, freeing them from the tyranny of overpowering Syracuse. Their generals had obviously been misinformed.

Nicias sold the slaves for one hundred and twenty talents and together with the thirty talents he was able to squeeze from the Egestians, was able to fund the enterprise for a while longer. The brutal treatment of the Hyccarans, however, deterred other towns from rushing to join the Athenians. The invasion had in fact made the islanders more united. As summer ended the fleet was still moored at Catana, going nowhere.

Due to the long sea voyage, the Athenians had brought few horses with them, bringing mainly cavalry personnel and tack. It was expected they'd acquire the necessary mounts on their arrival but finding few friends on the island, this was proving difficult, and in the coming months their tent encampment was constantly harassed by the Syracusan horse, forcing foraging parties to run for their lives. The horsemen went so far as to mock the Athenians, asking whether they'd come to settle at Catana, permanently.

The following winter, however, Glaucus announced to his crew that being so long in Lamachas' company, Nicias had finally grown some balls, because the normally hesitant general had decided to make a move. The Athenians had managed to trick the Syracusans into making a march on Catana, en masse, leaving their city unprotected, and during the night, the entire Athenian fleet sailed down the coast to moor in Syracuse's Great Harbour. As daylight broke the generals were able to choose their ground without hindrance, on a site where the enemy cavalry could do the least harm.

The Syracusans, on reaching Catana, realised they'd been tricked and quickly marched back to defend their city, and although not without courage, they were unused to fighting on such a scale and their lack of discipline caused problems. When a sudden storm arrived bringing with it thunder and lightning and heavy rain, it only added to their fears. They lost two hundred and sixty men. The Athenians lost fifty; due in the main to being fiercely pressed by the Syracusan cavalry. Realising their lack of horses was a severe hindrance to furthering their attack, they collected their dead and withdrew, hoping that this victory would now make the waverers think again. The great city of Syracuse with its mighty harbour, two miles long by one mile wide and large enough to contain all the harbours of the Pireaus, could be taken.

Feeling more confident, Nicias sent messengers to Athens requesting more money and cavalry.

For the rest of the winter the generals set their men to work in making bricks and iron implements. Come the spring, together with the extra help expected from Athens, they intended to build a siege wall around Syracuse, and for the fleet to blockade it by sea. After their victory at the Great Harbour they expected the Syracusans would then accept that resistance was futile.

Clytes assisted in the grim task of recovering the Syracusan dead and later tried to console his friend, Hermocrates, on the disaster.

'We were duped,' the politician moaned. 'We believed the information that the Athenians would be encamped some distance from their arms. We thought he was a friend of Syracuse. We cannot trust anyone!'

'I hope you're not suspecting me?!' answered Clytes, vehemently. 'I want them to leave as much as you do. My guidance has been focused on making them go back to where they came from, just as you were able to do nine years ago!'

'You're an honourable man, Clytes. No, I'm not suspecting you. I've taken your advice in making full use of our cavalry. We've kept our enemies from gathering food and accessing fresh water supplies, as you suggested, but we are unused to warfare such as this.'

'Don't be so defeatist, my friend. In my opinion, Syracuse could be just as great as Athens, one day. I'm at your service, Hermocrates, with any advice I can give, to help drive the fleet back to Athens.'

'You may have friends with the fleet, Clytes.'

'I'm aware of that, but they belong to another life. The sooner they leave, the less of them will be killed. Keep up the pressure with the cavalry and reduce the number of commanders. Too many can cause confusion and slow down decision making.'

Armed with Clytes' recommendations, Hermocrates held an assembly and addressed the people, telling them not to be disheartened and explaining that a want of discipline had caused the mischief, being an army of artisans opposed to the most practised soldiers in Hellas. He also proposed that the number of commanders be cut down from fifteen to three, which was accepted by the people, and they voted for Hermocrates, Heraclides and Sicanus. The rest of the winter was focused on providing arms for everyone and attending training sessions, together with preparing for a siege which everyone now thought likely.

They also sent to Sparta, where Alcibiades was living in exile, requesting their help.

FIFTY-FOUR

I N THE FOLLOWING SPRING, reinforcements arrived from Athens, with two hundred and fifty cavalry personnel, thirty mounted archers and enough silver to purchase four hundred horses from their Sicilian allies. Feeling more confident about taking on their enemy's cavalry, the army headed back to Syracuse. Moving swiftly and stealthily the soldiers took control of the Epipolae plateau above the city and the labourers immediately began building their headquarters; a large fortress which they called 'the Circle'. From there they began erecting the walls which were to cut Syracuse off from the rest of the island, and as soon as work had progressed sufficiently, the fleet was brought into the Great Harbour. The Syracusans were astounded at how quickly the Athenians made progress and being desperate not to be blockaded by land and sea they started erecting their own counter walls, and encouraged by Hermocrates, they fought hard against their enemy. During a skirmish, Lamachas became separated from his men by a corps of Syracusan horsemen and he was challenged to single combat by their leader, Callicrates, a renowned and fearsome fighter. The brave veteran could not refuse. Tragically, his first wound was a mortal one, but he was still able to inflict a similar wound on his opponent and the two warriors fell together. Nicias, who was in the Circle, being tended for his illness of the kidneys, had been left undefended and was in danger. When the Syracusans tried to storm the ramparts, he rose from his sick bed and ordered his attendants to gather the timbers lying about, which were for the construction of siege engines, and to set fire to them. Not a moment too soon, the Syracusans were driven off by a wall of flames.

The ailing general was now in sole command but being a man addicted to superstition and divination, he felt emboldened by his good fortune. Firmly convinced by his spies in the city that the people were about to capitulate, he paid no heed to the rumours that help for the Syracusans had arrived from Sparta.

In return for being granted sanctuary, Alcibiades treacherously promised the Spartans that he would render them aid and service greater than all the harm he had previously done them as an enemy, and when they received pleas from the Syracusans for help, it was Alcibiades who spoke most persuasively in favour of taking action against his own people. Believing his warnings that the Athenians were intent on seriously enlarging their empire, including an attack on Sparta, the ephors voted in favour of sending Gylippus, one of their most experienced generals, to help the Syracusans in defeating their assailants.

As soon as the general arrived on the island, he wasted no time in seeking out allies to boost his already diverse army, and due to the favourable stories of Brasidas still lingering in people's minds, they assumed that all Spartans must be alike and flocked to join him. For the Syracusans, his arrival with seven hundred marines, one thousand hoplites, a hundred cavalry, and one thousand Sicilians, was most fortuitous, since Nicias had almost completed the investment of their city. Faced with inevitable starvation, they'd been on the point of surrendering, but Gylippus' timely arrival changed all that. He quickly rallied the Syracusans and put Nicias under such pressure that the ailing general, so close to victory, was plunged into despair.

The northern wall on the Epipolae plateau was still incomplete and the Spartan general seized this opportunity, pouring his troops through the Euryalus Pass to capture the vital fort of Labdalum where the Athenians kept their supplies and treasury. It was a great loss to Nicias, and he was forced to create a new base on the Plemmyrium peninsular at the extreme southern edge of the great bay. Being more besieged than besieger he constructed there, three forts, but the site was ill-chosen being without a fresh water supply, and whenever scouting parties ventured out, they were constantly harassed by the Syracusan cavalry.

When the Corinthian fleet arrived to join forces with Gylippus, Nicias was left with little hope of his situation improving and dispensing with the usual use of heralds, he wrote a personal, desperate dispatch to Athens, urging the people to recall his own force entirely or to send a relief force equal to the first expedition. At the very least he begged to be relieved of his command due to his ill-health. His messages sadly conveyed the consequences of blockading the harbour for an entire year and being for so long partly encamped on unhealthy marshy ground.

Our fleet was originally in first-class condition; the timbers were sound and the crews were in good shape. Now, however, the ships have been at sea so long that the timbers have rotted, and the crews are not what they were. We cannot drag our ships on shore to dry and clean them, because the enemy has as many or more ships than we have and keeps us in the constant expectation of having to face an attack. We can see them at their manoeuvers, and the initiative is in their hands. Moreover, it is easier for them to dry their ships, since they are not maintaining a blockade.

If Nicias thought that his high demands in order to improve the situation would be too much for the Athenians to bear, he got it wrong again. They refused to accept that the expense so far invested in the enterprise had come to nothing, and they chose the second option. They replied that reinforcements would be sent, and that he was to remain at his post.

FIFTY-FIVE

DESPITE THE TENSIONS WITHIN the city, Hermocrates and Clytes continued their usual practice of meeting regularly at the public bathhouse to be cleansed and pampered by attentive slaves. After the day's grime had been scraped away and fresh oil massaged into their bodies, they relaxed in separate terracotta bathtubs, placed side by side. Partly shrouded in vapours arising from the heated water infused with scented bay leaves, the pair used these restorative occasions to seriously discuss the latest happenings.

'Our treasury is almost depleted, Clytes,' Hermocrates confessed to his friend. 'We cannot afford to fund Gylippus for much longer and now there's news of a second fleet being sent from Athens. We haven't much time left. The Spartan is suggesting we attack their ships in the harbour, before reinforcements arrive. What do you think, Clytes? Would it be suicide?'

'The Athenians have the best seamen in all Hellas,' Clytes answered, truthfully, 'but it would give them a fright to think you were brave enough to take them on. The men are sick from malaria, being encamped too near the marsh, and the ships are in a deplorable state. Gylippus has so out-manoeuvred them, I'm surprised they're still here.'

'They may be sick, but we are still no match for them.'

'Until they were attacked by the Persians, Hermocrates, the Athenians were landsmen......to a greater extent than you Sicilians. They were forced to learn.'

After his conversation with Clytes, Hermocrates joined with Gylippus in urging the Syracusans to put aside their fears and to try their fortune at sea, and between them, they conceived a strategy. Eighty Syracusan ships were sent by Hermocrates to attack the Athenian fleet and while they were distracted, Gylippus and his hoplites stormed the Plemmyrium peninsular, capturing all three forts. They took all the money, grain and supplies stored there, together with masts and other equipment for forty triremes. It was a colossal loss for Nicias, especially after having already lost their supplies and treasury on the plateau.

'We lost eleven ships to their three,' reported Hermocrates to Clytes, later, 'but it was worth the loss to drive them from the peninsular. They can't get their supplies past there now without a fight. I have to give credit to Gylippus; his plan worked beautifully!'

'He's as good a strategist as Brasidas ever was,' Clytes admitted, somewhat subduedly. His loyalties were now being torn between his love for the city which had given him refuge and purpose, helping him to finally conquer his morbid fears of Lykaon, and his concern for the lives of his fellow countrymen, which he thought were being needlessly squandered on a drawn-out enterprise with little chance of success. He may have friends with the fleet, even family, since his cousins could be amongst the oarsmen. He had hoped that when Gylippus gained control on land and the Syracusans showed that they were not afraid to attack them by sea, Nicias would be forced to leave, but the overburdened general had even more problems than Clytes could have imagined.

Demosthenes, the hero of Pylos, and Eurymedon, a veteran of the previous expedition to Sicily, were chosen to command the new fleet sailing from Athens; ultimately to replace Alcibiades and Lamachas, but until their arrival, the Assembly elected Euthydemus and Menander to be promoted from amongst Nicias' officers, to share his responsibilities. Wanting to distinguish themselves before their replacements arrived, they pressed Nicias to engage in another sea-battle. The general argued against such action, explaining it would be sheer folly when a well-equipped fleet was coming to their rescue, but he was outvoted.

Emboldened by their recent experiences, the Syracusans felt more confident going into a second sea-fight and on the third day of skirmishing with neither side having gained any advantage, they put to sea earlier than usual, attacking again by land and sea. At a given time, they then halted to take their lunch at a specially prepared food market at the shore's edge. Nicias, believing they'd done with fighting for the day because they felt they were being beaten, had his men disembark and to begin preparing their meal also. Suddenly, without warning the Syracusans remanned their ships and sailed against them again. The Athenians were thrown into confusion and with many still hungry, with great difficulty, they put out to meet them.

Learning from mistakes in their first sea-battle, alterations had been made to the Syracusan ships to strengthen the prows, which enabled them to do greater damage to the Athenian ships when charged head-on. In the tightly packed space of the harbour, the mighty triremes were unable to function at their best, especially when a myriad of small boats ran against their oars and barrages of javelins were discharged against their sailors. Fighting hard, the Syracusans were eventually victorious, sinking seven Athenian vessels and losing only two of their own, and that was only because of over-excitement when pursuing their fleeing enemies.

Feeling confident of victory at last, they prepared for a final attack, again by land and sea on Nicias' demoralised and diseased forces, but just when they thought they could see an end to their nightmare, a new peril appeared offshore. Demosthenes and Eurymedon arrived with a fleet of seventy-three resplendent ships. Carrying eight thousand able-bodied men; hoplites, javelineers, archers and slingers, as intended, the gleam of their arms and the tumult caused by the multitude of coxswains and pipers drove fear into the Syracusans. They looked on fearfully at the splendour and might of this new invasion force and felt they were back to where they started.

Sailing with the fleet were one hundred Plataeans, including Stephanos, Theomenes and Sebastianos, drawn into service by Demosthenes.

FIFTY-SIX

ON SEEING THE POOR condition of both men and equipment, Demosthenes accurately summed up the dire situation, and spoke with Stephanos, urgently.

'Nicias has lost the camp on the plateau and the forts on the peninsular. The men are succumbing to illness. We hit the Syracusans now and we hit them hard. I'm giving them no time to recover from the shock of our arrival. If we don't succeed, we take the fleet back to Athens. I'm not letting any more men die here, needlessly, when they are wanted to defend our homeland.'

'Nicias wasted too much time wintering at Catana,' answered Stephanos, who was also dismayed at the condition of the once proud expeditionary force. 'He had the advantage. He should have pushed harder when he had the chance.'

'He gave the Spartans time to send reinforcements. I'm not going to make the same mistake. We act quickly, while they're still deciding what to do.'

When Demosthenes revealed his plans, Nicias strongly objected. His spies in the city were telling him that the Syracusans had had enough, and sight alone of the brave new fleet was enough to bring about capitulation, but Eurymedon sided with Demosthenes and the ailing general was again outvoted.

Demosthenes realised that an attack on Epipolae in daylight would easily be repulsed, but knew that if they regained the plateau, Syracuse could quickly be surrounded, and the war would be over.

'Prepare your men, Stephanos,' the Plataean commander was ordered. 'We're going to attack the heights - tonight!'

'In the dark?' queried Stephanos. 'The terrain is unknown to us.'

'They won't be expecting a night attack. It's now or never!'

After first watch, taking supplies for five days, Demosthenes, Eurymedon and Menander, set off with the entire army, as well as masons and carpenters, to retake the plateau of Epipolae. Climbing

261

the hill, unobserved by the guards, they quickly took the Syracusan fort, putting part of the garrison to the sword. The rest escaped giving the alarm to the camps on the plateau, but the men stationed there were taken completely by surprise by a night attack and were easily routed by the Athenians, who successfully reached the Syracusan counter-wall and began pulling down the battlements.

When Gylippus arrived with his troops to defend the fortifications, the Athenians were so flushed with their initial victory that they advanced against them in disorder, so intent were they on attacking while their opposite number was still unprepared. At first, they were successful in halting Gylippus' forces, but there was one group unfazed by the situation. A contingent of Boeotians, attached to the Spartan's army, stood their ground and fought back. Demosthenes' infantry became disorientated, being on unfamiliar ground, and in the darkness, not knowing friend from foe, soldiers called out the watchword, hoping to be reunited with their unit. This was quickly picked up by the enemy, however, and used to confuse the Athenians even more. The rest of Demosthenes' troops were still making their way up the hill, and the plateau became overrun with hoplites from both sides, moving about in the dark, not knowing which way to go.

The Plataean contingent, which was split into two units, one lead by Stephanos and the other by Sebastianos, kept close to Demosthenes, as ordered by the general, and their discipline held better than most, until they became aware of Boeotians in their midst and could hear their mocking taunts in the darkness. Before they could be stopped, two Plataeans broke away from Stephanos' unit and went on the attack, never to return. Stephanos railed at his men to stay close together, for now friend was mistakenly killing friend in the terrifying confusion.

The situation had quickly changed from order to mayhem and the ensuing rout drove the Athenians to seek ways of escaping being massacred. With the way down from Epipolae being narrow and already crowded, many panicked and in desperation they threw themselves from the cliffs. Being unable to see how deep the descent was, many died in the fall. The following morning Syracusan cavalry hunted down and killed all those who'd ended up lost and were found wandering about the countryside, but Demosthenes, who'd been guided by men who knew the locality well, successfully fought his way back to the plain, guarded by the surviving Plataeans.

The Syracusans claimed they killed two thousand of Demosthenes' forces that fateful night, but the general disputed the number, due to the enormous number of shields and other weaponry which had been discarded by men who'd actually escaped. His bold attempt, however, had gone disastrously wrong and he and Eurymedon now both agreed it was time to leave.

FIFTY-SEVEN

NICIAS WAS NOW AFRAID that blame for the disasters at sea and on the plateau, both brought about by co-commanders who'd gone against his advice, would be laid at his door. Still believing the Syracusans were close to surrendering, he argued for the fleet to remain. He had decided he'd rather die in action than face trial and execution back in Athens, where it would be impossible to give a satisfactory account for the failure of the expedition.

Demosthenes and Eurymedon were persuaded to wait and while they waited, Gylippus, buoyed up by his success on Epipolae, was able to encourage the wavering cities on Sicily to come to the aid of Syracuse, and just as Demosthenes feared, more reinforcements arrived from Sparta. Seeing the approach of a fresh army and knowing the poor condition of their own, Nicias was forced to change his mind. Operating as secretly as possible, orders went out for the men to board their ships and be ready to sail at a given signal. It was a night with a full moon, and all was in readiness to evacuate the island when the sky suddenly started to darken. Men looked to the heavens, only to see the shining orb of the moon slowly being eaten by a dark shadow. Fear spread quickly as an eclipse was considered a bad omen, and Nicias, being particularly superstitious, cancelled the evacuation, preferring to wait until the following full moon which the soothsayers told him would be more favourable.

When rumours of the proposed flight reached the Syracusans they no longer feared the Athenians and went back on the offensive. Renewed activities began when they attacked the Athenian lines and Theomenes was involved in a disastrous cavalry incident. Sallying out from separate gates in their defences, accompanied by a small force of supporting heavy infantry, Theomenes and Makron, boldly led out their cavalry against the advancing forces, but several of their hoplites became segregated and were swiftly surrounded by the enemy. Without infantry support, the cavalry were vulnerable and they were forced to flee back to the camp. The gateways being narrow, however, made it impossible to get through quickly. Makron was knocked to the ground by a thrown javelin and killed where he fell, and seventy horses were lost to the enemy. They could ill afford to lose so many, and it was a terrible defeat for Theomenes. He narrowly avoided being brought down himself and was filled with remorse at the death of Makron and others well known to him from the unit. Memories took his mind back to when he first encountered the cavalryman, when they were both young recruits in Athens and the time Makron was thrown from Cyclops' back. Remembering the big white mule caused him to dwell on his family back in Scione, which only made him more disheartened. What were they doing here? Syracuse was a great city much like Athens. It was already a thriving democracy; they had a fleet and cavalry, much as Athens had. He'd even learned that they loved the Athenian playwrights and had a fine theatre where excellent performances were a regular occurrence. There was nothing to bribe the citizens with. Nothing to divide them.

The Syracusans now sought revenge for what they'd been made to endure. They no longer wanted their enemy to just leave - they wanted to entrap them. After a successful sea engagement when the veteran strategos, Eurymedon, was killed in a failed manoeuvre and an unprecedented eighteen Athenian ships taken, the Great Harbour became once again the domain of the Syracusans, and they immediately began blocking its mile wide exit with every available vessel. When the Athenians saw what was happening, they panicked and began manning all their ships, sea-worthy or not, with any men still of use, determining to break through the barrier.

Demosthenes, Menander and Euthydemus were to command the ships, while Nicias, with a small force to protect them, lined up every non-combatant and those too ill to fight, along the shoreline in front of their camp, to give encouragement.

Realizing how disheartened the men were, following their defeat at sea, he could not remain at his station on shore, but leaving the land troops he boarded a boat and passed along the line of the Athenian triremes. Calling each captain by name and stretching forth his hands, he implored them all, now if ever before, to grasp the only hope left to them, for on the valour of those who were about to join battle at sea depended the preservation both of themselves, every man of them, and of their fatherland. Those who were fathers of children he reminded of their sons; those who were sons of distinguished fathers he exhorted not to bring disgrace to the valorous deeds of their ancestors; those who had been honoured by their fellow citizens he urged to show themselves worthy of their crowns; and all of them he reminded of the trophies erected at Salamis and begged them not to bring to disrepute the far-famed glory of their fatherland nor surrender themselves like slaves to the Syracusans.

'I don't need to remind you how proud your father, Paramanos, is of your glorious career!' he called out to Iandros, who was captaining one of the triremes, which a year before had been the pride of the Athenian navy but was now a patchwork of inadequate repairs. 'My father will hear of our adventures from my own lips, general!' the trierarch shouted back in reply, endeavouring to give much needed encouragement to his men. 'We have the best crews and marines in all Hellas. They are more than ready!' he lied.

Gylippus and the Syracusan generals seeing that the Athenians had begun boarding their ships, addressed their soldiers also, implying that if they lost, Syracuse would be treated much like Scione and Melos. The men would suffer a fate most dreadful and the women and children a dishonourable one.

When all was in readiness, about two hundred ships filled the Great Harbour; the Athenians utilising anything that would float and the Syracusan alliance with over seventy well-preserved warships. The three commanders lead the charge and successfully reached the barrier but found the heavy blockade of fishing boats, cargo ships and out of service warships, effectively strengthened by ropes and iron chains. The fighting men on Demosthenes' trireme included twenty Plataeans, and Sebastianos and Stephanos were amongst those who fought valiantly, while others struggled desperately to break the cables. They succeeded in overpowering the ships stationed there, but the enemy warships, lined up on either side of the harbour, had been waiting their chance and now raced towards them, entrapping them while they were still trying to dismantle the barricade.

The Athenians had prepared themselves for the head-on ramming which had caused so much damage to their ships previously and had come supplied with grappling hooks, which would stop the enemy from being able to back away, but their new tactics had been leaked to the enemy, and the Syracusan ships came fitted with animal hides, making it impossible for the iron claws to take hold. With so many ships crowded into such cramped conditions, however, there was little room for *any* kind of ramming and for some time the battle raged with no clear winner.

Collisions were many and Glaucus and Cassa were hard pressed on the Thetis, being unable to manoeuvre their ship out of danger. The noise of other frantic helmsmen and boatswains also roaring out their orders, only added to the confusion. As marines leaped from ship to ship, it became more like a battle on land than one at sea, and the Thetis was boarded more than once. Akylas may have been abandoned by Alcibiades, but the aristocrat had made sure the young Plataean was left fully equipped, and in the fierce hand to hand fighting his weapons were put to good use. 'I wish I had my fucking axe!' was a curse the big Thessalian was heard to roar many times, as the Thetis became overrun. The helmsman on any ship was a sitting target, and if it hadn't been for Akylas bravely deflecting javelins and other missiles directed at the conspicuous redhead, he would have been killed. Whenever he saw Akylas confronted by an opponent, he bellowed out his encouragement, giving the inexperienced young warrior much needed confidence.

'Go for the knees, lad!' he bellowed. His shield is too high!' or 'Strike him again! Look there's a gap! Don't let him get up! To your right, Akylas! To your left!'

The walls about the harbour and every high place in the city were crowded with people, eyeing the battle with the greatest anguish of spirit, and as the battle raged one way and then the other, cries of 'we are winning!' or 'we are losing!' could be heard by Clytes and Hermocrates who were down at the shoreline. For the Eleusinian it was difficult to watch. His countrymen hadn't been able to break through to freedom as he'd hoped, and after a long battle, to cheers and shouts of jubilation erupting all around him, he witnessed their desperate flight back to shore, and in panic, the likes of which had never been experienced before, sought protection behind what was left of their encampment walls.

'Now we have them!' exclaimed Hermocrates, relieved. 'I'm sorry for your sake that it came to this, Clytes. They should have left when they had the chance. The people will not be lenient.'

'There'll be many who can afford to pay a ransom. I'll help in any way I can, in the negotiations.'

'My friend, there is so much anger, I cannot promise anything.'

Hearing the cries of anguish coming from the defeated, and seeing the wreckage of the once mighty armada, a feeling of deep foreboding engulfed Clytes at that moment, and he regretted wholeheartedly the support he'd initially offered the Syracusan.

One of the many wounded carried ashore was Iandros, son of Paramanos, and like so many others, the brave trierarch did not survive the night.

Fifty Athenian ships were lost in the second sea-battle, compared with twenty-five from the Syracusan side, and the two remaining commanders, Nicias and Demosthenes, agreed between them that they should make one last attempt at a break for freedom with the sixty sea-worthy vessels still in their possession. En mass, however, the men mutinied, so afraid were they to return to the ships, and they flatly refused to reboard. This left the generals with no other choice, and they ordered the ships to be set on fire so they would not fall into enemy hands. They were now without any means of escape from Sicily and were without food and water due to the generals assuming they'd be vacating the island and having cancelled their regular supplies from Catana. The still substantial army of forty thousand combatants, non-combatants and slaves, was in dire straits and it was decided to take it back to Catana, overland, that very night, while the Syracusans were celebrating their great victory and understandably getting drunk.

Hermocrates, however, had learned of their imminent flight and since the last thing he wanted was for the Athenians to establish themselves in another part of Sicily, and realising the citizens were not up to apprehending them, was forced to come up with a stratagem. As soon as it was dusk, he sent a friend to the edge of the Athenian camp and pretending to be one of Nicias' spies, he called out in the darkness for a message to be got to the general, urgently. He impressed that they should not leave that night, for their plans were known to the Syracusans; that the celebrations in the city were only a pretence and that forces were actually guarding the roads. The ruse worked. Fearful of another night-time disaster, the generals delayed their march until the second day after the sea-fight, by which time Gylippus and the Syracusans had blocked all routes north and put guards at every water supply.

FIFTY-EIGHT

I MMEDIATELY CLYTES HEARD OF the ruse to delay the Athenians, he made up his mind to get to their camp. He feared the worst now and needed to know if his cousins were there. Just before dawn he reached one of the guarded gates to their compound and called out to the watch, explaining who he was and asking if any fellow Eleusinians were in the camp. When he received only a vague response, he asked if there were any Plataeans with the army.

'There are Plataeans guarding Demosthenes,' came the reply.

'Can you get a message to them?'

'Depends on what it is.'

'Clytes of Eleusis. The Shield Company.'

Is that it?'

'It's enough.'

It was an anxious time waiting, while the men on watch, protected by the palisade, walked backwards and forwards along the top of the wall above him, but finally he heard a familiar voice from the other side of the gate. 'Is that really you, Clytes?' Stephanos asked, incredulously, trying to keep his voice low. 'I have Theo here with me.'

'My friends, it is so good to know you both still live, but it grieves me to know you are here. The Syracusans are blocking the roads as we speak.'

'There's no food in the camp and no water,' spoke up Theomenes. 'We have no choice but to leave and take our chances.'

'I'm well known in Syracuse, Theo. I'll use what influence I have to try and get you both freed from the camp.'

'We appreciate your offer, Clytes,' Theomenes answered promptly, and moved by his friend's generosity, 'but we cannot desert the rest of our men.'

'Or Demosthenes,' Stephanos added, determinedly.

'If things go wrong, I could be of help if the city leaders will accept ransoms. I pray me meet again but in better circumstances.

If you see any of my cousins tell them, I'll be praying for them also.' His talk shifted quickly to their mutual friend Glaucus and how he'd come across the 'Delias' on his journey to Sicily.

'What did I tell you, Theo!' exclaimed Stephanos, pleased to have been proven right about the stolen vessel.

'But what happened to Glaucus?' Clytes asked, anxiously, his body pressed close to the gate, to be able to hear clearly.

'He's the same as he ever was!' answered Stephanos. 'Only poorer!'

'Thank the gods!' exclaimed Clytes, who, until that moment, had feared the worst. 'I don't expect he'll be with the fleet. Probably too old for such adventures now, but tell him I have his axe, if you do come across him!'

'And I have something here that you should have, Clytes,' said Stephanos suddenly, and he received an affirming nod from Theomenes. 'I'll drop it from the palisade,' and he quickly ran up the steps while the watch was looking the other way. When Clytes drew the sword from its scabbard, even in the dim light, he knew immediately what it was.

'You shouldn't have done that,' he said, awkwardly, when Stephanos had returned to the gate.

'It's safer with you. It belongs to *you*,' emphasised Stephanos.

Clytes shuddered, trying not to associate the return of the sword with his own change in circumstances. 'It was disrespectful of me to leave it,' he forced himself to reply. 'Diokles entrusted me with it.'

'Theomenes has told me about your phobia, Clytes. Shit happens......to any one of us. It's just a sword. An expensive one but still just a sword. Now *I'm* entrusting you with it.'

As dawn approached, the friends parted, not knowing whether they would ever see each other again, and when walking back to their tent, life in the camp was just beginning to stir. They were passing through Nicias' section of the overcrowded, fetid encampment, when Stephanos and Theomenes heard something which stopped them in their tracks. From one of the tents in their path, men were just waking up, and the pair could hear the occupants' loud grumblings. 'Glaucus, your bloody snoring kept us awake, again!' a man moaned, only to be shouted down by a familiar voice complaining of his companion's farting.

'It can't be!' remarked Theomenes.

'Only one way to find out,' replied Stephanos, and he approached the bulging, moving canopy, from which mutterings could still be heard.

'What's going on here?' he asked, authoritatively, on lifting the flap, giving the occupants the impression they were being admonished by a senior officer. The large bulk of a man in the middle, struggled to sit up and on seeing Stephanos' grinning face, let out a roar.

'By thunder, you're a sight for sore eyes, my friend! You remember Cassa, don't you?' he bellowed, tugging at his shipmate's arm, 'and you know Akylas, of course!'

'Akylas?'

The blonde Plataean, lying on the other side of the large helmsman, and almost obscured from view, looked embarrassed.

'Theo, you'd better look in here,' Stephanos called out, and after talking with Glaucus, the pair got to questioning their fellow kinsman.

'We never expected to see you here! We thought you were safe back in Athens, as part of the garrison,' said Theomenes, in shock. 'You'd better transfer to our unit of Plataeans so we can protect you.'

'Humph!' exclaimed Glaucus. 'He doesn't need protection. He saved my life more than once. Didn't you lad?'

'I'd prefer to stay with Glaucus and Cassa,' answered Akylas, firmly. 'I'm in Nicias division, and I'd prefer to remain with him.'

'Well, we won't force you,' Stephanos told him. 'We know Glaucus will look out for you. I admire your loyalty. I'd be reluctant to leave Demosthenes.'

'I must say,' Theomenes said, with surprise in his voice, 'I hardly recognise you, Akylas. Not in looks, but your attitude. It has done you good to be out of Alcibiades' company.'

'You don't think it's because he's been in mine then?' asked Glaucus, feigning hurt.

'I don't doubt it!' replied Theomenes, with sincerity. 'You've helped Akylas to find his true self. A worthwhile teaching...... and most timely!'

When Glaucus heard that Clytes was in the city and that he had his axe, his great shoulders shook with genuine emotion and tears sprung to his eyes. 'That lanky landsman?!' he exclaimed, his great hands wiping furiously at his wet cheeks. 'By all the gods, I'd like to have seen him. He thought I was too old to be here, did he? I'll give him 'too old' when I see him next. I wish he'd brought my axe with him, though,' he added seriously. 'I'm going to need it!'

'Our situation is indeed desperate,' said Theomenes, soberly. 'Nicias is too ill to think rationally, and Demosthenes is more effective when he can act quickly. We're at the mercy of the gods now, and I'm not sure they're on our side.'

Stephanos had to agree with him. 'If Nicias can be brought so low, after all his splendid religious services, what hope is there for the rest of us?'

FIFTY-NINE

IT WAS A LAMENTABLE scene as the army prepared to leave their now foul-smelling camp. The dead were still unburied and lay in rotting piles, and when the sick and wounded realised they were being left behind without care or protection, they cried out in despair. Many begged for help and clung to friends or relatives, pleading to be taken with them, and when no help was forthcoming, some entreated for an end to be put to their miseries, believing it was a more honourable death than waiting for the Syracusans to finish them off.

One of the bodies left unburied and unsung was that of Pyrus, the Plataean archer. Having fallen at the attempt to break through the barrier, Theomenes was left with the sad task of removing his comrade's ring, to have it returned to his family in Scione. Another Plataean who would not be leaving Syracuse was the elder brother of Erastos. He was one of the unfortunates being left behind with the wounded. A vicious wound in his thigh had become infected and the whole leg was now black and turning putrid.

'Once we reach Catana, we'll reorganise our forces and we'll be back for you,' Erastos said to his gaunt kinsman, as he forced back tears. 'There'll be food and wine waiting for us. Once we've regained our strength, we'll put the fear of the gods into them again, you'll see!'

'You don't have to lie to me, brother. The Syracusans are just waiting for you to leave. We don't stand a chance and you know it. Don't tell our mother I died miserably, like this......please?!'

'You're not being abandoned, Zotikos. The army will reform and we'll be back. I'll find a surgeon!'

'Look me in the eye, Erastos. Do you honestly believe that will happen? No, I thought not. Do one last thing. Stay with me until the end? It won't take long. Which one of us has the sharpest blade?'

'You'll die a hero, brother. You saved me more than once in this debacle.'

'And you me! Promise me you'll get home. Our mother can ill afford to lose both of us.'

'Our commanders are shite, Zotikos. We lost the best when Alcibiades fled. I'll desert if I have to. If he can do it ....'

'I'm ready, brother.'

They prayed together quietly as the blood flowed freely into the earth, then Erastos gently closed his brother's eyes and released hold of his wrist. He was reluctant to leave him but nor did he wish to remain a moment longer in such a god-forsaken place. Furiously wiping away his tears he looked at the dead and the dying all about him and at the ships ablaze in the harbour, wondering what had gone so wrong. Men cried out for water when they saw him, but there was none to give. Some pleaded, in vain, for him to relieve them of their agony. After taking one last look at his brother and begging the gods' forgiveness, Erastos fled the stench and the horror and ran to catch up with the remaining Plataeans, every one of whom, like himself, had all too readily answered Demosthenes' call to arms.

Spurred on by their commanders, the entire army moved onwards, but in a mood of dejection and self-condemnation, since all their great hopes and their once magnificent ships were now gone. None dared look back, knowing that men were painfully dragging themselves after the retreating column, until inevitably their strength failed them, and their mournful cries could be heard no more. The march north was continuously hindered by attacks from the Syracusan cavalry, and since at every pass and ford the enemy was waiting for them, the Athenians were unable to make much progress. By the sixth day they'd only managed to cover a few miles and had lost so many men due to injury and sickness that Nicias and Demosthenes were forced to abandon their attempt to reach Catana.

'The men are in too wretched a condition to fight, Nicias,' Demosthenes was forced to admit, 'and many are deserting, especially the slaves and islanders. We'll have to turn back and head for the southern coast, while Gylippus still believes we are intent on going north. We still have some friends there.'

'But the enemy is also behind us!' Nicias declared. 'There'll be no 'element of surprise', if that's your intent.'

'We set the campfires as normal, and we leave tonight. They won't be expecting that!'

Despite being ill and without basic necessities, Nicias set off first with half the army, and stoically keeping the men in good order outpaced Demosthenes who fell behind with his division. By morning a gap had grown between them of five or six miles. When dawn broke and the Syracusans realised the Athenians were gone, it didn't take them long to discover the route they'd taken, and by dinnertime they'd caught up with the troops defending the rear of Demosthenes' column. Harassed mercilessly by the cavalry, his entire force finally became surrounded, and the isolated general was forced to call a halt in order to prepare his men for battle.

Theomenes, Stephanos and Sebastianos were some of the few in the Plataean contingent who were well-equipped and were placed in the front line, defending the less well-armed behind them, but their army's position was not a good one being enclosed by large groves of olive trees which the enemy used to their advantage. Finding it unnecessary to fight at close quarters and risk injury, the Syracusans rained down their missiles from every quarter on the exhausted Athenians and their allies, and many islanders who'd joined the Athenians now decided to flee back to their towns and villages. The Plataean, Erastos, was tempted to make a run for it also, but then Sebastianos was hit by a javelin, putting him out of action, and Theomenes ordered him to pick up his weapons and to take his place in the front line. Throughout the whole day the bombardment of missiles continued, and their numbers dwindled alarmingly due to injury, sickness, hunger and desertion, until finally seeing them so worn down and no longer a threat, the Syracusans offered to spare those still living, in return for them laying down their arms and surrendering.

Although what remained of his forces were in a wretched condition, Demosthenes refused to capitulate until he received further guarantees from Gylippus and the Syracusans that they would also not face death by imprisonment or through lack of the necessities of life, and these conditions were also accepted. Of the original twenty thousand, only six thousand remained to be taken prisoner, and these were herded back to Syracuse, like cattle. All the money in their possession filled the hollows of four shields.

Immediately after receiving confirmation that the troops would not be harmed, Demosthenes, filled with shame and dishonour at what had befallen his division, attempted to stab himself with his sword, but the enemy seized him, denying him the chance of dying at his own hand. Stephanos, becoming aware of his commander's desperate state, and seeing the brutal way he was being treated, fought to be near him, receiving a severe wound himself in the fracas. Both badly injured, they were borne, harshly, into custody together. Of the original one hundred Plataeans, less than forty now remained.

SIXTY

NICIAS' DIVISION WAS OVERTAKEN the following day, when he is informed of Demosthenes' surrender and is advised to do the same, but finding the news unbelievable, he asked if a horseman could be sent to verify the fact. On learning the dreadful truth, he sent a herald to Gylippus and the Syracusans, promising on behalf of the Athenian people, to refund all the expenses they had outlaid on the war, if they would allow his army to go free. They refused his proposition, and with no surrender forthcoming, they attacked Nicias' forces as mercilessly as they had Demosthenes'.

Glaucus and Cassa, being seamen, had no heavy armour and Akylas was once again their protector, deflecting the bombardment of javelins and missiles as best he could. The physical condition of the troops was deplorable due to lack of provisions and when Nicias ordered the division to push on again, Glaucus begged to be left behind.

'I can't go any further without food or water!' he gasped. 'I'm not built for walking!'

'We're not leaving you now, Glaucus!' Cassa told him, firmly. 'The men are saying there's a river ahead. Lean on me. I'll get you there.'

Akylas was unable to add his support, since he'd lost his servant long before, and was struggling himself to carry his heavy armaments and other essentials. Few in the army had slaves to help them now. Driven on by hope that they could breathe more easily if they made it across the river, the men dragged themselves onwards, but as the river came into sight, pandemonium broke out. The troops were so eager to escape from their relentless attackers, and so desperate were they for water, that many fell over in the crush at the river, only to be trampled by their comrades. The opposite bank brought no promise of freedom, since on top of the steep ridge, the Syracusans were already lined up to stop them, and their missiles poured down on the Athenians, killing many, so focused were they in trying to quench their agonising thirst.

CHAPTER SIXTY

The three friends made it to the river and Akylas bravely removed his helmet to use as a drinking vessel in order that an exhausted Glaucus could have his fill, but they were in the thick of it, and when Gylippus and his Spartans charged down the incline, the river quickly turned red, such was the ensuing butchery. Despite the blood, mud and other vile pollutants, the remaining Athenians still drank greedily, most even fighting to have it, especially an obviously deranged creature, wearing a head bandana, who broke away from a group of Euboean mercenaries, whooping and cheering as he splashed about crazily in the fouled water. The religious Spartans, believing the man was inhabited by spirits, restrained from firing on him and allowed the mad man to run off, but they soon regretted it. He stopped briefly at the top of the incline, turned to shout profanities, then let loose with a single javelin, which pierced the throat of one of their captains.

As the bodies continued to pile up, Nicias, seeing no end to the dreadful slaughter, was forced to surrender himself to Gylippus, trusting him more than the Syracusans, telling the Spartan that he could do whatever he wanted with him, but begged him to stop the killings. Seeing the sad state of the general and remembering how he had been a true friend of Sparta during the peace treaty negotiations, Gylippus ordered his troops to give quarter to the Athenians. Many of the prisoners were quickly hidden by the soldiery or spirited away by locals to be sold as slaves, and all Sicily became filled with them, but those who were left; a mere one thousand out of what had been a force of twenty thousand only eight days before, were taken to Syracuse, to be reunited with what remained of Demosthenes' forces.

With no other place to hold such a large number of prisoners, and intent on making their enemies suffer even more, the Syracusans sent every one of them, seven thousand in all and already in deplorable condition, to work in the limestone quarry, north of the city; a deep, precipitous pit with no shelter from the elements.

SIXTY-ONE

'THIS IS MONSTROUS!' CLYTES raged at Hermocrates, when he heard how the prisoners were being treated. 'There are men of great standing being put to work as slaves! Why aren't ransoms being asked for?'

'Don't push me, Clytes,' his friend responded in exasperation. 'The people are screaming for their heads, and if I cross them, they will want mine too. Demosthenes' terms were that they be spared. They've been spared.'

'The condition they're in! It's a death sentence and you know it!'

'What can I do?!'

'Talk to the Assembly. Their anger may cool. Try and persuade them to be more lenient. Those men are a valuable commodity. Why work them to death?'

'I am no longer listened to, Clytes. Eurycles is popular with the people now. They will follow what he says.'

'Well, try and persuade *him*! Get his wife to help. He's greatly influenced by her. I'm serious. He'll listen to her.'

'How do you know so much about his wife? No, don't tell me.'

Later, at a general assembly of the Syracusans and their allies, the popular leader, Eurycles, brought in a motion that after seventy days in the mines, Athenian allies, serving as members of the Delian League, should be released from their misery in the pit and sold into slavery, but that freeborn Athenians and any collaborators from Sicily or Italy should remain there. Demosthenes and Nicias, Eurycles insisted, should be executed. These propositions were readily adopted despite Hermocrates arguing strongly that a better use of victory would be to act nobly, and even Gylippus was vehemently shouted down when he demanded he be allowed to take the Athenian generals back to Sparta, as trophies.

'Nicias is nearly sixty and in poor health,' said Clytes, imploringly, to his Syracusan friend, on hearing what had transpired. 'They could spare him, surely?!'

'They wouldn't hear of it. I begged them. So did Gylippus. There was one proposition put forward though, which will interest you, Clytes.'

'Oh?'

'It was Eurycles' suggestion, but obviously inspired by his wife.'

'You talked with Entelina? Good! What did she propose?'

'That any of the prisoners who can quote from Euripides' works, will receive more favourable treatment.'

'Seriously?!'

'Apparently she and her friends admire his work above all others, and she was able to persuade her husband to put forward the proposal.'

'Hmm.'

'Would you have anything to do with their admiration, Clytes?'

'I'm glad my *recitations* have been appreciated.'

'Eunice was right to leave you. You *are* incorrigible. But what do you think? Will it help?'

'He's very popular. There'll be many who can quote his verses. May the gods bless the woman; she made a good choice. But what help is there for Demosthenes and Nicias?'

'None whatsoever! Not even Gylippus could persuade the assembly to spare them.'

'We need to get a message to them, Hermocrates. Nicias especially will be expecting favourable treatment from the Spartans.'

'I agree. A stoning would be an ignominious end to such a devout life. He needs to be warned.'

While the two friends were deliberating on how best to help the prisoners, an answer to their dilemma arrived, when a servant brought news of a visitor.

'Commander Styphon, wishes to talk with you urgently,' he announced, and then when told to let him enter, stepped aside quickly to let the Spartan stride purposefully into the room.

'I heard about what happened at the Assembly, Hermocrates,' Styphon declared, with urgency. 'That the Athenian commanders are to be executed......and that you argued against their sentences.'

'I was shouted down. Why are you interested?'

'I understand there's a Plataean with Demosthenes.'

'Yes, that's right. The man was wounded trying to defend him.'

'Is he also to be executed?'

'He has asked for the same fate as Demosthenes, I believe...... so yes, he will receive the same treatment.'

'Stoning?'

'So I believe.'

'That man was a good friend to me when I was held prisoner in an Athenian jail. I want to help him......as he would me, if circumstances were reversed.'

'In what way?'

'I have no sympathy for Demosthenes. His victory at Pylos was the reason I became a prisoner in Athens. Nicias, though, I have respect for, and for my friend......an everlasting gratitude.'

'What are you proposing?'

'That I be made part of the guard, so I can pass them a knife. I know which death I'd prefer.'

Clytes was intrigued by the Spartan's regard for the Plataean and was curious to know his identity.

'He is called Stephanos,' Styphon answered him, directly. 'A good man.'

'I know him!' groaned Clytes, on hearing the name of his friend. 'He is loyalty personified! He means it when he says he will suffer the same fate as Demosthenes. We have to do something!'

'It will be risky for you, Spartan,' said the statesman to the commander, but if this is what you want to do, then I'll make arrangements for you to be included in the prison guard tonight.

CHAPTER SIXTY-ONE

Impress upon them that there is no chance of a reprieve......for any of them.'

'I never met a braver man,' said Styphon, referring to Stephanos. 'What he did for our general Brasidas will never be forgotten. The Syracusans will not shame him in his last hours.'

The squalid quarters where the prisoners were held, reeked of infection and excrement and Styphon was appalled to find that no treatment had been given to the wounds suffered by Demosthenes and Stephanos nor any relief for Nicias' obvious distress. The Plataean was grey with pain and Demosthenes was drifting in and out of delirium. Nicias, too ill to sit or stand, lay pale and gaunt and shivered uncontrollably. Taking the opportunity to replace a fellow guard who wished to relieve himself, Styphon knew he didn't have much time. Quietly he called out Stephanos' name.

'Styphon?' the Plataean answered, joyfully but shakily, on recognition. 'Now it's my turn to be behind the bars.'

'I wish your future was as hopeful, friend.'

'What's happening?'

'The Syracusans want blood. Hermocrates and Gylippus have both tried to dissuade them but have been shouted down.'

'What will be the punishments?'

'Stoning.'

'For Nicias?! That's barbaric! The poor man's half dead already.'

'I've been talking with the guards here. There is so much hatred, they intend to make a spectacle of your deaths. You're to be stoned by a rabid mob, Stephanos, which Hermocrates does not want. He has sent me here with this. Hide it quickly.'

'You have my gratitude, Spartan, and I believe I speak for the others, also.'

'The guard will be returning soon. I'll have to leave you, my friend. I have a message from the actor, Clytes. He says the sword is safe and you can trust him to act honourably. I expect you know what that means?'

'I'm relieved. My friend is obviously himself again. Get a message to him, Styphon. Tell him Glaucus is here, with Nicias' contingent. And just one last request. Our possessions have all been taken from us, but can you see that my wife in Scione gets this,' and he quickly cut a lock of hair from his head, remarking appreciatively on how sharp the knife was.

'I sharpened it myself......to be sure.'

'It has been a privilege, Spartan.'

'Likewise, Plataean.'

As heavy footsteps approached, Styphon quickly resumed his post, giving no indication to the returning guard that anything was untoward, then without looking back he thrust the lock of dark curls into his pouch and left the fetid quarters, to take his place at the strongly defended entrance, knowing that by his recent actions he'd probably signed his own death warrant.

The following morning when the bodies were found, the Syracusans were so incensed at being denied their spectacle, they mutilated the corpses and then threw them outside the city gates to be devoured by wolves and packs of wild dogs.

SIXTY-TWO

O N DISCOVERING THAT GLAUCUS had come with the fleet, Clytes immediately set about trying to find him. He hadn't been able to save Stephanos but if the big Thessalian still lived, he was determined he would not suffer the same fate. He had influence in Syracuse and was prepared to use it. He also knew which officials to bribe. The quarry, he was well aware of, being close to the theatre where he was a regular performer, and he feared for anyone being sent there. Hermocrates, on learning of his plans, warned him to keep away from the place.

'It's worse than grim, Clytes. There are seven thousand down there with no sanitation and no care for the sick. Already there are bodies piling up. Stay away my friend.'

'Glaucus is like a brother. If he's there, I'll do whatever it takes to get him out. I won't be dissuaded.'

'Don't go too far or you'll end up down there with the rest. There's much anger in the city.'

'I'll take my chance.'

By bribing one of the officials to check the lists of prisoners, Clytes was able to establish that a Thessalian by the name of Glaucus was in the mines, and on further questioning of the guards, got the proof he needed when told that there was indeed a prisoner with red hair and a voice like a raging bull. There was no record of his cousins, and he prayed that they'd never left Attica. Relieved that his friend still lived, Clytes had the reassurance he needed and set about negotiating a ransom. His attempts were vilified. No prisoners under any circumstances, were to be released for at least seventy days, on the orders of the city leader, Eurycles, and any survivors were to be sent to the slave market to be sold to the highest bidder.

'Do you think your friend can last seventy days?' Hermocrates asked, sympathetically. 'Rations are meagre. Only a pint of meal and half a pint of water a day and there's the exposure to the elements to consider.'

'Eurycles likes his Euripides. I'll offer private recitals for him and his friends for as long as it takes, in exchange for more food and water being given to Glaucus. What do you think?'

'If you can bear to be in the company of that demagogue and his cronies, it's worth a try.'

For weeks Clytes entertained the city leader and his rapidly expanding number of friends, once news got out that the popular actor was giving the recitals, and although increased provisions were provided in return, word reached Clytes that Glaucus was failing.

'I need to go into the quarry myself, Hermocrates. I have to find out what's happening.'

'My friend, my friend! You are risking your life going in there. There's nowhere for the prisoners to relieve themselves. Disease is rife. Bodies are left rotting. You've done all you could.'

'Can you get me the permission?'

'To go in, certainly, but to get you out could be more difficult.'

'I'll recite every word Euripides has ever written, if I have to. If that fails, you'll have to promise to buy me at the slave market...... whatever the price. I won't be cheap!'

'Ha! You flatter yourself! I hope it doesn't come to that, but consider it done.'

Clytes, armed with his written permission to enter the quarry and talk with Glaucus, was eventually lowered down on one of the wooden platforms used for bringing the blocks of limestone to the surface. With the support of ropes and pulleys he swayed his way slowly down the rock face into the gloom; the stomach wrenching stench of decomposition growing stronger the deeper he went. Wrapping a thick cloth tightly around his nose and mouth, he moved amongst what had once been strong fighting men but were now living ghosts, and those too weak for the need of shackles anymore, pleaded with him for water, tugging feebly at his garments. Onwards he went, guided by one of the supervisors who was also heavily masked, gently pushing aside any who tried to delay him, but the man he found, his wasted body lying propped up against a limestone slab, looking more dead than alive, was not the man he remembered. His beard was still the distinctive flaming red but the hair on his head had turned white, and he no longer befitted the name 'big man'. He seemed to be sleeping and before Clytes could approach him, he was hailed by a voice he recognised.

'Thank the gods!' Clytes exclaimed with relief, when he saw that Glaucus was with friends, and on seeing Theomenes, he grasped his hands firmly. 'How are you?' he asked, concerned, on seeing his pitiful condition.

'What you see,' he answered, stoically. 'We are none of us what we were.'

Akylas was also close by, doing what he could to care for his wounded and emaciated stepfather, Sebastianos, who was suffering badly from the lack of necessities - as were all the Plataeans in their sadly, depleted group.

'What's happened to Glaucus?' Clytes asked, anxiously, as he looked towards his friend. 'I've had extra food and water provided for him for weeks, but then I received a message that he's failing.'

'Glaucus came here wounded, supported by Cassa and Akylas,' explained Theomenes. We could hear him bellowing on his arrival and had them join our group. How I wish I could hear that sound again! He was already in a pitiful state, but he's received no treatment, and even with your increased rations, it hasn't been enough to sustain a man like him. They're still meagre, and they expect extra work for them.

'That's inhuman!'

'They intend to kill us all, Clytes. We'd be dead men already if some of us hadn't been able to recite Euripides. Who would have thought that in a place like this, poetry would be appreciated.'

'You know your verses, then? Good!'

'I can remember some, but Akylas has been a revelation. He met the playwright many times at Aspasia's house and has been able to remember much of what he taught him. He shares his extra portions with Sebastianos and other Plataeans. It's not much, but it has made the difference between life and death for some of us.

'I remember Sebastianos from our exploits with The Shield Company' said Clytes, reflectively, 'and Akylas I haven't seen since The Shield was taken to Delphi.' He looked at the horrors happening all around him, and he shuddered, his emotions reeling between outrage and despair. 'What a place for a reunion!'

'It was Akylas who got the message to you, in return for relating stories of Aspasia's household to the guards. He's very fond of Glaucus, Clytes. Our Thessalian friend has been the saving of him. He knew how much Glaucus wanted to see you, before......'

I'm determined to save Glaucus, Theo,' he said passionately. 'If my recitations aren't enough, then he'll have to learn to recite also.'

'Prepare yourself, Clytes. I really don't think he has long.'

The prison guards had been only too willing to inform the trapped men of the brutal demise of their commanders, but it was Clytes who had the sad duty to let the Plataeans know of the heroic death of Stephanos. His loss was keenly felt, even after experiencing so much horror, and he discretely left them to their sorrow and to pray together over the passing of the best of them.

Reunited with Glaucus, Clytes believed he'd arrived in time to save him. 'If you could only memorise a few lines,' he told him, encouragingly, 'the guards will give you extra food.'

'It's too late, Clytes,' Glaucus answered him, weakly.

'I have a verse I know you'll appreciate,' said Clytes, with urgency. Are you listening?'

'I'm listening.'

'I'll recite it first and then you repeat it to me.' Softly, he began to sing.

'Famous were the ships
Which sailed along from Hellas to Troy,
When the dancing of oars without number
Joined in their journey the dancing sea-nymphs,
Where, drawn by the music of flutes,
Dolphins were leaping and rolling
Beside the purple-painted prows,
Bearing on his way the son of Thetis,
The light-footed leaper Achilles,
Who went with Agamemnon's army
To the rocky Trojan coast and the Simois river.'

'Your voice is as sweet as it ever was,' Glaucus told him, his sunken eyes bright with tears. 'To hear it one last time, is more than I could have hoped for.'

'No, no! You're going to make it, Glaucus!' exclaimed Clytes. 'Can you repeat the words for me? *Famous were the ships......*'

'Keep my axe well sharpened, Clytes,' Glaucus told him, his voice wavering with the effort. 'You never know when you'll need it.'

'I will, big man, never fear!' and seeing the obvious pain his friend was in, he tried to distract him. 'How did you acquire the axe, Glaucus? You never did tell me. It has some age, I think?'

'That's a story worth telling,' Glaucus forced himself to reply. 'I was young then and in Thrace when prince......'

His words suddenly dissolved into a choking gargle and his shrunken body shuddered violently. Then he spoke no more.

'Go on, Glaucus!' Clytes urged him, frantically.

'He's gone,' said Theomenes, coming up behind him.

'He can't be! Come on big man, stay with me!'

'We've lost him, Clytes. It's no good.'

Raging at his loss, Clytes grappled with the nearest guard, cursing him and his kind for their callousness and demanding that the men be given more rations, but he was quickly overpowered and put in irons, then forcibly removed from the pit, leaving Theomenes to try and console an inconsolable Akylas.

'You're well respected here, actor,' spoke one of his minders. 'I've seen all your performances, but if you didn't have the protection of the city leaders, you'd still be down there. Don't come back!'

Not long after, Cassa also succumbed to the vile conditions, the two friends together on the rotting pile which increased daily at an alarming rate.

SIXTY-THREE

AFTER GLAUCUS' DEMISE, CLYTES was no longer allowed into the mines, no matter how many recitals he gave, and the Plataeans were left to fend for themselves, but seeing for himself how weak they were, he argued strongly for their release after seventy days and for them not to be punished along with the freeborn Athenians who'd been sentenced to endure eight months.

'They are Athenian citizens, Clytes,' Hermocrates retorted in response to his pleas. 'Eurycles will make no exceptions.'

'Made Athenian citizens purely because their own city was destroyed! In their condition, they'll never survive eight months. I'm only asking for three lives. He's refused to see me, but can you persuade him?'

'If it's on this matter, you're wasting your time.'

'Tell him, I'll make it worth his while.'

'It will take more than your entertainment skills to make him change his mind.'

'I'm begging you, Hermocrates! There isn't much time. I've already lost people who were very dear to me.'

'Provoke the man and it will not only be your head that falls, but mine also.'

'I'm prepared to risk mine.'

'You owe me one, Clytes!'

Due to Clytes' persistence and Hermocrates' influence, Theomenes, Sebastianos and Akylas, severely emaciated, were released from the quarry after seventy days. Others, from states in the Delian League, who'd impressed the Sycracusans by their knowledge of Euripides and their educated manners were either bought in order to entertain at drinking parties, or in the case of the nobility, released on the promised payment of hefty ransoms. The freeborn Athenians, together with their Sicilian and Italian allies, were left to suffer from hunger, sickness and exposure, until after eight months had passed when the few survivors were taken out, branded on the forehead and forced into servitude, which after all they'd endured, they were grateful to accept.

'Clytes?' Theomenes asked, curiously, one day, while he was recovering at Catana. 'Where's the Theban sword?'

'Ah! Eurycles has it.'

'I thought as much! Is that how we gained our freedoms?'

'How else? You were expensive. Especially the son of Phalinus.'

'That was a great sacrifice, Clytes.'

'It was no sacrifice. I could think of no better purpose for it.'

'I hope you made him pay dearly. That sword has history.'

'Enough to get us home Theo, which is what we all want.'

'If Stephanos was here, he would have approved. We'll be forever grateful.'

'We both lost some good friends here. As soon as the seas are open again, we'll be leaving this island of death together. I have no future here......not now.'

'Does Akylas know that you used the Theban sword to save him? He was insistent at one time, that it should have been passed to him.'

'Then it would have become part of the spoils of war, and you would have died in that pit, which no doubt is what has happened to the rest of the Plataeans. I told Stephanos I would act honourably. I have no regrets. I had no other means of buying your freedom.'

'Let him believe it was taken when Stephanos fell. No need to tell him otherwise......not yet.'

'You may think I imagined Lykaon's curse on the weapon, Theo, but there's no imagining my own. May the Theban sword bring no joy to the man!'

'Add *my* curse also!'

In other parts of the island, a few individuals who'd fled from battle or escaped slavery, roamed the countryside living as bandits, until one by one a trickle of desperate men arrived at Catana seeking sanctuary. One such, was the Plataean, Erastos, who'd escaped capture at the river massacre, carrying stories of how men on the run had been given food by the locals in return for quoting anything from Euripides. Another unexpected arrival was the Spartan, Styphon. Warned by Hermocrates that following questioning and torture of the men who'd guarded the prisoners, it had been concluded that he was the only one who could have smuggled in a blade, and he was now part of Clytes' broken and demoralised group of escapees. He still carried the poignant lock of hair which he felt duty bound to give to Micca personally, seeing as he felt responsible for the death of her incomparable husband.

SIXTY-FOUR

IRST, THEY SAILED TO Italy on the earliest ship that
would carry them and then, by degrees, they finally arrived
at Pireaus and home territory to find Athens was suffering from
an invasion by the Spartans. Just thirteen miles from the city
they'd established a fort at Decelea, on the traitor, Alcibiades',
recommendation, cutting the Athenians off from their silver mines
at Lavrion and also their farmland beyond the city walls. They
were now totally reliant on the seas for their survival.

Immediately upon arriving in the confined city, Clytes sought
out the playwright, Euripides, to tell him of what had transpired
at Syracuse and to thank him for saving the lives of some poor
unfortunates. He then surprised Leon and Panthas by his
unexpected appearance.

'Clytes!' Panthas squealed on opening the door, and then he
dragged him, unceremoniously, into their cluttered quarters, filled
almost entirely with theatrical paraphernalia. 'Look who it is,
Leon!'

'I can't believe it?!' exclaimed Leon, fighting back tears of joy,
and he rushed forward to grasp him by the hands. 'When did you
get in?'

'You're looking very prosperous!' Panthas interrupted, going
over to feel the quality of Clytes' garments.

'Did you get my letters?' Clytes asked, trying politely to
sidestep Panthas' interference.

'We've heard nothing from you for the past two years!'
Panthas complained, while still running his plump fingers along
an embroidered detail of Clytes' fine cloak.

'It was to be expected,' responded Leon. 'There was a war on!
Before that, as well as your letters, we used to get regular news
from travellers on how well you were doing in Syracuse.'

'We couldn't have been more proud!' Panthas enthused.

'I had a very good life there my friends......until the fleet
arrived,' he added, grimly. 'But that's all in the past now.'

'Well, we are so glad you are back. It will be just like the old times,' said Panthas, enthusiastically. 'Now, tell us,' he then added, his voice deepening dramatically to a more manly tone. 'Just how bad was it?'

Akylas headed for Aspasia's house, to let her know of how Alcibiades had abandoned him to his fate in Syracuse. 'I did warn you never to trust him,' Aspasia told him, shaking her head in disappointment at the extraordinary behaviour of her most outrageous protégé, but she could not have been more proud of Akylas.

'You've matured beyond your years, Akylas. You're quite the man now!'

'A Thessalian called Glaucus looked out for me after Alcibiades defected. I owe my life to him.'

'I shall be forever grateful to the man. I hope I can meet him one day.'

'He's dead, Aspasia! Like all the others!'

'We have plenty of time for you to tell me about what happened. I won't rush you.'

'I'm not staying in Athens. I'm leaving for Scione with my stepfather and Theomenes.'

'You don't *have* to go, Akylas! You have friends here, and you can always rely on my support.'

'Alcibiades was wrong to say there is no Plataea. For as long as there are Plataeans, we will never give up the fight to return to our city. No-one else will protect our cultural heritage, and I want to play my part. We lost Stephanos in Syracuse......too many good men! Alcibiades betrayed us, Aspasia!'

Theomenes, after first reuniting with his ecstatic uncle, Hypatos, went to the cheese market in the agora, where he knew the Plataeans who'd refused to move to Scione, met every month. He needed to prepare them for the worst. To hear from Theomenes that he and his small group, could, in all probability, be all that remained of the original one hundred who'd left with Demosthenes, was heartbreak beyond belief and the shock was

THE SWORD OF THEBES

immense. On learning that Akylas still lived, though, brought great relief.

'There are rumours of the disaster spreading about the city,' said an elderly woman, already hardened by adversity and beyond tears, 'but the officials don't believe them. There's a prisoner in custody, who apparently says he was at Syracuse, and I've heard he's telling his torturers that he's a Plataean?'

'I know what happened to every one of us who went on that fateful venture,' Theomenes answered, grimly. 'Most likely a metic trying to pass himself off as Plataean to avoid punishment. It's been done before.'

'That's just what I said,' replied the aged cheese seller, nodding affirmatively towards her disconsolate, fellow stall holders.

All around the agora, Theomenes heard repeated garbled stories of the unkempt stranger who'd stepped off a ship at Piraeus, to immediately seek out a haircut, and talking as though the barber already knew about the disaster at Syracuse, was astonished to find himself being arrested and brought to Athens for questioning. His unbelievable tale about the loss of forty thousand men and one hundred and seventy-five ships caused furious anger in the citizens, and refusing to accept the appalling truth, the poor man was racked on the wheel to force him to change his story.

It became obvious to Theomenes that the man, whoever he was, was only telling the truth, and he asked Clytes, Sebastianos and Akylas to go with him to the archon's office, so they could relate their individual stories. No matter how distasteful, the city had to be told of the death of Nicias and Demosthenes, together with the loss of their entire army and fleet.

'So, you are part of the vanguard?' the archon asked Clytes, uncomprehendingly. 'Is that what you are saying?'

'No, we are not part of any vanguard,' replied Clytes, trying to keep his temper. 'Apart from a few individuals who may arrive over time, there will be no ships bringing back the men.'

'But you are here? If you escaped, then there must be others, surely?'

'Our circumstances were unusual,' ventured Theomenes.

'I cannot take your word alone,' replied the archon, shaking his head in an effort to dispel the news. 'We must wait until we receive Nicias' report, before we can be sure of anything.'

'You're not listening!' shouted Clytes, in frustration, leaning over the man's desk to face him directly. 'There is no Nicias. No Demosthenes. No men! No ships!'

'*Everything* is gone,' Theomenes stressed, his voice breaking with emotion. 'Our generals. Our army, archon. They're not coming back.'

Unable to entirely convince the official, Theomenes asked if they could be taken to see the prisoner who purported to be a Plataean, and even though they'd witnessed deplorable scenes while at Syracuse, the sight of the broken individual brought gasps of both horror and sympathy from the friends on entering the torture room.

'Untie the man!' Sebastianos shouted, angrily. 'He is only telling you the truth!'

The unconscious prisoner was taken from the rack and laid out on a bare wooden pallet where Sebastianos could examine him. 'I don't recognise him, but I don't expect his own mother would,' he said to the others. 'He's had a brand on his forehead, by the looks of things, which he's attempted to remove. Theo, do you recognise him?'

I'm not sure? There's something about him that is familiar,' and he turned to the guard to find out what the man had revealed about himself.

'He was rambling. Incoherent. We couldn't get a straight answer from him. The only thing he finally did tell us, was that he was a Plataean......if he can be believed. He was wearing this around his head when we brought him in. Obviously to hide the scar. He's an escaped slave, is my guess.'

Akylas, who'd been watching and listening carefully, came forward.

'I know this man!' he exclaimed, excitedly. 'He was with the Euboean contingent when Nicias surrendered. I recognise the bandana. He *was* at Syracuse!'

'Then who is he?' queried Sebastianos, puzzled. 'Fetch some wine,' he ordered the guard. 'We need to question him, ourselves.'

Gradually, due to their administrations, the prisoner regained consciousness, only to immediately cry out in pain, due to his injuries. 'More wine!' Sebastianos ordered, until eventually they were able to reassure him that he was with friends.

On hearing their names, the man began laughing and crying simultaneously, and he grabbed at Theomenes' garment, pulling him close. 'Did Angelos make it?' he asked, pressingly.

'Angelos? How do you know Angelos?'

'Not here!' he whispered, his eyes looking anxiously towards the guard.

'Who are you?!' Theomenes urged him.

'I was known as Strong-Arm. That's all I can tell you.'

'You've had enough time,' the guard, interrupted. 'You'll have to leave now.'

Theomenes thrust some coins into the guard's hand. 'We'll be back tomorrow. Get his injuries attended to, and make sure he's fed!'

On later discussing the individual and trying to solve the mystery of his identity, Theomenes suddenly burst out, 'It must be Iairos! Praise the gods, the man must have escaped from the mines and made it to Euboea! No wonder he's hesitant to let the guards know who he is. He's concerned they'll want to claim the ransom for a runaway. He's afraid he'll be forced back there!'

'It must be him!' Sebastianos agreed, enthusiastically.

'And no wonder he looked familiar,' Theomenes added. 'There's a statue of him in the marketplace at Scione. The man's a hero!'

Armed with strong evidence as to who the prisoner was, the friends were able to free him, and he was taken to Hypatos' house to recover from his dreadful ordeals. Here, he learned of Angelos winning at the Olympic Games and of how he was now a guest of Tissaphernes in Lydia.

'He made a good decision to leave when he did,' Iairos admitted, ruefully. 'I have a mind to join him. What is there to stay here for? The Athenians overreached themselves. They should have listened to Nicias.'

'Pericles' advice always was, never to take on an enemy far from home, while Sparta was still undefeated,' remarked Hypatos, sagely. 'They will recall his words now and weep.'

Two months later and still not fully recovered, Iairos, wearing a new colourful bandana was at the Pireaus, eager to leave for the shores of Anatolia and to seek out his friend, Angelos. He was not alone. Clytes had recognised a kindred spirit in Iairos, and being unable to settle into his old life, the intrepid pair had decided to travel together. He still owed Angelos an apology for leaving him at Sinope, without so much as a word. He also wanted to thank him for taking care of the Sword of Thebes, which he'd so recklessly left behind; a weapon which had proved to be worth so much more than its mere weight in gold.

Theomenes, Sebastianos and Akylas were there to watch him leave, as was the distraught pair, Leon and Panthas. He gave them all a final wave, then his long legs took him purposefully towards the waiting ship. Strapped to his broad back was Glaucus' freshly sharpened Thracian axe, the twin blades glinting in the sunlight, its faded tassels swaying as he went.

*

EPILOGUE

THE SECOND PELOPONNESIAN WAR covered a period of twenty-seven destructive years, both sides ignoring several opportunities to bring about an honourable settlement. At their end Athens was in ruins, its Golden Age consigned to history, and Sparta having no interest in maintaining an empire, allowed other factions to come to the fore.

It was ninety years after the fall of Plataea, before the city was finally rebuilt, and descendants of its displaced people were able to regain permanent possession. Inspired by the stoic Plataeans, who never gave up believing, Alexander the Great restored their plateau fortress to its former glory. The city of Thebes, he razed to the ground.

*